# SUGAR RAIN

*Other Avon Books in*
## THE STARBRIDGE CHRONICLES
### by Paul Park

SOLDIERS OF PARADISE

# THE STARBRIDGE CHRONICLES

# SUGAR RAIN

## PAUL PARK

AVON BOOKS ◆ NEW YORK

AVON BOOKS
A division of
The Hearst Corporation
105 Madison Avenue
New York, New York 10016

Copyright © 1989 by Paul Park
Cover art by Gary Ruddell
Published by arrangement with William Morrow and Company, Inc.
Library of Congress Catalog Card Number: 88-34499
ISBN: 0-380-71179-6

First Avon Books Printing: October 1990

AVON TRADEMARK REG. U.S. PAT. OFF. AND IN OTHER COUNTRIES, MARCA
REGISTRADA, HECHO EN U.S.A.

Printed in the U.S.A.

RA   10   9   8   7   6   5   4   3   2   1

FOR MARY AND NATHANIEL LAWRENCE

# SUGAR RAIN

# CHARITY
# STARBRIDGE

There is a fresco in the prince's library where it is all set out: the Sun painted on the black background of deep space, while around it spins the wheel of Earth's majestic orbit. And the rim of the wheel is made of numbers, tiny calculations of painted gold, for in those days the length of the year was a matter of dogma. Knowing it to be a lie, the bishop's astronomers had put the figure down as eighty thousand days precisely. They were in love with a vision of celestial harmony: four seasons of twenty thousand days, twenty phases of a thousand days each, ten months of a hundred days, ten weeks of ten, twenty hours of a hundred minutes each. The artist has painted a portrait of the bishop, enthroned within the circle of the Earth. In her hand she holds a silver sword. It is composed of numbers, the magical equation $1 \times 10 \times 10 \times 10 \times 20 \times 4 = 1$. Under her feet writhe demons and heretics, arbitrary and conflicting figures issuing from their mouths.

Closer in around the Sun and farther out in space, the nine planets of hell pursue their separate ways—tight, fiery circles and long, cold ellipses. Each is decorated with scenes of souls in torment. Men freeze in icy prisons or burn like torches; they burst apart or weigh a thousand pounds, depending on the differing effects of temperature and atmosphere. And beneath each planet the artist has depicted the kinds of criminals who inhabit it. Under Baqui Minor, for example, he has painted a seascape, a storm raging on a sea of liquid helium. Almost overwhelmed by the waves, a raft breaks through a cloud of spray. Clutched to the deck, miserable men and women huddle together for warmth, a murderer, a tailor, a paralytic, a smuggler, a homosexual, a man with yellow hair. Each carries, cut into his forehead or the muscle of his upper arm, the symbol of his vice.

In temporary orbit around Mega Prime moves Paradise, the source of life, a captive planet among the terrors of the solar system. Its towers and lakes and shining palaces are painted with a kind of wistful brilliance, and its complicated path among the planets is traced with ribbons of gold. Smallest of all the planets, it is also the greatest, painted as if lit from within, surrounded by halos of luminescence which spread out into darkest space. Angels and demons cavort in its upper atmosphere, and on the topmost tower of the brightest palace sits Angkhdt, dog-headed prophet of God, enthroned on a dais, surrounded by companies of the blessed, his mouth contorted in a doglike scowl. He has opened his hand and released a bird into the air, a falcon bearing a lantern in its claws, setting its wings over the wide abyss towards Earth.

The falcon flies over a recumbent figure, a sleeping giant painted on an empty section of the wall. The bones of his forehead have been stripped away, and within the caverns of his brain sit convocations of God's priests, holding the synapses of his system in their ancient, spotted hands.

The giant is symbolic of the body of the state. Along his shoulders sit regiments of Starbridges—judges, princes, generals, financiers, all in gorgeous uniforms. Lower down, craftsmen and artisans crouch among the giant's hands, the pennants of their guilds sprouting from his fingers. Along the passages of his entrails slog tradesmen and merchants in shit-colored robes, dragging enormous packages on sledges. Soldiers camp upon his thighs. And on his legs and feet squat crowds of men and women dressed in yellow rags, working people, slaves.

Yet even these are not the lowest. For the giant has relieved himself before going to sleep. A pile of excrement smokes near his feet, and in it squirm heretics and atheists painted in the shape of maggots—antinomials, adventists, cannibals, carnivores, and a dozen others, the marks of their heresies branded on their backs.

In the days when the fresco was first painted, men believed in miracles. When Paradise was in rotation close to Earth, people could see with the naked eye what looked like sparks and streamers falling out from its bright surface into space. They believed there was a spark of divinity burning in the hearts of men. They believed that from his companies of angels God had exiled some for punishment on Earth. And when a child was born in those days, a priest would come to cast its horoscope and pattern its tattoos. He would listen to its crying. For then, in the language of the newborn, the fallen angel in the heart of every child would describe the sins that had pulled it down, given it flesh and blood, molded its young bones. And some babies were arrested right away and beaten or condemned to prison. Others, less perverse, were permitted to learn trades. But most were condemned in their cradles to lifetimes of labor. For God marked the most sinful with certain signs. They were born into poor families, or their limbs were crooked, or their eyes were green.

The fresco's border is decorated with scenes from the life of the Beloved Angkhdt, painted in exquisite detail. In those days every citizen of Charn could recite the story of how the prophet left his wife and family to set out on his journey through the stars. He divided his goods among his friends: to Cosro Starbridge, his gun. To Nestrim Starbridge, his money and his books. To Bartek Starbridge, his livestock and his plow. In this way he divided all the earth. And at the time the fresco was first painted, in the early phases of spring, 00016, in the city of Charn, the descendants of these men held sovereign power. They were the priests and the administrators. They owned every bird and every stone, for their power was in trust from God. They were the wardens of the prison world.

Parts of the fresco are so complicated, they require a magnifying glass to decipher. Standing in her brother's library, the princess peered at it doubtfully. There was a crack in the wall under the image of the Sun, a tiny imperfection in the plaster. She reached out to rub it with her thumb, and then she turned away.

Outside her tower window the city stretched away into the rain and the dark night. She stood staring towards the east. There, still far away, her brother's fire turned the intervening houses into jagged silhouettes, lit from behind by green and silver flares, and the deep red burning. Closer in, the river had risen through the lowest slums and spread into a lake five miles around, drowning the miserable streets, making islands out of the highest buildings, the prisons and the temples. Neon steeples and gilded domes rose up above the water's inky surface. From time to time, fat boats full of lamplight would glide between them, carrying priests and soldiers on unknown errands.

She stood at the window of her brother's library on the thirty-seventh floor. Beneath her, throngs of people seethed around the first gates of the Mountain of Redemption, the monstrous prison at the city's heart. Horse soldiers with whips had kept the major streets clear, but there weren't enough of them to do more than that. Looking down from her tower window, Charity Starbridge could see where an entire shanty-town had sprung up around the gate, cardboard boxes and plywood shelters, and people sitting around bonfires dressed in urine-colored rags. Displaced by fire and flood, paupers had come from all over the city to gather at the mountain's base, to chant the names of rage, to recite in unison the fourteen reasons for despair. Some squatted in the mud or huddled under umbrellas, cowed to silence by the constant rain, but others swarmed against the barricades, shaking their skinny fists and shouting. Here and there in the crowd, men had erected symbols of revolt: a huge chamberpot made out of papier-mâché, dog-headed effigies of the prince of Caladon, inflated phalluses as tall as men. Someone had made wings and a tail and a huge beak for himself out of red cardboard, and he danced on a box above the crowd, a red bird of adventism. Elsewhere, rebel preachers gesticulated and prayed, surrounded by devotees. Charlatans juggled torches, and mountebanks ate fire. And sometimes a dark soldier of the purge would push his horse past the barricades around the gate, wading his horse contemptuously through the mob, clearing a circle around himself with his pistol and his whip. From her high window, Charity saw one of them raise his hand; she heard the shot and saw the man in the bird suit pitch backwards into the crowd, flapping his red wings.

After a few minutes the soldier retreated back into the shelter of the gate, and the crowd closed up where he had been. Charity stared down at him, admiring his black uniform without understanding what he was. Drugs and innocence and social custom had made a prison out of her mind, and she stared down out of her window as if through the bars. Somewhere among the edgeless days of marriage she had lost the ability to think. Or rather, not completely—a week before, she had stopped taking the personality relaxers prescribed to her on her wedding day, and already it was as if a giant bird which had nested in her skull had spread its wings and flown away. Already the precepts of the Starbridge marriage code seemed less consuming. It had been thousands of days since she had last stood before a window looking out. That kind of activity was frowned on in a married woman. But still, it was hard for her to make sense of what she saw. The scene below her was so various and complex, the significance of it so bewildering, that in a little while she gave up trying and took consolation instead in the patterns of color and the shapes of the buildings. Ten major avenues radiated from the mountain's base straight to the city walls. One, the Street of Seven Sins, emerged from the gate below her, and she took consolation in following the long line of orange streetlights out to the far horizon, where the fire her brother had started filled the sky.

Behind her came a scrabbling and a scratching at the door. She turned and backed away from it, holding her hands behind her as if hiding something. She backed into a dark corner of the room, where the lamps were arranged to make her disappear into a cleft of shadow. Each room in the apartment contained a similar place of refuge, for it was against the law for anyone except her husband or her closest relatives to see her face. But in the course of her marriage she had broken the law many times. And not so long before, she had pulverized it so completely that now she obeyed its strictures not out of modesty but out of fear. She was afraid. In the doorway stood a blind man and his seeing eye.

They hesitated there, a young priest in purple robes with the tattoos of an advocate at law. In his right hand he grasped the silken collar of his servant, a professional moron, scarcely human anymore, the marks of surgical incisions standing out all over his pale forehead.

"Are you there?" called out the advocate in his supple, castrate voice. "Woman, are you there?" His servant was an older man. He crouched down on his haunches, sniffing and peering like a dog, his master's hand still tight around his collar.

"Are you there?" called out the advocate. He was recently blinded, his sockets still raw where his eyes had been torn away. From time to time, reddish tears ran down his face. "Are you there?" he called out.

The servant sniffed and peered, his head oscillating back and forth on the end of a long neck. For a while his mouth had hung open; now it closed as he settled his attention on the dark corner where the princess stood. His whole body stiffened, and his face took on an eager, sad expression. "Woman," he said softly.

Charity Starbridge stepped backwards, and the floorboards squeaked under her feet. The advocate turned his ruined face towards the sound. "There you are," he said. "Don't hide from me. You have no reason to hide." He smiled, displaying perfect teeth.

"Please don't hurt me," whispered Charity.

There was a pause. The seeing eye moved his head. "Window," he said. "Books."

The advocate frowned. "Where are we?" he asked. "What room is this?"

"This is my brother's library," answered Charity.

"It is not suitable for you to be here. Where are your servants? There was nobody to let us in."

"I am alone here," said the princess. "My brother's been arrested, and my husband is dead. The servants have all run away."

"It is not suitable," repeated the advocate. "But I am not here to scold you. Not yet. I am here to console you. I bring a message from the bishop's council."

The seeing eye was holding a plastic attaché case in the crook of his forearm. The advocate bent down to take it, and then he straightened up and took a few unsteady steps into the room. "I've brought the clothes your husband was wearing when he died. Together with a selection of the personal belongings from his tent. There is also a letter of commendation and a promotion. He will enter Paradise with the rank of brigadier."

Charity made no movement, and the advocate stood holding some papers out and frowning. Reddish tears ran down his face. "There is also a letter," he continued, "describing the way in which your husband met his death. I was not there. But I am told that he died bravely on the battlefield and that he successfully fulfilled the obligations of his name and his tattoos."

Still in the doorway, the seeing eye peered this way and that. Freed of his master's hand, he had sunk down into a strange, doglike crouch. With his forearms stretched out flat along the floor, he drummed his fingers on the polished wood.

"I don't understand," said Princess Charity. "That's not what my cousin says. My cousin Thanakar. He said my husband died miles from the fighting. He said my husband was murdered by one of our own priests. I don't understand. My cousin says he was stabbed to death before the battle even started. By a priest of God, one of the order of St. Lucan the Unmarred. Is that your order? My cousin says you carry knives hidden in your socks."

Her voice, puzzled, anxious, hesitant, trailed away. The advocate waited for a moment before answering, and he turned his head to listen to his servant's fingers drumming on the floor. "You have seen Thanakar Starbridge?" he asked.

"No. He wrote to me. Please, I don't mean to contradict you. It's just that I'd like to know the truth. My husband was always kind to me. I'd like to know."

"Miserable female!" interrupted the advocate, his voice rising high and shrill. "How can you use his name? How can you even say it? Thanakar Starbridge! We will hang him when we catch him. We will hang him." He made an angry, dismissive gesture with his arms, and it was enough to throw him off balance, so that he staggered and might have fallen. But his servant was watching and rose to help him. The advocate's flailing fingers caught the old man by the hair; he yanked back on the old man's hair and kept himself upright that way. "Let me tell you," he continued softly, after a pause.

"Thanakar Starbridge is under indictment for murder and for treason. Adultery is the least of the crimes he is charged with."

"I don't understand. He's done nothing wrong."

"Hasn't he? Then be prepared." The advocate smiled and raised his hand to wipe the red tear from his eye. "Your cousin is a sick young man. He has picked up some moral virus somewhere, perhaps some physical corruption. Be prepared. He might claim he contracted it from you. We'll see. The purge went out tonight to bring him in."

Charity leaned back against the bookcase. She remembered a story her brother had told her when she was just a girl, about a magician escaping from the purge, who turned himself into a sentence and escaped between the pages of a book, safe in some bookish landscape where the soldiers never found him. She leaned back and closed her eyes. She felt like crying, but the lawyer's bloody parody of tears had robbed her of the impulse, and left her with a knot in her throat and no way of getting rid of it. Inside her, feelings fought and struggled without the armament of words. Thoughts struggled to be born.

"Say something," demanded the advocate. "Let me tell you, the judge is disposed to be lenient. Moral contamination is hard to prove, and frankly, we believe that Thanakar Starbridge was a criminal long before he met you. The judge is disposed to think that if there was contamination, more likely it went the other way. He is willing to be lenient. But you must cooperate."

Charity said nothing. Thoughts of Thanakar had brought him back so vividly, it was as if he were standing near her, somewhere in the library, out of sight behind her shoulder or behind a turning of the wall. A pale, dark man with such beautiful hands, the hands of a healer. How could she have resisted, when he touched her with those hands?

"So," continued the advocate. "You have nothing to say." He wiped his cheek. "You think it will be his word against yours. Not quite." He smiled. "We have other evidence. Learn from this. A criminal pollutes everything he touches. He left a mark, a stain on your bedsheets. The woman who does your laundry alerted the police."

"She had no right."

"True. She had no right. And she has already been condemned for her impertinence, if it is any consolation to you. For slandering her superiors. Injected with the fever, if it is any consolation. The sentence is already carried out. But the evidence remains."

Charity stepped out from her dark corner. She turned to the window, her mind empty. She stared out to the horizon, where the fire burned bright. She watched a sugarstorm gathering above the river, the raindrops burning as they fell. Outside, far below, the crowd struggled and shouted. Wisps of chanting, fragments of revolutionary songs rose up to the tower window. "Where is my brother?" she asked suddenly.

"Prince Abu Starbridge is being held at Wanhope Prison. In the psychiatric ward. He too is in deep trouble, deeper than yours. For him there is no way out. But you—let me finish. I told you, the judge is inclined to be lenient. Thanakar Starbridge is a known criminal, and there are extenuating circumstances. You are a widow, after all. But we need your cooperation. We need your testimony to condemn him." He fumbled with the papers in his case. "I've prepared a statement for you to sign. It is a confession of adultery. Sign it and we will let you live. The bishop's council has found a refuge for you in the home of Barton Starbridge, your mother's second cousin. Seven hundred miles south of here. You would be free to collect your husband's pension."

From the window Charity could see down into the courtyard of a small shrine, where an execution was in progress. A thicket of gallows rose from the center of an open space, protected from the crowd by a circle of the spiritual police, the black-coated soldiers of the purge. As the princess watched, a priest performed the last rites for a condemned prisoner, cutting the mark of absolution into his face, checking his passports.

"Woman, say something!" cried the advocate behind her. He held out the unsigned confession, not realizing that she had turned away from him. Squatting nearby, the seeing eye drew back his lips to reveal long teeth filed into points. "Window," he said softly.

"God damn it, woman, pay attention," shouted the advocate. "Don't waste my time. You have no choice. If you refuse to sign, the council will vote to terminate your duties here. They'll send you home, and I tell you, the journey will be hard and long. Paradise is in orbit near the seventh planet. More than seven hundred million miles from here."

"I'd like to see my brother," said Charity after a pause.

Down below, the priest had strung up several prisoners. They hung suspended from the highest gibbets, their bodies revolving slowly in the rain. On the scaffold below, the priest danced a quiet version of the dance of death, lit by a spotlight from the temple tower. He was a good dancer, graceful and sure, but even so, the crowd was angry. They shouted and threw bottles. A bottle hit the priest on the shoulder as he danced; he stopped and stood upright, but Charity was too far away to see the expression on his face. He was in no danger. The purge stood around the scaffold in a circle, with automatic rifles and bright bayonets. In a little while he started to dance again.

"I'd like to see my brother," repeated the princess.

"That's not possible. God damn you, why do you even ask? Here. Here he is, if you really want to see." The advocate stretched out his hand, palm up, and Charity turned back to watch him. In a little while the air above his palm started to glow, and then a tiny figure materialized out of the air, a man sitting on a bed, reading, too small even to recognize. The advocate closed his hand, and the image disappeared as if crushed between his fingers.

"Now," he said. "Would you like to see him die?" He opened his hand again, and Charity could see a tiny pyre of logs. Here the scale was even smaller; Charity could see a throng of tiny figures, red-robed priests and black soldiers. Through the middle of the crowd, a pickup truck moved slowly forward towards the pyre, a single figure standing upright in the back.

The seeing eye sat up on his haunches and stared at the bright image, licking his lips with his long tongue. Charity, too, stood mesmerized until the advocate closed his hands again. "There," he said. "Are you satisfied?"

She was not satisfied. She began to cry. At the sound, the advocate tilted his head, listening intently with a puzzled expression on his face, though he must have been used to hearing people cry. He listened, and then he reached his hand up to touch his cheek, where his own red tears had left a scum.

He held out the paper for her to sign, but she had turned away again. In a little while he opened his fingers and let the paper settle to the floor. "I'll leave it," he said quietly. "Don't be a fool. I'll send my clerk tomorrow morning, and if you still refuse, at ten o'clock I will come back to send you home. I will pump the blood from your body, and I won't be gentle, either. That I promise. Women like you are a disgrace to us. You don't deserve your own tattoos. If I could send you to hell, I would."

All that day the churches had been packed with worshipers, and when the priests had rung the bells for evensong, the crowds had taken to the streets, jamming the roads, moving in slow streams towards the center of the city, down towards the Mountain of Redemption, where they had spread out around its lower slopes. The gigantic prison blocked out the sky. Even in those days it was the biggest building in the known universe, a huge, squat, unfinished tower, circle after circle of black battlements. It held a population of one million souls. And all around its lowest tier, sticking up like the spikes of a crown around a great, misshapen head, rose smaller towers, the Starbridge palaces, white and graceful, glinting with lamplight. Below, the streets were full of people chanting and singing. They looked up towards the windows while the rain fell steadily in dark, viscous drops, tasting of sugar and smelling of gasoline, coating men's clothes and crusting their skins. Here and there, preachers in the crowd spoke of the apocalypse, and some preached slowly and softly, and some ranted like maniacs. Numerologists had made a magic number out of the date: October 44th, in the eighth phase of spring. The forty-fourth day of the eighth month—some had daubed this number, 4408800016, on cardboard placards, which they waved above their heads. According to some long-extinct rule of prosody, this number duplicated the meter of the so-called apocalyptic verses of the Song of Angkhdt, the verses that begin, "Sweet love, you can do nothing further to arouse me. It's late—don't touch me anymore . . ."

An old man recited the lamentations of St. Chrystym Polymorph in a loud voice; naked to the waist, he whipped himself listlessly with a knotted scourge, not even raising a bruise. The sugar rain coated his shoulders. It was dismal weather, a dismal season. The food reserves, which previous generations of priests had stored up through summer and fall, were almost gone, and the daily ration of rice soup and edible plastic was scarcely enough to keep a child alive. Hunger had made men crazy. Strange sights and visions had been reported. An old woman had seen huge figures stalking her street in the hour before dawn—the angels of the apocalypse, she cried: war, famine, and civil war, she cried, and she had taken a photograph. People stood around her and passed it from hand to hand, studying the dark, unfocused image. The old woman was an adventist. "Sweet friends," she cried, "the hour is here. All my life I've prayed that I would live to see it. The powers of Earth are overthrown. The bishop herself has been imprisoned. The soldiers fight among themselves. And the Starbridges..." She paused to spit, and shake her fist at the pale towers above her head. "Every morning they are fewer. Every morning I have seen them at the southern gates, their motorcars loaded up with food." It was true. In their lifetimes people could remember when the windows of the Starbridge palaces lit the streets for miles around, but now more than half the windows were dark, and some whole towers stood empty, abandoned. The Starbridges had retired south to their estates, waiting for better weather. In summertime their grandchildren would return to rule the city.

The old woman had long gray hair, a long nose, and thin cheeks branded with the mark of heresy. "Sweet friends," she cried. "Old Earth is finished. But lift yourselves up, lift up your hearts, because a flower will grow out of this wreckage, and a garden that will cover all the earth. Birds and fish will speak. And there will be no more bloodshed, no, and no more hunger, and all these things will be like memories of nightmares. And God will wash the world between his fingers, and he will wash away all the priests and tyrants, the judges and the torturers. Look!" she screamed. "It has already been accomplished!" She grabbed back her photograph and held it up above her head.

A young woman stood away from the crowd, under the shadow of the gate. She shook her hair back from her face. She tried to comb some of the tangles out between her fingers, but the sugar rain had turned her hair into a sticky mass of knots. Yet she pulled at it restlessly, and her other hand moved restlessly over her body, touching her skin wherever it was exposed, her neck, her temples, her wrist. She was on fire. Already her temperature was way above a hundred, and the parson had told her that it would keep on rising at a steady rate until her heart burst into flame. One degree an hour, he had said. Then he had given her a glass of water and released her from the hospital, for there was no sense in keeping her. So she had wandered down into the streets, and all evening she had wandered with the crowds, and followed the crowds down into the center of the city, more desperate and distracted every minute. Now she stood at the barricade around the gate and raised her hand to gain the attention of the guard.

"Please, sir," she whispered, her voice burning in her throat.

"Please sir," she whispered, holding out her hand. But when the guard came to peer at her palm, she was suddenly afraid he wouldn't let her pass. Her tattoos were forgeries, a little vinegar would wash them clean, and she was suddenly afraid that she might have smudged them in some places and that tonight of all nights, the last night of her life, the guard wouldn't let her pass. She closed her hand into a fist. The soldier frowned. "What do you want in there?" he asked.

"I have some work to do."

The soldier looked up at the gate. "Go home, sister," he said. "Come back tomorrow. The laundry's closed."

"Please, sir. I have something that can't wait."

She pulled her hair back from her face, and the guard noticed for the first time how beautiful she was, how sweet her skin, how proud her eyes. He smiled. "What is your name?"

"Rosamundi," she answered. "Like the flower."

The soldier smiled. "Rosamundi. This is what I'll do. The gate's closed for the night. But give me a kiss, and then we'll see."

They stood on opposite sides of the barricade, a line of wooden sawhorses painted red. She ducked underneath and tried to run past him, but he grabbed her wrist in his heavy glove and twisted her against him, forcing her wrist up between her shoulder blades. He was a handsome man with long black hair, handsome in his black uniform with the silver dog's-head insignia; he twisted her against him, forcing her hand higher when she tried to pull away. He bent down to kiss her and she turned her face away, but even so he was close enough to brush his lips against her cheek. It was enough. He released her suddenly and pushed her, so that she stumbled and fell down. "My God," he cried. "My God." He touched his glove to his lip, where her cheek had burned him. Then he spat, and mumbled part of a prayer of purification. "Unclean," he said, and then he made the sign of the unclean, touching the heel of his palm to his nose and ducking his head down once to either side. In the guardpost underneath the gate, other soldiers of the purge stopped what they were doing and looked out.

Farther on along the barricade, an officer turned his horse and came towards them, flicking his whip against his leg. "What's this?" he asked when he got close.

"A witch, sir." The guard was rubbing his lips and pointing.

The captain looked down from his horse. "What makes you think so?" he asked. He was an older man, and he wore his gray hair fastened in a steel clasp behind his neck, in the style of a previous generation.

"Her skin, sir. She's not human."

The captain frowned. "Superstitious jerk," he muttered, and then he swung himself heavily out of the saddle. He squatted down on the cobblestones near where the girl had fallen, and with the butt of his whip he pushed the hair back from her face. "Why, she's just a child," he said. He put his whip down on the stones, and then he stripped away one of his black gauntlets so that he could touch her face with his bare hand. "Poor child," he said. "Injected with the fever. What crime?"

"I don't know." The words burned in her throat. "I don't know," she cried. She reached out to hold his hand against her cheek. "Please, sir. Please let me in."

"The gate's closed," he said gently.

"Please, sir. My mother runs the elevator above Cosro's Barbican. I want to see her. This is my last night."

Soldiers had gathered from the guardpost and stood around them in a circle. The captain glared at them, and the circle widened as the men drifted away and stood whispering in little groups. The captain touched Rosa's forehead with his fingers.

The gate loomed above them, one of ten set into the mountainside, a square brick edifice two hundred feet high. "Of course, child, of course," he murmured. He stood and helped her to her feet, and together they passed up the steps and under the brick archway into a high, vaulted chamber stinking of urine. Wasps had made their nests among the pillars, and bats hung from the vault. At the far side, ninety-foot wooden doors led into the first tier of the Mountain of Redemption. But they were locked and barred. Rosa stood in front of them with restless hands, touching her neck, picking at the soft hair below her jaw while the captain hammered on the postern with his fist.

Nothing happened. Rosa turned to look back through the arch, behind her up the Street of Seven Sins, barricaded from the crowd on either side, patrolled by soldiers of the purge. "Don't worry," the captain reassured her. "Someone will come." He looked at his wristwatch. "How much time do you have?"

"I don't know."

"Poor child." He fumbled with a pouch at his belt and found a steel pillbox. "Let me give you something for the pain. If the pain gets too bad." He held out a small white pill.

"No. My pain is my own. Every minute of it." She scratched at the skin below her collarbone. "No," she repeated. "Besides, I need the practice." She laughed, and pulled down the bodice of her dress to show where the parson had marked her. He had filled her veins with fever, and then he had marked her shoulder with the sign of Chandra

Sere, the fourth planet, close in around the Sun. "I need the practice," she repeated, pulling at the strings of her bodice. "It's hot where I'm going. Stone melts, they say."

"Hush, child, don't bother about that. Those are just legends. Parsons' dreams. Don't worry about that. What's dead is dead."

"Legends!" she cried. "It is my faith. My God is sending me to hell. It is my God," she cried, wiping the sweat from around her mouth. "Don't try to console me. I will not be consoled. But one day I will wake in Paradise."

"Sooner than you think, child. Sooner than you think."

"Don't lie to me!" Daughter of a prostitute, she gripped religion tighter for having come to it so late. Paradise, she thought. For a few nights she had seen it, the last time it had passed close to Earth. Before the sugar rain had started—she had stretched her hands out to it as it rose above the hills.

"My father was a Starbridge," she continued. "That's what my mother said. That counts for something, doesn't it? I told that to the priest this afternoon, but he just laughed. Half-Starbridge, he said, that would take me halfway to Paradise. Tonight Chandra Sere is just halfway. The fire planet—how could he be so cruel?"

The captain said nothing, but he hammered on the postern with his fist. It was a small metal door to the right of the main gate, once painted red, but now streaked and dented, and in some places it had almost rusted through. But a panel on the door's upper part had recently been repainted with a portrait of St. Simeon Millefeuille, the last of the great teachers. The saint's face was pensive, but his eyes were vacant and flat white. As Rosa watched, they shuttered inward and disappeared. Behind them, through the saint's left eyesocket, she could see another eye blinking out at them, and then a bulbous human finger protruded through the hole, curling down over the saint's cheek. "Hold on," came a voice from inside. "Who's there?"

A beam of silver light shot out from the saint's right eye and played upon their faces and their clothes. There was silence for a moment, and then the voice spoke again. "Gate's closed, friends. Try the next one over. Deacon's Portal. Half a mile along the wall, and they don't lock up till one o'clock. Come back in the morning, better yet."

The captain stepped forward and held his palm up so that the light shone on his tattoos. "Ah, Captain," said the voice. "I didn't recognize you." There came the sound of bolts being drawn back, and then the door swung inward, revealing a fat man standing in the gap. "Evening, Captain, miss," he said. He took off his cap and stood rubbing his nose.

"Hello, Dim. Can you let this girl inside?"

"Don't know why I should."

"On my responsibility. I'll answer for it."

"That's all very well," said the little man. "You know the rules."

"It's only a few hours, Dim. She's got the fever. She says her mother runs the elevator up by Cosro's Barbican. Can you let her in?"

"Don't want to, Captain. Doesn't seem likely, anyway. Not unless her mother's a man."

The Captain squinted. "What do you mean?"

"Styrene Denson's run that barbican as long as I can remember. I reckon he's alive and well."

Puzzled, the captain turned around, but Rosa was too quick. The fever gave her strength; she jumped into the doorway and pushed the little man in his fat stomach so that he sprawled back against the wall. The captain swore and reached out his hand, but she was already gone, running barefoot down the corridor inside. The captain drew his pistol, but it was already too late. She was gone around a bend in the passageway, and he could hear her bare feet slapping up the first of thirty-seven flights of stairs. "It doesn't matter," he said. "She can't go far."

"I don't see why not," replied the little man, touching his stomach where the girl had pushed him. "We're not chasing her."

"Well, maybe you should ring the alarm."

The little man looked up at the wall above his head, to where a red handle was connected to a frayed blue wire all covered with spiderwebs and dirt. "Hasn't worked in my lifetime," he said. "Not unless they fixed it recently."

Princess Charity lay sleepless on her bed. She raised herself up on one elbow and looked around, half-dazed and suffocating in her airless, windowless room. In a little while she sat up against the wall and drew her knees up to her chest. At some parts of her life she had been able to sleep all day in that bed, and all night too. For weeks at a time she had been awake only for a few hours in the evening, when her maids had brought her food. Dreams had become more real than life. And this night, too, she had been drowsy. It was her last night on Earth, and she had meant to sleep it through. Already yawning, she had made dinner for herself with her own hands, sitting at the kitchen table peeling strawberries and golden oranges, eating the last of the hashish ice cream straight out of the can. But now, in bed, sleep receded from her grasp, and all the tricks that she had ever learned to coax it closer failed. She leaned her head back against the wall. She hadn't signed the lawyer's paper. She hadn't even read it. She had forgotten all about it.

A silver lamp stood on the table beside her bed, a clump of silver wildgrass, with tiny lights hidden in among its stems. She reached out to turn it on, fumbling with the switch, and then she swung her legs over the side of the bed and stood up unsteadily. The room was in a whirl around her. She caught a glimpse of her naked shoulder in the mirror hung above her washstand, a glimpse of her hand holding on to one of the carved bedposts. Though it had been months since she could smell it, she could taste the odor of her scented wallpaper in the back of her throat. It sickened her. All around her, queasy combinations of pink and gray fought queasy warfare on the walls—colors high up on the bishop's scale of visual eroticism, mixed into horrifying patterns by a blind priest. He had lit incense and spattered her mattress with drops of holy oil. He had consecrated her bedroom as a shrine of love. A grotesquely phallic statue of Beloved Angkhdt crouched in one corner over an oil lantern. Her shelves were lined with devotional literature, and the night table was still crowded with unguents and powders, and aphrodisiacs, and strange mechanical devices. She had inherited them from her predecessor in that room, the old man's second wife. They were neatly arranged and carefully dusted, never opened, never used.

She looked across at herself in the mirror above her washstand, the outlines of her famished body, her dark hair. Mesmerized by her reflection, she walked towards it from across the room, wondering, as her face came into focus, at what point, at what moment she had departed from beauty, for she had been a beautiful child. When she was a child, she had been able to make a silence just by walking into a room. Now, sitting down to stare at herself in the spotted surface of the glass, she wondered at what moment that had changed. There must have been a single instant, she thought, when misery and disappointment had broken through the surface of her features, changing not their shape but their significance. It couldn't have been long ago. She had been born in spring, and spring was not half gone. She remembered her wedding party when she was just a girl, the day she had married the old man. Then she had been beautiful, in her white dress. And she remembered her friends and schoolmates crowding around to say goodbye, young girls, and boys in their first uniforms. "We will meet again in Paradise," they had said, loudly coached by the deaf parson who had performed the ceremony. Except for one—she remembered her cousin Thanakar, with his long hair and his long face, limping through the crowd. "It's a goddamned shame," he had said, scowling, and when the priest had reached out to restrain him, Thanakar had pushed the deaf man's hand away, his face twisted up with loathing. He was the only one whom she had seen again.

On a table next to the washstand stood vats and jars of makeup—eyeliner and mascara, vermilion, and aromatic powders wrapped in leaves. Idly, she mixed some colors on her palette, wondering if she could draw some beauty back into her face. She had always been skillful with her hands. She raised her brush up to her eyelid and then hesitated, staring at her face in the mirror. What had gone wrong? Nose, ear, lips, cheek, skin—everything was perfect. Nothing had changed. And yet, something had been added that had ruined it all. In her eye, perhaps. In the center, in the bottom of her eye, there lurked some poisonous new thing.

She put down her brush and unscrewed one of the jars. Long before, her mother had gone home to Paradise. And the night before she left, she had put some makeup on her face, in a style that had occurred to her in a dream. She had not wanted to arrive in Paradise dressed out of fashion, to be laughed at by all her friends that had gone before. She was a vain woman. And the night before she died, she had put silver makeup on her cheeks, emphasizing the ridges of the bone. When Charity and Abu, her young daughter and her son, had come to say goodbye, they had run to her and put their arms around her neck, and she had pulled away, ever so slightly. Smiling, she had pulled away. She had not wanted them to spoil her makeup, but Charity had reached out to kiss her on the cheek, and had come away with silver pigment on her lips.

Now Charity opened a jar of the same color and mixed it experimentally on her palm. And then she stopped and turned her head, because the door behind her had opened partway, and it was as if a gust of hot wind had come in from the darkened antechamber, and she could feel the temperature of the air around her rise a little bit. At the same time she was conscious of a noise, a sound of roaring, labored breathing. Rubbing the ball of pigment into a puddle in the center of her palm, Charity touched almost unconsciously the tiny lion's head tattooed below her index finger, the symbol of immunity from fear. She turned her head.

A young woman stood in the doorway, Charity's own age, or perhaps a little younger. Her black hair was matted and tangled, and she wore a long ragged dress of yellow nylon. She had loosened the bodice from around her neck to give herself air. Her skin was flushed and dark.

They stared at each other for a moment, and then the girl dropped her eyes. She bowed her head and made the obligatory gestures of respect, pressing the knuckles of her right hand up against her forehead.

Princess Charity crossed her arms over her chest. She was wearing a robe of purple spidersilk, and she pulled it up around her shoulders. Some silver pigment had come off on the collar; irritated, she turned to clean her hands with cotton wool and cold cream, and then she pulled her collar down to clean the spot, rubbing gently at the spidery material. "Who are you?" she asked, not looking up. "How did you get in?"

"Please, ma'am, the door was open." The girl's voice was harsh and full of breath. "They've all run away. They nailed a notice to your door. Pink. Moral contamination."

"And you're not afraid?" asked Charity, smiling gently, rubbing at the spot. She looked up. The girl was pretty, she decided. Again she wiped her hands and smoothed the collar back from her shoulder, arranging a fold of material over the damp patch.

"No, ma'am. I'm not afraid. I'd come to see what they had done to you."

Charity looked up at her. "Who are you?" she asked.

Rosa paused to wipe her lips with a corner of her shawl.

Her other hand moved restlessly around her body, touching, scratching. "I do the laundry for this floor," she said. "Used to. These four apartments."

Charity Starbridge stood up. Again she crossed her arms over her breasts. "Yes," the girl continued. "I turned you in. I did my duty as a citizen, and I hope they hang you for it. Look what they have done to me."

"It serves you right," said the princess softly. "It was no business of yours."

Rosa wiped her face with her shawl. Sweat ran down from underneath her hair and along the insides of her arms. She stripped the shawl from around her shoulders, wadded it up into a ball and rubbed her neck with it, and then she threw it into a corner of the room. "Oh, God," she moaned. "I'm burning." She reached out to catch hold of one of the bedposts, and then she leaned against it.

Princess Charity stood looking at her for a moment. Then she bent to rummage in a small refrigerator beside her washstand, pouring bottled water into a glass. "Here," she said, standing up and taking a few steps across the room. The girl reached out and took the glass and drank the water down. She held the glass against her head. "Oh, God," she moaned. "I ran up all the way. I thought my heart would burst."

Princess Charity gave her the bottle and took back the glass. Rosa drank. From the bedpost hung a linen towel; she pulled it down and poured water over it with shaking fingers, and then she held it up against her face. "Oh, God, I'm sorry," she cried. "I never would have told them if I had known."

"What's done is done," murmured the princess. Confronted with weakness, she felt strong. "Never mind," she said. "It doesn't matter. Only tell me, why did you do it? Was I so cruel a mistress?"

"Oh, ma'am, how could you be cruel? I worked here for a thousand days, and I never even saw you. But your husband, he was kind to me. He once gave me a dollar and a half."

"Ah. So it was for his sake."

"No. It was for my sake. Oh, ma'am, I hope they hang you. Don't you understand? I washed your sheets a thousand times. It was my fate, and I was true to it. Was it too much to ask the same of you?"

The princess put the glass down on her washstand. She rubbed her hands together, her fingers stroking the marks of all her obligations: courage, kindness, modesty. She stroked the golden ball and chain tattooed on the lap of skin under her thumb, the mark of marital fidelity.

Rosa had collapsed against the bedpost, gasping, out of breath. The princess went to her and took the bottle and the towel, and with her own hands she wiped the sweat from the girl's face. Rosa submitted and suffered Charity to lead her to the bed, where she sat down. "I feel so tired," she said. "I ran up all those stairs."

"Hush," murmured the princess. "It's the fever. You may lie here for a little while. But first tell me, what was the stain you found? On my bedsheet. A bloodstain, was it not?"

"Part of it. I know what it was. I'm not a child."

"No, but a bloodstain. Didn't that mean anything to you? I was married more than twenty months—two thousand four hundred and one days. My husband never touched me. Look at my hands. I have other obligations, too. Fertility—look—and love. I thought you might have understood. You might have pitied me."

She had been fussing with the girl while she was speaking, stroking her down onto the bed, stroking her hair. But now Rosa started up. "Pity you?" she cried. "God in heaven, pity you? You must be insane. Even now, when they have filled my blood with poison and charted my soul's flight to Chandra Sere. Pity you, is that why I came all this way? No, I wanted to see what they would do to you. I hoped they'd hang you. They've been hanging Starbridges, I hear. I've seen posters for your lover in the streets. But not you. No luck. I know already. They're sending you back."

"Yes," said the princess. "They come tomorrow morning." She spoke gently, softly, but the girl pulled away and buried her face in the pillow. "It's not fair," she sobbed.

Charity reached out to touch her hair. "Never mind," she said. "Not many of us believe in Paradise anymore, or in hell either."

The girl turned towards her, her lips pulled back. "You don't even believe it! You work us like slaves—who gave you the right if God does not exist? Hypocrite! Don't touch me." Delirious, she made the sign of the unclean, pressing the heel of her hand against her nose. But she didn't have the strength to pull away; she collapsed against the pillow. The silk turned yellow where her cheek touched it, seared by the heat of her skin.

Charity waited, and in a little while she reached over and wiped Rosa's face again. "I think you think my life must be more pleasant than it is," she said, touching the girl's hair. She couldn't keep her hands away. She was fascinated by the girl's beauty. The two of them were similar in every part, only the girl was beautiful. I lost my beauty with my freedom, thought Charity. It is freedom that illuminates a face.

She was sitting next to Rosa on the bed, her back to the door. Someone staggered in; she jumped up and pulled her robe around her, and turned her face away. A man crouched in the doorway, leaning up against the frame. He held up his hand. "Don't worry, ma'am. Don't worry. I won't bother you. I won't even look." He pointed to the bed. "It's her, ma'am. It's her I want."

He was a renegade parson, his voice full of alcohol, his red robes torn, his face dry and spotted, his nose broken and red. His scalp showed in strips through his lank hair. "Don't let me disturb you," he said. "It's her I've come for."

At the sound of his voice, the girl sat up. She stared at him in horror for a moment and then sank back onto the pillows. "Don't come near me," she warned. "God damn you, can't you let me go?"

The parson cringed against the doorframe, smiling nervously, picking at his lips. "I've come to fetch her," he said. "I've come to take her home."

The girl pointed at him from the bed. "Don't come any closer," she commanded. "Drunken pig! Eunuch! Can't you let me alone?"

"Oh, Rosa, how can you say such things?" whined the parson. "After everything I've done for you. I followed you halfway across the city tonight, just to bring you home."

"Don't you understand?" cried the girl. "I'm dying. You've gotten all you're going to get from me."

"Rosa, how can you talk like that? After I've cared for you all these months. Fed you and kept you. Don't you trust me yet? Look, I have medicine for you." He stepped towards her into the room, holding out a little package of aluminum foil.

"Please, ma'am," cried Rosa. "Don't let him touch me. Don't let him come any closer."

Princess Charity stepped forward into the light. The parson turned to face her, bowing humbly. "Excuse me—I'm sorry. I don't mean to disturb you. Raksha Starbridge is my name, formerly in holy orders. Eleven months ago I found this girl abandoned in the street and took her in. She's been like a daughter to me."

"Daughter?" cried Rosa. "Lecherous pig!"

"Don't listen to her, ma'am. It's the fever talking. The fever's in her brain. If it weren't for me, she would have starved to death." He had opened up the foil package, and he rubbed some of the red powder it contained into his gums. And as he twisted the foil back up, he paused to wink heavily. "And would you believe it? When I met her, her palms were naked as a baby's."

He had the face of someone who drinks more than he eats, his eyes bloodshot, his cheeks covered with scars and broken blood vessels. On the bed behind him, Rosa had started to cry.

"Yes, ma'am," continued the parson. "I can see she fooled you with all her spiritual talk. She's got no right to talk like that. Her mother was an atheist. An antinomial whore. She didn't even have a name until I gave her one. Rosamundi, like the flower. When I met her, she could hardly talk. Just a few words and bits of songs. She was singing in the streets for pennies. Now look at her—everything she is, I taught her. I taught her how to work. Every morning I drew those tattoos on fresh. Oil pencil. She used to beg me to make them permanent. But I'm not such a fool."

He was a mendicant preacher, a Starbridge who had lost his destiny. Expelled from his congregation, he lived by his wits among the common people, saying mass for a dollar or a bottle of wine, healing the sick, telling fortunes. And among the common people he had found something to love. Now he turned and sat down on the bed. "Oh, Rosa," he said. "Isn't it better to tell the truth, now that it can't hurt you anymore? There—don't cry. You don't really think I'd let them send my little girl to hell?"

She looked up at him, tears running down her face. But her cheeks were so hot, they evaporated before they were halfway down. She pulled her bodice down to show where the priest had marked her, the horned circle on her shoulder, the sign of Chandra Sere. "You're too late," she said. "I'm on my way. One or two hours, not more. I saw him cast the spell."

Her voice was a dry creaking in her throat. She had stopped sweating, and her skin was assuming a dry, papery look; in some places it was even turning dark, like paper held over a flame. The parson, too, had started to cry. But in everything he did there was a mixture of sentiment and slyness, so that even as the tears rolled down his nose, he turned to the princess and winked. "I know," he said. "Poor girl." He reached out for Rosa's hands, and this time she did not resist him; he took her hands and chafed them between his own. "I know," he said. "But stranger things have happened. I've heard that there is someone bound for Paradise tonight. More than one, though truthfully, the conjunction of the planets is not ideal." He turned and gave the princess a sharp look. "Maybe we could get someone to give up her place."

"Gladly," said the princess.

"I thought so," muttered the parson. "God knows I'm in no hurry to go back."

Rosa lay back slowly on the pillows. "Only Starbridges..." she croaked.

"And don't I have the power to make you a Starbridge?" cried the parson, tears in his eyes. "Aren't I still a priest of God? Look, I have brought my tools." He turned her hands palm up on the bedsheet, and then he started fumbling underneath his robe, and from hidden pockets he drew out scalpels, needles, lotions, inks, books of numbers, astrological charts. He laid them all out on the surface of the bed. He took the towel the girl had used to cool her face, and squeezed out some liquid from a tube, and cleaned her hands with it until her palms were clean and white. "Come here," he said over his shoulder. "I need you for a model."

Charity moved close, knelt down, and put her own hands on the coverlet. All trace of palsy had vanished from the parson's fingers; with his tongue in the corner of his mouth, he drew quickly and expertly. Flowers grew and spread along the hills and valleys of the young girl's palms—castles, faces, lists of privileges. And when the time came for him to make the cuts, his work was easy, for the blood had receded from her hands, and the incisions were as dry as scratches on a piece of paper. All the while Rosa looked on, the breath rattling in her throat, her eyes wide with wonder, her expression changing gradually until there was something like happiness in it, something like contentment. The parson muttered incantations and made quick, deft gestures in the air. And when he moved the needle through the cuts, the colors seemed to spread out by themselves, mixing and making patterns, secondary colors, a whole world. It was perfect. And then he spread a sealer over it, and then, finally, he reached up to her shoulder. Under his needle, miraculously, the mark of Chandra Sere became less distinct, and out of it spread crowns and halos and the head of a dog, silver and golden, the mark of Paradise.

The parson leaned back. His face was covered with sweat. Rosa had closed her eyes. With one hand he reached out to touch her forehead, while with the other he took her pulse. "What time is it?" he asked.

"Twenty past two," answered the princess.

"Then it is time." He consulted an astrological chart, a map of the solar system, and then something that looked like a railway timetable. "Dear child," he said. "It's time to go." Again he touched her forehead. She opened her eyes and smiled, and brought her palms up to look at them. "Already?" she whispered. She looked down to her shoulder, and then she turned to rub her face against the parson's hand. The pillowcase was singed where she had lain.

"You leave at two-thirty," he said softly. "Look. This is the way." He opened his hand to reveal a pill held between his fingers, a clear capsule with some liquid in it.

For an instant she looked doubtful. Then she turned to the princess, who smiled a little bit and nodded. Rosa smiled back and then, hesitantly, like a little girl, she opened her mouth and put out her tongue. The parson blessed her with his fingers and then laid the pill upon her tongue. She closed her mouth and settled back and closed her eyes. That was the end. At two-thirty precisely, her breathing stopped.

"I wasn't to go before morning," said the princess after a while. "Ten o'clock."

"Shh," whispered the parson. He looked up at the ceiling. Tears trembled on his chin. He sat still for a few minutes, and then he reached into his pocket and drew out a pint of wine.

By three-fifteen, Charity began to understand that she was free. She went to lie down on a sofa in another room, and when she returned, the parson had passed out on the floor. The girl was lying back in bed, her body cool, her face peaceful. Charity stood in the doorway watching her, fascinated by her beauty. After a few minutes she went to stand above her, and with the priest's scalpel she reached down to cut the buttons off of Rosa's bodice, and cut away the hooks that held it closed, and then she slit the yellow nylon down to the girl's waist and peeled it back, exposing skin so beautiful and breasts so strong and perfect, it made her want to cry. If only she could be like that, lie there like that. She cut away the ragged skirt. Shifting the body to one side, she pulled the whole dress away, crushed it into a ball, threw it to the floor, and then she stood up to look at the girl as she lay naked, her skin clear and brown, the light from the bedside table catching at the soft hair that grew along her stomach, along the outside of her thigh.

Then, scarcely knowing why, Charity went to her washstand and gathered together a hairbrush and some pots of eyeshadow and rouge. She sat down on the bed, and with an expert hand she brushed the girl's hair quiet and put a little paint onto her face—only a little, where death was already robbing the color from her cheek. She darkened the girl's eyebrows and stroked some indigo into the corners of her eyes. She paused, her brush suspended above Rosa's face, and then sat back and smiled. She was making the girl into a Starbridge, for the lower classes were not allowed to

paint their faces or wear jewelry. But more than that—
she unclasped from around her neck the silver necklace
with the bloodstone pendant that her brother had given
her on her wedding day. She paused, and then she drew
the necklace around Rosa's neck and arranged it so that
the pendant fell between her breasts. In some ways the
girl was very like her.

The princess laughed. She pulled the silver combs out of
her own hair and shook it wildly about her head, and
rubbed it into a mass of tangles. Then she stood up, and
with the barest glance at the parson to see if he still slept,
she shook her robe from her shoulders so that it fell around
her feet. She stooped to pick up Rosa's dress. It stank of
sweat and fever and was slit so that it no longer closed in
front, but it fit the princess as if it had been made for her in
the palace dress shops. She took it off and sat down at her
table to repair it.

With a silver needle and a silken thread, she sat mending
the yellow dress, sewing up where it was torn, patching it
with pieces cut from a golden scarf. After about half an
hour she paused to roll a marijuana cigarette and smoke it
thoughtfully. The parson had fallen away from her onto his
side; she turned around and studied him, and studied the
dead girl, trying to understand her feelings. "Rejoice at
every death," advised the Starbridge Catechism. Nevertheless, there was something eerie and disagreeable about
death, Charity decided, even when it was swift and merci-
ful. She sucked the smoke deep into her lungs, trying to
relax. Her fingers were shaking. In spite of everything that
had happened that night, it was hard not to feel optimistic.
She was free. The girl lay on her bed, wearing her jewels,
marked with her tattoos, looking so much like her. Not that
it even mattered, thought the princess, for not more than a
dozen people had seen her face since she was married, and
of those most were dead or gone away.

She stubbed the roach of her cigarette out in a crystal

ashtray, rubbing it reflectively over the image of Angkhdt the God of Matrimony incised into the bottom. The forces that had shaped her life so far had been so inexorable, the routine of it so deadening, that now, suddenly free, she felt giddy and off balance, as if she had suddenly stepped outside into the sunlight after months in a dark cell. Already she imagined she felt changes in herself. She got unsteadily to her feet.

And when she was ready to go, barefoot, dressed in yellow rags, her shawl clutched tight around her shoulders, she knelt by the parson to wake him up. She had left a suicide note by her night table, a last farewell in complicated calligraphy. Farewell to whom? And yet it seemed appropriate. She was a different person; she had coated her palms with greasepaint and powder to obscure the marks of privilege. That was the last stage of her transformation; when it was complete she laughed aloud, and laughed to see the parson, shaken out of sleep, stare at her slack-mouthed. She could feel him cringe under her touch, could hear the whimper in his throat. He pulled away and lay back against the wall, swallowing heavily, breathing through his mouth. His wits were diluted with liquor. But in a moment he began to understand; he looked over her shoulder and saw the dead girl on the bed, dressed in a silken nightgown, her lips painted, her hair brushed and arranged. For a moment the fear in his eyes gave way to sadness, and then his face cracked open and he smiled, showing rotten stumps of teeth. "You won't last a day out there," he said when he could speak.

"We'll see."

"Your voice, your movements, everything is wrong."

"I'll learn. Listen: Eunuch. Drunken Eunuch. Pig. Drunken pig." Experimentally, she sharpened her voice into the accent of the starving class. "When I want your advice, I'll ask for it, drunk pig. Now get your things and let's go."

# EXECUTIONS | 2

When Prince Abu was a boy, he enjoyed playing with dolls long after the age when most children tire of them. His father had died when he was young, one of the last casualties of the winter war. Shortly after, his mother had drifted into orbit near a planet of her own, a silent world of penance and religious ceremonial. He and his sister were raised by servants, by married aunts, by loud, bearded uncles home on leave. These would bring him legions of toy soldiers, Starbridge officers on horseback, beautifully painted, their banners streaming in the wind. But their faces were so fierce. Arranging them together, the young prince found it hard to imagine conversations of any subtlety taking place among them. On horseback with the wind so strong, the men would have to shout just to make themselves heard above the jingle of their bridles and the beating of the flags. It was hard to imagine anything but harsh cries of defiance. To be sure, the banners on their backs made some kind of dialogue, announcing in Starbridge pictographs each man's name and obligations. "I am brave," said one. "I am not so brave as you, but braver than he," confided another. "I am scarcely brave at all, but I am fearfully intelligent," confessed a third. "Nevertheless, I will die next Tuesday from a wound in the throat."

For Prince Abu it was not enough. Instead he preferred the more fluid conversations that took place in the hallway of his sister's dollhouse. There an elderly gentleman pointed towards the sideboard. "Do you see that envelope next to the bottle of pills? It contains six photographs and a letter for my friend. You must bring it to him quickly, for I will not leave this house again. Wait there for an answer. As for these pills, take them once an hour. These fits of weeping will pass."

"Yes, sir," answers the servant girl. But her white china face is so ambiguous. Surely she realizes that by the time she delivers the letter, it will have lost its meaning.

On the last night of his life the prince found that he could remember many of these conversations clearly. He stood in the middle of his cell in Wanhope Prison Hospital, whispering them to himself. These ones from his childhood had a strange, disjointed quality. What photographs? What pills?

Once, driving through the city in his motorcar, Prince Abu had told his cousin a whole story he had spun up out of nothing while they were waiting for the traffic. Their chauffeur had stopped the car behind a convoy of episcopal trucks. Up ahead, a man had been crushed beneath a cart, and the traffic had been halted all along the street while the police pried the man's body from the mud. In an instant their car had been surrounded by a swarm of beggars. Thanakar had put his window up, but Abu had rummaged in his pockets and pulled out a big handful of change.

His cousin had sat back, smiling cynically, his eyes half-closed. And even Abu was not paying close attention; he was listening to the sound of his own voice against a background of murmured prayers, and beggars chanting the nine benefits of generosity. But in a moment the cadence was interrupted by a scream of rage and the sound of fists drumming on the roof. Prince Abu hastily rolled up his window. His handful of stone currency had contained a silver dollar; concentrating on his story, he had handed it out with the rest. A beggar's fingers had closed on it and disappeared, but as soon as the man had realized what it was, he dropped it in the mud, shaking his fingers as if they had been burned. Gold and silver were the Starbridge metals, forbidden to the poor, and in an instant all the men were shouting, outraged, pressing their faces up against the glass.

"How can you be so careless?" Dr. Thanakar had cried, after the police had come and gone and sent them on their way. "How can you make fun of them? Next time they'll roll the car. We're that close to a revolution, and you have to play the fool."

"I don't think they would have hurt us," Abu had replied. "I thought you'd welcome a revolution."

"You can't expect everyone to be like you. Not everyone can share your zest for self-destruction. This system is absurd, but at least we're at the top. At least we're better off than that." Thanakar had motioned out the windscreen of the car to where a crew stood working on the road, leaning on their shovels, listening to the instructions of a young priest in scarlet robes.

Alone in his prison cell, Prince Abu remembered his friend's words. A passion for self-destruction, he thought. He examined the binding of the book of poetry in his hand and cast it wearily onto the bed. On the table stood the remnants of his dinner: curried plums and ginger, and walnuts in a silver dish. Not trusting him with a knife and fork, the curates had given him a spoon. There was no glass or porcelain that he could break and use against himself. He had felt like a child with his spoon and metal cup.

Above him a window was set into the quilted wall. He pulled a chair out from the table and climbed onto it so that his face was level with the bars. But he hesitated for a minute before he looked out, leaning his head against the wall, rubbing his cheek against the yellow silk, examining the pattern up close. It was against Starbridge custom to wear corrective lenses. Abu, who was myopic, took pleasure in looking closely at things, for at a distance of a few inches his eyes could magnify small objects into images of great clarity. What from far away looked like specks upon the surface of the silken wall, up close he could see that they were insects, tiny black insects, clambering with difficulty over the uneven surface as if over the hairs of a man's arm. The lamp from the table threw a soft, oblique light. Abu could see the shadows of the insects on the wall.

He reached across to the window and chafed his thumb along one of the silver bars. The guildmark of the silversmith was sunk deep into the metal, a centaur carrying a machine gun, and Abu chafed the ball of his thumb against the tiny figure. The silver had thickened slightly around the base of the bars, and the metal was soft there, soft enough to take his thumbprint. The bars were wearing thin up at the top as the metal softened and ran down. Abu wondered whether the prison guards had to reverse them in their frame from time to time, to keep them from draining away.

He gripped the bars and pulled himself up to the windowsill and looked out. His cell was on the third floor of the psychiatric ward, overlooking the courtyard. For an instant he saw everything clearly, and then the blurred mist of his myopia settled down over the courtyard. But even so, he knew the space was packed with people standing patiently in the rain, staring up at his window with a focused concentration that felt like heat on his bare cheeks. An arc light switched on down below and reached its blue beam up through the bars of his window to seize hold of his face; he stood balanced on his chair, blinded and blinking, while from the courtyard below him a sudden noise rose up, a roaring from a thousand throats. He couldn't understand what they were saying.

He stood at the window, blinded, his mouth open, and

then he turned away. A guard had entered the room behind him, a hospital orderly in a white robe. He was making the gestures of respect. When he was finished, he stood erect, a young man with a dark, heavy face. "Congratulations," he said. "They're cheering for you."

"I can't understand what they're saying."

"They're saying, 'Save us! Save us!'"

Embarrassed, Abu smiled, and rubbed his lips with the back of his hand.

He had not washed in the week since he was taken, nor had he changed his clothes. He stood balanced on his chair, the back of his head against the window. To the orderly, only the outline of his big, soft body was visible, only the outline of his balding head. He stood leaning back against the bars, lit from behind by the arc light, a cloud of blue radiance shining around his head.

"I took one of your undershirts to rip up and sell as souvenirs," said the orderly. "To pay for the postage and all that. I thought you wouldn't mind."

Prince Abu smiled. "No, I don't care," he said. "Did you get what I wanted?"

"Yes, sir." The orderly slipped a quart of whiskey out of a paper bag. "I mailed the letter to your sister," he said. "Charity Starbridge. The courier had run away, so I took it directly to the post office." He sighed. "The mails are undependable these days."

"Thank you."

"My privilege, sir. You're our most famous client now. There must be fifteen hundred people in the courtyard, and I hear they are already lining up along the streets you'll pass tomorrow. The police are expecting twenty thousand just around the bonfire."

"How gratifying."

"I know what you mean, sir. But if you're not doing it for the effect, why are you doing it? You could just stop it any time you want. You could just walk out of here, just by raising up your hand. Not that it wouldn't be a sort of anticlimax."

Prince Abu smiled. "Well, that's it, isn't it? I've let things go so far." He brought the palm of his right hand up in front of his nose, so that he could see in minute detail the mark of the golden sun, the most powerful tattoo in Charn. He examined it mournfully. It had been the curse and burden of his life, a long, sad practical joke, for what use was power without strength or will or faith? "No," he said. "It's too late now. Where would I go?"

In that phase of spring, many people still believed that diseases could be spread by music, that sickness could be wakened in the blood by certain combinations of notes. Priests and bankers used this fear to guard their holy places. They decorated bank vaults and granaries with musical notations set into the tile. And when a Starbridge woman married in those days, the priest would mark the threshold of her husband's house. He would paint a line of notes along the inside of the sill, using a mixture of attar and albumen, invisible, yet potent too. In those days it was against custom for a woman to step outside her husband's house until she was past childbearing age.

Raksha Starbridge squatted over the doorjamb of the princess's apartment, trying to make it out. He had rubbed the faceless marble with a mixture of lemon juice and wine, and now he moved a lighted match along the stone. Gradually a line of notes came clear, blackened by the flame.

"There," he said. He sat back on his ankles, the match trembling in his hand.

"What does it say?" asked Charity. The parson had already crossed over and sat in the hallway, but she still lingered in the door.

"Oh, God, I don't know," complained the parson. "It's been so long. It's coded to your name." He rubbed the matchstick along the line of notes. "I thought you didn't believe in this shit."

"Just tell me what it says."

The parson smiled and showed his rotten teeth. He gave her a sly wink and then started to hum a little tune. Charity put her fingers in her ears. "Stop it!" she commanded. "Just tell me."

"Oh, I don't know. It's about remorse. Self-hatred. An outbreak of self-hatred. It says you'll be dead in two months if you cross over. Suicide."

The princess laughed. Relieved, she stepped over the threshold. "Then they're too late," she said. And then she looked back through the open doorway, suddenly afraid. The atrium stretched into the shadows, lined with cabinets and family portraits. Here and there she could see glimpses of frescos, tapestries, and carpets through the open doorways bordering the hall; she had lit all of the lamps before she went and run quickly through each room, passing her hands over the marble busts, touching the spines of her favorite books, inhaling, suddenly resensitized, the fragrances of her lifetime in those rooms: dust, hashish, cedar, and old stone. Suddenly resensitized, she had seen as if for the first time the beauty of a ewer of cut glass. She had batted it to the floor, and it had broken into a thousand parts. "What's that?" Raksha Starbridge had cried. He had been looting the kitchen cabinets for food, looking for money in the pockets of her husband's suits.

But as she hesitated on the threshold, it was as if she were searching for reasons to be afraid. As soon as she stepped into the outside corridor, then she was no longer superstitious. In that one moment she shed the whole impossible burden of her marriage, laying it down inside the door where she had picked it up the only other time that she had crossed that sill, the day she had married the old man. She felt like a child again. And though the old man had always been gentle, and though she had cried until her eyes were sore the day she heard that he was dead, and though he and her brother had been the only two companions she had had to help her carry the burden of that house, still she left the old man's memory there too. She ran down the outside corridor towards the elevator banks, suddenly remembering what it had been like, her wedding procession along that same hall, up from her mother's apartment on the thirty-fourth floor. As she ran, the empty months fell away, as if even the memory of them could not exist outside the perfumed atmosphere of her husband's house. She remembered how it had been before; more than that, she felt it in her body. At Starbridge Dayschools she had been eighth in her class, winning prizes in physics, mathematics, archery, and law. She had written a thesis in silver ink, using a whole arcane vocabulary of knowledge. So long ago—now, running down the corridor towards the elevator, the only word she could remember was *syzygy*.

Raksha Starbridge hurried after her. Sick of him, disgusted by his ugliness, she ran fast, trying to lose him in the empty passageways. At the elevator banks she kept her finger on the button, hearing the bell ring somewhere far below. But no one came. Once she heard one of the express cars at the end of the row rattle past her, ascending rapidly, but it didn't stop. Out of breath, she leaned against the metal doors. The corridor was dark here, the carpet dusty, the walls faded and stained. A statuette of Angkhdt the God of Light crouched in a niche above the button for the elevator, his tongue a small electric bulb. Loose in its socket, it flickered miserably.

Raksha Starbridge appeared at the turning of the passage. "These are all broken," he announced. "We'll have to take the service car from the floor below." But at that moment the door she was leaning against opened, revealing a gnomelike operator, perhaps the same one who had taken her upstairs on her wedding day. Then he had bowed almost to the floor and made an elaborate dance out of the gestures of respect, for she had been dressed in purest white, with a necklace of flowers from the bishop's own garden. But now he peered at her with eyes full of hostility. Astonished, she stared back at him, expecting him at any moment to drop his eyes and bring his knuckles to his forehead. Then she remembered her new clothes.

"What do you want?" asked the gnome.

"Please, sir, can you take me down?"

He didn't answer, and Charity was afraid she had gotten the accent wrong. He shook his head and stared at her, and then he said, "That guard tell me that girl run loose up here. That girl break in. That girl you?"

"No sir." She took a step backwards, suddenly glad that Raksha Starbridge had come up beside her. And when he put his hand on her shoulder, she didn't pull away. "She's with me," said the parson. He winked.

Deeply suspicious, the gnome peered out at the parson's ragged cassock, the neck of his wine bottle sticking from his pocket, his filthy hair, his broken fingernails. Then, slowly, as if unwillingly, he put his fist to his forehead and bowed low. He was powerless to do otherwise, no matter what he thought. He stepped back into the car and gave them space to enter.

All the way down, Charity could feel the pressure of his stare itching between her shoulderblades. The elevator was a small one, paneled with exotic carvings, upholstered in green velvet. The lights had burned out, but the gnome had hung a lantern of his own devising from a hook in the ceiling; it was touching, thought Charity, how closely he still clung to his duty, even though the city was on fire and most of his masters had already run away. These positions were hereditary. No doubt the gnome had spent his whole life in that car. Perhaps he had even been born on the overstuffed banquette. He carried some priest's crude rendition of an elevator's button panel etched into the skin below his little finger.

Charity had covered her own palms with paint; they felt sticky and unclean as she tightened and relaxed her fists. She thought she could understand something of the gnome's deep disapproval, his fear of pollution, his feeling of possessiveness about his little car. She too felt polluted by the parson's hand on her bare shoulder. When the doors opened on the ground floor, she jumped out quickly. "Please," she said, turning back towards the gnome to apologize, but then she stopped. Without thinking, she had used the honorific appropriate to their stations, a princess and a palace servant. She stopped when she saw the look of horror on his face, but the parson was behind her and grabbed her by the arm. "Filthy slut," he muttered. "Don't give yourself airs."

Then he pulled her away through the enormous gallery at the bottom of the building. Their footsteps echoed over the empty tiles, stirring up eddies of tiny green birds. Clouds of birds migrated through the distant vaults, following constellations set into the stone, mosaic figures of the zodiac. Charity looked up with an open mouth. Wineshops, bookshops, dress shops, and delicatessens stretched around her in a circle. Many were boarded up and dark, but the lights were on in a few restaurants, and in a few of the offices priests and seminarians kept late hours, dozing over the ledgers and accounts.

Charity stared up, entranced. "Is that the sky?" she whispered, but the parson didn't answer. Instead, he dragged her away, onward through passageways and colonnades, through waiting rooms and mirrored halls. And finally they passed through the first gates, into a vast deserted courtyard under the open sky. It was almost morning.

Underneath the statue of Cosro Starbridge and his nine sons, they rested in a thicket of stone legs. Charity was eager to go on. The parson lagged behind, leaning against the ankle of the youngest son.

He hung back, out of breath, and with trembling fingers he unscrewed the top of his pint of wine. He threw his skinny head back to taste the last of it, and then he pointed forward, the bottle still in his hand. Across the yard stood an ancient gate, flanked on both sides by seated statues of Beloved Angkhdt. A quote from holy scripture was carved into the pediment between them: "Set me on fire, fill me with your seed."

Giddy in the open air, Charity danced over the pavement

and stood beneath it, and there was something in the stone muzzles of the god that made her pause, puzzling out the uncouth words, obscure in any language. "What does it mean?" she asked as the parson staggered up.

Scowling, he turned his head away. Among the refuse of his mind he groped for the continuation of the text, learned in seminary long before, when he was young. And in a little while he found it: "'. . . For I am yours, my beloved, now especially, while the morning is still sweet, and the morning stars are hidden in a gauze of mist . . .'"

"What does it mean?" repeated Charity.

The parson scowled. "It means the world belongs to us," he said. "To Starbridges. To you and me." He flicked his empty bottle away over the stones, and it shattered in a corner of the wall. And as if that were some kind of signal, the doors trembled and grated open with a hollow booming noise, splitting away from Charity as she stood on the threshold, showing her world for the first time. From where she stood, a small stair led down into the garden of the same temple she had seen from far above, where the gallows stood like a clump of trees, poisoning the air with bitter fruit. Soldiers patrolled the steps, paying no attention to her in her yellow dress, though they saluted the parson as he hobbled down beside her.

The air was warmer here and it was full of smells. That was the first thing she noticed, the air so rich that it seemed hard to breathe, so thick with odors: cinnamon and cloves, urine and gasoline, onions and wet mud. A woman sprawled out on the steps next to the captain of the guard, dressed in the peach-colored uniform of the guild of prostitutes, smoking hashish from a metal pipe, and as Charity passed, she threw her head back and laughed aloud. Farther below, a boy gnawed furtively on a radish. And below him the garden was full of people, clustered around the bases of the gibbets, talking with strange urgency, gesticulating and pointing. Charity stepped down into the mud. Immediately she was surrounded by a mass of people jostling against her, jabbering in languages she didn't know. Happy and excited, she reached out her hands. The warm air, the sweat on her bare skin, the mud between her toes, all filled her with an ecstasy that was close to nausea, a feeling of pollution more vital than anything she had experienced before. She was ready to begin.

In those days it was the fashion for the priests of Charn to mutilate themselves. The bishop's secretary had approved a new translation of the Song of Angkhdt, and one new verse was widely quoted: "Break me in pieces, oh my beloved. Have I not hands, mouth, eyes, feet, heart . . . ?" And so all spring the streets were full of flagellants, and priests would mutilate themselves on their own altars, in bloody public rituals. Individually, it gave them some authority. It was an impressive sight to watch an old man get up at the altar rail to preach, his eyes burned out of his head.

But nothing was more pathetic than to see a crowd of priests together, and that morning in the council chamber of the Inner Ear, on October 45th, in the eighth phase of spring, there must have been two hundred slouching in their chairs, rows and rows of blind, footless, fat old men. Many were already dead, mere skeletons wrapped in gorgeous robes, their miters slipping from their polished skulls. Many more were almost dead, carried up from their apartments on the backs of servants. For no one had wanted to miss that meeting, dead or not.

The council chamber was built in the shape of a shallow amphitheater, high in the central tower of the Temple of Kindness and Repair, on a hill overlooking the city. In front of the chamber was a raised dais, and behind it stretched a great flat pane of solid glass, forty feet from edge to edge, mined unbroken in a single piece during the reign of the eighteenth bishop. From the dais you could see the city spreading out to the horizon, held in its cup of hills, and in the distance, miles away, the Mountain of Redemption loomed through the mist and smoke. Between the temple and the mountain, the valley floor was covered with a congeries of streets and walls and spires and gilded domes. You could see the river snaking through down to the port, or where the port had been before the war with Caladon had throttled it.

On the dais stood the bishop's throne, but it was empty. Beside it in a smaller chair of carved obsidian sat Chrism Demiurge, the bishop's secretary. He was an old, emaciated man, with the face and gestures of an old scavenger bird. With long, bloodless fingers he plucked restlessly at his robe. He looked around at the assembled company.

Presently he lifted his pocket watch up to his face, and with his left hand he pulled back his eyelids so that his right eye bulged out of its socket. In that way he could tell what time it was, for he was afflicted with a peculiar kind of blindness. He could perceive color and movement, but not form. Holding his watch an inch away from his right eye, he could see the motion of the hands.

And when the watch hands had aligned themselves into an angle that he thought he recognized, he produced a bell from among the folds of his robe and rang it. It had no effect. There was no lessening in the noise around him after the clear, sweet tone had died away. The buzz and twitter of the voices of the council continued as before, until the secretary stooped to touch a golden cord that ran over his feet. Long, sinuous, metallic, it ran away from him on either side in a great circle around the auditorium, looping through the banks of seats. It ran through the fingers of the assembled priests, a golden serpent with a golden voice, a cord of telepathic sorcery that linked the members of the council. As the secretary chafed it with his thumbnail, the priests fell silent one by one.

"Gentlemen," said Chrism Demiurge. Quiet and insistent, his voice filled the chamber. He said, "We don't have much time left. There is no time for us to argue. Instead I want to show you what I saw. It gives me pain to do so, but a minister of God has certain duties to the truth. The truth," he repeated gently, and then he held out his hands. He had replaced his bell and watch back in the pockets of his robe, but in one hand he still grasped the telepathic cord. With the other he made a soft, caressing gesture. A brazier was set into the stone floor in front of him, and on it burned a small red smokeless fire. It flared up suddenly under his fingers and then subsided as the light in the chamber faded down to darkness. Mist gathered outside the window behind the secretary's back, and the rain beat down. Soon the shadows lay thick in all the corners of the room, and there was no sound except the old man's soft, gentle voice. "I saw her," he said. "God help me."

An image formed out of the shadow, floating above the little fire. At first it was just a cloud of radiance, amber-colored, soothing to the eye. Yet it didn't seem to lighten any of the dark around it; it just hung there over the fire, and gradually it acquired mass and bulk and shape and became the figure of a woman sitting cross-legged in the air. She was naked, surrounded by a nimbus of amber light, and her hair was black and fell in heavy curls around her shoulders. In a little while she raised her head, and all around the room the golden cord glowed dimly as the priests recognized her, even the blind ones.

The thirty-second bishop of Charn had the pale skin peculiar to the children of that season. It had a richness to it, like something edible, some sweet kind of dessert. She had been born in the third phase of spring; now five thousand days later she was still almost a girl. Her body had a kind of awkwardness about it, because it was still changing. There was some clumsiness in the way she pushed her hair back, the way she shifted her position and stretched out her legs. Naked, she had not yet learned self-consciousness. But her face was a woman's face, with a gravity beyond her age. Last child of an ancient family, she had been raised by priests in the fastness of the temple, and the endless round of rituals had left their mark upon her face, had given her an appreciation of futility unusual in one so young. But there was arrogance, too, burning in her clear black eyes, for she had lived her whole life in the courts of power and learned much.

She stretched out onto her back, arching her spine so that her breasts flattened down. She raised her arms above her head, in a gesture so languorous and inviting that it would have changed the breathing of most normal men. But in that chamber full of eunuch priests and half-dead corpses, the golden serpent glowed dully. There was no interest of that kind. Perhaps a few of the observers, keener and more perceptive than the rest, might have realized that the image made by Chrism Demiurge possessed a physical perfection beyond even that of the original. The bishop's skin wasn't that sweet, nor her hair that heavy, nor that black. He had made her perfect for reasons of his own, out of a sentiment that was perhaps the last spark of feeling left in his old breast. Or perhaps it was out of a sense of contrast, to make the change more poignant when the cat materialized between her legs, a huge rough yellow tomcat with a missing ear. And when it leaped between her legs onto her stomach and lay down, its paws made dirty prints on her white skin.

The apparition of the cat made chaos in the chamber. One priest shouted aloud, and others muttered prayers. The golden cord glowed hot white for an instant. But in a little while, above the noise of the outrage came the ringing of the secretary's bell and his soft voice saying, "It is true. I saw her with the demon, not ten feet from the altar of our God. I saw her. With my own . . . eyes."

As he spoke, the cat became a demon indeed, under the influence of his caressing hand. It grew huge, bigger than the bishop, with a distorted, masklike face, all lips and gaping eyes. It licked her breasts with its great lolling tongue, and scratched her shoulders until the blood came. And when it pushed her legs apart to penetrate her, even in that circle of eunuchs there were some who cried out, astonished that her small body could accommodate so furious an attack.

On the morning of October 45th, in the eighth phase of spring, the council passed a vote of censure, and in a rider to another bill, the bishop was condemned to death, for witchcraft and for heresy. The vote was close, the roll call taken in complete silence. Everybody understood the importance of what was happening. And when Chrism Demiurge cast his vote, a sigh rose up around the chamber, an exhalation of relief. Everybody knew that they had taken an irrevocable step. Later historians, describing the events that led up to the October Revolution, wrote that the council at this time was overtaken by a kind of frenzy, like a pack of starving dogs that, for want of further prey, finally turn upon themselves. They point to tyrants and oligarchs of other years, who by combinations of good judgment and good luck managed to keep their governments intact almost to summer. They conclude that the council of the Inner Ear, that spring, must have been in the grip of some collective madness, to persist so long in policies that led up to their own destruction. This is not true.

In fact that day, which was to end with the mutiny of the bishop's private guard and two regiments of her soldiers, started in an atmosphere of calm. All night the crowds had rioted around the Mountain of Redemption, but by dawn they had dispersed back to their own parishes, where food was still being distributed at the end of morning prayer. And at nine o'clock the weather broke, and the sun came out for half an hour. Charity and Raksha Starbridge had stopped in a vacant lot where some buildings had been torn down. The princess climbed up on a hunk of masonry to look back at the palace where she had lived her whole life, while the parson squatted below her, wrapped in his filthy robe. "Come down," he cried. "Don't waste your time."

Waste? thought Charity. The Starbridge towers rose above the house, delicate spires of glass and stone, glinting in the sun. Behind them the mountain filled the sky, tier after tier of battlements, and Charity could see soldiers pacing back and forth along the nearest parapets. The mist had parted on the mountain's crest, and even at that distance Charity could see the work up there, the cranes and winches, the great soaring arches of unfinished stone, all covered with black scaffolding.

A wind blew down out of the mountain carrying noises from the work site, a muted throbbing and the grind of gears. Steel cables hundreds of feet long dragged a load of bricks and sand up towards the summit. Charity followed it with her outstretched finger. "What's that?" she asked. Living on its lower slopes, she had never guessed the prison's bulk. But the parson looked up grimly. "The time is coming," he muttered, "when all men will be free. Women, too" he muttered, smiling suddenly. That morning he had eaten three or four white pills, and his hands were shaking. When he got to his feet, he staggered and almost fell. "Come on," he cried, lurching back across the lot to where a small alleyway led down towards the river.

Charity looked at his greasy head, his spotted neck. She too felt giddy, drunk from sensation, and she was staring wide-eyed at every new thing. She was standing on a broken block of carving two yards high, a piece from the shoulder of a fallen statue. She sat down and swung her legs over the side, kicking at the ridge of an enormous ear. She spread her hand over the surface of the stone. The rain had painted it with sugar scum; it was rough and pitted to her touch, and pools of sugar had collected in the joints between the stones. She brought her fingers up to her face, smiling at the sweet, nauseating odor, the taste of honey mixed with gasoline. So much smiling was making her cheeks tired.

Strange sounds came down the alleyway and drifted out into the lot near where the parson picked his way among the rubble. Charity could hear drumbeats and the sound of bells rising above a muddled, whining chant. The parson stopped and rocked back on his heels. He looked anxious and afraid, but the princess was happy because there, framed in the entrance to the alleyway, painted on a large square standard, was the portrait of a face she knew.

Caught by the breeze, it bellied towards her out of the opening, supported from behind by men carrying long poles. They strutted out into the yard, and behind them marched a procession of perhaps forty men and women. They blew whistles and rang handbells, and they had looted drums out of some temple, long black hollow logs covered with carvings. Each drum took two men to carry it; they took careful steps over the uneven ground, while others beat a ragged rhythm using sticks wrapped in red flannel.

Sitting on the fallen statue, Princess Charity clapped her hands and laughed, because the banner above them was unrolling on the wind, and the face that it carried was the face of her brother, Abu Starbridge. In a little while the marchers had found an open space, where the ground was clear for a circle of thirty feet. They put the banner up on poles stuck in the dirt.

They were a troupe of traveling dancers, and beneath the banner six or seven men and women went through a pantomime of recognition and welcome, embracing each other and slapping each other's palms. The rest spread out in a circle around them, and Charity jumped down from her perch and came close, standing next to Raksha Starbridge in the crowd. The lot was filling up with people. Men straggled in from neighboring streets, and groups of children rolled their hoops and pointed and chattered to each other in high voices.

"What is it?" asked Charity.

"Passion players," answered the parson. "It's a play about your brother's trial. Look, there he is." He pointed to a dancer who was putting on his costume and his mask.

"Why? What happened?"

The parson looked at her. "I can't believe you haven't heard," he said. "You must be the only person in Charn who doesn't know. Today is his execution day."

Suddenly there were tears in her eyes. "Don't say it," she cried. "They will not dare."

The parson shrugged and turned his attention to the play. Around them the crowd was quieting down. One of the dancers had put on a quilted jacket and a mask: a bald head and a high white forehead. He drank liquor out of an empty bottle and made a mime of drunkenness, stumbling and staggering around the circle until the crowd roared. Then he held his hand up for silence. His palm was painted with the symbol of the sun.

"How dare they?" whispered Charity, tears in her eyes. "How can they make fun of him? He is a prince of Charn."

"Hush," warned the parson, and put his fingers on her arm. "They mean no disrespect," he muttered. "On the contrary. You'll see."

The play started. It was in pantomime and hard to understand for someone who knew nothing of the story. In most cases people seemed to know, and those who didn't know were quickly told by others in the crowd. All around there was a hum of talk. Charity plucked the sleeve of her companion after every scene, whispering, "What is happening? What is happening now?"

"How can you be so ignorant?" grumbled Raksha Starbridge. "The whole city knows this story. Look, there's the church. You know, where the fire started."

Four dancers sat cross-legged on the ground, joined at wrists and ankles with gray scarves, indicating manacles. Above them stood another dancer, dressed in the red robes of priesthood. His mask was grotesque and distorted, painted half face, half skull, and he held a pillow out in front of him to indicate his fat.

"Parish chaplain," muttered the parson as Charity tugged his arm. "Can't you see? He's delivering a sermon to the prisoners."

The parish chaplain stalked around the circle, gesticulating and shaking his fists, while below him the prisoners groveled and hung their heads. But then Prince Abu stumbled in. Standing in the middle of the circle, he raised his right hand to show the tattoo of the golden sun. For an instant no one moved. And then the prince and the chaplain were struggling in elaborate mock battle, full of kicks and pratfalls, until the chaplain tripped and fell, and it was over. The prince stood above his fallen adversary. He took a drink out of his empty bottle, and then he squatted down among the prisoners, pulling the scarves away from their ankles and their hands, helping them to their feet.

But then more dancers were leaping into the circle from the crowd. Dressed in black, with black, empty masks, they joined hands around Prince Abu and the knot of prisoners. Again, the prince raised his hand, and for an instant everyone was still.

Then one of the prisoners jumped forward, swinging his gray scarf, and one of the black soldiers of the purge fell, holding his head. He had hidden some red paint in the palm of his hand, and as he fell, he streaked his hair with it, leaving a long red smear.

It was a signal for pandemonium, as prisoners and soldiers struggled together. They formed a spinning circle around the prince; he stood untouched. Then suddenly all was quiet. The dancers threw themselves to the ground, frozen in various attitudes of prostration, while a young girl stepped over them into the middle of the circle, and twirled a graceful pirouette. She was dressed in a ragged shirt of orange and red, and her mask was red, and her naked arms were decorated with a motif of flames as she raised them to the sky. Then she began to dance, graceful and slow, moving among the other dancers, and when she touched them, they collapsed and lay still.

"She's the fire," whispered Raksha Starbridge, as the princess tugged his arm. "Oh, you know. Your brother broke into the chapel while the chaplain was preaching to the condemned prisoners. Your brother freed them on his own authority, but then there was a fight. The building caught fire, that's all."

The girl danced around the circle, making exquisite gestures with her hands, while musicians in the crowd beat a rhythm on the drums. The drumming worked up to a frenzy and then stopped suddenly with a single hollow beat. The dancers got up and dusted themselves off and mixed in with the crowd, but the play wasn't over. But it had changed direction, and for the princess the second part was easier than the first to understand. It was as if the first part were describing events that everyone already knew, and therefore did not have to be explained. But the second part was news. It was the story of Prince Abu's trial and condemnation; a boy stood up to tell it in a high, sweet voice. He was dressed in white. As he spoke, one or more of the dancers behind him acted out the words. When the time came for dialogue, they supplied it, their voices faint and muffled through their masks.

"I know these things are true," the young boy was saying, holding his hands up for silence. "I know these things are true because I saw them. I am witness to the truth. I was there, and when the roof of the chapel fell, I saw him shield my mother's body with his own. I saw him on the floor, crushed under a fallen beam, his face covered with soot. And when they took him up and carried him to prison, they didn't recognize him. They put him with the rest of us. This was in the Mountain of Redemption, in the second tier. I know it because I went with him. I was by his side when he woke up. There were three hundred of us there in the long hall, men and women and young children, and he lived there with us, and he shared our water and our food. We knew what he was, a prince sent down from Paradise to help us. At any time he could have raised his hand and made them set him free. He carried the tattoo of the golden sun. But he had covered it with soot and dirt, so that he would not be recognized. And the guards who came to bring us food never guessed who he was, but we knew. His flesh was sacred, and he had the healer's gift. He touched us with his own hands. His pockets were full of candy, and he shared it with us. He showed us games like hop scotch and the jumping rope. And we were happy, until the day we came before the judge."

A dancer near Charity was putting on his makeup and his mask. And when he stepped into the circle of the stage, there were shouts of anger from the audience, and people spat and shook their fists. She touched the parson's arm. "Who's that?" she asked.

"Lascar Starbridge. He's the judge. They've really done him up. Look at his arms."

Lascar Starbridge was taking his seat on the back of one of the other dancers, who knelt down on her hands and knees. He was a little man with trembling hands, and his skin was painted white, and streaks of black ran up his arms, to emphasize his veins. On the mask his eyes were painted red and black, and he had black teeth, red gums, and a black tongue.

"He's an addict," explained Raksha Starbridge. "Look how they hate him! Bastard! He knows he won't live long. It makes him careless with the lives of others."

Again people in the crowd were shouting and hissing, and some even threw stones. "I saw him once," continued the parson. "In his court it's a heresy to speak in your own defense. He says that in the time it takes to argue, other criminals might go free. He sits for six hours at a time, handing out sentences as the prisoners file past. He projects their tattoos onto a screen. He's always mixing up the slides. He's too high to see straight."

Lascar Starbridge's voice was slurred and feeble. As the dancers moved past him, he asked their names, and they would pantomime putting their hands into the projection machine. Another dancer held a spiral pad of drawing paper up behind the judge's head, and as each dancer passed, he flipped another page over from the back, to show the different tattoos. Each page had a hand drawn on it, and on each palm was drawn one of the recurrent symbols of the criminally poor: a spiderweb, a checkerboard, a pick and shovel, a hangman's noose.

In the audience, men and women rubbed their own hands together and they groaned. For Charity there was something poignant in the sound, so that for the first time the drama came alive for her, and she could see a picture of the strange scene in her mind as it must have been, the line of broken prisoners, and among them her own brother, Abu, not the dancer with his greasepaint and his mask but her own sweet brother, standing fat and tall.

"What is your name?" asked the beadle.

"Abu Starbridge. Prince...Abu Starbridge." He was sweating heavily, and the light shone on his bald forehead. His face was dirty and his clothes were in rags, but at the sound of his voice, there was sudden silence in the courtroom. A dozen clerks stopped writing and looked up. The magistrate sat back in his chair, grimacing and showing his teeth. He looked terrified. Lifting his gavel, he half-turned so that he could see the slide of the prince's hand, projected on the screen behind him. The tattoo of the golden sun seemed to spray the room with light.

"What's the charge?" mumbled Lascar Starbridge, grimacing and shuffling his papers.

"Disturbing the peace," said the beadle. "Inciting to riot. There must be some mistake...."

"Enough," interrupted the magistrate. "That's enough. The prisoner is remanded to the psychiatric ward of Wanhope Hospital for observation. Next case." His cheek was twitching and he raised one hand to smooth it. The pupils of his eyes were shrunken down to pinpricks, and his skin had an unhealthy pallor.

Prince Abu smiled. "There is no mistake," he said. "Cousin, please. Might I remind you that the last nine men and women up before you on this charge were all sentenced to death?"

The magistrate glared at him and leaned forward over his desk. "Are you mad?" he hissed. "You must be mad. Take him away. No, stop," he shouted, as the guards moved forward. "Don't touch him. He's a Starbridge. Are you insane?" he asked, stroking the twitch in his cheek.

He was not insane, not yet. But he was tired. All night he had sat drinking and listening to voices in the crowd outside his cell. Unable to sleep, he had pulled a chair up under the window and sat back with his head against the wall. And from time to time the wall would resonate to the sound of some speechmaker shouting through a megaphone. Once or twice he had stood up on the chair to look out through the bars, and then the noise of the people had risen like a wave. A thousand people stood outside his window, in the courtyard of the hospital, in the rain.

He had sat with a pen and notebook in his lap, thinking to write a poem before he died, something magnanimous and fine, but nothing came. And towards morning he must have slept, for he was jolted awake by the sound of gunfire and breaking glass. Spring sunlight was prodding gently through his window, making a white mark on the floorboards at his feet. The lamps had all gone out. His pen and his paper had fallen to the floor. And one of the hospital orderlies stood before him, holding breakfast on a silver tray.

Jolted from sleep, the prince woke with a cry. He heard bangs and smashes coming from the courtyard, and the sound of bells. "What . . . ?" he stammered. "What . . . ?" His eyelids fluttered with the effort of speech.

"A great change has come," said the orderly. Sepulchral and grave, he stood like a statue, dressed in a white smock. His face had taken on that look of respectful reproach so familiar to the prince, and Abu closed his eyes to block it out. His mouth was foul with drinking, and his neck was sore.

"There's been a change," repeated the orderly. He was a middle-aged man. In those days superannuated and wounded soldiers were put to work in hospitals and prisons. This man's cheek and neck were rough with scars, and his left hand was made of wood. His head was shaved in a style forbidden by law except to certain grades of soldiers.

Prince Abu rubbed his forehead with his hand. "Are they trying to set me free?"

"No, sir," replied the orderly. "Where do you want this?" Without waiting for a response, he turned back towards the table and put down his tray.

The prince rose to his feet. He stepped up onto his chair to look out his window into the courtyard. It was a weak, milky morning, and the rain had stopped. The crowd was still there, in diminished numbers. But it had lost its singleness; no one looked up towards Abu's window now. People stood arguing in groups or sat glumly on the ground. The torches and the bonfires had all burned out, and columns of pale smoke rose up from the cinders.

"What happened?" Abu asked.

Behind him the orderly stood still, his wooden fingers clamped around the saucer of an empty coffee cup. "Forgive me, sir," he said. "I want to ask you something. I've never met a prince before. I've never seen one, not up close. What I want to know is, are you a different kind of man? Physically, I mean. Genetically."

The prince leaned forward until his bald head rested against the silver bars. He had such a headache. Behind him the orderly was still talking: "Forgive me, sir. I feel that I can speak freely, because soon you will be dead. It's just that you don't seem to be behaving rationally. Not just you. When I was with the army, the priests and the officers behaved like crazy men. I saw a priest set fire to a powder wagon. He blew himself to pieces and twelve of his own soldiers. Coffee, sir?"

"Thank you. Milk, no sugar."

In the courtyard, in the crowd, a group of soldiers stood arguing. One of them was making furious gestures with his fists; he broke away from the others and ran a few steps forward, and then he stripped his black cap from off his head and stripped off his black tunic, and threw them down into the mud. Abu watched him.

"It's not rational," said the orderly behind him. "And you're just as bad, sir. I mean no disrespect. But I can tell, you're going to let them kill you. And there's no reason for it. You could just walk out of here. They'd do anything you said. They'd have to."

Prince Abu raised his fingers to his head. "I refuse to claim my privileges under a system I despise," he said. In the courtyard a scuffle had broken out. The man who had taken off his coat was being kicked and beaten by two of his companions.

"Tell me what happened," said the prince.

The orderly raised Abu's coffee cup to smell it and then lowered it again. "The council's voted to condemn the bishop," he said. "The announcement just went up. Tomorrow night she burns."

Abu's cell was large and spacious. Its walls were lined with silk. The door was set into an alcove, behind some curtains, and as the prince turned around he saw that someone was standing there. Someone had entered without knocking, an old priest in purple robes.

As Abu looked at him over the orderly's shoulder, the priest smiled and put his finger to his lips. Unaware of him, the orderly was still talking: "I'm not a religious man. But even so, it's lunacy. You make someone into a living goddess and then you burn her at the stake. I tell you, they must be insane. Whole regiments have taken oaths of personal allegiance to the bishop. Half the city worships her. If the council tries to burn her, there'll be civil war. There'll be a revolution."

"How interesting," said the priest behind him. "How very . . . interesting." He was an old man, with white hair and a predatory face. On his collar he was wearing the ensign of the Inner Ear, an anvil, stirrup, and an eardrum, fashioned exquisitely in gold. Unlike most priests, he wore no other jewelry. His robe, too, was plain and unembroidered.

Abu had not seen his uncle since he was a little boy, yet he was sure this man was he, Lord Chrism Demiurge, secretary of the council. It was not that Abu recognized his face. But his voice seemed to speak out of the quietest recesses of the prince's childhood. Gentle, barely audible, it seemed to linger in the air and fill it with softness and dry menace. The silence that surrounded it was absolute. In perfect silence, the orderly turned his head. In silence he replaced the prince's coffee cup on the tray. In silence he began to make the gestures of respect.

"Don't," said the priest, still smiling, holding out his hand. "In the past minute you have already committed two crimes. You have slandered the bishop's council and you have spoken the word *revolution*. Both are forbidden under emergency Statute Two-twenty-one-J, among others. The Prophet Angkhdt tells us... but no matter. No, don't go," he continued, as the orderly changed his gestures to imply an urgent duty elsewhere. "I am interested in what you have to say. Only be careful, I warn you."

Prince Abu stepped down off his chair. "Please, Uncle," he began, but the priest held up his forefinger. He had a circle of silver lips tattooed around his fingertip, and his fingernail protruded like a tongue. The mark entitled him to talk without being interrupted. "Go on," he said. "Speak, my son. Go on with your analysis. Only be careful."

Slowly, stiffly, the orderly went down on his knees. His face was slack with fear, and he stammered when he spoke. "My Lord," he said. "Oh God, please..."

The priest smiled, as if the name of God contained a private joke. "Ah," he said gently. "Perhaps it is not true, then, that you are not a religious man. But to call on God now, in this context, couldn't that be called hypocrisy?"

"Uncle, stop," said Abu. "Don't bully him." But again the old man lifted up his forefinger. There was silence for a full minute, and then the orderly began to speak. Kneeling on the floor, his head bowed and turned away, amid much swallowing and hesitation, he said, "I knew it. It's true. You're not human, are you? You have no hearts. My mother used to say that. Starbridges. From another star. And now I know it's true."

Lord Chrism chuckled, a dry rustling in his throat. "Your mother sounds unorthodox. Is she still alive? It would surprise me if she were still alive."

Ignoring the old man's uplifted forefinger, the orderly leaped forward, and grabbed up at his throat. The priest stepped back and made a little gesture in the air. And whether it was magic, or perhaps some subtler power, the orderly never touched him. He stopped as if he had run into a wall of glass. His arms grew slack, and his wooden hand caught fire suddenly and flared up.

And that was all. In perfect silence he knelt down again and bowed his head as his hand burned down to a cinder and burned out.

The old man's voice was soft as spiderweb. "Correct me if I'm wrong," he said. "You were a soldier once."

The orderly said nothing, but he bowed down to the floor. And in a little while the priest continued: "Yes, I see. You are a brave man. A commendable quality in a soldier. Very . . . commendable. You may go now."

"Sir?"

"Go in peace. I am not as interested in you as you might think. I thought perhaps that I could goad my nephew into some display of strength. Yet I find he could not raise his hand to save an innocent man. Is it because he lacks the courage of a common solider?"

But before he had even reached the end of speaking, the orderly had scuttled out the door, while the curtains whispered after him. Lord Chrism took no notice. He was smiling, and his blind eyes glistened and shone. "Well, Nephew," he said softly. "Say something. I know you're there."

Abu reached down to pick up the whiskey bottle from beside his chair. There was a glass beside it with some whiskey in the bottom; he picked it up and rinsed his mouth out with the dregs, sucking it around his teeth before he swallowed it. Then he poured himself some more.

The old priest cocked his head to listen to the sound. "Ah," he said. "They treat you well."

"I don't complain."

"No? But that's good. And what is this—breakfast?" He stepped to the table and passed his hand over a basket of croissants, picking at the crust.

The prince's bed stood along the far wall, across from the window. Unused the night before, it was still neat, piled high with blankets and silk pillows. Abu walked over and sat down. He felt ashamed, mocked, soiled, suddenly filthy in the clothes he had been wearing for a week. His teeth felt furry and ill used.

When he was a child, his uncle's presence had been enough to frighten him into fits. He looked down at the tattoo on his palm. "Is that why you came?" he asked. "To laugh at me?"

"No. Or rather, not entirely. It was too long a trip just for that. I came from Kindness and Repair. Six miles, underground. The streets this morning are unsafe."

"It will get worse."

"Indeed. Burning you will not be popular, I fear. Burning my bishop, that will be a national catastrophe. But what choice do I have? She was guilty of an imperfection, poor child. A chemical impurity. It is . . . unfortunate."

"So you don't care if there's a civil war or not."

The secretary smiled. "I am an old man," he said. "And there are always wars. It is God's way. Perhaps when I see Him I will ask Him why, if I remember. It doesn't matter. On Friday I return to Paradise."

"Are you sure?"

"Yes. I have seen it in my dreams. The streets are paved with silver. The women all have flowers in their hair. I will have a palace of my own, built of lapis lazuli. And God will take me in His arms, and He will make me young again."

"You don't believe that."

"But I do. I have seen it. And something else: My palace has a dungeon, below the level of the street. It is not like this one, no. It is much . . . harsher. It is all prepared. There is one cell for your sister and one for you."

"My sister . . ."

"Yes. It is what I came to tell you, partly. She is on her way. Last night she took poison. My agents found her body, but her soul had fled. Like you she had no courage. No courage and no brains."

Prince Abu sat back on his bed and drank deeply. The whiskey in his glass was almost clear, a grade reserved for princes and for priests. It came from far away, distilled from the flowers of some distant southern desert, harvested by hand among the sand dunes. Popular among lovers, it was called Heartsbalm.

The prince lifted the bottle into the light. There was more than a third left. The old man was still talking, but Abu couldn't listen anymore. He felt the first effects of drunkenness—it seemed impossible to do more than one thing at a time, and right then he was thinking about his sister. The Heartsbalm had a mildly hallucinogenic effect, and when he closed his eyes, he could see her clearly. Her black braids were tied up around her head, and she was turning from the bathroom window, a pencil in her hand. He took another swallow of drink and watched the image fade. In his mind's eye he saw her change—Charity Starbridge, older now, soon after she had married the old commissar, bending down over a bouquet of herbs, her small body constricted in the tight, soft robes of matrimony, her face already tired. And then again—later still, her cheeks pale and her hair unkempt, smoking marijuana from a silver chillum, in bed in the middle of the afternoon.

He opened his eyes and looked down at the whiskey in his glass. He swirled it in a circle around the bottom. "Where is Thanakar?" he asked suddenly. "My cousin Thanakar?"

"With the army. Not for long. My agents have gone out to bring him in. I tell you, burning you will be my melancholy duty. Hanging him will be a pleasure. Ever since he was a child, he has thwarted me. Broken my law. Debauched my niece. He has . . . thwarted me."

Abu closed his eyes. In his mind he saw his sister. Once she had stopped eating, and he had persuaded his brother-in-law to consult a doctor. The old man had chosen Thanakar. And within a week she had been better. He remembered her standing in the hall, looking at the clock, waiting, counting the time until her consultation, and when he had laughed at her, she had turned towards him, blushing, angry. How pretty she had looked.

"She poisoned herself," he said.

"Yes. A peculiar kind of poison. It seemed to burn her from within. One wonders how she purchased such a thing."

"I would like to see her."

"Ah. In fact, there is nothing left to see. So I am informed. My agents were attacked outside the gate. As they were bringing her to me. The crowd broke into her bier. They were looking for jewelry. Her body broke apart under their hands. Inside, there was nothing left but ash."

"Rejoice at every death," counseled the Starbridge Catechism. Nevertheless Abu felt tears on his cheek. The old priest stared at him, peering intently, but in the manner of the blind, he missed Abu's eyes. He could see movement and color, but not form, and Abu had not moved in a long time.

The old man peered into a corner. As always, it was as if he were surrounded by a mist of light, as if he stood swaddled in color, the pink walls and the red carpets and the changing morning, the silver tray, the golden tablecloth all smearing into one another all around him. Looking down at his own body, he saw a smear of purple and scarlet, mixing together as he raised his arm.

"Are you . . . crying?" he asked softly, lifting his arm. "Be comforted. You will see her soon, in Paradise."

"In a prison cell."

"Be comforted. A prison cell in Paradise is better than the richest palace here. It will be summer there."

"I'm surprised you want to go," remarked the prince. "I'm surprised you think that God will be so glad to see you, after you have wrecked this city and brought it to the brink of revolution." He poured some whiskey for himself.

The old man shook his head. "You still don't understand, do you? You still don't understand what I have done. You must think that I'm a madman. No, but listen: Do you think I don't know what is happening outside? There are demagogues on every street corner preaching revolution and predicting the apocalypse. I had to creep here through the catacombs, six miles underground. I was afraid, I, who have ruled this city since before your birth. Don't be a fool; if I were so in love with power, wouldn't I have contrived some way to keep it? If I had believed in power. No."

The old man made a gesture, and all around him the glowing mist started to dim; to Abu it was as if the sun outside had gone behind a cloud. The room settled down to darkness and deep shadow, and the old man's voice grew louder, more intense.

"There is a myth," he said, "about a world where the seasons change so fast, two hundred, three hundred times in a man's lifetime, and the harvests just a few short months apart. If such a world exists, they must have no such thing as war. Fathers, sons, and grandsons all must understand each other. But here, when I was born, it was already winter, and winter is a season that requires strength of will. Therefore I have ruled this city with a desperate jealousy. And I am not ashamed; now, only now have we run out of food. In my great-grandfather's time half the diocese was dead by this phase of spring, and even Starbridges were eating straw. I am not ashamed.

"But it is spring now. Already times are not as hard. Soon there will be food to eat, birds on the trees. I have designed a system where men worship their oppressors. In winter that was necessary, but times have changed. Can I now go before my ministers and tell them Paradise is just an empty rock, that the God who granted them the right to rule does not exist? Can I go before the people and explain that all their misery has been for nothing? No—let them find out in their own way. The best I can do is make the change as quick and sudden as I can. Therefore I will burn my bishop, and there will be a revolution. The council will ascend to Paradise, and for twenty thousand days the name of Angkhdt will be forgotten. New politics will come. But don't misunderstand—I have planted a seed. Now, even now, all over the city, actors and musicians are spreading word of you. They are in my pay."

Prince Abu stared at him. He suddenly felt very drunk; lifting his glass to his lips, he slopped whiskey on his shirt.

"I have planted a seed," repeated the old man. "I have been dreaming of this moment ever since your mother came to me when you were just a baby. Have you ever wondered why I gave you your tattoos? Why I put such power into your hands—you, a weakling and a fool? It is because I needed a seed for a new faith, not now, but fifty thousand days from now. Here, now, perhaps you think you symbolize something new, a spirit of resistance, perhaps, of godlessness and revolution. But I have seen a vision of a new church. Fifty thousand days from now, no one will remember then your foolish scruples. No, they will remember the myth that now, right now, I am devising: of how a Starbridge prince suffered for them and led them to salvation. And fifty thousand days from now, when winter comes, they will be eager to surrender all their freedom into the hands of your ministers and your family. Just as they were eager to let me rule them, when I was a young man. All the temples and the shrines will be rebuilt, and your face will be on every altar. That is my dream."

Prince Abu sat forward. He had heard enough. Summoning strength, he rose to his feet. "I forbid it," he said. "I won't be part of it; I've changed my mind. Set me free." He raised his hand. But in the darkness and the shadow, the great golden tattoo was invisible. It had no power to illuminate. And Lord Chrism laughed, a dry, feathery sound. "Too late," he whispered softly. "Too late." He made a gesture with his little finger, and two soldiers stepped out of the curtains behind him. Each held in his hands a length of purple rope. Like Lord Chrism, they were blind.

Charity broke away from the circle of dancers and pushed away out of the crowd. She felt stifled by her own breath. "They won't kill him," she said aloud. "They can't." She pushed out through a mass of people, holding her hands spread out in front of her, and when they saw her blank, tattooless palms, people stood aside to let her pass, afraid of the pollution. Her palms had begun to itch under the greasepaint; her whole body had begun to itch.

She broke away into an open space and ran up a small slope of rubble, towards where an alleyway came out onto the yard. Once there, she rested in the shadow of the gatepost, looking back towards the dancers and the actor who was playing her brother. And then she turned away. In those days her attention span was short. The world was various and new. And in a little while it was as if she had forgotten; she bowed her head until her breathing slowed, and then she squatted down to look into a tiny shrine set into the wall of an old house. Remembering part of an old prayer, she looked under the brass arch and past a double row of oil lamps. The back ones had burned out, and the image itself was covered up in shadow. But its eyes were made of mirror, and Charity could see them shining in the darkness. This god was very old. The level of the street had risen up around her knees. It was Angkhdt the God of Children.

Charity leaned forward to sniff the smoke that rose up from the lamps. Drunk from sensation, she was fearless the way drunkards are, so that she didn't even turn around when she felt somebody grab her from behind. He had to pull her out, and then he hit her hard across the cheek, but she took no notice. She put her hands up to her face.

"Don't run away like that," said Raksha Starbridge. "Don't make me chase you."

He grabbed her by the back of the neck and twisted her head around to make her look at him, and then he thrust her past the gatepost into a narrow, stinking alley, out of sight from the yard. He was stronger than he looked. Or perhaps the drugs had made him strong—he was sweating, and his whole body shook. And there was something different in his eye, too, as if violence had awakened something there. From her neck he ran his hand down the muscles of her shoulder, and pushed his trembling fingers into the soft flesh above her collarbone. She could smell his breath, a mixture of alcohol and rot. It was too rich a smell; she gagged and turned away, and then she pushed him in the chest so that he stumbled backwards and fell down. He hit his head on the brick wall behind him. A protruding brick cut a gash in his head, and he sat down in the mud and covered it with his hands. Charity watched him, fascinated by the black blood welling up between his fingers. And she was fascinated by the sound he was making, a low gurgle in his throat. Then he put his head back, and she could see tears on his cheeks, real tears. "Don't be afraid of me," he sobbed. "Please don't be afraid. I can't hurt you. I was in holy orders. They took my manhood when I made my vows. Only I need to touch someone sometimes. Is that so bad?"

Fascinated, she bent down to look at him. "I need you," he confessed. "You're like my little Rosa. And don't you understand, you need me too. You won't survive out here, with no money and no food."

She reached out and pulled his hands away from the cut on his head. But suddenly he grabbed hold of her thumb and twisted it back and then jumped up, twisting her arm back behind her. Tears were trembling in his eyes, but then he winked. "I need you," he said. "Don't you understand?"

He held her by the wrist, in a special hammerlock known only to parsons. And then he pulled her away and led her down narrow and deserted streets, along high, windowless brick walls. Underfoot the mud was covered with a sugar crust, and in the corners sugar had already begun to accumulate. In some places the drifts were six inches high and still damp, for it had rained all night and looked to start again any minute. In the middle of the roadway the crust had split apart over a gutter full of water and raw sewage, and as they went on, the water spread across the street. Soon it lapped the bricks on either side and then grew deep, so that they were wading through water past their ankles. And always they were going downhill, and at a choice of ways they always took the one that led downhill, until they stood at the top of a broad set of stairs with the water cascading down. It led down into what had once been a market, but now it was all drowned. Remnants of tents and canvas awnings still stuck up above the water.

From where they stood, they looked out over a small lake. A wind had sprung up out of nowhere and chased itself in circles out over the water and raised whirlwinds of dust and newspaper into the air. Yet the surface of the lake was undisturbed. A layer of rain had built up on the surface like a layer of oil, and there were no waves or ripples on the lake, but only oily swells, rushing towards them up the steps and then sucking away.

The parson put his fingers to his mouth and whistled shrilly. Across the lake a boat broke away from a group of others and came towards them. It was brightly painted and cut swiftly through the water. Charity admired the strong strokes of the oarsman. He was dressed in yellow trousers and a green shirt, and when he got close she could see how big he was. He had long arms and a big, burly frame. But his hair and beard were streaked with yellow.

"I'm surprised he owns a boat," said Charity.

"All things belong to God," replied the parson. "He rents it from the church." And then he grinned. "Don't give yourself airs. You're lower down than him. He may not let you in the boat."

When the boatman saw who had hailed him, he laughed and waved. "Monsignor!" he shouted. He pulled up to a mooring pole, one of several near the steps. A makeshift jetty ran out to it, put together out of ladders and loose boards. The parson pushed Charity along it while the boatman shouted encouragement. He had a wide, freckled face and a smile full of teeth. When the parson tripped and almost pitched into the water, he stood up in his boat and clapped his hands. And then he made the gestures of respect. While they staggered towards him over the jetty, he bowed and capered in the boat, closing his eyes and pressing his knuckles to his forehead.

He was using forms that were old-fashioned even then, unnecessarily servile and complex. But his laughter put irony into everything he did. At the very end he bent down to touch his toes. He was laughing when he straightened up, but the parson's face was dark with anger. The boatman didn't care. He reached his hand out for Charity to grab, but when she stepped down towards him, he pulled his hand away, and the laughter faded from his mouth. He had seen her palm.

"Not your usual, is she, sir?" he asked. He sat down by the oars and stared at her, while she stood uncertainly on the jetty. But then the parson pushed her from behind, so that she collapsed into the bottom of the boat. He stepped down after her and sat down in the stern.

The boatman hawked a wad of spit up from his throat and blew it over the side. "Where are you going?" he asked.

"Spider Ghat. Not far."

"Any money?"

The parson shook his head.

"Any food?"

"No."

The boatman frowned. "Got to be something, my master."

Charity wore a talisman she had gotten that morning, pinned to the front of her dress. One of the dancers had distributed them to the crowd, a tin button painted with her brother's face. The boatman pointed to it. "I thought they were atheists," he said.

Charity opened her mouth to answer, but the parson shook his head. "Her mother was an antinomial. I'll purify the boat once we get back."

"Thank you, my master. That's not good enough."

"It will have to do. The harm has already been done."

The man stared at them a long moment, and then he bent down for his oars. He had a boat tattooed along the outside of each finger, and perhaps he had had something in his horoscope, or perhaps the priests had seen some promise in him when he was a boy, but the work was finer than was usual for people of his caste, less monochromatic, better drawn. Each boat was different: a steamboat, a sailboat, a barge, a tug.

He pulled out swiftly into the lake. Drops from the blades of his oars made rows of circles in the water. "Antinomial, is she?" he asked. "Can she sing? I've never heard one sing."

Again Charity opened her mouth to speak, and again the parson shook his head. "I'll give you twenty cents," he said.

"All right. But I have a sick friend."

"No drugs. I'm sorry."

The boatman rowed for a while in silence, and then he smiled. "You're not good for much, are you, monsignor? You might offer me a drink, at least. This is thirsty work."

The parson squinted up at the sky. A rip had opened in the clouds above them, and the sun was shining through. The light made swirling patterns on the water. Charity looked at her reflection over the side. She trailed her fingers in the lake, joining hands with her reflection. The lake gave off an acrid, sweaty smell. Smiling, she turned around and watched the sweat gather on the boatman's forehead and drip slowly down into his eyes.

"I'll say this for her," the man said. "She's easily amused."

They were coming in among some buildings and the tops of flooded tenements. Charity looked through the windows into the apartments. Some were still furnished and intact, and some had rowboats parked outside, tied to the fire escapes.

She saw no other people. But soon the water was much shallower. Ahead she saw a group of wooden houses built on stilts. It was a style that had been popular in winter, when the snow was very deep.

"There is one thing," said the parson. "I could write you a charm. In lieu of payment. What kind of man is he? Your sick friend."

"Like me. He has a fever." The man put his oars up and let the boat glide from its own momentum into Spider Ghat.

"Understand, I don't guarantee results. It's a question of faith."

"I understand."

"Just so you know." The parson fished a ballpoint pen out of a pocket in his robe. From some other place he produced a book of rolling papers, and he took one out and ripped it in half. He spread it out on the gunwale and bent over it, hiding it from Charity as he wrote. Then he handed it to the boatman. "Have him roll it up and take it like a pill."

"What does it say?"

"It is a verse from holy scripture. A very potent verse."

One of the houses had a wooden porch built along three sides, and steps ran down from it onto a wooden landing. The landing floated on the shallow water, lashed to oil drums at either end. "There," said Raksha Starbridge. "Take us there."

A scum of Styrofoam and driftwood covered the water near the landing, wreckage from the submerged apartments, pieces of furniture, and broken chunks of roof.

Charity pushed aside some saturated sofa cushions and stared down into the water. She could see the concrete curbstone two feet down and, superimposed, the reflection of the house as they drifted to the landing. It was one-storied and dilapidated, with cracks in the sheathing. The windows were broken and boarded over, the walls covered with graffiti. The porch and the landing were crowded with objects salvaged from the flood—crates and chains and spools of wire, a child's tricycle, a broken rocking chair.

Charity raised her eyes. The boatman was still sitting in his seat, puzzling over the fragment of paper. He spindled the paper in his hand, curling it around his finger while the parson stepped out onto the landing. And then he made a tiny gesture with his head, a gesture of dismissal. Charity got to her feet, and the parson grabbed her around the wrist and pulled her from the boat. He let go of the painter. But the man just sat there in the boat with the paper curled around his finger, until the parson pushed the gunwale with his foot, and the boat drifted away. Charity stood looking after it, while the parson held onto her wrist, forcing his fingernail into the vein beneath her palm. The man in the boat backed water slowly, but it wasn't until he was out of sight behind the wreckage of a wall that Raksha Starbridge permitted himself to laugh. "He'd better pray there is no God," he said.

Five miles away, Lord Chrism stood on Bishop's Keys, beneath the belly of the temple. From Wanhope Prison he had traveled underground, along a web of waterways that stretched for miles under the city. Returning to the temple he had traveled underground, in his somber, hearselike barge of state, all gilded wood and purple hangings, poled by silent members of his guard.

He stood at the edge of the stone pier, looking back into the darkness the way they had come. He could remember when that whole enormous cavern had been ablaze with light. When he was a young man, each member of the council had kept a boat here at the docks beneath the temple. The catacombs had been full of noise and messengers in livery and soldiers transporting grain. In winter they had used ponies to pull sleds over the ice, smart brown beasts with sharpened hooves and ribbons in their manes.

Then, standing on Bishop's Keys, he had been surrounded by a storm of light and brilliant colors and the high, strident voices of the priests. Now everything was dark, save for the torches in his guardsmen's hands. He could hear the water slapping against the wooden bottom of his barge as the men stowed it along the slip and covered it with tarpaulin.

He shivered, and with cramped, arthritic fingers, he plucked at the sleeves of his robe. Then he turned and walked quickly over the stone promenade. His men fell into place a step behind him. Their torches spit and flared, grabbing at the cavern's roof unsuccessfully until they passed under a lower vault. There the echoes of their footsteps seemed flatter and less resonant. Rough carvings protruded down into the light, though Lord Chrism's blindness robbed them of detail. Even in his memory they had no detail.

This part of the temple had been built during the reign of the ninth bishop, in winter many years before. The principle of the elevator had been forgotten then. From Bishop's Keys the architects had built stairways that reached toward every section of the temple, hollow fingers of stone that stretched up half a mile, some of them, a lot of steps for an old man.

Here the cavern had assumed a disklike shape, the walls still out of sight, the ceiling not more than nineteen feet above their heads. In front of them, the first of fifty stairways rose up from the floor, a narrow spiral cased in stone. It stood alone, like a tree with the ceiling in its branches. Farther on, the stairways grew closer together and more numerous, until the three men were walking as if through a stone forest, among groves of trees irregularly spaced and sized. These were the servants' stairs, leading up to kitchens and guardhouses. At the base of each there was a door, black now, mostly, though some still showed a feeble glow. That was how the chamber had been illuminated in the old days—the staircases were sheathed in alabaster, and inside, the spirals had been lined with lights, red, green, violet, the colors coded to their destinations and the caste of people who could use them. Then each stair had formed a column of light nineteen feet from floor to ceiling, the colors bleeding through the thin, transparent stone.

Then this entire chamber had been alive; now it was dead. Lord Chrism hurried on. Ahead of them, a wall stretched to both sides. Lord Chrism turned to the left and walked along it, past a gaping doorway. A single bulb hung from the keystone of the arch. Once guards had been stationed there around the clock. It was the entrance of an old granary, one of one hundred and seventeen cavernous storage bins cut into the rock beneath the temple. The electric light gave contour to a mass of carving all around the arch, a beautiful woman in a variety of different poses. Each granary was dedicated to one of the one hundred and seventeen lovers of Immortal Angkhdt; this one, named after the so-called White-Faced Woman, had served the Church of Morquar the Unkempt, and all the shrines between the river and the Morquar Gate. All winter and well into spring, for more than a lifetime, it had fed the people of that district. Now it was empty. They were all empty, and people everywhere were forgetting God.

In the summertime and autumn, generations of men and women had slaved to fill these granaries, working with increasing desperation as the weather grew colder and the power of the priests increased. When Lord Chrism's father was a boy, the episcopal wheatfields had stretched for ninety miles around the city, land that was all barren now. Winter had scraped it clean, down to the red rock. And when the snow had come, and the countryside was empty, and the country people had all come in through the gates, then these caverns had been full of light, and soldiers pulling carts and sledges loaded with fat red grainbags, each one stamped with black dog's head of Angkhdt. Their labor had been a kind of worship, and they had chanted songs of worship while they worked. They had pulled the sledges over the ice and through the catacombs down underneath the city. They had pulled them through the crypts beneath the churches, where the grain was off-loaded and turned over to the parish priests for distribution to the multitude, between the sermon and the invocation, in small plastic bags.

Farther on along the wall, Lord Chrism stopped for breath next to another doorway. The carvings here had been among his favorites when he was a boy, and even though he could no longer see, he put his hand out to stroke the smooth neck of the brass statue. He slid his finger down her spine. In scripture, this woman had no name. The God's encounter with her had been brief and furtive, and the granary itself was insignificant. But the statue was delightful. As the old priest stopped to catch his breath, he let his hand stroke the curve of her buttocks.

This granary was empty, too, and the light in the archway had burned out. But nearby there was another, prouder entrance cut into the stone and a wide rampway sloping up and to the right. It led up to Lord Chrism's private quarters in the Courtyard of the Rights of Man, a long and weary way. Fingering the statue, Lord Chrism prayed to God for strength and muttered charms to slow his breath and smooth his heart. He turned back to his men, standing behind him in a pool of light. "Don't wait for me," he said. "Don't . . . wait."

He made a gesture with his finger, and they bowed their heads. They could not speak. Their lips were sewn shut with a metal thread. But they touched their knuckles to their foreheads, and then they walked past him up the ramp without looking back. At intervals along the walls extinguished torches hung in metal brackets. As the two men walked up the ramp, they lit them from the torches that they carried, so that a line of guttering blue lights followed them along each wall. Lord Chrism smiled. In the darkness, his eyes made out a curving double line of blue. He fingered the head of the prophet's metal penis and fingered the ring of mystic symbols carved around the woman's lips.

He waited a few minutes and then went up another way. Leaving the torches and the ramp behind him, he turned aside into an ancient doorway and up an ancient, dusty stair. Even though it could not help him in the way it helped a seeing man, he took a torch down from its bracket. For comfort's sake, he lit it with an effort of his mind, a small effort, but he was tired. And soon, as he climbed the stairs, the light settled into the rhythm of his breathing. When his lungs were full, it burned up bright. When he exhaled, it glimmered out. Breathing hard, he was wrapped in alternating cocoons of light and dark.

At the seventh landing of the seventh stair he stopped to rest again. Soon he would rest for all eternity. If God existed, then on Friday he would be in Paradise, and God would cleanse his heart, and he would feel no fear or sadness anymore. If God did not exist, that, too, would be a kind of rest, mute blackness to the end of time. Either way it made no difference. He still had work to do.

But even so he stood a while longer, letting alternating images of doubt and faith possess his mind, until his breathing settled down and the torch cast a more even light. He murmured a prayer to smooth his ragged heartbeat and then pressed on, past storehouses and armories and warrens of useless, empty rooms. Ten thousand monks had lived in Kindness and Repair when Chrism Demiurge first came to stay there, a young priest, newly gelded. Then he had come up this same way. Raised in splendor in his father's house, he had been shocked and frightened by this humble stair, for even then his footsteps had been muffled in the dust, and it was cold, so cold, with the winter thick outside. And even though he had been born to glory, and his tattoos specified that he was to be a great commander of the faithful, still there had been no ceremony to greet his coming. He had been given a cell in a section of the temple that, even then, was ancient and disused. On the way his father had terrified him with stories of the catacombs, and told him stories of vast conclaves of heretics who worshiped alien gods down in the darkest crypts, among the stone sarcophagi. When he became a man, his first act had been to send soldiers down through every corner of the catacomb, but they found nothing. It had been winter then.

In spring, of course, new heresies sprouted from a thousand seeds. Somewhere in this labyrinth there lurked a race of refugees and criminals, men and women who had run away from all the duties of their caste, who scavenged from the city and worshiped a strange god, an incarnation of the White-Faced Woman. On six successive nights Lord Chrism had seen her in a dream, a woman standing in a field of whitened bones. She had worn an onyx necklace, and her face was as white as wax. Each night he had woken up sweating, and once he had cried out. The dream had held the force of premonition.

At the fifteenth turning of the fourteenth stair, Lord Chrism stopped and peered back down into the darkness. A narrow door led from behind the landing; Lord Chrism fumbled through and pushed it shut behind him. He bolted it. It was the border of the realm of light. In a high, empty hall he threw his torch away, for light was coming in through the high windows, a cool, soft light, mixing with the smell of dust and dreams, and books and rotting tapestries. Lord Chrism wrinkled up his nose. There was something else here too, a smell of gasoline and perfume, and a sound like gravel thrown against the window. The rain had started up again. High above him, one of the casements had split open and the sugar rain was pouring through, soaking the tapestries and biting at the cloth, so that underneath the windowsill the fabric hung in strips. The sugar phosphorescence had penetrated the room, so that to the priest's blind eyes one whole wall was lit with silver fire.

Muttering, he turned away. That vision of Paradise was not for him; he turned away and fumbled for a secret doorknob carved into the wall. A panel of the wall was carved into the likeness of the thirteenth bishop, a bibulous old man, and when Lord Chrism found his swollen wooden nose, the panel levered back to show another secret stair, which twisted up into a secret tower. Here were cells reserved for Chrism's private enemies. His predecessor was still alive in one, an ancient paralytic, deaf and blind, still fed three times a day.

Wide, straight flights of steps rose up around a square central well. There was a landing at each corner, and Lord Chrism stopped at the first one. He turned the key in the lock of a small door and pushed it open without entering. He stood back against the wall. "Come out," he said. "Come out now." But nothing happened. There was no sound, and for a moment Chrism was afraid the boy had died. Like all antinomials, the boy worshiped freedom as if it were a god, and for an instant Chrism was afraid that even a few days' captivity had been too much, and no bad treatment either. But then he heard a deep, gutteral breathing, even and untroubled, like an animal's.

The boy was sitting on his bed with his back against the wall. His huge hand moved delicately through the fur of the cat on his lap. It was the only movement he made, until he raised his head to stare out through the open door. He had been sitting in darkness, the shutters pulled closed over the window. The light from the open doorway cut diagonally across his face.

Like Prince Abu's, his cell was large and luxurious, reserved for prisoners of the highest rank. That had not made any difference to the boy. He had defecated next to his bed and urinated in several places along the wall, ignoring the chemical toilet built into the windowseat. His blankets had been pulled apart and rearranged into a kind of nest. The room itself had taken on a hot, sweaty odor. The boy's enormous body was glistening with sweat. He was naked to the waist.

"Come out," repeated Chrism Demiurge. He peered inside, but his sight was too dim to distinguish the soft caress of the boy's hand, the slow ripple in the darkness as he raised his head. The old priest was listening for some change in the boy's breathing, to see if he was sleeping or awake. But then suddenly he caught a flash of blue, as the light from the doorway was thrown back at him, reflected in the boy's alien, criminal blue eyes.

Lord Chrism shuddered. He had not seen the boy since he had come upon him in the bishop's chamber, and he had forgotten his blue eyes. Criminals in Paradise, atheists and cannibals on Earth—these antinomials, God had marked them so that they could never hide. He had marked them with their hairless skins, their gigantic bodies, their repulsive eyes. Reflexively, Lord Chrism made the sign of the unclean, dropping his chin into each armpit, muttering a little spiteful prayer.

The boy had no way of understanding the language of the prayer. But he understood its rhythm and its tone. Like all his kind, he was sensitive to music, and he heard the venom in the old man's voice. He turned his head so that he could savor it more carefully. And because he was sensitive to dancing, he watched each motion of the old priest's hands, though he cared nothing for barbarian ritual, as a rule. Yet this one seemed to concern him closely, so with music the boy put a note of interrogation into the air, a few notes of the melody called "talk some more."

But when he heard it, the old priest staggered backwards and stuck his skinny fingers in his ears. And when he spoke, his voice contained nothing of its usual gentleness. "Silence!" he shouted. "No blasphemy! Do as I command."

These words meant nothing to the boy. He understood

their pitch, their tone, even their definitions, but not their sense. It was a barbarian way of talking, a way of using language as a kind of power. That was all he knew. He had no way of appreciating the complexity of form, when a Starbridge and a prince of the church stooped to address a piece of human filth. And in fact he was not interested, because there was something else, too, some other music in the air. He turned his head to listen.

The tower rose eleven stories around a central stairwell. On every floor the stair was lined with cells. And when the old priest made his exclamation, the sound drifted up through the stairwell, finding resonances in the ancient tower, awakening prisoners in their beds, disturbing them at their desks or at their meals. In a little while the whole building shook to the sound of their weak shouting, and their weak fists drumming on the doors. They recognized his voice. And some were banging on the pipes, so that the sound made up a kind of music.

The boy sat listening, trying to analyze its parts, to break it down into its voices, as if he were walking up the stair with his hand on the bannister, pausing at every door. There could be something vital to him, if he could separate it out. If he could disregard the muffled curses and the cries, and break apart the rhythm of the pounding, and travel up each step of that long stair, then perhaps he would hear something. He would hear it separate from the rest, a song that he had taught her with great difficulty, for she was ignorant of music.

The cat jumped to the floor. It stretched, and arched its back. He stood up too, swiftly and unhurriedly. In the doorway the priest muttered a charm to calm the boy and sap his strength. But the antinomial knew nothing about magic. He pushed the old man aside, so that he fell back against the wall. The boy was free; he leaped across the threshold and leaped up the stairs.

As he ran, he pulled his thumb along the rods of the bannister. It made a quick, even patter on the wood, mixing with his heartbeat and the slapping of his footsteps. He was humming part of a melody, a tune called "think of me." And all the time he strained to hear another music blending with his own, badly sung and out of tune perhaps, but recognizable. He passed by doorway after doorway. He heard all the melodies of desperation in the frenzied banging and the strange, half-human cries; the music he was searching for was different from that.

He stopped on an upper landing. There were six doors in a row, but one was different from the rest, grander and more solid. It was built of oak and studded with nails. The whole surface of it was covered with symbols drawn in chalk, charms to reinforce the hinges, for the bishop was a powerful sorceress. She could have broken any ordinary door. But this one was sealed with magic. It was set into a recess in the wall, and on each side the frame was carved into a likeness of the God of Chastity, her lips clamped shut, her wooden fingers locked over her sex. In one of her five hands she held a spindle, and with each of the other four she passed a strand of thread back to her sister on the other side.

Between them, the doorway was sealed with a web of magic. But the boy cared nothing for barbarian superstition. He swept the edge of his palm down across it, and the web broke apart. The threads pulled back under his hand and writhed and tangled in the air, fringing the door as if with seething snakes. But the boy was ignorant of danger. He bent down to listen at the keyhole, and then he struck the door with all his strength.

Coming up behind him, Lord Chrism heard the hollow booming. "Stupid, so stupid," he muttered, laboring up the stair, leaning on the rail. But at the landing he stopped, and from the chain around his neck he produced a silver key.

Already the boy's hands were bloody, his knuckles mashed. His lips were pulled back along his gums, displaying long, carnivorous teeth. With a cry of rage, he smashed his naked shoulder against the studded door. But when he saw the priest, he turned around. The old man held the key out towards him at the end of its chain.

Then for a moment everything fell silent. For a moment the protests of the other prisoners fell silent, and in the interval the old man heard another sound, hesitant, unclear, a woman's voice, and even his barbarian ears could hear the music in it, though he couldn't understand it. In front of the door the antinomial was grimacing in pain. He reached his hand out for the key. "Give it to me," he said.

In one moment all the boy's violence had drained away. Lord Chrism disliked violence. Yet even more, he disliked sudden change. These antinomials were great, empty casks of flesh, yet they were dangerous and unpredictable. Lord Chrism muttered prayers against pollution. But then he shuffled forward, dangling the key, while with his other hand he made stiff, arthritic gestures in the air.

He never thought the boy would understand the working of the lock. But the antinomial had grown up in Charn. Though he loved freedom, he had never known it, even in his mind. Locks and keys he knew; he had been in prison more than once. So he grabbed the key and held it up. Grimacing, he rubbed it between his fingers and fitted it carefully into the lock.

The door swung open. At one time, the cell beyond had been the richest in the tower. In his strange, sad way, the priest had loved his bishop. Now, that love mixed with his blindness, and it took a moment for the old man to realize what had changed. For a moment, as he looked in through the door, he saw his memory of the way the room had been, imprinted on his ruined retinas. He saw the cushioned wallpaper, the chandelier, the carpets, and the giant bed where Angkhdt himself had once made love. But then the vision faded as his nostrils caught the smell of smoke. With a jolt of bitterness and pain, he realized she had wrecked the room.

The wallpaper had been white, and decorated with a floral pattern. Lord Chrism had chosen it himself, a mixture of forget-me-nots and lilies of the valley. Now it was gray and scorched and soggy. She had lit the room on fire and then extinguished it with water. The furniture was battered into pieces, the bed turned on its side, the mattress ripped apart and oozing soggy cotton. The chandelier had fallen to the floor. And in the middle of the wreckage stood the bishop, straight as a candle flame, dressed in her immaculate white shirt.

To the old man's eyes she appeared as a luminous white glow on a background of dark gray. But then a stain spread across the image as the antinomial leaped forward and took her in his arms. Lord Chrism turned his head aside and spat. The boy was his peace offering, his gift, but already he regretted bringing him. It nauseated him to see the sacred couple willingly with the unclean, nauseated him and broke his heart. Almost he regretted having come.

Before his eyes the candle flame burned free again. She had twisted from the boy's embrace and turned towards him. "Well?" she asked. "What have you to say to me?"

For the last time in his life the old man made the gestures of respect. He looked down at the floor. "It is my painful duty to inform you," he mumbled, "of the results of this morning's roll call. The vote was one hundred and seven to ninety-five with twenty-one abstentions—"

The bishop interrupted him. "Don't you think I guessed?" she cried. "My window overlooks the courtyard."

She pointed, but the old man did not raise his head. He could not have seen, even if he had wanted to, what she was pointing at, out the bars of her window, over the retaining wall, in the Courtyard of the Sun and Stars. "It is my scaffold," said the bishop. "They have been building it all morning. When is it to be?"

"Tomorrow night."

"I am surprised you won the vote. You must have lied to them."

"No, ma'am. Not entirely. Forgive me. But if I had told

the truth, they would not have voted to convict. It was a question of . . . political expediency. And better for you, too, in the long run. When your great-great uncle was bishop of this city, he was tortured to death by the revolutionary tribunal, almost exactly one year ago."

The bishop stood in the center of the room. The antinomial had moved over to the window. Lord Chrism leaned against the doorpost, looking down. Otherwise, he would have missed the smear of golden orange on the dark wood as the huge cat slunk across the threshold. It picked its way over the ruined carpet to rub up against the boy's legs.

The bishop also looked down at the cat, so that her black hair obscured her face. A week's imprisonment had not changed her, even in memory, her black eyes and heavy eyebrows, her petulant expression, her skin like edible sweet cream. Sadly, Lord Chrism recognized the reason he had come. He had wanted to see her one last time.

"I had to lie," he said. "If I had told the truth, it would not have been enough. Though it was enough for me. They did not see what I saw. If they had found you naked in your chamber with this . . . this . . . this . . . carnivore."

"And wasn't that my right?" she cried, looking up with angry eyes. "I am Bishop of Charn."

"It was your right, but it was not well done. In part, I blame myself. These atheists, I should have burned them all. And I ask myself, how did you find him? Through what crack did he crawl?"

"He climbed up to my tower window. He was starving and wet through. Do you blame me? I was brought up in this temple among men like you. Old men, blind. I thought he was the God Himself."

Standing at the window, the antinomial scowled and frowned. He tugged on one of the bars of the window as he looked back into the room. Outside, the weather had closed in, and it was raining.

"I do not blame you," said the priest. "I chose your education. I might have known the effects that so much holy scripture would have had on a young girl. Only I wish you had chosen something worthier. Some worthier object for your . . . love. It is unfortunate."

The cat was pacing back and forth under the window. The old man paused, and then continued. "It was his cat which gave me the idea," he said. "I told the council I had found you coupled with a demon. The demon from the ninety-second psalm—you know, Palagon Bahu, in the shape of a cat. I showed them in a living image, and they trusted me. Now I am sorry, but to tell the truth, what else could I do? Believe me, child—dear child—you will hardly feel it. I'll give you a drug, and you will hardly feel the fire. Or just a little bit—you will fall asleep, and you will wake in Paradise. Believe me, I have prayed for you. Every night of this past week, I have prepared a room for you. In the house of our beloved Lord."

"I think you are a monster," she said.

"Don't call me that. I am being generous. This afternoon my nephew burns, my own sister's son, and I have cursed him. Or rather, I'm not sure. I still have plans." Lord Chrism smiled at his own cleverness, and yet it was a guilty smile. He felt a compulsion to shame himself by telling everything. Yet he was gleeful, too, and proud, because the bishop, after all, was just a little girl. She could not be expected to understand.

"I came here to ask you for absolution," he said. "But now I see it is a wasted trip. Nevertheless, please try to understand. I have prepared a miracle. I have made my nephew's double. Surgically. Or rather, I have caused him to be made. I have made a man who looks just like him, from a distance. Understand: I want to make a miracle, to burn one and then use the other, as if God had saved him from the fire. Only I haven't yet decided which to burn."

"I think you are a monster," she repeated.

"Yes. Well, perhaps." Lord Chrism swallowed, and then he looked away. His voice had risen defiantly, but now it resumed its soft, insinuating tone. "But in a sense, it doesn't

matter what you think. You are deposed. You lack...
authority."

"I am Bishop of Charn."

"Yes. Perhaps. For a little while longer, I suppose."

That day, all day, there was chaos in the streets of Charn.
At nine o'clock, in Soldan Square, the spokesman for the
Inner Ear had nailed up a pronouncement, confirming
rumors of the bishop's condemnation. A crowd of seven
thousand people waited for the news under a light rain, and
when it came, they raised a howl that could be heard for
half a mile. They pelted the council's spokesman with excrement and mud; he was an old, fat, blind man, and they
almost killed him.

By noon the news had spread throughout the city. The
churches and chapels were all packed for morning prayer;
after the distribution of the grain, the parish priests stood up
to give the news, and later many of them took refuge in the
crypts, cowering among the tombs while the crowds ram-
paged above their heads. One at least, the chaplain at St.
Soldan's Gate, stripped off his miter and went down to join his
angry congregation. With his own crosier he beat in the
stained-glass portrait of Lord Chrism Demiurge above the
altar, and with his own hands he rang St. Soldan's Bell and
called the folk to arms.

"Which one of you has not received some comfort from
her hand?" he asked rhetorically. "Which one of you has
never felt the comfort of her grace?" His name was Ripon
Starbridge, and within a month he would be dead, broken
on the gallows of the revolution. For the sake of his name
and his tattoos, he would be broken and condemned, but on
that day he was a hero of the revolution, the first to raise his
hand against oppression. Later chroniclers would call that
time the Starbridge Uprising; from the 45th of October to
the fall of the temple five days later, much of the violence
against the government was led by rebel officers and priests,

seeking first to free the bishop, later to avenge her death.

Too late these men would realize their own danger: They were rousing passions that would overwhelm them. That day, when Ripon Starbridge rang the bell above St. Soldan's Church, he rang the tocsin for his race. All over the district men and women stopped what they were doing and looked up.

When Raksha Starbridge heard the sound, he was squatting over the workbench in his house on Spider Ghat, a beaker of what looked like urine in his hand. He turned his head and squinted up into the air. "What's that?" he asked, but he already knew. And there was no one else to tell him; to Princess Charity the bell was just a noise, another cadence fighting with the squall of rain upon the tiles, the slap of water on the pilings underneath the house. Or more than that: After a while the sound of the bell seemed to drown out other rhythms. Charity shivered, and wrapped her skinny body in her arms.

She stood near the doorway of the parson's house, leaning back against the bare studs of the wall. The house was larger than it looked from the outside, a single room, packed to the rafters with huge piles of junk. Near Charity, a mass of broken bicycles, scrap metal, and electrical supplies loomed up above her head. In front of her, occasional rodents wandered among bales of paper, chimney stacks of books.

Charity shivered, and listened to the tolling of the bell. After her morning in the streets, she was relieved to be inside. The outside world had proved so varied and intense, it was a relief to get away; concentrating on a single sound, she felt her strength return. In time she was secure enough to feel bored; that morning Raksha Starbridge had dragged her to his house. But once inside, he had abandoned her and disappeared. After an hour, she pushed away from the wall and walked down a pathway between boxes, following a line of revolutionary slogans painted on the floor. There, in an open space in the center of the house, Raksha Star-

bridge kept his bed and kitchen. There he kept his laboratory, a strange, eclectic cluster of burners and pipettes and
dusty bulbs of colored liquids. And there he crouched over
his workbench, stirring a beaker, while with his other hand
he added pinches of some dark and dirty powder.

He was talking softly to himself. Standing above him,
Charity noticed a new purpose in the way he moved, a new
anxiety. "It's Soldan's Bell," he said aloud, anticipating
what was on her lips to ask. "God help us all," he said.

Baffled, she shook her head, and he turned back to stare
at her. "My God, you're ignorant," he said. "Even Rosa
would have understood—listen," he said, rising to face her,
cradling the beaker in his hands. "Listen, why do you think
I brought you down here? It's because I needed you for my
experiment. But I didn't guess I needed you so urgently."

Baffled, she shook her head. He tried again. "I have a
friend in Kindness and Repair. He told me this: Last
Wednesday Chrism Demiurge, returning late from midnight
mass, surprised the bishop of this city coupled with a
stranger, before the altar of her private shrine. Lord Chrism
had them both arrested, and the bishop was indicted for
witchcraft and impurity. That was on Sunday. This morning
the council was to meet, to vote on the indictment, and I
was sure she'd be released. That bell tells me I was wrong."

The parson's face was full of movement, even when he
paused. Drugs and alcohol had penetrated every part of
him; his eyes were dilated, and his eyelids twitched. Clouds
of angry rashes and discolored skin seemed to move over his
cheeks; his mouth was never still and never dry. Charity
stared down at his trembling hands, watching the uneven
surface of the liquid in his beaker.

He wasn't finished: "I was wrong. The chaplain of Saint
Soldan's church is calling for armed demonstrations and a
general strike. He is Lord Chrism's cousin, but he is the
bishop's man. What can that mean, except she was condemned? What can that mean, except the moment I have

feared and hoped for all my life is here at last, and I am unprepared?"

Raksha Starbridge held the beaker in one hand. The other he spread open, and Charity could see his strange tattoo: a dark thicket of leaves and underneath, almost invisible, a single seam of gold, a tiny lizard hiding in the grass. "Once their power splits," he said, "then it will fall. I used to think, yes in my lifetime, yes in one thousand or two thousand days, the people would rise up. But that bell means that in a week—no more—the people will be hunting Starbridges through all the streets, and they will murder all they find." He stared down at his palm, and with the forefinger of the hand that held the beaker, he touched the seam of gold. "And I mean to survive."

Then suddenly he took her hand and led her over to another bench, under the shadow of a wall of books. "Stand here," he said. He put the beaker down upon the bench. "I needed you," he said. "For my experiment. Just for a moment—you will hardly feel it. The experiment has been complete, only I need the test. My own blood was never pure, and I have ruined it. Besides," he said, glancing down at his mottled forearm. "I find it hard to raise a vein."

With trembling fingers he lit a spirit lamp and then chose four test tubes from a dusty box. He rubbed them with a piece of cloth, then poised them upright in a row, balanced in a wooden rack. Then he crouched down. Under the bench there was a small electric cooler; he opened it and took the only thing that it contained—a china beaker covered with tin foil. Standing again, he poured two of the test tubes full of a thick liquid. It was dark blue and almost black.

"This is human blood," he said. "Ordinary. Starving class. But this"—he broke the seal on a sterile bag, and drew out a thick needle, which he connected to a plastic tube—"this," he said, and then he grabbed the princess by the arm and jammed the needle into the big vein inside her elbow. She grunted with surprise and pulled away, but he was stronger than he looked. He held her by the arm and then let go; it only took a moment for him to fill two test tubes with her blood. He yanked the needle out almost before she had a chance to say a word, and clamped a piece of gauze over the wound. Then he let go and turned back to the test tubes.

With a chuckle of delight, he held one up against the flame. "Perfect," he said. Her blood gleamed amber-colored in the lamplight; he shook it, watching the residue settle, and then replaced it in his rack. "Perfect," he said again. Charity said nothing, only she held the gauze clamped tightly over her arm.

Then he took the other beaker, the one that he had first prepared, and with a pipette he dripped seven drops of liquid into each tube.

In the two tubes of ordinary blood there was no change. But instantly the Starbridge blood turned color, and let forth an evil smell. When it was gone, the four tubes were interchangeable.

"What does it prove?" asked Charity.

Raksha Starbridge laughed. "Nothing," he said. "Nothing at all. But you and I are not religious. If we were, we'd find this demonstration most significant."

"What do you mean?"

Raksha Starbridge held the tubes up to the light, one after the other. "There are millions in this city who believe the myth we taught them, that there are differences between the rich and the poor. There are millions who will find it hard, even now, to rise up against their masters. They will think, 'What is the use? Our masters are like gods. To kill them is to send them straight to Paradise.' Now, to such a one, I would think this demonstration might be most significant. If they could be convinced there was a drug that could eliminate that difference, they might feel a revolution might succeed. A pill, perhaps, or an injection—something that would neutralize the sacred essence of the Starbridge blood...well, then they'd feel their hands were free to strike at their oppressors. And more than that, might they not be grateful to the man who gave that drug to them, who freed them from the burden of that myth? Might they not give him a high place in their counsels, and if he is a Starbridge, might they not forgive his blood, forgive his past?"

"My God," said Charity. "You'd sell us to the mob..."

"Ah yes, my family," interrupted Raksha Starbridge, and again he raised his hand, so that she could see the gleam of gold along his palm. "Ah yes," he said, looking around the filthy room. "My family, who have treated me so well. No, it is their own stupidity that has betrayed them. I have not brought them to this place. But I plan to survive—what are your plans?"

Charity took the gauze from her arm and looked down at the patch of amber blood. "I miss my cousin Thanakar," she said, tears in her eyes. "My cousin and my brother. He'd know what to do. The bishop's been arrested—he could free her. Just by raising up his hand."

"Yes. Perhaps. He has the power, but he lacks the strength. And Chrism Demiurge is burning him this afternoon. Had you forgotten?"

She had not forgotten. Tears were in her eyes. He went on: "No. These stories are all coming to an end. Your brother and the bishop. The Starbridge power in this city is coming to an end. The storm is coming, and I mean to ride it. I mean to survive."

"I, too," said Charity. "But not like that." She seized the beaker from the table and tried to pull away, but the parson had grabbed her by the arm. She tried to pull away, and then she turned and dashed the contents of the beaker back into his face, so that it ran down his clothes.

Raksha Starbridge laughed and licked his lips. "It doesn't matter. Rat piss and dopamine, that's all it is. I know the formula."

The bell had stopped. Charity pulled away, and he released her suddenly, so that she staggered and fell back. "Go," he said. "If you're not with me, you're against me. Don't come begging, later on."

He turned back to his test tubes. And Charity felt a sudden rush of terror, because, disgusting as he was, in all the vicious city he was everyone she knew. Almost, already, she felt like begging his forgiveness; the house on Spider Ghat seemed like a refuge, dark and peaceful, from the crowds outside. But then she gathered strength. She turned and walked up through the piles of junk, into the open air.

"What are you doing?" asked the boy.

In Kindness and Repair, part of the bishop's cell was still intact. When the old man had gone and sealed the door behind him, the boy sat on the windowsill, his cat upon his lap. He watched with a strange, silent absorption as she lit the candles of her private altar. From her own chamber in the bishop's tower, she had brought an old four-handed statue of Angkhdt the Charioteer. It was about ten inches high, carved of blackened bronze. The God was dancing, His arms making a circle around His head, and in each hand He held a symbol of the four great mysteries—love, war, poetry, and faith. His face was human, and there was nothing vulgar or deformed about His sex. The statue had been for children in the ancient time.

The bishop mixed some kaya gum into a bluish paste. At the same time, she was reciting vespers in her clear, low voice. She poured water into a row of small brass bowls, so that it trembled on the lip of overflowing. "Oh my Father," she intoned, "teach me how to love, for my love is the joy, the passion, and the flame."

At two o'clock, the bells started to ring again in churches all over the city. The bishop sat back on her heels to listen. She brushed a strand of hair back from her face. The boy watched her from the window, and with the thumb and index finger of his right hand he stroked the fur under the cat's right ear. Once again, the clouds outside had. broken apart, and the afternoon sun was coming through the bars into the room, touching his golden hair, his golden skin. "There is part of you that I don't like" he said.

"I am sorry," replied the bishop. She didn't turn around.

"This is slavery," he said. "In your mind. Leave it and come with me. Can you break the door?"

The bishop made the mark of Paradise above her forehead and her heart, tracing it in water. "I cannot," she said. "He has sealed it with an incantation, which will not be released until my death."

The boy hummed a few notes of a song called "come with me." Outside the window, the sun was shining with a clear, straight, golden light. It shone on the backs of the soldiers laboring in the courtyard around the scaffold, and it made their shadows long and black. They had built a pyramid of logs. Soaked with rainwater, scented with perfume, now it was smoking in the sunlight and the unaccustomed heat. The great pile of wood with the heavy stake on top pointed dolefully up towards the sky. The shadow of it stretched across the yard and touched another, smaller gallows by the wall. "Tomorrow night," said the bishop. "Tomorrow night we shall be free."

"In Paradise," said the boy, his voice a music of contempt.

The bishop frowned. Again she pushed the hair back from her face. "Not quite that far," she said. "Watch this."

In a dark space near the altar an image gathered shape. It spun and twisted on the floor, a coil of snakes, a white stag, and a cloud of butterflies. A mixture of illusions in a space six inches high, and then another image: a tree growing from a pyre of burning logs, spreading its limbs, its leaves and branches catching fire. A silver apple on its topmost bough spun in the light, detached itself, and floated up into the air. It was the Earth, a tiny simulacrum of the Earth, spinning, changing color, changing season.

The bishop frowned. "I can make a dream as real as flesh," she said.

Six miles away across the city, Prince Abu watched the sun for the last time. He stood on the steps of Wanhope Prison, squinting myopically into the glare. "How warm it is," he said. "This is real spring weather, after all." These were his last words, and later people argued constantly about their meaning. And in fact it was the hottest day in Charn so far that season. That, and the unsettled weather, were things that people would remember later, when they sang songs about his death.

The priests had ungagged him and untied his hands, so that they could shrive him. Lord Chrism had asked them to perform this ceremony in public. So they had put up saw-horses and barricades in the open square before the prison steps, and the purge was holding back the crowd. There were fifteen hundred people in the square. "Abu, Abu, Abu," they shouted. The prince smiled and waved. He felt like a fool. He had been drinking steadily all day, and now he could scarcely stand. He wasn't thinking at all clearly, but he liked the feeling of the sun on his bare cheeks.

For a while he had thought to make a gesture. When the priest approached him with the cup, he had thought to knock it from his hands so that it clattered down the steps. In his mind he had rehearsed how he would strike it down and then raise up his hand, so that the people could all see the symbol of the shining sun. But when the moment came, he saw that for his benefit the sacrificial balsam in the cup had been replaced by rum, a good, solid shot of rum, a last present from his uncle, and no doubt liberally drugged. So instead, he grabbed the cup and raised it to his lips, and all around him the cheering was redoubled. It was something they would all remember, how Prince Abu grabbed the cup and drained it, instead of kneeling to accept a sip.

He wiped the sweat from his bald forehead. He was happy, even in that circle of repulsive priests. Only, when they brought him the mask and gauntlets, for a moment he turned away. "Wait," he said. He turned back towards the sun and closed his eyes. So that he wasn't even paying attention when they tied him and locked the silver gauntlets to his wrists. They strapped the silver mask over his head.

And when he opened his eyes again, he found that he could scarcely see. The mask was padded so as not to hurt him, and the eye slits were several inches from his eyes. He didn't care. The world of his sensation was closing down. But he could still feel the sunlight, and his body chafing in his clothes. And he could still hear the chanting of the crowd, cheering for him, though doubtless for the wrong reasons. It didn't matter; reasons didn't matter. But the cheering seemed to fill his heart.

They put his hands in gauntlets and led him down the steps. There a procession was waiting for him, a double row of seminarians, young serious boys in pink and silver robes. Their hair was combed back straight, or parted in the middle. They were carrying handbells. And interspersed among them were a number of old flagellants that the council had raked up from some asylum. Since the procession had not yet started, most were still squatting in their places, scratching for fleas, smelling their fingers, muttering to themselves. Their hair and beards were long and wild, their backs ridged with scars.

At the end of the procession stood an ancient pickup truck, freshly painted black and decorated with the symbol of the Inner Ear. It was a mark of the council's favor that they had made such a vehicle available, for there were very few in Charn, all relics from the previous year. This one ran on a mixture of methane and solar power; the driver touched off the old-fashioned gunpowder ignition plate, and the engine shuddered to life, spewing clouds of evil smoke. And as if that were the signal, the seminarians opened their missals, and some had tambourines and tiny cymbals. The flagellants got to their feet, combing out their scourges, and it was they who provided the first rhythm of the march, tentative at first and then stronger as they got used to their own stroke, and the anesthetic paste that they were chewing took its grip.

Then the boys started to sing, and even Abu was not too drunk to smile at the irony of that choir, the eldest of whom had already been emasculated, singing such a triumphant celebration of the phallus of Beloved Angkhdt. "It is hard as iron," they chanted, a cheerful, hopeful song, and it filled Prince Abu's heart with laughter as they led him to the tailgate of the truck. There in the bed of the pickup stood a large wicker cage, and they prodded him inside and strapped it closed.

The symbolism of this was lost on him, but the crowd understood it. Ever since they were children they had heard the story of how Angkhdt had been carried in a cage through those same streets. Prince Abu's silver mask had been carved into the scowling muzzle of a dog, and he peered through eyes of yellow agate. The prince was not aware of how he looked. But he knew the crowd was cheering, and he waved and clapped his hands as the truck started across the open square. It turned into the first of the long streets that led out to the municipal gallows and the burning ground.

All through the city where he was to pass, the streets were lined with people. Near the Morquar Gate, Princess Charity was standing in another section of the crowd, among some factory workers. They were big, rough, drunken men.

Their leader was Professor Sabian. Later he was to found the first of the labor caucuses that were to rule the city, but at that time he was still a public obstetrician, having given up a good position in the house of a Starbridge financier. He was very small, almost a dwarf, and by nature he was stooped and mild, with careful manners and clean clothes. But when he spoke in public in those days, he was transformed. His frailty and indecision vanished, and his voice, normally quiet and precise, rose to a shriek.

That afternoon he was standing at the curbside, on a platform of barrel heads. Five hundred people had gathered to hear him, and when the funeral procession appeared at the bottom of the street, the professor shook his fists in the air. "Citizens!" he shouted. "Don't let this distract you. Don't be taken in. Now is the time to stand up strong and show that you will not be satisfied with the deaths of one or two or ten of these, for I tell you, the time is coming soon when we will wash our streets clean with their blood. Starbridge parasites! I tell you, not one will escape. Not one!"

Charity stood listening in an open section of the crowd. She leaned her back against a concrete wall abutting the wide sidewalk. Her eyes kept closing by themselves. She had come on foot from Spider Ghat, following the crowds, and now she waited with the rest, hoping to catch a glimpse of Abu's funeral cortege. She could not think further than that.

The day before, she'd been in bed, asleep in her palace on the thirty-seventh floor. Out of that womblike stasis she had been expelled onto the street, and now she stood, weary in her deepest heart, her bare feet torn and bruised, her dress covered with mud. Around her the world that she had known was sinking fast, subsiding as the sun went down, yet still she stood, waiting to sever one last link.

"Citizens!" cried the professor. "This is just a piece of theater. Do not let yourselves be fooled. But look around you now and feel the power of your numbers, and ask yourselves who else can stand against you when these princes, lords, and bishops turn upon themselves!"

His voice was drowned out in the crowd. A chant came rolling up the line, people shouting in unison. "Starbridge!" they shouted. "Starbridge! Starbridge! Starbridge! Starbridge! Starbridge!" And at that moment, Abu Starbridge's procession turned into the bottom of the street, and Charity could hear the music of the tambourines. Over the heads of the assembled multitude she saw soldiers on horseback trotting by, and then she stood erect and pushed into the crowd, pushing herself forward until she stood in the front rank.

But by the time the prince's truck arrived, the crowd was so excited that it had broken past the barricade into the street. Men squatted down to pull the cobblestones out of the roadbed, and soon the air was full of rocks and flying debris, raining on the shoulders of the flagellants, banging dents in the old truck. Prince Abu was awakened by the sound. Tired out from adulation, he had fallen into a drunken doze, but now he woke to the sound of stones pattering around him and the rhythmic, hostile shouting of the mob. "Starbridge! Starbridge! Starbridge!" they shouted. Abu peered out through the slits in his mask.

But they did not get a chance to harm him. Within minutes a mounted company of soldiers had ridden back from the head of the column, clearing the street with their nightsticks and their whips. The rebels staggered back, but not before several of the boldest had penetrated to the truck itself. One, taller and stronger than the rest, a glass miner from Caladon, raised his pick above his head. Tottering, off balance, he swung it in a circle; he lifted it up high above the prince's cage. But Charity had followed him into the street; before he could bring it down, she reached up to grab the spike of it as it hung down behind his back. The miner shook his weapon free, but even so the stroke went wide. It smashed down on the tailgate of the truck, puncturing the ancient metal, and then it was torn from his hands. But for a split instant, the truck's forward progress was slowed, and it gave the princess time enough to leap up into the bed. This also became part of the legend: how Prince Abu, even at the very last, still had the strength to raise himself and offer comfort to a woman of the starving class, a laundress, an atheist who had not discovered God until that moment. She was dressed in yellow rags, covered with mud, and her feet were bare and bruised. But in the moment before the soldiers in the truck had pitched her out, Prince Abu scrambled to his feet to stand beside her, gripping the bars of his cage between his silver gauntlets. And some people reported later that he had reached out to bless her, that he had touched her on the hand, that they had pressed their heads together, and even had exchanged some words.

It was over in a moment. The soldiers pitched her out. She fell to her knees in the rough street.

# THANAKAR

**T**he city of Charn stands at the base of a broad promontory, thirty miles from the sea. It rises out of a circle of small hills, broken to the east and west by flat, rocky gorges, and the river running through. From the Harbor Bridge the river unwinds nineteen miles to the port—in those days a long reach of abandoned buildings and collapsing docks, where rusted cranes stood fingering the sky. Warfare with Caladon had closed the port: The estuary and the lagoon were blocked with the wrecks of sunken ships. The water there was shallow, too, because in that season the ocean had receded back ten miles beyond the littoral, leaving the lagoon covered with a brackish sheet of water, out of which rose the hulks of the abandoned warships, their gundecks canted over in the sand.

By the middle of October in the eighth phase of spring, the war had reached a cautious stage. Argon Starbridge, King of Caladon, had pulled his army back across the border. A strong commander would have marched on

Charn, to take advantage of the change in government.
But Argon Starbridge had recently been beaten in a
bloody fight, his army broken by the bishop's on the Serpentine Ridge. And he was by nature a cautious ruler.
Ancient and immensely fat, he sat immobile on his throne
in Caladon, a hundred miles from the border, two
hundred miles from the gates of Charn. He had been king
for longer than old men could recollect, for his father and
his grandfather had been the same as he—the same
name, the same habits, the same bulk.

That season the seat of power in Caladon was the cathedral, a maze of windowless low buildings on Kodasch Promenade. There King Argon sat upon his throne, accessible to
any of his subjects with the strength to penetrate that labyrinth of shrines. Even the most urgent couriers had to allow
a full day, from the time they passed under the cathedral's
low, unguarded portal, to the time they stood at last in the
round chamber of the sanctuary. There the rituals of state-
craft moved unaltered, whatever the message, whatever the
hour, whatever the day—the gold mosaic of the walls glinting in the candlelight, the acolytes dancing to the music of
the flute and tambourine. And in the middle Argon Starbridge sat on his pierced and padded throne, surrounded by
a circle of soldiers and ministers. In perfect rhythm to the
music, they would pass him documents to sign or bend to
whisper in his ears. Every hour they would help him change
his clothes; it was the only way of judging time in that place,
to see what he was wearing. As the day wore on, golden
robes would give way gradually to scarlet ones. At nighttime he was clothed in regal black, changing to gray and
pink as morning came.

And every hour or so his courtiers would help him to his
feet, and he would walk down the steps of the dais to the
altar. There he would make the round of sacred objects. He
would raise each one according to the ancient custom, and
his hands would describe patterns in the air. His hands were

long and eloquent. They were not the hands of a fat man.

At other times he sat immobile on his throne. Or rather, he gave the impression of immobility. But the impression was a false one: From time to time he would take a book from one of his courtiers and study it for minutes on end. He would rearrange the rings upon his fingers. And although rumor claimed he never slept and never ate, a careful watcher, waiting for an audience among the banks of pews, would soon perceive the truth: The king was mortal. Occasionally his masked head would fall forward on his breast for minutes at a time, and he would be heard to snore. At other times, his seneschal would pass him little golden plates of candies and thimble cups of vegetable stimulants. .

In summer, Caladon City had risen out of endless fields of flowers, two days' journey from the nearest imperfection in the plain. Tulips, hyacinth, and sun trumpets had grown in hundred-acre paddocks, separated from each other by narrow, straight canals. The trunk road had passed over dozens of small bridges; travelers coming down out of the hills had found their sinuses assaulted by a mist of fragrances, so that houses and villages had seemed to rise out of a fog.

In summer, Caladon had been a wealthy place, famous for its merchants and its women. The city ramparts had been covered up with earth; there had been gardens and fountains and low bungalows. But by the eighth phase of spring, 00016, endless weathering had stripped away the soil, down to its foundations of soda ash and lime. That spring a flat, white, caustic plain stretched to the horizon in all directions, and the city was surrounded by walls forty feet high, built of limestone blocks, discovered course by course all season by the searching wind. The citizens were glad of the protection. In the streets they wrapped scarves around their faces; women and children shivered in their houses and rarely ventured out.

By midspring the rains had come, and turned the soda plains to mud. In some places the roads were washed away. Farther up into the country they were pitted and ridged, with gullies that could break a wheel. And in the high hills near the border there were mudslides, and the roads were full of carts and beasts of burden and soldiers shouting and cursing at the rain.

In October of the eighth phase of spring, there was new activity on these roads. Argon Starbridge had garrisoned a series of hill forts along a ridge of mountains to the sea. In the village beneath each one there was a customs post—a stone building surrounded by hotels. The border wound over the hills between these posts. In those days it was marked by a fence of luminous barbed wire, twice as tall as a man. Even in daylight it seemed to glow, but at nighttime travelers from far away could see it burning over the hills, in places red, in places livid green. Closer to hand, they saw the fire resolve into its separate strands, and then it seemed a barrier of nervous handwriting, a scrawl of giant, illegible letters across the landscape, lighting up the sky, marching to the sea.

Thanakar Starbridge saw it from far away, sitting in the boat he had taken from the wreck of Charn. It came down from the hills and made a barrier along the beach, and then it came out towards them on poles progressively longer, though the water there was shallow, close to land. Farther out, it was supported by pontoons, continuing on past them, out of sight across the glass-flat sea.

Thanakar turned the boat and came to shore, following the lights. There was a place where the wire had come unstuck from its pole and sagged down almost to the water. He could have crossed it there, and in the weeks that followed, he would look back to that moment in frustration, wondering if everyone along this border was given just one single chance to cross, and that was his, and he had missed it. But that first night, as he rested on the oars, he was not anticipating trouble. That first night he was happy and relieved that he had led them all to safety, down the river from the burning city.

He had been with the army when the news of his indictment came. He had been indicted for adultery, and Chrism Demiurge had sent the purge to take him in. But he had managed to evade them and return to Charn, arriving on October 46th. There he had found news of Charity's death, the bishop's condemnation, and the streets had been full of revolution. So he had left the city the next day, taking his family's boat down through the catacombs and down the river.

And he had taken flotsam from the city's wreck: Mrs. Cassimer, his family's housekeeper; and Jenny Pentecost, an orphan who had been his patient. Refugees, they had slept along the riverbank under the constant rain and skulked for food around the outskirts of the towns. In the estuary Thanakar had fished for hours in the dark with a small, pale flashlight tied to a piece of twine, trying to tempt an old sea cucumber from its hole. At night they had camped on the lagoon among the broken battleships, and they could smell the sea and hear the cry of the birds.

But in time they had passed under the reach of the lido, and out onto the cold, flat sea. For a week they had motored up the coast until the engine gave out, and there was no more fuel. Then Thanakar had rowed until his delicate white hands were split and blistered, while Mrs. Cassimer boiled seaweed on the primus, and Jenny Pentecost stared straight ahead over the bow.

That had been the first sign of her illness. An ordinary child, bred in the slums of Charn as she had been, would have looked around herself with eyes full of wonder. And maybe she would have been frightened, and maybe she would have cried about the weather and complained about the food—still, anything was better than just staring up ahead. Thanakar felt like shaking her, turning her by her frail shoulders, forcing her to notice when a small sea dragon flopped over the bow, forcing her to notice when the border came in sight, gleaming through the darkness like a wall of fire.

He himself was too excited to speak. That first night he saw it, the wall of burning letters spelled out safety to him, and freedom, and success against all odds. Mrs. Cassimer was sleeping in the bilge; he pulled the boat in towards land and beached it on the shore, and made camp. In the morning he washed his face in the last of the fresh water, and limped up through the sand dunes to the village.

It was a poor, muddy place, thatched one-story houses built out of driftwood and flat stones. But there was one imposing structure, a new stone customs house rising from the central square, and near its steps a new stone statue of King Argon Starbridge, holding in his arms his infant son.

Behind the king, facing the other way, stood one of his ministers, and between his marble hands he hoisted up a strand of glowing wire, part of the wire fence that straggled in across the square and cut the town in two. This was the border midway between Caladon and Charn, decreed by Angkhdt Himself, drawn by Angkhdt Himself across the map of the world. Throughout the chaos of the endless war it had never shifted, though in fact it had no practical significance. In the last phase of the fighting, Argon Starbridge's armies had driven past it almost to the walls of Charn, and though they had been defeated there and been pushed back, still the intervening countryside had not been recaptured. The town on both sides of the border was the same. The people spoke the same language, lived the same lives, and passed freely through the gate at one end of the square.

The gate was a hole in the wire fence, perhaps twelve feet wide, and no guard seemed to be on duty there. Thanakar limped towards it across the square, along the facade of the customs house. He limped through a group of children playing marbles, dirty kids with runny noses and ripped undershirts. And he had gotten past them, and past some women carrying pots, and past a child playing with his hoop, and almost to the gate itself, when he was stopped. A little boy ran after him, tugging at his sleeve. At first Thanakar thought he was a beggar, and he fumbled with the change in his pocket and tried to pull his hand away. But the boy held on tight and dragged him towards the steps of the stone building. "Coming, sir," he cried. "Please, coming, sir," he cried, his voice a high singsong, and he was pulling with all his strength on Thanakar's cuff. And there was something in his face, too, some poignancy, some reserve of childish power, that sapped Thanakar's will. He allowed himself to be pulled up the stone steps, under the lintel and the rough plaster frieze along the pediment: vultures feasting on St. Morquar's brain.

That should have warned him, that and a dozen other things. Inside the building, clerks scurried down the narrow passageways, and patient janitors pushed carts of wastepaper. But still Thanakar didn't pay attention; he allowed himself to be led into the deep recesses of the building. And it wasn't until he stood inside the door of the main waiting room with the child still hanging onto his arm, watching the first of the emaciated, veiled figures stalk towards him over the tiles, that he cried out and tried to turn away. By then it was too late. The door had closed behind him.

With a curse, Thanakar flung the boy aside and started back, but the door was locked. On each side a Caladonian soldier stood unblinking, and though their backs were rigid and their faces stiff, still it seemed to Thanakar that they were mocking him. Flight and resistance seemed suddenly undignified, so with a gesture of disgust he turned around and allowed the veiled figure to lead him into the room, past rows of chairs, mostly vacant, though old men watched him anxiously from some of them. He allowed himself to be led down an aisle between the seats, into an inner chamber made of movable partitions.

There, behind an old desk piled with papers, sat another of the veiled creatures. It was swaddled in black gauze, and the thin angularity of its body made it look inhuman, more like an insect than a man. Its face was covered with black cloth, and through it Thanakar could see its eyes and the hint of a long face.

Thanakar put his fingers to his cheek and made the gestures of contempt. He had heard about these creatures. In Charn they had been exterminated one full year before, in Thanakar's great-grandfather's time. Somewhere among the endless revolutions of that spring an angry crowd had set fire to the prison where they lay—there had not been many of them, even in those golden days of paperwork. But obviously some had survived in Caladon, and Argon Starbridge had found work for them. Unravelers, they had been called, part of an ancient and hereditary cult of civil servants, descendants of Lord Laban Coromex, who had been (or so he claimed) the Prophet's catamite.

In Charn they had been arrested and imprisoned with other ritual practitioners of homosexuality, for the revolutionary council had been strict that spring. It was unclear how they reproduced. Popular songs of the period described them hatching like insects from the mold of books—it was ridiculous, thought Thanakar. Doubtless somewhere there existed a race of women as angular and secretive as they. The one in front of him could easily have been a woman. Thanakar experimented with the thought and then decided it was so just as the creature opened her mouth. Later he was to have trouble telling them apart. Later he would look back on this one with a kind of wistfulness, for her voice, at least, was sweet and sympathetic.

She sat back in her chair and looked at him, while with one finger she hit the space bar of an old typewriter on her desk. It had no paper in it.

"Please sit," she said, and then she turned her head and looked past him towards a corner of the wall. In her wheeled armchair, her whole attitude was one of listless melancholy, her drooping neck and shoulder, the line of her arm. "Please sit," she said again.

"I don't expect it's necessary," Thanakar replied. "I don't expect to be here long."

The absurdity of this statement didn't seem to strike her. She heaved a long, melancholy sigh and rapped idly on the space bar of her typewriter. "No," she said. "Not long."

She stared past him at the wall. And then, after a good minute had gone by, she looked briefly at his face. She picked up a piece of paper from the litter on her desk and then cast it aside. "How old are you?" she asked.

The question took Thanakar by surprise. But it seemed as good a place as any to begin. "I was born on the twenty-second of December, in the eighteenth phase of winter," he said.

"So. Ten thousand days." She reached her hand out towards her desktop calculator and then let it drop. "Almost . . . ten thousand," she repeated. "Where were you born?"

"Wanhope Hospital. In Charn."

"In Charn," she said, as if she heard the city's name for the first time. "And . . . who are you?" she asked.

Thanakar rubbed his nose. "I am called Thanakar Starbridge," he answered, feeling that strange mix of arrogance and shame that afflicted him whenever he had to name himself. It was arrogance for what he was, shame for what his family had made out of the world.

"Starbridge," said the woman softly, and Thanakar could see her frown under the veil, as if the word brought up images and associations she was striving to recall. "King," she said. "Argon Starbridge is our king. Are you a relative of his?"

"Not a close one."

"Then . . . who are you?"

"I am a surgeon," replied Thanakar uneasily. "I was a surgeon in the army of the late bishop of Charn."

"The late bishop—is she dead?"

"She is dead."

The woman sighed. "So many dead. Six thousand... almost seven thousand of our soldiers. Almost exactly seven thousand, in our last battle with the bishop's army, on the Serpentine Ridge. Were you there?"

"I was there," he said. "I was a doctor."

"And now you wish to enter Caladon. Do you have some proof of your identity?"

Thanakar put out his hand. He had washed that morning, so that the lines were bright and clear, the silver dog's head and the yellow briar, the emblems of his father's family. He turned his palm a little, to show the golden key tattooed under his thumb, the key that opened all doors.

With her little finger the unraveler hit the space bar of her typewriter. "Starbridge," she said softly. "Are you carrying a passport?"

Thanakar opened up his shirt, and from a secret pocket sewn into the seam he took out his passport and his letter of safe conduct, and laid them on the desk.

The letter of safe conduct was an impressive document, issued to Thanakar's great-grandfather and hereditary in his family, signed by the emperor himself. The unraveler perused it wearily. On her desk stood an array of stamps and inkpads; she reached her finger out to touch one, and then looked up at him again. "Are you traveling alone?"

"No. My housekeeper and adopted daughter are accompanying me."

"And... where are their passports?"

"They don't need passports. The letter states that clearly: 'Thanakar Starbridge, his family, and whatever property he wishes...'"

The unraveler stared at him a moment and then turned away. "The document refers to relatives by blood, not by adoption. And your housekeeper, is she also a member of your family?"

"Of course not. She belongs to me. She was my mother's servant."

"Nevertheless. Perhaps in Charn a human being is considered property. Not here."

There was a long silence. Thanakar broke it by pulling a chair from the wall behind him and sitting down, for his leg was hurting him.

The unraveler leaned towards him. "So," she said. "You understand what I am saying. You, I am powerless to prevent. These others, well. Perhaps I am not powerless."

"What do you suggest?" asked Thanakar.

"You must return to Charn. I will provide you with a list of documents you need. Then we will see."

"I can't go back. How can I go back? I escaped from the city with my life and nothing else."

"I'm sorry," she said. Her voice was soft and sympathetic.

Thanakar possessed a sapphire ring. He twisted it uneasily on his finger, but the unraveler guessed his thoughts. "Please don't try to bribe me," she said. "I cannot be bribed."

He let his hands drop to his lap. The unraveler leaned back in her chair. "Come back tomorrow morning," she suggested. "Please don't give up hope—there's always hope."

Thanakar went back the next morning and again each day that week. He moved Jenny and Mrs. Cassimer into a hotel near the square. But on the morning of October 78th he went for a walk outside of town, to a small half-ruined chapel out of sight of the sea, bombed months before by the Brothers of Unrest. He had heard there was a priest there, like himself a refugee from Charn, and one morning he came out of the rain and stood in the shadow at the back of the church, leaning on an old umbrella, waiting for the priest to finish morning mass.

A dozen men and women clustered near the altar rail,

where the roof was solid. They were dressed in the colors of the Caladonian working class, muted grays and browns. But it was not their poverty that made Thanakar feel self-conscious. He was used to that. No, it was their devotion, the way they bowed their heads and pressed their knuckles to their foreheads, the tears in their eyes as they repeated the words of the general confession, the humility with which they touched the sacred image of Immortal Angkhdt. It made Thanakar unhappy. The rite was unfamiliar, but he recognized parts of it, enough to smell the sickness that had spread from Charn all over that northern country. Here, too, men worshiped their oppressors. He had hoped it would be different.

He looked up at the crack in the roof above his head, the white sky showing and the sugar dripping through. Then he turned back towards the priest. He would have felt better, he decided, if he could have found it in his heart to hate the man. But as always, circumstances had combined to frustrate him. There was nothing contemptible in that gentle face. There was nothing contemptible in the way the old man moved among his people, bending down to touch them and to whisper words of consolation in their ears. He moved down the line of kneeling figures, holding the sacred image out for them to kiss, the lingam of Beloved Angkhdt, giver of life. Then he opened his cassock, and into each pair of outstretched hands he thrust a small package of rice flour, though he himself looked as though he could have used a meal, thought Thanakar.

The priest made the sign of absolution, and the parishioners started to disperse. Thanakar waited until he was alone, standing by the altar, wiping out the vessels with a greasy rag. But he turned his head when he heard the patter of the doctor's limp and the click of the steel spike of his umbrella coming towards him over the stone floor. For a moment he looked frightened. But then Thanakar took his hat off and stepped out from the shadow of the arch into a circle of candlelight. He saw relief wash into the old man's face, together with that humble look that never failed to irritate him, the more so when it seemed sincere. He raised his hand.

"My lord," said the priest. He bowed and made the gestures of respect.

Thanakar stared at him sourly. All his life he had hated priests, hated their arrogance and power. This one seemed different, his ragged clothes, his tired face. His humility seemed genuine. The first of a new breed, thought Thanakar.

"You are from Charn," he said. "I had heard you were from Charn."

Again the old priest bowed. "God was kind to me," he said. "I was smuggled out in an empty wine cask. Of my convocation, I alone am not a martyr."

"You sound sorry."

"I am not sorry. Life is sweet. Come," he said. "We will be safer in the open air. I am followed everywhere I go."

He led the way down the aisle and out onto the porch, walking quickly and then waiting for the doctor to catch up. The front end of the chapel had collapsed, but the porch was still intact. The priest waited there.

Outside it was raining, a slow, scummy drizzle. The chapel stood in a countryside of fields, divided from each other by stone walls, and Thanakar was encouraged to see some greenness there, and some signs of agriculture. It was greener country than around Charn. The soil was not so pitiful, and even the rock gorges were not barren, as they were back towards the city. A green fungus grew over the rock, and Thanakar knew that it was edible, for he had seen children in the evening scraping it from the stones, and women boiling it in huge kettles.

This close to the sea the land was kinder. The people here ate seaweed and set traps for sea vegetables, the first of the season. Nevertheless, wherever Thanakar went, he was surrounded by a swarm of beggars. Several had followed him up from the town, and they stood in the shelter of a gray stone wall as Thanakar and the priest looked out from the porch.

"Do you have anything to give them?" asked the priest.

"I had brought something for you."

"Let us eat it here, and we will share it."

Thanakar had brought a kind of pie, cheese baked in a thick pastry and wrapped in silver foil. He undid the upper buttons of his overcoat and fished it out from an inside pocket. It made a messy meal, and he and the priest sat on the steps to eat it. With his pocketknife the old man cut aside a small portion for themselves, and he sliced the remainder into strips and placed it on the lowest step. They settled down to wait, and in a little while the beggars came close, timidly at first, making exaggerated signs of self-abasement. One of them, finally, a gap-toothed, red-haired man, squatted down below them and stretched out his hand, once, twice, until the priest nodded his head. And then the beggar grabbed the food and hurried off with it and carried it to the shelter of a pile of rocks not far away, where the rest clustered around him.

"They distrust you," remarked Thanakar.

"They have been shamefully abused," replied the priest. "Their own parish chaplain has run away. Between here and the city, most have fled. They have heard terrible rumors, most of which are true. I cannot blame them."

"And you?"

The old priest shrugged. "I do what I can," he said. "Tomorrow I move on."

"Where to?"

"Caladon City, eventually. I am carrying the daily execution lists from Charn, until one week ago, when I escaped. My late master thought that they might interest the king."

"Can I see them?"

The priest turned away and stared out over the green

fields. "I have no wish to cause you pain," he said. "They contain the names of many relatives of yours."

The doctor put his fingers to his head. "They are in Paradise," he said.

The old man's eyes were tired and old and rimmed with yellow. "That's just it," he said. "We can't be sure of that. Not anymore." He swallowed, and then went on: "The new tribunal contains a defrocked priest. I am ashamed to say it. January First, he calls himself—he has developed a vaccine. It reacts with what is sacred in the blood. When my late master was condemned, this man visited him in his cell. He injected him with this vaccine—my late master was condemned to hell, and so were all the members of the bishop's council, those they found alive. Down to the ninth planet, do you know what that's like? I have seen photographs. The surface pressure is enough to flatten steel."

"January First?"

"Raksha Starbridge, his name was. He changed his name to January First. There is a motion before the new assembly to reform the calendar. The new majority speaker changed his name." The old man shook his head. "Tell me, is it possible? The desanctification vaccine—God help me, the thought of it has hurt my faith. You asked me if I were eager to die, to accept martyrdom like so many others. I tell you, I am afraid."

Thanakar shifted on the stone step and stretched out his crippled leg. "I don't believe it's possible," he said. "Tell me," he continued. "Tell me what has happened. Who is the leader of this revolution?"

"Raksha Starbridge!" muttered the old priest, making the sign of the unclean. "Traitor! No, he is not the only one." He turned towards Thanakar, a doubtful expression on his face. "I can't believe that this is news to you."

The doctor shrugged. "I left the city thirty days ago, after the bishop's execution. I have heard many rumors, but no news."

"You are here alone?"

"With my adopted daughter. She is sick."

The chapel stood on the outskirts of the town. From where Thanakar sat, he could see the slate roofs of the houses and the end of the main street, where it stumbled out into the fields. A procession of a dozen men was coming along the muddy track, partly hidden by the stone walls and the hedgerows. They were pushing wheelbarrows and carrying baskets full of seaweed up to the drying shed at the end of town. It was a wooden building set on stilts above the soaking ground, wall-less, open to the air, the roof supported by posts at the four corners. Some women were already there, raking out the morning catch with long wooden rakes. And the village shaman was there also, in a white, featureless paper mask and a loose white shirt with flapping sleeves. He was moving in a circle around the perimeter of the floor, ringing a wooden bell.

This was a ritual practiced in the seacoast towns. The shaman was frightening away ghosts, scaring away the ghosts of anyone who had ever died of hunger in that town. The people feared their starving ancestors, afraid that their spirits might gather like birds to feed upon the crop, and pluck away the ghost of nourishment hidden in the heart of their poor food, and leave only the worthless husk.

Thanakar settled back to watch. At his side, the priest settled back against the stone pillar of the porch and cleaned the blade of his pocketknife against the skirt of his habit. "After the bishop died," he said, "the city fell apart. It was as if the center of our life was gone. The simplest tricks no longer worked. There was no power anywhere. The army and the purge split into factions. Chrism Demiurge and his council were besieged in the temple. When the rebels finally broke in, they found that most of them were gone, fled to Paradise. Some were arrested with the hypodermics still in their hands—that was in the middle of the month, October 50th, old style. Chrism Demiurge had disappeared. It was thought he knew some secret bolt hole below ground. He was never found."

In the drying shed the shaman danced and rang his bell. Thanakar sat watching him, and with the nail of his little finger he picked some cheese out from between his teeth.

"Now there is no magic left in Charn," the priest went on. "All those who practiced it are dead. On the fifty-second of October, Raksha Starbridge had the bodies of the council dragged to Durbar Square. He built a huge bonfire out of pews and statues from the temple. That was the beginning of the cult of Desecration. He damned them all to hell. Tell me—is that possible?"

Thanakar shrugged. "It is not possible," he said. "It's just more fakery. New lies to replace the old."

"He had the great bronze statue of Immortal Angkhdt carried down from the temple. The workmen dragged it on wagons through the streets and then smashed it into pieces with their sledgehammers. That was the start of it. By the time I left, there was not one shrine still intact in all of Charn. The sanctuary of Saint Morquar had been turned into a barracks for the Desecration League. The Rebel Angels. They were copulating on the altar. They brought wagonloads of excrement into the shrine and smeared the faces of the statues."

In spite of himself Thanakar smiled. "And whose idea was that?" he asked.

The old priest shuddered. "I don't know. Raksha Starbridge is a monster, but he is not the worst. There are others—they had been waiting for their moment, and with the bishop gone and the council dead and the army broken into pieces, well, it seems there was a whole rebel network that had flourished underground. It all happened so fast—a man named Earnest Darkheart, a black man, a foreigner. He held rallies every night in Durbar Square. He divided the city into wards, and now each street is electing officers into a new assembly. They meet daily in the old bathhouse behind Wanhope Prison. They are drafting a new constitution. But until it is finished, they have appointed an executive tribunal, a committee of four men. Raksha Starbridge, he's one. And the commander of the army, Colonel Aspe. And that black man, Earnest Darkheart."

"And the fourth?"

"That's Professor Sabian. A dwarf."

In the drying shed the shaman had taken colored ribbons and pulled them tight around the wooden posts at the corners of the building, making a multicolored barrier. Inside, men and women threshed the piles of seaweed with long flails, threshing out the eggs of various sea creatures. Though broken by the flails, these would be returned to the sea. The villagers were the strictest of the seven kinds of vegetarians.

The old priest was still talking. He chafed the edge of his pocketknife along his palm. "Listen," he said. "Listen to me. Who could have believed this a month ago? In those first days after the temple's fall Professor Sabian had all the Starbridges arrested, all the ones that he could find. He put a hundred of them to work along the levee filling sandbags. But Fairfax Starbridge wouldn't do it. He let himself be whipped to death, and after that the rest refused. They threw their shovels down into the water. It was the excuse that Raksha Starbridge needed. Since then, every day he has gained power. January First, he calls himself, and that's the day he means. October sixty-sixth, old style. Twelve days ago—the day he pushed his so-called bill of attainder through the assembly. Now the Desecration League is hunting Starbridges throughout the city. They are given public trials, but not one has been acquitted. The men are crucified in Durbar Square, the women buried alive. Raksha Starbridge is the judge."

Above their heads the sky had shown signs of clearing, but now it started to rain again, a sudden downpour, the drops exploding like firecrackers where they hit the stones. Sugar dripped down from the eaves.

Thanakar put his fingers to his head. Charn seemed far away. And his feelings, too, seemed far away from him— old bitterness, old anger, old regret. Yet he felt sick at heart: "It's strange," he said. "This man Raksha Starbridge. It's strange that a man could be so bitter against his own family. Who was his father?"

The priest shrugged. "He panders to the passions of the mob. His ferocity is all a sham, I feel sure."

Thanakar turned his head away to listen to the rain. "It's a terrible thing," he said. "Still, you are wrong. Any sane man could have seen it coming months ago. It's the price we are paying for our arrogance."

The priest stared straight ahead. "It was our right," he said. "It was the way God made us. We could not have acted otherwise."

"Come now," said Thanakar. "Surely now we can let go of this charade, after what has happened. Paradise above us and all that. You're an honest man; be honest with yourself. Tell me it was more than just a pack of lies, of magic tricks and sleight of hand, to keep ourselves in power. Tell me Chrism Demiurge was a religious man."

The old priest stared straight in front of him into the rain. When he spoke again, it was in a softer, sadder voice. "My lord," he said, "I understand what you are saying. Human beings pollute everything they touch. Religion is no different. My lord, it is not difficult to make us look like hypocrites. And I know what you are saying—in the past, so much of what we did was empty ceremony. Illusion mixed with politics—I know. But it is different now. In this past month I have been given a great gift. I have been given certain knowledge of the truth. You must know what I mean."

Thanakar smiled. "I suppose you are referring to the

martyrdom of my cousin, Abu Starbridge."

The old priest stared at him. "My lord," he stammered. "I had no idea." Again, reflexively, he made the gestures of respect, but then he broke off in the middle. "Then you must know what I mean."

"I think I do," Thanakar began, but the old man interrupted him. He leaned forward, speaking low and urgently, and his hand hovered above the doctor's knee. "The fire burned for two and a half hours. But in the evening, when they cut him down, there was not a mark on him. Listen to this—" The priest lowered his voice still further and tapped the doctor's leg. "He was seen drinking in a tavern that same evening, the evening that he died."

"Did you see him?"

"No. But hundreds did. There were a hundred witnesses."

"I don't believe it," said Thanakar. "You didn't know him as I did. He was an atheist."

"But don't you see, that is always the way. He was innocent until his death, ignorant even of his own holiness. No, do not cheat yourself. You must believe it. Listen—that's not all."

The priest clasped his hands in front of him in an attitude of prayer. He bowed his head, and his voice was barely louder than a whisper. Yet even so, Thanakar could understand him perfectly, because his articulation was so precise and clear, as if he were reciting from memory. And as he spoke, his wrinkled face took on a new softness, a new color. His yellow-rimmed old eyes shone brightly. "This I saw," he said. "This I saw with my own eyes. I was in the temple when they burned Cosima Starbridge, Cosro Starbridge's daughter, thirty-second bishop of Charn. There must have been three hundred of us around the scaffold, though most by now have followed her to Paradise. Still, there are some who can bear witness, as I do. Listen— when the fire was laid on, there was silence for the space of half a minute. Then we looked up through the smoke and saw a great tree growing up through the logs of the scaffold, breaking them apart. There where we had seen her, dressed in white, tied to the stake, the smoke just starting to coil around her, there was the trunk of an enormous tree. And as we watched, it spread its limbs over the courtyard and covered the sky with a canopy of leaves, as if it were midsummer. And all around I heard a singing noise, deafening my ears—it split my skull. I bowed my head and put my hands over my ears, but still I could hear it, and when I raised my eyes, I saw a red bird fly up from the top branches and fly up straight into the night. Most had hid their faces, deafened by that noise, but I saw it with my own eyes, my bishop's soul ascend to Paradise, and it was as if a voice had cried out in my heart. Because it was true, after all, you see. After all the lies and violence, it was still true. All night I watched that tree burning, and in the morning it was like a skeleton against the sky."

The rain had ended as suddenly as it had begun, leaving behind it the same soft drizzle out of the low sky. The sugar hung in strings from the stone eaves of the porch, unwinding in the gentle air.

Thanakar shifted his seat. "And if it were just more magic?" he asked quietly.

Furious, the old man turned on him. "It was no magic," he hissed. "I have spent my whole life behind the altar. Do you think I still can't tell the truth from a lie?" He looked away, silent for a minute, and then he let some softness come back into his voice. "You think that since so much of it was rotten, then everything was rotten. But you are cheating yourself."

Below them the beggars had come back. During the rainstorm they had kept within the shelter of the wall. But now they crept in close, three women and a man. Having finished their food and licked their fingers clean, they wanted more. They squatted in the mud below the lowest step, raising their open palms above their heads. The old priest looked at them. "Besides," he said. "It would be cowardice, now, to give it up. When I was in Charn, God kept me fed when all around me men were starving. Now they break His image into pieces in the streets, and it is a crime to speak His name. Yet even so I will continue, spreading the news that I have seen. It would be cowardly, now, to turn my back on Him."

"Tell me," said the doctor after a pause. "I heard a rumor, and I don't know whether to believe it. Prince Abu Starbridge had a sister." He stopped, unable to continue.

"She took poison," said the priest. "The night before her brother's execution. She meant to cheat the jailer, is that what you had heard? She was convicted of adultery, posthumously, the next day. It was probably the council's last official act."

"That's what I had heard," said Thanakar.

"It was a terrible thing," continued the old man. "Her husband was a hero. He was a soldier, dead upon the Serpentine Ridge. All the while, that woman had been—"

"And the lover?" interrupted Thanakar.

"He was not named in the conviction. But the rumor was, he was a member of her family. Also an army officer. He was not named—he must have escaped in the confusion. Is that what you had heard?"

"That's what I had heard."

This was the part of the conversation that Thanakar took with him when he left. He carried it down the hill under his umbrella, like a box in his hand. And the jewel in the box, the memory he uncovered when he broke apart the words in his mind, was an image of the princess, Charity Starbridge. It was a memory he had kept a long time, in divers secret places, an image of her asleep, curled up away from him, with her naked foot making a small kicking motion at the end of the bed. In his mind she turned over onto her back.

Once, that single memory had been enough to keep him happy, when he was apart from her. Then there had been a hope of future images that he could piece together with the first. But now his memory of her had acquired a different beauty; it was too beautiful to bear. It was too heavy for his strength. Limping back down the hill into the town, he hid it back inside himself. I will not take it out again, he thought.

Yet he was sick at heart. Abu had been his only friend, and he was dead. Charity had been less than that, and more. This is not the season for romantic friendships, thought Thanakar. This is not the weather for a sentimental friendship. He had barely known her.

Nevertheless, once it had been enough to make him happy, just to think that some day he might know her well.

At the bottom of the hill the road divided. He took the way back into town, along a row of houses. He had the impression that people were watching him from the upstairs windows, and he bowed his head. And at a turning in the road, he passed a covered carriage parked before the gate of some new guesthouse.

He recognized the escutcheon painted on the carriage door. Day by day the town was filling up with refugees, priests and Starbridges from Charn, running from the revolution. Late enemies of Argon Starbridge, now they were imposing on his mercy, hoping to cross the border into safety.

Thanakar lowered his umbrella to hide his face. He had no wish to meet the owner of the carriage. Some members of his family had even registered in his hotel, but he had no wish to see them. Always a misfit for the sake of his politics and his crippled leg, now he was isolated for new reasons. These refugees were seeking safety from the revolution and the new laws of attainder. Though Thanakar, if he had stayed in Charn until the end, would have been persecuted as harshly as any for his name and his tattoos, still he had

not stayed. He had fled, not from the revolution but from
Chrism Demiurge.

Thanakar thought that this difference was enough to
place him, in the minds of other Starbridges, with the forces
of rebellion. And even though he might not give a damn
what they might think, still he had no wish to draw attention
to himself. The old priest had been too senile to guess the
name of Princess Charity's lover, but Thanakar assumed
that others would have no trouble guessing. He had no wish
to hear himself blamed for her death; so, at the entrance
to his hotel near the square, he pulled his hat down over
his ears.

He need not have bothered. The instant he crossed the
threshold into the common room, he heard his name
shouted from the corner by a relative of his, a second cousin
on his mother's side, a boy named Oxus Starbridge. Thanakar had known him in the army.

"Cousin!" he shouted. "Cousin Thanakar!" He was very
young, with a thin, nervous face and bad skin. "Thanakar!"
he shouted. He came hurrying from across the room to
shake the doctor's hand. He looked pale and exhausted, as
if he hadn't slept in far too long. A sad new beard was
trying feebly to hide his features, and he picked at it nervously and smelled his fingers as he talked. He was wearing
the remnants of his army uniform; his shirt was ragged and
his pants were torn.

A row of greasy couches ran along one wall. The boy
collapsed onto one and drew the doctor down beside him.
Elsewhere around the room, people stopped what they
were doing to stare at them. They included a group of Starbridge officers playing cards at a round table, two married
women with veiled faces, and an old bearded gentleman
wiping his hands on a black-and-white-striped handkerchief.

"Thank God you've come," said the boy. "I don't know
anyone here. Yours is the first familiar face I've seen."

Thanakar put his hand out to touch the boy's shoulder.

"I'm glad to see you," he said gently. "I'm glad to see that you've escaped."

The boy made a gesture with his arm, as if dismissing recollections too painful to mention. "I swam the river," he said. "My God, I've lived for weeks on garbage and stale bread. And now, I can't believe it. I have an uncle in Caladon City, only they won't let me across. They won't let me go. I can't believe it. I told them who I was." He held out his hand so that Thanakar could see the silver bluebird tattooed on his palm. Then he stared at it himself. "They didn't seem to care."

Thanakar smiled. "Ignorant swine," he said.

"It's an outrage," continued the boy. "When I get across, I'll have them all locked up. Filthy bureaucrats! My uncle knows the king."

"The king is paying them to keep us here. They take the place of soldiers."

"I don't care. Who are they, to go against my will? My father was Baroda Starbridge. By God, I'll have them flogged."

Suppressing a gesture of impatience, Thanakar made as if to stand, but the boy was clinging to his coat sleeve. And there was something in his face that made the doctor pause, some underlying seriousness. His voice was high-pitched and precarious, as if he understood his own futility but was searching for a way of hiding it from others. Surely that was forgivable in one so young, thought Thanakar. And there was something else: The boy was close to tears. "They broke into my house," he said. "The Desecration League. I got a message from my sister to come back, and I left my regiment and rode all night. On the morning of the fifty-eighth, I reached the gates of Charn just after dawn, and it took me until one o'clock to go the last few miles, there were so many people in the streets. They had torched that whole block of houses, from Cosro's Barbican almost to the river. My own house was gutted—all the furniture was thrown out into the street. And they had written their obscenities on every wall, and everywhere the mark of the red hand—my mother lived there. And my little sister. They were gone."

With great delicacy and care, the boy pushed a strand of hair back from his face and curled it behind his ear. "I ran away," he said. "I swam the river, and I ran away."

He seemed to expect no response to this, so Thanakar said nothing. He relaxed back onto the couch, feeling the familiar mix of pity, irritation, and embarrassment that so often possessed him when he listened to tales of other people's misery. He put awkward fingers on the boy's hand and twisted his face into a rictus of compassion. The boy had been afraid. He was confessing cowardice, and for a Starbridge that had always been the most desperate of all crimes. The boy knew it and he felt it; suddenly embarrassed, he turned his face away. But he turned back after a moment, when Thanakar had risen to his feet.

"Please," he said, and when he raised his chin, Thanakar could see the movement of his epiglottis, a shudder in his narrow throat. "Please," he said. "I had no money when I came away. This thief of a hotelkeeper is charging me six dollars a night. He has given me a mattress on the floor."

Relieved, Thanakar fished some money from his coat, two fifty-dollar bills. The boy reached out to grab them. He took them and crushed them between his fingers. He crushed them into little balls, and as he did so, his face took on a sudden expression of hostility.

"Let me give you a receipt," he said. "You understand—this is a temporary loan. I'll pay you ten percent a month."

Outside there was a crash of thunder, and the rain came down redoubled on the greasy windows. The common room was darkened; light came from a small fire on the stove, where three Caladonian merchants sat smoking hashish from long pipes. Light came from the table, where the officers played cards around an oil lamp; they had stopped in the middle of a hand and were staring at the doctor as he looked around. They were playing for money. Loose coins lay scattered across the table.

What is it? thought Thanakar. What is it about me? He turned and walked away, spurning the receipt that the boy thrust at him. His boots struck an uneven rhythm on the floor as he crossed the room and pushed through the low door into the courtyard. Outside the raindrops danced and spattered on the flagstones, while the horses in their stalls licked up the sugar and scraped the scum from each other's backs with the sharp edges of their beaks, standing head to tail in the rain.

The ostlers were bringing straw. One saw him and made the gestures of respect, but Thanakar turned aside and limped up the small covered stairwell that led to his quarters on the second floor. At the top he rested, ducking his head, for the ceiling in the corridor was very low. He leaned his head against the doorframe. From along the corridor there came a sound that tore his heart, the sound of a girl crying.

When Charity Starbridge was a little girl, she had played on the soccer team at Starbridge Dayschools. She had been a good runner, graceful and strong, stronger than most girls, and sometimes after school she would practice by herself in the playground. She would run as fast as she could, back and forth across the deserted field, the silver ball floating in front of her—she never seemed to kick it. She would be dressed in silver spandex, her black hair wild around her face, and sometimes Thanakar and Abu, her brother, would stand out on the balcony of the Upper School, watching her practice on the playground below them. Thanakar's leg had never let him run like that.

In his hotel on the frontier Thanakar thought, She's dead. Why think of her? One night he got up from his bed, and limped over to the window of his hotel room, and watched the streetlights shining in the rain. They shone on the statue of Argon Starbridge in the middle of the square, shone on the facade of the stone customs house. He watched the wire fence gleaming in the rain. By day Thanakar's mind was a strong citadel, but at night his thoughts rioted and raised rebellions. God curse all Starbridges; the priests of Charn had murdered everything he loved, and yet, and yet. Those palaces had been his home. It was not welcome news to hear of their destruction.

At night he found it hard to sleep. And in the morning— every morning for three weeks in the last part of October— Thanakar went to the customs house. Every morning the unravelers granted him an interview. Even in those tempestuous days, when their antechambers were packed with supplicants, they never seemed to have anything to do. They sat in their cubicles surrounded by stacks of unread documents, their eyes fixed upon nothing, as if contemplating some ideal vision of bureaucracy, infinitely removed from mundane paperwork. Their desktops were crowded with the tools of their profession—silent telephones, broken calculators, pens with no ink. Always they exuded an impression of lassitude and deepest melancholy, their soft, slow speech punctuated by silences and dismal sighs.

This melancholy was deceptive, thought Thanakar, because at some moments, deep beneath the surface, they seemed full of glee. They took care to end each interview with some words of optimism, some hint that no matter how insuperable the barriers might appear, some forward progress might be possible, given time. This was the essential part of their power, thought Thanakar later. He would meet supplicants who, even after forty interviews, were still hopeful. Thanakar himself, against his own better judgment, found himself seduced by an illusion of progress: After the first few visits, no further mention was made of Mrs. Cassimer's and Jenny's missing passports. It was as if that hurdle had been crossed. Instead, he pursued the unravelers in new and hopeful directions. They listed the addresses of people he might stay with in Caladon City. They speculated on his chances of finding a job. But always there was some new obstacle. Once Thanakar arrived to find that his file had been mislaid. Thanakar asked himself what his file could possibly consist of, since no one, at least in his presence, had ever done so much as write down his name. Nevertheless, that day they had had to start everything again.

Or once, after a long interview, the unraveler had implied that he was finally satisfied, and that all the doctor would have to do was show up the next morning to pick up his visa. Some inner wariness prevented Thanakar from celebrating; he had seen other supplicants come back from the customs house triumphant and boastful, and take exaggerated leave of everybody in the hotel, only to reappear at breakfast a few days later. Sure enough, Thanakar arrived at the customs house the next morning to find that the unraveler in charge of his case had been transferred.

Yet even so, despite these setbacks, there were intimations of progress. On each unraveler's desk stood a number of rubber stamps, including one large, important-looking one with a metal faceplate bearing the Caladonian coat of arms. Though never actually stated, it was implied that this stamp was the coveted visa—multiple entries, six months. On Thanakar's first visit the unraveler had touched it with her forefinger. On his seventh, the unraveler had actually picked it up and weighed it in his hand before replacing it with a sigh in its little metal stand. And on his seventeenth, the man had reached for it forcefully, only to hesitate at the last minute, think better of it, lean back in his chair.

During Thanakar's twenty-seventh interview, the man mentioned for the first time another set of documents. This man was unusually tall, even for an unraveler, and he was dressed in a dilapidated uniform of yellow gauze. His veil was wrapped closely around his face, so closely that the cloth over his mouth was alternately convex and concave as he blew in and out.

Thanaker had seen him several times before. Most he couldn't tell apart, but this one had a distinguishing eccentricity of speech: a kind of stammer, and a habit of qualifying everything he said, so that often the sense of it was lost, mislaid in a fog of vagueness. "I-I don't know if you know," he said. "At least, at least I hope you do. But there have been questions asked. There have been . . . inquiries."

"Yes?" prompted Thanakar.

"Well, it has been noticed that you have not yet submitted certain documents, which may or may not be needed, at-at least not at this time."

"What documents?"

"They-they still may not be necessary," demurred the unraveler. "Not yet. Nevertheless, I have heard rumors . . ."

"What documents?" asked Thanakar between his teeth.

"C-certificates of health. Witnessed by a licensed physician."

"I am a physician," answered Thanakar. "Give me these certificates, and I will fill them out."

"D-don't misunderstand me. I am not sure these documents exist, in triplicate, or otherwise. The question is, are you licensed to practice? In Caladon?"

"Licensed? My father was a prince of Charn. God help me, what do you want from me?"

"I understand," said the unraveler. "Don't misunderstand me. You are an eminent man. Eminent. At least, I myself have never heard of you. And I am not talking about you anyway. But your companions, that is something else."

At last Thanakar understood where the conversation was heading. He sat back and put his fingers to his forehead.

"Now," continued the unraveler. "I will take your word for it. We trust you, you see. We can see you are in perfect health," he said, glancing down towards Thanakar's crippled knee.

He had laid Thanakar's passport and letter of safe conduct out before him on his desk, together with three blank pieces of paper that Thanakar had come to recognize as visa forms. These he aligned with great solemnity. And then he picked the stamp up from its cradle and frowned at it. With his other hand he flicked open the top of his stamp pad. "Now," he said. "Mrs.-Mrs. Cassimer. Your ... housekeeper."

"She is in good health."

"Fine. Excellent. And your daughter?"

For more than a minute Thanakar looked at him and then turned away. The unraveler closed his stamp pad with a sigh. "At least now you appreciate the difficulties," he said softly. "Although we try to be of service."

"She has a mental condition," said Thanakar at last.

"Yes. We had heard rumors, you see. But never mind, mental illness is not unknown in Caladon, as you'll soon see. And in your case, it may not be significant. Perhaps we can waive these restrictions in your case, if ... if in fact they do exist. Perhaps we can make an exception in the case of such an eminent physician, whose father was a prince of Charn. I will talk to my superior. If you could come back tomorrow..."

This conversation was the lowest point in Thanaker's negotiations with the unravelers, and after it was over, he stood in the rain underneath the statue of Argon Starbridge with his heart full of hatred and misgivings. It was evening and the barbed-wire barricade gave off a sullen glow. At the Caladon Gate a single soldier warmed his hands over a fire in an old oil drum, while a woman sat at his feet against a pile of bricks, smoking a cigarette. Along one wall of the customs house someone had put up a canvas shelter, and a few men sat at tables underneath it, playing dice by the light of paper lanterns, while nearby two children argued over a wicker ball.

The pedestal of the statue was painted gray and daubed with adventist grafitti, proclaiming the second coming of Immortal Angkhdt. Underneath, some dissident had painted the red hand, symbol of the Desecration League, and though subsequent zealots had smeared the place with mud, it was still visible. It was a small hand, a child's hand, beautifully rendered, the five fingers long and delicate, the thumb stiff and decisive.

The beauty of the drawing made it ambiguous as a symbol of revolt, thought Thanakar. He remembered talking to the unraveler. "She has a mental condition," he had said. It was the first time he had said so; standing in the rain, he wondered whether he believed it. Surely the vagaries of Jenny's life, the strangeness of the last few weeks, the violence and perversion she had seen in Charn did much to explain the peculiarity of her behavior. Her parents had been dead less than a month. These days she hardly spoke, but what was that? She had always been a quiet child. In Charn, when she was his patient, Thanakar had first been drawn to her because he sensed she was a misfit like himself, branded like him with the sign of God's contempt, the birthmark on her cheek, his crippled leg. And now they had another bond: They were alone and far from home. Abu and Charity, her mother and her father—the priests of Charn had murdered everyone that they had ever cared about. Now it touched him more than he could ever say, that she seemed to have accepted him in an alliance against all the world. That morning she had sat upon his lap, crying uncontrollably, her fingers locked around his neck.

He reached out to touch the painted picture of the child's hand. But there was more to it, he thought. It was not just sadness; there are a hundred reasons to be sad. But at times it was as if some outside force had become part of her, and the strangest evidence of that was the way that she had learned to draw. Since they had been in the hotel, she had sat at her table all day, every day, and up into the night. She had covered hundreds of pages with her drawings, so that every morning Mrs. Cassimer had gone out shopping for more paper and new pencils.

She had begun naturally enough, sketching geometric symbols on the backs of envelopes and menus. Soon she was turning out the wastebaskets for paper to draw on, and she had broken Thanakar's silver fountain pen by throwing it against the wall. That had been the second morning in the hotel; she had cried and cried until he had come back with a ream of typewriter paper and some colored pencils. By midnight she had covered five hundred sheets with circles and crosses, scribbling all day with a dark scowl on her face.

In the days since then she had made tremendous progress. Now she would spend hours on a single drawing before crumpling it up and throwing it across the room. When finally she lay asleep, curled up tight in a corner of her bed, Thanakar would gather them up. He would uncrumple them and spread them out, staring at them in amazement as every day they grew more competent and more complex.

And it was not just their sophistication that made him get up from his chair and go into her room, and sit down to watch her as she slept. It was their subject matter—tapirs and watercats and centipedes and naked apes, creatures she never, ever could have seen, even in photographs. She drew mountain villages in the snow, and fields of summer flowers, and portraits of old men in uniform. "Where have you seen such things?" he asked, but by that time she wasn't speaking. Only once she climbed up into his lap and put her arms around his neck and put her lips next to his ear. Yet even then he could barely hear her when she whispered, "In my mind."

A beggar came out from an alleyway and ambled towards him across the square. Thanakar pulled his hat over his eyes and turned to go.

He walked back over the uneven stones, and back to his hotel. Mrs. Cassimer was waiting for him at the threshold of his suite. She had her finger to her lips. "Hush," she said. "The girl's asleep." But when she saw the doctor's clothes, sodden in the lamplight, gleaming faintly from the phosphorescent rain, she found it impossible to keep quiet. "Look at you," she said. "Oh, sir, how can you? Where is your umbrella? You must have stood out in the rain for hours to get so wet. Give me your coat—I swear to God, it's as if you were a little boy again. No respect for anybody else's feelings."

A constant diet of unpleasant surprises had turned Mrs. Cassimer into a shrew. It was a way she had when she was worried: "Look at you! I swear to God, your own mother used to say you had the weakest mind in your entire postal code. 'Mentally weak,' she used to say. Mind you, she was one to talk. But it takes one to know one, as the rapist told the judge."

Smiling sheepishly, Thanakar gave her his overcoat. "Please, Mrs. Cassimer," he said, "could you make me some tea?"

"Tea! You think I've got nothing better to do than make you tea? You come in here, soaked to the bone, and the first thing you can think to do is give me orders."

The doctor put his fingers to his eyes. "Please, Mrs. Cassimer," he said. "Just do it, please. I've had a difficult day."

"Oh, and I suppose you think it's been a party here," cried Mrs. Cassimer, furious now. And she would have said a good deal more, only at that moment Jenny woke up, and Thanakar could hear her thin, even whining from across the hall. He motioned for Mrs. Cassimer to be silent and then walked across to Jenny's bedroom.

When she saw him, she stopped crying and sat up in bed. Her face was smudged with ink where she had rubbed it with her inky fingers. And the inside of her mouth, too, was dark with ink, for she had been sucking on her thumb.

Thanakar stood in the doorway with his finger on the light switch. She sat up in bed staring at him, the patterns of ink on her face mixing with her freckles and the birthmark underneath her ear. Around her the bed and floor were littered with discarded drawings. From where he stood, Thanakar could see the same pattern endlessly repeated, a round black smudge in the center of each paper, with six jointed legs.

Thanakar kicked through them as he limped across the floor. He brushed them aside as he sat down. He put his hand, palm up, open on the coverlet, and waited. And in a little while she uncurled from the corner of the bed, where she had sat hugging her knees, and came close to him. She was as timid as an animal. But finally she came and sat by him and put her arms around his neck.

"Why is she—why is she yelling?" she asked at last, whispering, with her lips pressed up against his ear. From where they sat, they could hear Mrs. Cassimer grumbling to herself and moving things around back in another room.

Thanakar smoothed the little girl's hair back from her forehead. "It doesn't matter," he said. "It's because she is afraid."

There was a piece of paper laid out on her pillow. It seemed to be the finished drawing for which all the rest were merely sketches: a large, careful drawing of an insect, minutely detailed, its hairy legs carefully articulated. It was blind. It had sharp claws, and a sharp, heavy, long proboscis, for taking blood.

"What is that?" asked Thanakar gently, stroking back the little girl's brown hair, his hand moving over the crest of her skull.

"A flea," said the voice inside his ear.

"And where have you seen such a thing?"

"I never saw it," said the little girl. "I felt it—there. There where your hand is now." His hand was resting on the back of her head, where her skull swelled out behind her ear.

Once when Charity Starbridge was a little girl, she had set fire to her brother's house of dolls. Returning unexpectedly from school, Thanakar and Abu had caught her with the match still in her hand. Thanakar would always remember the look of passion and betrayal in her eyes, when Abu summoned servants to take her to her room while he assessed the damage. He remembered her squirming in her housekeeper's grip, her eyes on fire, while his friend turned to him and smiled apologetically.

Thanakar remembered. Later, at her wedding, it had infuriated him to see a drugged, complacent look in eyes that once had burned so bright. Later, much later, that squirming girl had almost disappeared. Standing in his hotel room on the square, watching the border lights make patterns on the walls, Thanakar remembered her lying asleep, curled up away from him, her foot making a small kicking motion at the end of the bed.

At night he found it difficult to sleep. Instead he would stand alone at the window of his room, staring at the customs house across the square.

On the morning of October 99th, the unravelers kept him waiting for the first time. He sat on a bench in the large, empty, circular chamber that made up the heart of the customs house. The ceiling had been painted to look like the inside of a dome, and Thanakar sat staring up at it, cursing inwardly. Yet he was encouraged, too, because that day there was something different in the atmosphere of the place. It seemed colder, and the air had a crispness it had lacked before. Soldiers had come down out of the hills during the night; he had passed their horses stabled in the square, and in the customs building he could feel their presence. He could hear the sharp crack of their boot heels in the corridors, and occasionally the sound of hurried voices. In the porch he had passed soldiers making a game of who could spit the longest, until the stones were spattered with the black juice of their snuff.

The ceiling of the waiting room was painted to look like a circle of faces peering down over the rim of the supposed dome. Thanakar glared up at them for as long as he could stand it, and then he got to his feet and limped towards the door, vowing inwardly that he would not be made a fool of any longer. But at that moment, as if to demonstrate that this was not yet quite the case, a clerk appeared under one of the archways and beckoned to him and led him down a flight of stairs into a basement lined with concrete blocks. It was a part of the building he had never seen, and this encouraged him, until he passed a row of open doors and saw the unravelers sitting at their desks, staring off into space.

The clerk left him in an office that seemed larger than the rest. And the man at the desk gave the impression of seniority, or at least of bulk. He took up more space than others of his kind, and his voice was soft and clear, unmuffled by his veil. "Please come in," he said. "Please sit down."

Thanakar stood. The man had dyed his hair, pink on one side, orange on the other. It looked grotesque over his pale forehead.

Thanakar's patience had already been eroded down to nothing by the hours of waiting. But the dyed hair was too much; something bent in Thanakar, and then it broke. "Listen," he said. "I won't wait anymore. It doesn't matter—I don't care if I die here in this town, but just let me explain to you before I do, how sick of you I am. All of you. You make me sick. And I wonder, how can a man like you keep from despair? Or are you a man at all?"

The unraveler sat back in his chair. His veil covered his nose and mouth but left his eyes uncovered. They were red, as if from weeping.

He stared at Thanakar for a moment, and then he looked away, past him, towards a calendar on the wall. He sighed, and then he turned his plump, red hand over on a pile of papers on the desktop so that Thanakar could see a cage tattooed on his right palm and a small black beast inside of it.

The unraveler's voice was soft and clear. "And do you never . . . nauseate yourself?" he asked. And then he dropped his eyes and closed his hand. "We do our best with the fate God gave us," he said. "Who can do more?"

A philosopher, thought Thanakar bitterly. He cursed him, mentally willing him to stop, but he went on: "Besides," he said, "you are unjust. My brothers and I have worked long hours on your behalf. We have overlooked many restrictions. Today it was to have been my pleasure to inform you that our efforts had been successful, and that your application had been approved. Now, of course, the pleasure is all gone."

Thanakar held his breath. Wearily the unraveler uncovered the file on his desk and removed three visa forms. He laid them out in front of him, and then he opened his stamp pad. He picked the rubber visa stamp from its cradle and reset the date and then rolled it in the ink. As Thanakar watched, he lowered it to within an inch above the paper, and then he stopped. "May I see your passport?" he asked.

With quivering fingers, Thanakar drew out his passport and laid it on the desk. The unraveler squinted at it for a moment, and then he frowned. "Not that one," he said.

"What do you mean? It is my passport."

The unraveler frowned, and then he smiled. "Don't you have a new one? That one is no longer valid. There has been a change of government in Charn."

Thanakar stared at him. Then, with a cry of rage, he leaped across the room and around the desk. The unraveler tried to twist out of his chair. But Thanakar was too quick. He forced the man back down into his seat and stood behind him with his arms locked tight around his neck, twisting his head until he felt the bones stretch to their uttermost. His cheek was close to the man's cheek, so that he could smell his rank perfume and see a drop of sweat run down his neck under his veil.

Thanakar could feel the fat of the man's neck between his hands. The unraveler was fat and powerful, yet he never moved. In Thanakar's arms his body felt completely passive, completely vulnerable and receptive. There was something sickening in the way his fat flesh yielded to the doctor's touch; caught up in the sensuality of violence, Thanakar twisted the man's neck still more, until he heard his soft, sweet voice. "Don't," said the unraveler. "Please don't . . . hurt me." He could easily have been saying the reverse.

Thanakar raised his head. The papers on the desk were spattered with ink where the unraveler had dropped his rubber stamp. The stamp had fallen on one of the blank forms and then rolled over, leaving a printed image. Thanakar recognized it. It was no visa stamp. It was an image popular in all those northern lands. It was the beast with seven heads, symbolic of the seven kinds of loneliness, and underneath, the endless knot of the unravelers.

For a minute and a half Thanakar did nothing, only tightened his grip, and though his brain was moving, he was not thinking. He was staring at the endless knot, following each complicated strand until it found itself again. He bent the man's neck back until he heard a groaning noise deep in the bone. "Tell me," he said. "Who guards the border here?"

The unraveler still had not made the least resistance. His arms still rested on his chair, and Thanakar could see that his muscles were completely loose. "We have not the power . . . some people . . . ascribe to us," he admitted, finally.

"You have no power to grant visas, am I right?" asked Thanakar.

"We have the power to deny," admitted the unraveler.

"Then tell me, who guards the border here?"

The unraveler said nothing. Thanakar could see the sweat run down under his veil, streaking the powder on his neck.

Later, as he waited in the darkness of the square, Thanakar wondered why the man had made no effort to stop him when he left. He had not moved when Thanakar released him. Only he had touched his neck and whispered, "Please. Do not tell the others. Please."

There was a bell on the desk in front of him. He had not

rung it, though Thanakar had walked all the way up through
the building thinking he would hear it ring. But the soldiers
in the porch were friendly as he came into the open air; they
were laughing and chewing kaya gum, happy because there
was a break in the weather. The flags outside the customs
house were flapping in the new salt air: the red swine of
Caladon, the silver dog's head, and the endless knot. The
mist had broken, and there were traces of a sunset. Thanakar felt his heart lifting as he limped down the steps. Later
that night, standing in the darkness with his knapsack on his
back, with Jenny's fingers clamped so tightly around his
thumb that she was hurting him, with Mrs. Cassimer beside
him bitching underneath her breath, still he felt easy in his
heart.

In front of him across the square, the gate shone in the
night, a tangle of glowing wire stretched taut against the
darkness, green and violet, and deep black-red. Near it, five
soldiers stood talking. Thanakar could see the glow of their
cigarettes and hear the mutter of their voices. From time to
time one word would stand out clear against the rest, the
resolution of a story or a joke.

One of the soldiers was telling a story. Thanakar could
see the gesticulations of his hands and hear the sounds of
laughter. Another soldier squatted down. He took his cap
off and rubbed his head, and threw back his head so that he
could laugh more easily. That was when Thanakar knew
that it was going to be all right. Mrs. Cassimer had settled
down to silence, and Jenny was quiet too, holding his hand
as they walked forward towards the gate.

The soldiers paid no notice. One stood away from the
rest, lighting a cigarette. In the quiet air there were still
some remnants of rain, and as the soldier brought the match
up to his mouth and shook it out, the flame caught at some
lingering phosphorescence near his hand.

Thanakar could smell the acrid marijuana smoke as he

came opposite the barricade. He nodded to the soldier, and the soldier nodded back, a barely perceptible movement of his head. "Good evening," he said, in a harsh, flat, northern voice. And as the travelers crossed over, it seemed to Thanakar that even those small words could hold some promise in them, like a seed.

# CHARN | 4

**W**hen Charity Starbridge was a little girl, she had had a nurse named Mrs. Greer, a hard, melancholy woman with a fondness for punishment. Justly despised by little Charity, the nurse had terrified her brother, who never once could summon up the courage to defy her. That had been before he was given the tattoo of the golden sun, but even so he was a prince of Charn and head of the family after their father died. Mrs. Greer had no authority to punish him, and yet he let himself be punished with a fatalism that had infuriated his little sister. Even worse, he had allowed her to be punished, had allowed her to be locked into her bedroom, when all he would have had to do was walk in and release her. Who could have refused him? It was pure spinelessness, and it hurt Charity more than the punishment itself. Those nights she would lie on her bed, and she would beat with a spoon upon the solid silver water pipes that joined her room with her brother's on the floor below: "Fuck you, fuck you, fuck you," in the Starbridge code.

But one night, towards midnight, after an impassioned round of signaling, she heard a message coming back to her, very slow at first, hard to distinguish, because her brother wasn't as proficient in the code as she was. He was slow with languages; that night she had cursed his stupidity and listened with her ear against the pipe. But in a little while the beat grew stronger, and she had had to run to get a pencil and write down the message on the wall, so that she could remember:

> *How can it fill me, unless I*
> *offer it*
> *an empty cup? Ah sister,*
> *it is in surrender that we taste*
> *our*
> *lives.*

These words stayed with her all the time that she was growing up. When the mark of the pencil finally faded from the plaster, she retraced the lines in ink. Later, after she had married the old man and moved upstairs, she had painted them in her new bedroom, on the wall above the statue of Immortal Angkhdt. There she had used an alphabet of her own invention. She had drawn a gathering of horses on the wall, and each one was a different letter, distinguished by a variant position of its legs, the curl of its neck or horns or tail, or a new color.

She would lie in bed and smoke hashish and watch the letters stampede towards her on the wall. It was an alphabet known only to herself, and that was appropriate, because by that time the words had taken on a private meaning that she could not have explained to anyone.

"This is my empty cup." For her the words had no real meaning. It was like a prayer that monks repeat in temples. But on the day of her brother's execution, perhaps then she understood for the first time. She heard the words as if for the first time when she was kneeling in the Street of Seven

Sins, watching the pickup truck recede into the distance. She dragged herself into the gutter, where she lay in the shelter of a cardboard box.

That was the way Mrs. Soapwood found her, later, after the sun was down. "Pretty," said Mr. Taprobane. "Pretty skin." Crablike, he was moving up the center of the street, scavenging for food among the garbage left by the departing crowd while his mistress waited in the shadow of the wall. He was a twisted little man, the line of his shoulders set at right angles to his pelvis, and he moved sideways with his shoulder to the ground, now on four limbs, now on two. He had a green hat on his head, and he sang to himself under his breath as he combed through the mud. "Pretty skin," he crooned.

Charity had dragged herself to the side of the road, where she lay propped up on the curb. Mr. Taprobane squatted above her, and he lifted her head up by her hair and pulled it back so that he could see her cheek. "Pretty," he said, and then he staggered back, for she had put her hand into the middle of his face and pushed him away. He grunted and fell down in the mud, while Mrs. Soapwood laughed.

Laughing, she stepped out of the shadow of a doorway. Uncovering a lantern, she raised it high above her head. Blinded in all directions except one, the light cut sharply across the road. It cut Charity in two, shining in her eyes.

"Taprobane!" laughed Mrs. Soapwood. "Come here— that's enough. Find me something I can use."

"You said garbage," answered Mr. Taprobane, rubbing his nose; he sat lopsided in the mud. "She's garbage right enough. Look at her clothes."

"But she's alive!"

"Not for long," contested Mr. Taprobane. He rose up on his hands and feet and scuttled sideways to the curb, where his mistress was standing with her lantern.

Charity had been asleep when Mr. Taprobane first touched her. In her weakened state, she was not careful.

"Cripple," she said softly, using a language of abuse reserved strictly for the highest classes. "Mental, moral, psychic cripple. Your ugliness is symptomatic. Your damnation is assured."

Like most Starbridge curses, this one was a quote from holy scripture. It was a story known to everyone, Great Angkhdt's chastisement of the leper, and Charity recited it in an exhausted voice. Nevertheless, it had an impact. Mr. Taprobane jumped back still further and made a sign against the evil eye. Mrs. Soapwood kept on laughing. "God rescue me!" she cried. "Where did you learn that?"

She was a bulky woman, muffled in a woolen cloak, already six months pregnant by that time. She owned a brothel in the river ward, but even so she was kindhearted. It would have been hard for her in any case to walk away and leave someone to die of hunger in the street, harder to leave a woman, a young and pretty woman, a woman who had made her laugh. Besides, she was already considering the possibilities of a woman who could mimic Starbridge manners. Such a woman might be quite popular with certain types of men, if she were dressed in the right clothes.

She put her lantern down. Squatting with difficulty, she rummaged underneath her stomach and pulled out some bread wrapped in a sequined cloth and a tin bottle full of wine. She put them down on the concrete curbstone, then searched in her pocket for a cigarette. Deep in the crevice of the lining, she found a small and dirty one, bent into the shape of a beckoning finger. She drew it out. "Let's take a look at you," she said.

Mrs. Soapwood's hotel was on the Python Road, about a mile away. It was a tall, narrow building made of wood. The recent fires had burned whole blocks along that road, though because of freakish winds the south side of the street had not been touched. But on the north side, not one house in fifty was still standing; Mrs. Soapwood's hotel rose out of a block of smoking ruins. Formerly one of a row, it had survived because the firemen, frequent guests, had blown the houses up on either side. A week after the fire, the hotel was still surrounded by a perpetual mist, which leaked out of the piles of blackened rubbish and the drifting rain. The smoke rose in a curl around the house, and the sign out front creaked in the wind. Though burned and seared, the painting on it was still visible—a black bird with a flower in its mouth.

Charity Starbridge lived at this hotel for most of a month after the bishop's council was dissolved, after the change of government. This was during the worst part of the terror, when January First was speaker of the National Assembly, and the Rebel Angels and the Desecration League held rallies in the streets. They broke into the houses and filled the jails with Starbridges, with sympathizers and collaborators. During the month of November, in the eighth phase of spring, as many as a hundred prisoners were burned alive each day in Durbar Square, or buried alive in dungeons underneath the city.

Captains of the League came regularly to the house of the black bird, but Charity escaped their notice, for a time. She worked in the stables behind the house and in the kitchen, and she washed the sheets and swept the stairs. She slept on a mattress in the laundry room and went to bed early every night before the gentlemen came. She never left the house, except in the mornings when it was still dark, and she would wash herself next to the outhouse in the greasy morning rain. Then she would go back and work all day, changing the beds, scrubbing the landings, scouring the pots, working hard for two reasons at least. She wanted to make herself indispensable to Mrs. Soapwood. She tried to satisfy the woman, so that she would never think to put her to another, more distasteful labor. But more than that, she found a comfort in the work. She remembered a loose line of holy scripture—"God created work to be the consolation of the poor." And it was true, at least for her, for working was a new activity, and it soothed her mind and wore her out, so that she could fall exhausted into sleep each night.

She polished the metal plates and saucers until the scratches on them started to resolve. She was fascinated by her own productivity. Also, she felt happy to be useful to the other women in the house, because that month she had some friends for the first time since her marriage. There was Arabel, who had a constant cold, and Licorice, tall and dark, and then Charity's favorite, Marcelline, who was practically her own age. She especially would seek Charity out, in the morning when the gentlemen had left, and she would lie on Charity's bed to watch her do the ironing.

Charity wore rubber gloves most of the day, and only took them off in privacy, where she could retouch the greasepaint on her palms and cover them with powder. Among prostitutes it was bad manners to talk about the past; most of the women in the house wore gloves, though of a more expensive kind. But Marcelline was too young to have completely lost her sense of wonder. "Are you a cannibal?" she asked one day, when she had surprised Charity without her gloves. Then she blushed, because it sounded so stupid. But in Charn, in those days, only antinomials had no tattoos.

"No," said Charity, frowning. She put her gloves back on. She was ironing a pleated shirt and was not sure how to do it. "I am from another country," she said.

"Where?"

"South of here."

"Where?" asked Marcelline, and after that she would come every day to hear Charity's stories. And Charity would tell her stories about the country she was from, south, where the land was rich and it was summer all year round. She told Marcelline about the farm her father owned, and the catbirds, and the elephants, and the wild dogs. She told Marcelline about her seven brothers and her sisters and her mother, who was very fat.

"And did you have a lover there?" asked Marcelline.

"Yes," said Charity. That day she was ironing the sheets and, she paused for a moment in her work and put the iron up into its stand.

"What was he like?"

Charity ran her glove back through her hair. "He was dark, like me," she said. "He had a high, pale forehead and long hair," she said. "He had a beard."

"Was he handsome?"

"No." She frowned. "I don't think so. Or at least—to me he was. He had beautiful hands."

Often Mr. Taprobane would come down into the laundry, too, to listen to these stories. After a period of sullenness he had become fond of Princess Charity, and often came to help her with her work. Sometimes he brought newspapers for Charity to read aloud: Professor Sabian's *Free Word,* as well as broadsheets from the Rim. These were full of accusations, rumors of hoarding and profiteering, and every morning they would publish a list of the condemned. Marcelline would lie on the mattress underneath the stairs, dressed in her expensive underwear, while the little man would sit in an untidy heap, twisted around his knees. Fascinated, they would listen as Charity read out the obituaries of princes, soldiers, lawyers, priests. It was practice for her, to see if she could read the names without inflection. But sometimes a description would conjure up a face into her mind, a cousin or a family friend, and then her tongue would stumble. And once she stopped and put the paper down when, in a list of miscellaneous names, she came across this one: "Starbridge, T."

"What's the matter?" asked Marcelline. "Sweetheart, what is it?" and she got up and put her arms around her, and held Charity's face against her breast.

"I don't know," whispered Charity. "I just wish I knew sometimes. I just wish I knew for sure."

Then she looked down, because Mr. Taprobane had gotten up too. He was holding up a flask of whiskey with a solemn expression on his face.

Charity smiled and reached down for it, and that was a mistake. In a little while she felt better. In a little while she was sitting cross-legged, drinking whiskey on the bed with her arm around the cripple's shoulder. And then she let herself be coaxed upstairs, for drinking made her easy to persuade. "No wonder you're unhappy," said Marcelline. "This room would get the best of anyone."

The laundry had no windows, and it stank of bleach. "No wonder you're depressed," said Marcelline. "Look at you, why do you wear such clothes? You're such a beauty; why do you hide it?"

Though it was dangerously near evening, Charity allowed herself to be coaxed upstairs, and soon she was sitting in Marcelline's bathroom, while the younger woman cut her hair. "I hate to do it," Marcelline confided. "It's beautiful stuff, but not very stylish, unless you keep it clean. Real Starbridge black, we used to call it; not very popular nowadays."

I deserve a bit of cosseting, thought Charity, and after her haircut she found herself taking a bath in Marcelline's huge bathtub. Mr. Taprobane had gone back to work, but Charity had barely noticed his departure, her head was so full of liquor. The windows were clouded up with steam, and Charity lay back and let herself be stroked, and rubbed with perfumed oils.

Marcelline was a big girl with a fine, full figure. Her skin was flushed from her exertion, and in the damp air of the bathroom, her hair hung wet around her face. Her legs were naked, and Charity could see her skin through her wet camisole, her nipples and her hair. "The gentlemen would love you, that's for sure," she said as she scrubbed Charity's arms. "I mean it. I don't understand why—oh my God."

The girl had scraped her thumbnail along Charity's palm,

and the greasepaint, weakened by the water and the soap, had given way. Charity opened her eyes and jerked herself upright, splashing water on the floor. She tried to pull her hand away, but the girl wouldn't let go. She was stronger than Charity, and she held Charity's fingers open while she studied the scrape in the greasepaint that her thumbnail had made. She was staring at the tattoo of the silver rose. Then she let go suddenly and sat back on her heels beside the bathtub, bowing her head and making the gestures of respect.

Charity jumped to her feet. Terrified, she ran into Marcelline's bedroom, covering her nakedness with a bathrobe of red silk. Then she hurried out into the hall and down the staircase, not thinking and not listening. Otherwise, she would have heard the stamp of heavy boots coming towards her up the stairs. But as it was, she ran down the steps until it was too late, and she saw on the landing below her the figure of a man.

In the middle of the stair she tried to stop herself, clutching at the bannister, slipping down onto the steps. Panicked, she turned her head away, not bearing to look as the boots stamped towards her and then stopped. She closed her eyes and did not open them again until she felt a man's fingers on her chin, gentle and strong, pulling her face around. Then she opened her eyes and found herself staring into the face of a young soldier standing on the step below.

He was dressed in the uniform of the Desecration League, and his fingers were dyed red. The throat of his tunic was closed by a pin in the shape of a child's hand. He was a handsome man, with a hard, clean-shaven face, and he was smiling. "What have we here?" he asked.

Charity's forehead was still hot, and her hair and skin were still dripping wet. She had tensed every muscle of her body; one hand held her robe closed, and the other was locked into a tight fist. This was the palm where Marcelline had scratched away the paint, and in her mind Charity uttered a prayer she did not think she knew, when the soldier reached down for her hand and started to caress her fingers, as if to loosen them.

"Please, sir," she said. "Please, sir, may I go?"

The soldier smiled at her a moment, and then he bowed and stepped aside.

A week after this incident on the stairs, Mrs. Soapwood called Charity to her bedroom. By that time she was so pregnant that it was hard for her to move; her arms and legs were bloated, her skin shiny and green. Charity had heard rumors that she could no longer stomach solid food. Charity had heard that she had sent Mr. Taprobane out all over the city, searching for olive oil and mince pie, but then had vomited them up onto her bed.

Charity found these stories easy to believe. Already past the time of any natural confinement, Mrs. Soapwood lay gasping on the bed. The room stank of disinfectant and perfume, but there was another smell underneath those, the smell of something poisonous and sick.

Yet Mrs. Soapwood's mind seemed clear enough. "A gentleman has come to see me about you," she said. "He's been here twice."

Charity looked around the room. New municipal regulations had forbidden the private practice of religion, yet even so there was a shrine next to the bed. The icons had been removed, but the candles were still burning, and there was a brass bowl full of water, surrounded by framed photographs.

The blinds were drawn, and it was dark. Mrs. Soapwood lay on her side, breathing heavily, while the rain rattled on the windows. "You're a pretty girl," she said. "What do you think?"

"I'd rather not."

"Very well. But think about it. There are worse than he. And it would be easier than the work you're doing now."

"I've thought about it."

"Very well. But remember, it wouldn't have to be what you have seen. I was thinking of something . . . elegant. Expensive, like a palace. You know the Starbridge language. I'd have them treat you like a princess."

"No," said Charity.

"You could wear a veil. You could make the illusion as perfect as you want. Only you would have to use the Starbridge language. That's why they would come."

For a moment Charity was afraid that Marcelline had betrayed her. Then she remembered how she had cursed at Mr. Taprobane and pushed him down into the mud. "I don't know much," she said. "Mostly abuse. Words I picked up from my mistress."

"But that's all you would need. Mostly abuse. That's why they would come."

"Thank you, ma'am," said Charity. "I'd rather not."

Mrs. Soapwood turned over onto her back. "Very well," she said. "Just think about it. I make no demands. Only I would like you to wear some better clothes. Dress as if you worked here. There—I have put some clothes out by the closet. Some of mine. Alter them to fit yourself. I can't wear them anymore."

The sheets where she had lain were rumpled and wet. They were thick and made of silk, but they had ridden up along one side to expose an old and rotten mattress stuffed with straw. Mrs. Soapwood groaned and shook her head. "I am very sick," she said.

Charity came to her and sat down. "It will be over soon."

"Yes. For better or worse. God help me, I am so afraid. Touch me. Put your hand on me."

Charity slid her hands underneath the bedclothes. "Touch me!" cried Mrs. Soapwood. "Do you feel anything alive? Do you feel anything struggling? God help me, I have carried life before, and it was not like this."

Every spring in Charn, with the coming of the rain, there

was a plague of monstrous births. According to religious doctrine, this was a natural event. The twenty-seventh bishop had raised six women into sainthood for bearing children to the rain. But in recent generations even the priests had had their doubts. Chrism Demiurge himself had once expressed his skepticism. "I cannot believe that this rain is the literal semen of Beloved Angkhdt," he had once remarked. His words had provoked riots in the slums.

Nevertheless, there had been no other theory. Books about the sugar children had been violently suppressed. Professor Sabian had spent four months in prison, and on a public scaffold in Durbar Square the priests had made him eat the pamphlet he had written on the subject, page by page. But now all that was different since the change of government. Mrs. Soapwood had a copy of the pamphlet by her bed, annotated and reprinted in an edition of ten thousand. "Sabian," she said. "Promise me you'll get me Sabian, when my time comes."

During the first months of the new government, the National Assembly of Charn met in a converted bathhouse behind Wanhope Prison. The building had been abandoned since the end of winter, when it had been one of nine similar facilities. In winter, poor people would come from all over the city to stand naked in the enormous steam rooms, separated by concrete barriers according to their castes. The bishop's secretary had been afraid that they might freeze to death in their unheated homes.

In warmer weather these bathhouses had been abandoned, and some had already been torn down. The one behind Wanhope Prison had been the largest of the nine, a single great amphitheater of stone, windowless, but domed with milky glass. In it, in November of the eighth phase of spring, the National Assembly had gathered to draft a new constitution. On November 12th, old style, a resolution came before the Board of Public Health, and the four members of the board had put the matter to the full assembly so that they could hear the debate before they voted.

The issue had originally been under the jurisdiction of Professor Sabian, for he was the board member for food and medical distribution. He had hoped to dispose of it quietly, to present the Board of Health with an accomplished fact, but members of the assembly who were hostile to his interests had caught news of it.

That month the assembly was bitterly divided. On the lowest levels of the amphitheater, in a circle around the dais, sat Professor Sabian and his moderates, sober men in dark clothes. Most had been professional men under the old Starbridge regime, clerks and small officials. In the amphitheater they formed a central fortress of middle-class solidity. But they were beleaguered in those days, surrounded by circles of extremists. That month especially, it seemed that every day in the debates, men would leave the lower seats and walk up through the upper benches, to where the followers of Raksha Starbridge sat along the highest edge.

In November the extremists formed the largest single group. They called themselves the Rim. Orange was their color; the delegates wore orange armbands, though many were distinguished better by their loud, strident voices and their drunkenness. Many were from the lowest classes, unused to any power but bitterness, full of a new importance that was breaking them apart.

Among them sat Raksha Starbridge, now called January First. He was slouching in his chair. By his side stood another prominent member of the Rim, a man named Valium Samosir. Still young, he had gained influence in the assembly by the beauty of his voice and his ability to transform the harsh and bitter hatreds of his party into polished words. Outside the assembly, too, he had become famous for his personal beauty. The common people had nicknamed him the Bishop of the Revolution. His austere, noble features were on posters all over the city.

He was just finishing his speech. "Gentlemen," he said. "Far be it from me to impugn the honesty of any member of this council. Who can forget the first glorious days of our rebellion, when men like Martin Sabian stood alone against the forces of oppression? Who then could have doubted his patriotism, when he first raised the standard of revolt in Durbar Post Office? What man among us does not love him—let him dare to raise his hand. Who does not love him for his kindness, his compassion, his steadfast courage in the people's fight? No one has loved him more than I. Even now I find it hard to raise my voice against him.

"But there are crimes of silence, as well as speech. That is what he stands accused of, and I too would be guilty if I were to remain silent. Even now he has not lied, gentlemen. Don't think that. He has not spoken one word of falsehood in this chamber. But there are many kinds of lies—gentlemen, every day we have heard him speak. Every day we have sat mesmerized and listened in respectful silence while he outlined the minute details of public policy. Yet in this matter, which affects us all, he has said nothing. We have honored him with the most important post in our new government—minister of distribution. Yet now we learn that he, of all people, has conspired to release half a million criminals onto our streets. He is minister of distribution, let him tell us now what plans he has made to feed and clothe this multitude. What plans has he made to find them shelter, in a city where the recent fires have left one hundred thousand homeless, where most of the sixth ward is still under water? Gentlemen—I have seen them sleeping every night under the Embankment—these people are subsisting on five grams of artificial rice a day!"

Throughout the speech of Valium Samosir, the noise in the assembly had been building, until finally it blocked out his words. Delegates from the outer circles of the amphitheater stood on their chairs to hurl abuse down on the moderates, while the president of the assembly rang his bell. One drunken member, wearing an orange headband, beat the back of the chair in front of him with a wooden club. Raksha Starbridge said nothing, only slunk down deeper into his seat and made a cage out of his trembling fingers. Then suddenly, a smile passed over his lips; he turned towards Valium Samosir and winked.

The young man still had not finished. "Mr. President!" he cried, raising his hand. "Mr. President!" But it was no use. So in a little while he gave up, and crossed his arms over his chest, and stood scowling contemptuously out over the pandemonium that he had made.

He was a fastidious young man, well washed, his white shirt beautifully laundered. He was over six feet tall, but fine-boned, with high cheekbones and pale lips. So that when Professor Sabian stood up, even his supporters saw the contrast, the beautiful young man and the tiny old professor. Emaciated and intensely frail, Sabian stood leaning on his desk, supporting his weight on his knuckles. He seemed very tired, his neck bent, his head bowed low, as if overburdened by the weight of his features—his big eyes, his enormous nose and ears.

"Gentlemen," he said, and the sound of his high voice succeeded where the bell of the president had failed, for all around him the assembly settled down to listen. "Gentlemen," he said. "I sense an accusation in what my... honored colleague says, and yet I don't understand it. What he says is true: I have given orders for the release of all the political prisoners of the former government, a number which my sources put at not above three hundred thousand. And it is true: I did not think it necessary to advise this assembly of my decision. That is not a mark of my contempt for this assembly, as the honorable gentleman has implied, but of my trust: I still cannot believe that any citizen of this city could find it in his heart to disagree with my decision. But it seems I was mistaken."

Professor Sabian raised his head for a moment to peer

around the room, and then he looked back down at the notes upon his desk. "I was mistaken," he said quietly. "Now we have heard this morning from the honorable gentleman, introducing Motion Number Four-four-one-c and d before the Board of Public Health. Several gentlemen have spoken up in favor of this bill, and still I don't believe it. That any delegate of this assembly should seriously introduce a motion proposing that the gateways of the Mountain of Redemption be walled up and that three hundred thousand men and women there be left to starve, whose only crime was that they were enemies of our great enemy— brothers and sisters, these prisoners are the first heroes of our revolution. Many are in urgent need of medical attention."

He paused for a moment, then went on. "Now I know. No one understands, as I do, the burden this will place on our resources. But in all conscience, we have no other choice. And there is a way—for the past week I have been working on the preliminary arrangements. They are practically complete. And I believe that with courage and confidence, and with God's help . . . ," but after that he could go no further. The assembly, which had been listening in silence, suddenly broke out into an uproar of shouting and abuse. It was a serious political mistake, to bring the name of God into that debate, for it touched everything that Sabian had said with the stigma of reaction. It was a slip of the tongue, and political observers later claimed it never would have happened if Professor Sabian had not been so tired, so broken down with working. He was not a religious man, not in the old sense.

Later analysts would claim that if it had not been for that one mistake, Sabian's party would have carried that vote, as it had so many others. But what use are such speculations? For a moment the professor tried to make himself heard above the din. Then he sat down. He took his glasses off to rub his eyes, and then he looked up towards the other members of the Board of Health. Raksha Starbridge sat slouching on the upper rim, scratching and smiling nervously. Below him and to the right, Earnest Darkheart sat sucking on a pencil.

Darkheart was unpredictable in these debates. He was a man of intense and violent principles. Yet it was as if he understood that the time for his ideas had not yet come; he favored the abolition of all property, collective labor, and equality for women. Traditionally, such experiments were part of the political climate of another season, late spring or early summer. In spring it was too early in the year for him to speak his mind, except to a few chosen followers. Instead, he wavered, voting sometimes with the moderates and sometimes against them, according to an inner criterion that Sabian had yet to understand.

With him sat his wife, a big woman, as handsome and as black as he. As Sabian tried to catch his eye, she leaned over to him and whispered in his ear. He nodded, and wrote a few words on a slip of paper. Raising his head, he stared down at the professor for a moment and then lifted his hand. A messenger sprang forward, a young girl with her hands dyed red, who took the slip of paper from his fingers and then started down through the rows of seats. She moved quickly through the banks of shouting delegates, until she stood at Sabian's side. The dye from her hands had come off on the paper, but the sentence on it was still legible, a rough, heavy scrawl. It said, "I am with you."

Sabian felt a surge of hope. He turned to look back up behind him, to where the fourth member of the board sat surrounded by his officers. This was Colonel Aspe, commander of the army, still in the black uniform he had worn in the service of the bishop. He too was unpredictable— born an antinomial, a warrior chieftain of the frozen north, he had been broken by a life of service in the army, broken but not tamed. He had no politics and seemed to vote at random, but on the other hand, he had abstained from six out of the last seven votes. Again this time he showed no sign of listening to or understanding the debate, but sat heavily in his chair, his gaunt, enormous frame dominating that entire section of the chamber. His fierce eyes were fixed on nothing. One of his hands was made of steel. With the other, he tightened and untightened the screws that moved his fingers.

Professor Sabian came to a decision. He motioned to the president of the assembly, signaling for him to adjourn so that the Board of Public Health could stand apart and vote. But Raksha Starbridge had anticipated him. His drugged, dilated eyes missed nothing, and he had seen the note pass between his rivals. Guessing what it said, he was already standing up and speaking, and his harsh, nasal voice cut through the uproar and the noise of arguments.

Fearing defeat, or at best a deadlocked vote before the Board of Health, Raksha Starbridge called upon the president to put the motion to the assembly as a whole, where he knew he had the strength to win. "Mr. President," he said. "You understand I have no wish to threaten the authority of the board, of which I am a founding member. Together, my colleagues and myself have worked long hours in the people's name. We have accomplished much that could not have been accomplished otherwise. Yet from time to time it is my fear that we forget the power on which our power rests. In love with our own arguments, we forget that we are mere extensions of the people's will. Mr. President, today is such a time. Mr. President, I ask your permission to read this motion in front of the entire assembly. What I want to know is, is there a precedent for this?"

In those days Raksha Starbridge was an intimidating sight. He had traded his parson's cassock for a style of clothing then in vogue among the delegates of the Rim, the old, urine-colored uniform of the starving class. It was ripped and filthy. His face, too, had not been washed in days; it was streaked with dirt and with the purple kohl that he used around his eyes.

In those days his methamphetamine addiction had started to affect his entire system. His legs, his fingers, and his head were all afflicted with a constant trembling, and his arm was shaking as he lifted it to point down at the president at the conclusion of his speech.

The president was sitting at his high desk on the dais in the center of the chamber. It was a rotating position among the members of the assembly, and that day the president was a weak-willed man, a lawyer underneath the old regime, in love with legal precedent and terrified of Raksha Starbridge. He rang his bell, and in the hush that spread around the room, he let his voice sink to a whisper. "There is a precedent," he said.

He spoke so softly that the upper benches couldn't hear him. He cleared his throat and started to repeat himself, but in the gap, with the whole assembly silent and straining to hear, Professor Sabian stood up in his place. He took off his spectacles and shook them in the air above his head.

"Citizens!" he cried. "How long will you stand for this? Does this not sound familiar to you? Am I the only one among you who remembers? God help me, when I was a child I remember standing up in Durbar Square to hear my father read a proclamation from the bishop's council, when Marson Starbridge was the minister of family planning. Does no one here remember? One hundred thousand children were rounded up that day—my own brother was condemned—and taken to the mountain. God knows, perhaps he is still there. Brothers and sisters, can you have forgotten? Can you have forgotten your own suffering, that you let our ship of state be captained by this Starbridge parasite, this Starbridge and his band of sycophants, who sanction murder as a public policy, as they have since I was born . . . ?"

He would have continued, only he was interrupted by the president's bell, and by the shouting of the Rim, and by the voice of Raksha Starbridge rising up above the crowd: "Do not call me that! You are lying—I have changed my name!"

"Fool!" shouted Professor Sabian. "Show me your hands, Raksha Starbridge. Do you think it is that easy?" And then suddenly his voice was overwhelmed, and the assembly was conscious of another sound, darker and more ominous, coming from the right, where Earnest Darkheart and the Rebel Angels sat. They were stamping their feet in a slow rhythm till the floorboards resounded, and pounding on their chairs. "Starbridge!" they were shouting. "Starbridge, Starbridge, Starbridge, Starbridge, Starbridge!"

Resolution 441 passed narrowly that evening, after a long debate. When it was over, Professor Sabian loaded his briefcase full of papers and walked slowly down into the hall. He ignored all offers of assistance, all inquiries about his health, and when a colleague approached him and invited him to dinner at his house, he turned away. Instead he walked down alone through the gates and out into the street, past the expensive carriages of Valium Samosir and other prominent members of the assembly. A group of lobbyists and petitioners sat waiting for him on the steps underneath a headless statue of Sebastian Starbridge. He forced himself to stop and listen for a moment, and accept the pamphlets that they thrust into his hands. But as soon as he could, he left them and stepped down, planning to walk the half mile to his lodgings in the Street of the Old Shoemaker.

There too, all around the gate of his building, people were waiting for him with petitions and complaints. He had let it become known that his door was never locked, that night and day he was accessible to any man or woman in the city who might seek him out.

Also in those days he still had a public practice as an

obstetrician. Throughout the city there was a shortage of trained doctors, for most had fled away, and many more had been imprisoned. The ones that remained worked overtime; Professor Sabian's house was built into a tower above Shoemaker's Hospital, and the lobby of the tower was full of pregnant women.

His wife was one of these, though she was past the age when women generally conceive. She waddled out to meet him in the courtyard, and pushed away a supplicant, and took his hands. "What happened?" she asked.

"We lost. The soldiers go tomorrow to wall up the gates. They have enough food for a week inside the prison, maybe more. But after that . . ."

The woman said nothing; only she took his briefcase and led him from the crowd, back into the house, up into the tower, into their private rooms. She had some dinner waiting on a hot plate: nothing much.

She put him down into an armchair, and he sat there without speaking for a long time. Outside it grew dark, and after seven o'clock it began to rain again, big, heavy drops that hit the windowpanes and stuck there like old pieces of gum. He ate rice porridge out of a bowl, and then he put it aside to take his wife's hands again as she pulled up her chair by his. From time to time they were interrupted, but she had given orders to the servant girl to keep the people out. It was only the most strident of supplicants that managed to get past, and even they went away quite soon, because they saw quite soon that there was nothing to be done. Professor Sabian was sitting with his eyes closed.

But at nine o'clock, the hour before midnight, a young woman forced her way up the stairs of the tower and into the professor's room, not through violence or loud language but by the pressure of her need. She didn't say a word. The professor was asleep. He woke from the middle of a dream to see her standing there, her back against the door. How long she had been there, he had no idea. His wife had disappeared.

The woman was standing with her hands behind her. She had black eyes, high cheekbones, and black hair cut short, and she looked around the room with quick, nervous movements of her head. She was very thin, but in those days that was not unusual.

Mrs. Sabian came in through another doorway. "Don't," she said. "Please don't disturb him. Can't you see that he's asleep?" She crossed the room to take the woman's arm and lead her out. But the woman shied away and put her hands up to ward her off. Sabian noticed for the first time that she was wearing gloves. That in itself was not unusual; since the revolution, it had become the style in Charn. But not gloves like these: beautiful white linen gloves up to the elbow, and covered with blood.

Mrs. Soapwood's time had come that evening, when the top part of the house shook with her screams. Mr. Taprobane had closed the door that afternoon and marked it with black chalk to keep the gentlemen away. But when the screaming started, many of the women fled as well, fearing contagion. Even women who were used to childbirth blocked their ears and hid themselves away, for the birth of sugar children was a terrifying thing, and was always presaged by that terrifying sound. It was a roaring and a gibbering, as if someone were torturing a monkey in an upstairs room: That was the signal. The pious thought that Angkhdt himself was speaking through the mother's lips, and they feared what he was saying. When Charity came up from the basement, summoned by her mistress's cries, the house was dark and empty. Only Marcelline and Mr. Taprobane were left.

They were in the bedroom, and Marcelline was holding Mrs. Soapwood by the wrists while the cripple held her head. "Oh, ma'am," she said. "Thank God you've come."

She had called Charity "ma'am" since the incident in the bathtub, and could not be persuaded to stop. Fortunately Mrs. Soapwood was past noticing. She lay on her bed with her spine bent like a bow, while Mr. Taprobane sat above her on her pillow and held her shoulders down. There was froth on her lips, and her eyes were rolled back in her head.

Suddenly her left hand broke free, and she grabbed a spoon from the bowl on her night table. She stabbed it up into her face and managed to draw blood out of her cheek before Marcelline could wrestle it away. "This part of it started last night," said Marcelline. "She's tried to hurt herself." And in fact the woman's lips were bitten, and her arms and cheeks were badly scratched. Her hair was bloody where she had tried to pull it out.

"Help me tie her hands," said Marcelline. Charity tore one of the silken pillowcases into strips, and then together they tied the woman down and tied her hands in front of her. "What shall we do?" cried Marcelline. "She'll die like this. You know she will."

"Shut up," answered Charity. She was sitting on the woman's legs, with the woman's belly in her hands. "Tell me," she said. "Have her contractions started? Did her water break?"

Mr. Taprobane was crying quietly, the tears running down his face. Mrs. Soapwood was babbling and shouting, the words like curses in the language of the gods. She was bleeding heavily from between her legs, blood mixed with water. Charity's gloves were soaked in it.

She jumped down off the bed. "Stay here," she said, "and hold her still. I'll go get help."

"Where?"

"Shoemaker's Hospital. It's not far, is it? Professor Sabian has a clinic there."

Marcelline turned towards her, horrified. "Not Sabian," she said. "You can't go there. You won't fool him. Not him. One look at you, he'll know."

"You shut up," answered Charity. "I fooled you, didn't I?"

Nevertheless, she took precautions. She sent Mr. Taprobane out for a rickshaw, and while she waited, she examined herself in the mirror in the hall. She found some lipstick in the pocket of Mrs. Soapwood's raincoat, and with careful fingers she rubbed some color in around her eyes. It was a common shade, yellow mixed with brown—a shade most Starbridges would rather die than wear. She tied a rayon scarf around her shoulders, the peach-colored emblem of the guild of prostitutes. She tied it in the knot of bondage and was searching for clean gloves when the rickshaw came.

It was not far. But when she got to Sabian's house, she felt afraid. There was nothing to worry about; Marcelline had showed her how to streak her hair, and now the solid Starbridge black was streaked with red. It was a good disguise, but that was all it was. It had not changed her. Courage was still the obligation of her caste.

She told her rickshaw driver to wait, and then she stepped across the road and under the archway of the building. There she hesitated, for the court was full of soldiers, a detachment of the revolutionary police. They were playing bowls by torchlight, wrapped in yellow capes against the rain, and some were eating vegetables out of a bucket.

One of them saw her and made a gesture with his fork. He whistled, and others turned to stare at her. She felt the pressure of their staring on her naked cheeks; even though it had been most of a month since she had fled from home, still she was not used to the glances of strange men. It was pollution, and that was a feeling that had lost the thrill of novelty in the filthy streets of Charn.

She pulled her collar up around her face and walked across the yard. The soldiers were staring at her, and two of them had their mouths open. But none of them tried to stop her, and none said anything. And in the house itself no one asked her where she was going, though the rooms and staircases were full of nurses and ink-stained secretaries working late.

She continued up the stairs, slipping past servants and orderlies from the hospital, ignoring their questions. "I can see him," she said. "Any citizen can see him, that's what the posters say. Don't tell me it's a lie." And after that they let her pass. They asked her name. "Rosamund," she said.

They let her pass. And in an upper room she found him, sitting asleep, a small, big-featured man with something childlike in his face once sleep had smoothed away the lines. His glasses had fallen down into his lap.

Unsure of what to do, she stood with her back against the door. She put her hand out towards him and then drew it back. But then an inner door swung open and a fat woman came in. "Ssh," she said. "Don't wake him. Please go away." But he was awake already. He put his fingers to his eyes.

"I'm sorry to disturb you," said Charity. "My mistress has gone into labor."

"Please go away," repeated the fat woman. "How did you get in? You need a midwife, that is all. Does my husband have to deliver every baby born in Charn?"

"No midwife will touch her," said Charity. "It's a sugar birth."

Professor Sabian was having trouble focusing. He sat looking from one woman to the other, blinking his eyes. But when his wife went to the door to call to the people in the outer room, he spoke. "Sugar birth?" he asked.

"Yes, sir. I knew you had an interest," answered Charity. Then, as the fat woman took hold of her arm to lead her away, she continued, "Sir, you've got to help her. She'll die if you don't come."

"Sugar," repeated the professor, still not quite awake. He rubbed his eyes and put his glasses on. "Let go of her," he said.

His wife tightened her grip. "Martin," she said. "Look

what she is. She's with the guild; look at her clothes. Don't let her fool you."

Sabian frowned. "Let go of her." And then, to Charity: "Don't be afraid. Tell me what you know."

"Please, sir, she's forty days beyond her time. At least that's what she told me."

"How long has it been?" asked Sabian.

"Almost seven hundred days. That's not normal, is it, for this time of year? My mother carried me that long, but that was wintertime."

"It's far too long. Why is this the first I've heard of it? Surely she had time enough to make arrangements."

"I don't know. She was afraid."

"Afraid? But there is nothing supernatural about this. It is a natural phenomenon."

"She was afraid," said Charity.

Professor Sabian got to his feet. He was grumbling to himself. "Where are you going?" asked his wife. "You sit down. Why is it always you—can't you send somebody else?"

"She asked for you," said Charity. "She asked for you by name."

At that, Professor Sabian looked her full in the face. His eyes seemed enormous underneath his glasses. He frowned and then he shrugged his shoulders. "Today my government condemned three hundred thousand people to a cruel death," he said. And then he turned back to his wife. "I have a debt to pay."

A little before midnight he followed Charity out into the rain, where her rickshaw was still waiting. The driver recognized him and bowed his head and pressed his knuckles to his forehead. "Stop that," said Sabian. "We are all equal under God."

Sitting beside him as the rickshaw wheeled out into the street, Charity turned her head away. He was still very sleepy, and he looked at her benignly, nodding his head to the rhythm of the wheels. "It's what this revolution is about," he said. "It is a change in public thinking above all, so that we can free ourselves from the slavery of these myths." He held out his palm, and a raindrop splattered onto it obligingly. He rubbed it into a viscous ball between his fingers. "According to the myth," he continued, "this is the semen of Beloved Angkhdt. It falls from heaven every spring, and where the soil has been depleted by the winter weather, the rain builds it up over the course of time, so that once again it is capable of supporting life. That is quite reasonable; to call it sperm is just a metaphor. But the myth goes further. We've all heard stories of how, when the rain builds deep enough, all kinds of life erupts from it spontaneously: trees, flowers, insects, animals, all the species that have disappeared over the winter. But who has ever seen this, an animal erupting from the earth? Growing from a seed—in fact, this rain is much like other kinds of rain. Its overwhelming component is water. Only it has varying amounts of a trace chemical, which we call sugar, though of course there is no sugar in it."

He spoke slowly, lazily, fingering his earlobe, his head back against the seat. "These priests," he said, "they took a religious metaphor and turned it into an instrument for political repression. That is what we can never allow to happen again. Like all tyrants, they based their power on the people's ignorance. How shall we progress, how shall we break out of this cycle of tyranny, unless we can learn to look at these natural phenomena for what they are? Otherwise, these myths breed a kind of fatalism that poisons every enterprise, for we are powerless against the will of God. But these plagues and scourges are natural phenomena. That is why I find it so discouraging to hear that your friend took no precautions, made no arrangements for what she knew was happening to her."

"She was afraid," said Charity.

"Precisely. It is terrifying to give birth to something that is not human, particularly if you've seen in every church, ever since you were a little girl, images of a not-quite-human god. It is a terrifying thing to feel yourself impregnated by the seed of that fierce god. Nevertheless, if she could only have understood that these myths are born out of the phenomenon, that the phenomenon is the reason that we picture God the way we do. That the phenomenon came first and that all the myth has done is prevented us from understanding it. Then, perhaps, she would not have been afraid."

They had reached the house. It was completely dark, save for the window at the top, and even from the street they could hear the gibbering screams. Professor Sabian looked doubtfully at the sign of the black bird, as the rickshaw slowed and stopped. "Here?" he asked. Charity nodded.

Mr. Taprobane was waiting on the stoop. When he saw them, he came running out into the road and fished the professor's bag out of the boot, gesturing to him to come quickly. Unsure, the professor hesitated, but then he shrugged his shoulders and stepped down and followed Mr. Taprobane into the house.

The cripple took Professor Sabian's coat and ran back along the hall with it slung over his shoulder. And when he reached the stairs, he started up them without pausing, clambering on his hands and feet, with a strange, corkscrew motion of his twisted frame. He paused at the first landing and looked back. "Come on," he hissed. "Come quick." It was unbelievably fast the way he moved, like a monkey or a rat, with the professor's coat hanging down the steps behind him. "Come on," he said, and the professor followed him slowly, peering up into the dark.

Having paid the driver, Charity entered the house last of all and turned the lights on in the hallway. From the stairs Professor Sabian looked back at her, a puzzled expression on his face.

In the rickshaw he had not even asked where they were going. Looking up at him, she could tell that he was thinking for the first time whether he had been wise to come alone. She smiled at him to reassure him, and gestured with her head.

She had not planned to follow him upstairs. But in the end she did. She was confident in herself. But Marcelline almost wrecked it from the start. She got up from Mrs. Soapwood's bed, her hands and dress covered with blood, and came to meet the princess at the door. "Oh, ma'am," she said. "It's worse and worse."

"Shut up!" said Charity between her teeth, and she grabbed hold of the woman's upper arm. But Professor Sabian had his back turned, and Mrs. Soapwood's screams were drowning out all other noise. Charity relented. "Get some rest," she said more kindly. "It's my turn now."

Marcelline would have curtsied, only Charity was holding her upright. Instead, she bowed her head and went away, and Charity turned into the room, towards where Mr. Taprobane and the professor wrestled with the woman on the bed. One of her hands had gotten loose, and she was holding it above her head, every muscle tense, her fingers splayed out wide. "Let me go!" she shouted in a voice that was not her own. "God damn you, let me go!"

They were tying her across the body with long silken strips ripped from the bedclothes. They tied her to the posts. "God damn you!" she was shouting, and the voice inside her mouth was as low and harsh as an animal's or a man's. "You will freeze in hell," she cried, and then was silent, because Mr. Taprobane had seized hold of her jaw, and Sabian was trying to gag her with a strip of cloth tied through her mouth, around her head. But she was stronger than he was, and she was twisting her head back and forth and banging him with her free hand until Charity grabbed hold of it and held it down. Then, finally, the woman was overpowered, gagged and trussed, though her back was still arched and her legs still thrashed and kicked.

Professor Sabian prepared a syringe full of tranquilizer and shot it home into her neck. Then she was quiet, though her feet still spasmed periodically while Sabian made his examination. "Will she be all right?" asked Charity.

The professor shook his head. "She has already started her descent." He worked for a little while and then sat back and pushed his glasses back onto his nose. "I think that she will live," he said. "She's a big woman—nature has been kind. There is no need for extraordinary measures."

Nevertheless he shot her full of drugs, to relax her and to kill the pain, and to dilate her as far as possible. And after that it was just waiting. Mrs. Soapwood had lost consciousness. They ungagged her and untied her hands. Charity took her head onto her lap and washed her face out of a basin of hot water that Mr. Taprobane had brought. She cleaned the spittle from the woman's lips.

Professor Sabian sat back and watched her. "Who are you?" he asked.

Taken by surprise, she answered hesitantly, but he seemed not to notice. He grunted and then looked away, and took the conversation onto different subjects, because for a long time there was nothing they could do but wait. He told her about the new constitution of the city while Mr. Taprobane fell asleep, curled up in a corner of the room with his arms around a pillow. He asked her questions about her life, with a puzzled expression on his face, his eyes big and liquid underneath his spectacles. And even though she had prepared answers in advance about her birth and up-bringing, still she was taken by surprise. Because he was asking her about her opinions, about her dreams, about her hopes for government, and as she answered, she couldn't help but think that she was making some mistakes, taking positions that were not appropriate. So, after a while she was silent, but by then it was already too late, because already his attitude towards her had begun to change. His gestures and his way of talking took on a certain formal quality, very gradually at first, as if he were not yet aware of it. In a dozen different ways he was more distant, deferential, and at first Charity thought that he was making fun of her. But later she decided it was something true to him: later, as the night wore on, and everything he did became a ceremony, a gentle ritual of manners. His voice, his grammar, his vocabulary changed. When she handed him the forceps from his bag, he murmured his thanks and made a little bowing motion with his head.

There was something in Professor Sabian that brought back memories of servants. For a revolutionary there was something strange about his little bows, his mastery of the nine degrees of self-abasement. How strange it is that he is such a snob, thought Charity. Small wonder that he hates us so. In fact there was no hatred in the way he was behaving. When the crisis came and they were working hard together, he seemed glad that she was there, though he was careful not to touch her hands.

"There," he said, when it was done. Mrs. Soapwood had lost consciousness, but when the crisis came, she had cried out, and Charity was afraid that she was dead. "Please don't concern yourself," said Sabian. "Please don't—I entreat you." He pushed the woman over onto her side, and in a little while they could hear her breathing, hard and deep.

What had come out of her had no real shape, and it was dead. Professor Sabian wrapped it in a pillowcase. "I'll take it back with me," he said. "Permit me. Such specimens are rare."

Charity woke up Mr. Taprobane and laid him down beside his sleeping mistress. "I'll send somebody up to clean the room," she said.

Professor Sabian was standing with his bag next to the door. He had wrapped his bundle up into his raincoat. "Thank you for your help," said Charity, and he bowed low and motioned for her to precede him through the door. But for the first time there was a complicated expression in his face, uncomfortable and tentative.

She, on the other hand, felt very calm. She walked slowly down the stairs, down the hall, and out into the street. It was early morning, and the sky was gray; a soft rain was just starting. The professor followed seven feet behind her, as propriety required.

In the street she turned back towards him, but he dropped his eyes, embarrassed, and raised his hand to stop a rickshaw. "Thank you," she said again, and again he bowed, elegant and formal. This time, for the first time, the gesture seemed a little overdone, as if he had allowed some irony to mix with his respect. She smiled, and as a mark of special favor, she stripped off her glove and put her hand out towards him, turning her palm so that he could see the tattoo of the double ring, the symbol of good fellowship. She wore no greasepaint; it was her naked skin, and he bent over it, careful not to touch her, to pollute her with his breath. He closed his eyes. "I thought it might be you," he said. "I used to read about you in the social page, when you were just a little girl."

The rain was insubstantial and as fine as dust. It made a mist around them as they spoke. "Go back," he said. "There's time to sleep for a few hours."

He turned and walked across the street to where the rickshaw waited. From the seat he made a little wave. And late that morning, after breakfast, he sent round the soldiers.

# THE WHITE-FACED WOMAN

5

Later, of course, there was to be some semblance of justice as the city grew more prosperous. Later in the season, when the farms outside the city had begun to function, the tension in the streets grew less. By then, too, the revolution had already eaten its first children. Raksha Starbridge, Valium Samosir, Earnest Darkheart all followed each other, willing and unwilling, to the scaffold. They were replaced in the assembly by less passionate, less imaginative men.

Later that same season the effects of a new religious movement were first felt, the Cult of Loving Kindness. In summer it was to consume the politics of all that northern country. But in the time we speak of, at the end of the eighth phase of spring, 00016, in the first days of the revolution, there was no compassion in high places. The judicial system had not been much altered since the bishop's days; only the names of the judges and the criteria for condemnation were different.

If anything, the trials were even shorter, the chances for acquittal even thinner. The trial of Charity Starbridge was quicker even than her brother's had been under the old regime. She did not once appear before the revolutionary tribunal, nor was she notified of the charge. But on the seventh evening of her arrest, she was taken from her precinct cell to a new prison near the Battle Monument, where she was visited by Raksha Starbridge. He said, "I was wondering when we would find you. I never thought you'd be so stupid as to search us out."

Charity shrugged. "I was working as a laundress. I was tired of it."

"Ah. So what appears to be stupidity is really self-destruction. It must run in your family."

"Yes," answered Charity. "Where I am going, there are no dirty clothes."

Raksha Starbridge laughed. "Don't be so sure. No reliable reports have made it back."

He took a tablet from the breast pocket of his shirt and laid it on the tabletop near where she stood. "The desanctification vaccine," he said. "Now in tablet form. People who have taken this will never wake in Paradise."

"I'll pass," she said.

He laughed. "Don't worry. Since I saw you, I have changed the formula." He took a few more from his pocket and popped them in his mouth. "Aspirin," he said. "Mostly."

"I'd rather not."

He smiled. "I don't want to have to force you. After all, we both know it's nonsense. I feel sure that where we spend eternity will not be influenced by a pill. All the same, I have a duty to my government."

The desanctification pill was not the only drug he was taking. His pupils were dilated and his fingers shook. Charity reached out to touch the tablet with her finger. "Where will this one send me?" she asked.

The pill had a small number stamped on its underside. "Proxima Vermeil," said Raksha Starbridge. "The third planet. Not the worst alternative. It has water. Some kind of atmosphere. A tribute to your youth and beauty." He winked. "You made quite an impression on poor Sabian. It was a wrestle with his conscience to turn you in at all."

"How gratifying."

They were standing in a small, narrow, high-roofed chamber, with one wall of shoddy wooden bars. It looked out along a corridor of similar spaces, all occupied.

Since the closing of the Mountain of Redemption, there was a shortage of prison space in Charn. This building was a converted stable. Formerly it had housed a troupe of circus elephants. Months before, they had all been requisitioned by the army, leaving behind huge mounds of dirty straw. Most of this was stored in the central courtyard, but there were also piles of it in every cell.

Charity had made a nest out of her pile and covered it with a blanket. That evening, when Raksha Starbridge left, she sat down on it and took the pill into her hand, to study it and wonder if it were poison. Why had he come? In the end he had not forced her. No doubt he made a round of all the Starbridge prisoners, administering his vaccine. It was not fatal, she had heard, but perhaps this pill was different. Perhaps, as a mark of special favor. . . . She rolled the pill between her finger and thumb and then pitched it across the room through the bars of her cell. It rolled a short distance along the floor of the corridor.

Staring after it, her eyes met those of another prisoner. He was in the cell opposite hers, squatting by the open wall, his hands protruding through the bars.

"That was January First," he said.

She nodded.

"Who are you?" he asked. "You must be important."

She shrugged. "I knew him once." She stood up to look across the hall. The man had melted a small candle to the bars of his cell, and it illuminated a face that seemed familiar. There was something familiar in his features, his bulk, his balding head. Familiar and not familiar; now that she looked at him straight on, she saw that his face was very red, very white, and covered with small scars.

"Who are you?" asked the stranger.

For an answer she stretched her hand out through the bars so that he could see the silver rose, the emblem of her father's family, tattooed in the middle of her palm. It had an effect on him. Instantly his eyes filled up with tears. He put his fist up to his mouth, and then he stood and backed away into the recesses of his cell. Later he came back again to stare at her, but only for a minute—again the tears came to his eyes, and again he turned away.

How strange, thought Charity. And there was something else: The cell beside his was in darkness, and she had thought it was unoccupied. Only now she heard a sound there, barely audible, as soft as breath. And even though she had scarcely in her life heard any kind of music, yet she had read about it. Now, listening, she found she could identify it. The sound started to lengthen and contract, moving up and down the scale. Charity listened, her heart beating faster. She had no way of guessing how the sound was made; she only knew it was not made with one of the instruments sanctioned by the bishop's council in the old days. The thirty-first bishop had banned everything but percussive instruments: the xylophone, the drum, the cymbals, and the gong. He had banned every music that was not molded to a central beat. He had banned any music that was not dampened by religious singing—melody alone could light a fire in your mind, he had said. Listening in her cell, Charity wondered whether it was true. The man opposite her was weeping for no reason as the music of the flute went up and down. He was pressing his forehead against the bars of his door.

The sound from the dark cell stopped suddenly, interrupted by a deep, low coughing. The man turned his head in its direction. And in the silence that followed, he took a piece of paper from inside his shirt, a creased and wrinkled scrap of paper. He handled it reverently, as if it were a precious jewel or a religious amulet, and he unfolded it with special care. "I have a message for you," he said. Then he looked towards Charity across the corridor, a strange, yearning expression on his face. "At least, it is you, isn't it?" He turned the paper over so that she could see what looked like a name and an address written on the outside, though she was too far away to read the words.

"P-princess Charity Starbridge," said the stranger slowly, running his finger over the first line. "That's you, isn't it?"

She nodded.

"It's from your brother. Shall I read it to you? You don't mind, do you? I've read it so many times."

"My brother," she said softly.

"It's very short. They blocked out the whole first part. Chrism Demiurge—look." He held the paper out to her across the corridor, and she reached out her hand. It was still more than six feet beyond her fingertips, too far away to read, but Charity could recognize her brother's awkward handwriting. The first two paragraphs had been painted over with gold ink.

"Read it," she said. Suddenly it was terrifying how much the stranger looked like Abu, the way he fumbled with the paper and peered at it shortsightedly.

"Please excuse me. I can't read very well," he admitted. "I believe I used to have some education. Not anymore. It was among the things they stole from me."

"Read it," said Charity.

The stranger rubbed his hand back over his forehead and the bald crown of his head, a parody of a gesture painfully familiar to the princess. But his voice was not like Abu's. It was lower, hoarser. But his trick of hesitating was the same, his tendency to stammer.

When the man started to read, she closed her eyes. "The first part of the page is all blocked out," he said. "But then he writes, 'As you can see, it hasn't been too bad. They give me enough food. They've got litchi nuts and pickled ginger, and...' Something else I haven't been able to make out. 'Nothing to drink, of course, but that's just as well. The man I'm sending to deliver this...' Something else is crossed out, then he writes, 'Anyway, I wanted you to know that I'm all right, and that I've not been treated badly. No torture, nothing like that. But it gave me time to think. Charity, I believe a change of government is coming. Now I know you may not think that my opinion is worth much. But I worry about your safety. Now that I am gone, and your husband too, I've heard, you'll need someone to help you. Get in touch with...,' and then there is a name beginning with a *T*. It's been blocked out."

"Thanakar," said Charity.

"That's right. It's got a *K* in it. 'Get in touch with Thanakar. Send a message—he is with the army. Or if not, then he has gone to Caladon. He always talked of emigrating, and if I'm right about the government, then you should join him. Take money from the bureau drawer. There's nothing for you here. He likes you very much. He told me so.

"'You must forgive me for rambling on, but I'm in a philosophic mood. I wasn't a religious man, now I regret it in some ways. But I feel these questions of belief are too much stressed. These questions of faith: Faith comes from the outside in. How can our hearts be dirty, if our hands are clean? I always thought they were peculiar, these priests who murder people in the name of God. Don't they understand that kindness is the only thing?'"

The man stopped speaking for a moment; then he continued. "The end is all blocked out, except for the signature. And the date: 'Wanhope Prison, October 44.' The day before he died. And look at this—next to the date, he's drawn a picture of the Sun."

Again Charity heard the sound of a deep, hard, hacking cough from the dark cell. The stranger was holding the letter out to her, pointing at the signature. "Yes, I see," she said. "It's strange—you look very like him. You must know you do."

For the first time a flicker of what looked like anger passed across the stranger's face. "Of course I look like him," he cried. "Of course I do. How do you think I got this letter?"

"I don't know. I was going to ask."

Again tears came to the man's eyes. "How could you know?" he asked irrationally. "How could you guess? How could anyone guess something so cruel? I got this letter . . . ," here he shook it in the air. "I got this from Chrism Demiurge, may he suffocate in hell. He bought it from your brother's messenger."

"Why?"

"Why? I don't know. I don't know—he never told me his whole plan. Or if he did, I have forgotten. There's so much that's been wiped clean. What does he say? Your brother, here: 'How can our hearts be dirty, if our hands are clean?' But that's just foolishness, because he never knew. I could have told him how a man could be the center of the most perverted schemes yet keep his innocence. I don't remember my own name!"

The man was crying, leaning his bald forehead against the bars of his cell. His words were wild and full of tears: "How can our hands be dirty, if our hearts are clean? But a man who stumbles in the mud, is he not still defiled?"

"Calm yourself," said Charity. "You'll bring the guard. If you didn't know what you were doing, then you can't be blamed."

"I blame myself. Don't you understand? This"—he shook the letter in the air—"this was a great man. 'Faith comes from the outside in,' is anything more true than that? He was a great man. And I am his counterfeit. Yes, I look like

him. Don't you see the surgeon's marks? I don't even remember what my own face was like. And look here."

He stretched out his right hand and opened up his fingers.
His palm was covered with a silver membrane, bonded to
his skin, obscuring whatever tattoos lay beneath. But in the
center of his palm was painted, red and gold, the shining
Sun in splendor, Abu Starbridge's tattoo.

"I understand," said Charity. "They made you in my
brother's image."

"Yes," croaked the man, interrupting. "So that Chrism
Demiurge could kill the prince and still use him somehow.
He wanted people to believe the prince had died and then
risen again, like a god. The night after the execution, they
took me to a bar in Beggar's Medicine. I sat there drinking
the whole night. God help me, I was just fresh from the
hospital. I didn't understand why they were staring. I didn't
understand why no one came to sit with me. I had enough
money to buy drinks for the whole bar."

From the dark cell beside him came the sound of coughing and the clinking of a chain. Charity turned to peer into
the shadow, but saw nothing. "And after that?" she asked.

"That was the only thing I did. If Demiurge had other
plans, he never told me. The revolution came too fast—a
week later he was dead. I was arrested in my cell in Kindness and Repair. They took me for a Starbridge. Then they
weren't so sure. I told my story to the guards, to everyone.
They brought me before January First, and I told him. He
laughed. I thought that he would let me go. But yesterday
he sentenced me to die. He said the revolution has no place
for oddities left over from the old regime. God knows he's
right."

The next morning when the soldiers came, Charity was
standing by her door. She stuck her head out between the
bars of sawn-off two-by-four, so that she could see them
open up the dark cell and drag out the prisoner. Four men

went in, and two more stood guard in the corridor with rifles in their hands. But even so it took a long time, and there were sounds of fighting and swearing and the cracking of a whip. And when the men came out again, one of them was limping, and one was bleeding from a cut over his ear.

The prisoner was unconscious. They dragged her face down along the floor past Charity's cell, by a chain knotted around her wrists. She was a big, muscular woman, with coarse, gray hair. She was dressed in rags, open down the back, and Charity could see blood on her shoulders and the welts of frequent beatings.

"Not a pretty sight," said the guard who was opening her door. "Antinomial scum. They should have shot her out of hand."

"What is she accused of?" asked the princess.

"She's a savage. She eats dead animals. She had trapped a falcon when the soldiers caught her, and torn two of its wings off. She put two men in the hospital when they arrested her."

He was the man who had been cut over the ear. He had been carrying the woman's flute under his armpit; now he held it up for Charity to see. "Look at this," he said. "A real souvenir. Made out of a bamboo club. Someone must have broken it over her back the night she lit her cell on fire. She must have kept the piece."

Charity reached out to touch it. It was a marvelous thing, made of a broken stick of split bamboo, hollowed out, punctured at intervals, bound back together with twine and copper wire. One long split down the back had been filled in, patched with soot and melted wax.

The guard handed it to Charity, and she brought it to her lips. "Stop that," said the guard, snatching it back. "Behave yourself. You don't want to be dragged out like her."

The princess smiled and shook her head. "I don't know how to play."

The night before, she had tried to learn how to listen.

After the stranger had gone to bed, after he had blown his candle out and lain down on his pallet with his arms crossed over the face that was not his own, then Charity had sat up to listen. The whole night she had listened to the music from the dark cell. She had tried to understand what music meant, and she had failed. But even though she didn't know the language, even so the music spoke to her, comforted her, and quieted her heart. She sat on scraps of straw, leaning with her back against the bars of her cell, her legs stretched out, her head bent back, listening. Once the flute player broke off into a fit of coughing—that too for Charity became part of the music. Then, when the melody started again, she could hear the imperfections of the flute, the buzz of the split along its back in the lower notes, as if someone were singing with something loose caught in the back of her throat. But after the first few notes, Charity couldn't hear it anymore, after the song had taken hold. It was telling her of freedom in a language she would never know—she understood why it was banned. Why musicians were hunted down and killed.

In school she had read about the antinomials. She remembered an illustration: men and women riding together in the snow, standing in their saddles to look forward as the snow erased their tracks. It was an illustration from her anthropology text; shaking her head, Charity reached behind her, above her head, and took hold of one of the wooden bars of her cell. She thought this music was the first and last that she would ever hear. And when it stopped, she had felt too sad to sleep. But in the morning she found that the music lingered with her, or rather, not the music but the picture, the giants in the snow, their harsh, bitter faces, their horses and their dogs. It comforted her and opened up a space in her where she could live apart, some protection around her when the soldiers came, and beat the antinomial, and dragged her away.

"Stop it," said the soldier, and he snatched the flute out

of her hand. "You don't want to go like that." He nodded up along the corridor after his companions.

Charity smiled and shook her head. Her face was calm, and she looked pretty, standing in the milky morning shadows. For that reason the soldier was gentle as he tied her hands, and gentle when he led her out, down the stone corridors, out into the courtyard where the tumbril waited.

It was an open cart drawn by donkeys, their shaved heads oscillating, their meager voices whining. The antinomial was already in the back, lying with her head against the side. She was conscious, though her yellow eyes were swollen down to slits. Charity nodded to her and received a hard, contemptuous stare.

Then they brought the stranger out, whimpering stupidly, his hand still clasped around Prince Abu's letter. They threw him up into the back of the cart, and he sat down clumsily as it began to move. He was whimpering and hiding his face. He was no Starbridge, Charity decided. He could not be reconciled to his death. Charity alone kept to her feet, her hands tied in front of her, resting on the rail. She felt very calm.

There were only a few soldiers in the courtyard, but when the tumbril passed the gate into the street, its way was hampered by a crowd. There were perhaps a hundred people come to watch, encouraged by the weather. It was nothing like the crowd at Abu's execution. His had been a spectacle, with marchers and men beating drums. That crowd had been delirious, stirred by currents that had since subsided.

Less than a month ago; it seemed ten months. Since then the people had gotten used to these processions. But even so, a cry went up when she appeared, a crude, angry shouting like a crashing wave. "Starbridge!" shouted the crowd. "Starbridge, Starbridge, Starbridge, Starbridge, Starbridge!" The people had been well rehearsed. But even so, among the angry faces she saw others that were not as angry, and some people even made the gestures of respect.

The ritual touched her in a way it never had before.

She had thought that she would never hear any more music. But as the sounds of the crowd crashed around her, she heard part of another sound. "Shut up!" groaned the stranger, and the man who drove the donkeys turned back from his seat and snarled. He lifted his whip above his head, but the antinomial didn't care. She was beyond his reach. She sat in the bottom of the cart, staring at the sky with her head bent back, humming a wordless song.

Charity looked up too. Above them, the sun had broken through the clouds. It shone fiercely above their heads, deluging the city with cascades of amber light. Men and women in the crowd looked up blinking, their faces pale and astonished, for the sun had not been visible for weeks. And not for months had it been visible like this, shining unimpeded, making rainbows in the upper air. Later chroniclers would remember how the sun shone briefly on the day of Abu Starbridge's execution and then not again until his sister Charity was pulled through the same streets; they would make a point of it, for religious reasons. But in fact there was no comparison—on the day that Princess Charity was buried alive beneath the Morquar Gate, the sun burned brighter than it had since the beginning of the rains. And all the while the antinomial stared up at it, scowling fiercely, singing her wordless music louder and louder.

In the crowd, people made the sign of the unclean or put their fingers to their ears. The driver whipped his donkeys like a crazy man. He stood up in his seat and goaded them with a stick thrust up their anuses until they screamed aloud. He had twisted their tails together and tied them to the reins; he pulled their tails as cruelly as he could as they clattered up the Street of the Seven Sins out towards the gate.

In those days, in Charn, in the first days of the revolution, people were desperate for entertainment. New regulations had constricted the flow of drugs and alcohol into the city—on November 1st, workmen had built ten tons of sinsemillian into a pyramid in Morquar Square. Once on fire, it had burned for days, filling the streets around the gate with thick, intoxicating smoke, incapacitating the people in that neighborhood. In such quantities, the drug made it hard for them to walk.

On November 2nd, six marijuana profiteers were crucified along the north edge of the square. That same morning, Rebel Angels visited every public tavern north of the river, smashing bottles and destroying stocks. Pools of alcohol collected in the gutters, and men and women filled their buckets and their boots. The next day the *Free Word* published a photograph of men passed out under a hoarding, under a line of posters condemning public drunkenness.

Useless in the long term, these laws combined with others to encourage sad short-term effects. On November 3rd, Professor Sabian gave a speech before the National Assembly about recent increases in violent crime. "It is not the looting that appalls me," he remarked. "It is not the activity of the black markets or the reports of profiteering. Those seem to me regrettable but legitimate by-products of the current emergency. No—it is the other kind of crime. In the past five weeks alone, the incidence of rape in the sixth ward has risen ninety-two percent. Murder has risen thirty-six percent; violent assault by sixty-four percent.

"Of course," he continued, "there are reasons for this. The previous government of this city based its power on violence and coercion. Now we are seeing reaction, like a spring that is released from pressure. But that is not the only factor—brothers and sisters, the tyranny that once held us in slavery has loosened from our lives. All the outward trappings of that tyranny have been destroyed: the shrines, the idols, and the icons—though I am told that many still worship them in secret. But, brothers and sisters, noxious as it was, the ceremonial of the old regime contained some public benefice. It distracted the aggressions of us all. This benefice is something we have not been able to replace."

Swayed by the professor's speech, the assembly sat far into the night, and by daybreak it had appointed a commission. Raksha Starbridge, the majority speaker, received the task of drafting a new civic religion. It was to favor ritual over content. It was not to involve the worship of any deity of any kind.

Raksha Starbridge was delighted with the resolution. He laughed and clapped his hands. But Professor Sabian was horrified, even though his speech had been the seed of the idea.

Yet even he could never have anticipated the malice and the ingenuity that Raksha Starbridge brought to his new job. For almost one hundred days he used his power to terrorize the city, until even his own party turned against him. From October 94th, when he was inaugurated as director of the Desecration League, to November 87th, when Earnest Darkheart beat him senseless on the floor of the assembly, he presided over such a reign of violence in Charn that a generation later it was forbidden to allude to it, by imperial decree.

Nevertheless, later historians would agree that the most hideous of all the crimes of Raksha Starbridge was the sealing of the Mountain of Redemption and the abandonment of almost half a million prisoners to slow deaths from starvation. This work was started on the 13th of November. It was accomplished by the Desecration League, for even though the job was authorized by the assembly, neither the Rebel Angels, nor the police, nor the army, nor the guild of bricklayers wanted anything to do with it. The guild went on a strike of public protest, which ended with the arrest and disappearance of its leaders. And for weeks the League kept guards around the mountain's base, for fear of sabotage to the wet masonry.

For weeks, on every street corner, wherever the summit of the mountain could be seen, crowds gathered with telescopes and binoculars. And whenever there was a break in the mist, cries of anger and disgust rose to the skies, for the crowds could see the prisoners swarming on the mountain's upper slopes. From time to time, a prisoner would jump down from an upper balcony. Though the bulk of the building would prevent him from ever reaching the street, still he might fall a thousand feet before he disappeared.

This was the worst crime. But there was another that was even more spectacular, and in some ways more symbolic of the season. On November 9th, Raksha Starbridge opened the so-called Sugar Festival, on the fairgrounds out beyond the Morquar Gate. It was to run for more than ninety days. But within a week of its opening it had become the center of the life of Charn. All day and all night the festival was packed with noisy, celebrating people, and they scarcely noticed, or they scarcely cared, that every day among the carousels, the colored lights, and the free candy, dozens of prisoners were being hung, shot, buried, crucified before their eyes. For many, it was the reason they had come.

On the morning of November 21st, when Charity Starbridge was scheduled to die, the fairgrounds at the Morquar Gate were still only half built. Yet to come were the ferris wheels, the electric roller coasters, and the bumper cars. Yet to come were the circus acts, the trapeze artists and the tightrope walkers, the tumblers and performing dogs. Yet to come were the bandshells full of drummers, and choirs singing new patriotic lyrics to old hymns.

Nevertheless, the heart of the fair was already then in place; hundreds of small cardboard booths, housing potshies, gunshoots, soothsayers, wheels of fortune, guess-games, cardswaps, number tables, duckstools, finger-switches, and a dozen more, games of skill and games of chance. Already in place were the distribution booths, where script won in the games could be exchanged for clothing, and blankets, and liquor, and painkillers, and little bags of new synthetic meal. Already in place were the massive canvas awnings, stretched tight from poles over the cardboard streets, sheltering them from the weather and the constant rain. And in the center, beneath the shadow of the Morquar Gate, the execution grounds were already in place, the whipping posts, the burning pits, and around them a circle of steel crosses, forty feet high, bolted together, held up with steel wire.

In the sixth ward, the city walls had been demolished long before. The Morquar Gate stood by itself in the middle of the fairgrounds, a gigantic structure of carved brick. On it the League had hung a series of enormous banners proclaiming the maxims of Raksha Starbridge's new civic religion. Prisoners on the cross could spend their last remaining hours pondering these messages. "Life is senseless suffering," cautioned one, white words on a gray background. "I am the spirit of denial," claimed another: "Through me lies the gate of joy."

Charity squinted up towards another banner, hanging from the end of a long pole. "What have you got to lose?" it asked ambiguously. Another was more simple: "God does not exist."

"Small consolation," murmured Charity, as they rode in through the gate. In the early morning light, the carnival looked tired and unprofitable to her. The sun bleached out the colors of the neon and the crystal lanterns, and gave the crowds a pasty, furtive look.

"Morning crowd's never the best," remarked a soldier of the League. He was standing by the donkeys, wiping down their bellies with his hand. "Dark's the best, or in the rain. Then you can see the lights."

"I was expecting more excitement," Charity confessed. She had heard about the carnival from Mr. Taprobane.

"Ah. They are a lot of cowards really. They are frightened of your friend."

As soon as he had stopped the cart at the loading platform underneath the gate, the driver had jumped out and disappeared. Now Charity saw him, standing in a group of men next to a few wretched-looking canvas stalls. He was pointing back at them and shouting, and making the sign of the unclean.

"He's frightened of the singing," continued the young soldier. He was dark-haired and would have been good-looking, except that when he smiled his teeth were full of holes. His brows met in a line over his nose. He had loosened the bridle on the lead donkey. The dye from his red hands had made a smear across the animal's cheek and on its belly, too, in the place where the scales joined the flesh. "Life is meaningless," he said. "What can it matter if we sing or not?"

Ordinarily there was more of a ritual in these proceedings. But the sunlight put a weight on things. This was only the first of sixteen tumbrils expected at intervals throughout the day, and the mode of execution was not spectacular. Even so, ordinarily there would have been a crowd. This morning, frightened of the antinomial, the people retreated back into the fairgrounds, where some squatted down to watch from a safe distance.

Another soldier had come forward and climbed up into the cart. Smiling, he forced the stranger to his feet, but the antinomial rose by herself. She stood up straight in the back of the cart, her legs spread wide, and now she started to sing in earnest, staring at the sun.

The stranger put his hands over his ears. He was gibbering with fear, and when the soldier touched him, he cried out. Charity looked at him, surprised; he was afraid of death.

Fear required a concentration that she did not have. Reflexively she touched her lion's-head tattoo. It was good to be a Starbridge, but it was not necessary. All around her were distractions.

The handsome soldier was still stroking the donkeys and untying their tails. But in a little while he came to help his friend put down the tailgate. Grinning at each other, they helped Charity to the ground. Then they dragged out the stranger; he was kicking and biting until they hit him on the head, and then he began to cry. They threw him out onto the concrete, and he knelt, weeping, on all fours. Charity went to him and raised him up. "Hush," she said. "You're not dead yet." It was no consolation. He put his face into her neck and wept.

The antinomial jumped down unaided, singing all the time. Singing, she followed the others to an open space of poured concrete a hundred feet away, where a metal cover was set into a concrete ring. The soldiers opened it, and they poked down a ladder that was lying to one side. They held it steady for Charity and the stranger, and then they stood up, waiting. But the antinomial was busy with her music. She looked up at the sun; it was burning like a fire overhead. She sang part of the fire song while the two soldiers smiled at her. And then she climbed down the ladder until she stood in darkness, and she was still singing very quietly, just whispering, because she could still see some sunlight through the little hole above her head, until someone pulled the ladder up and closed the cover with a clang.

There was air from someplace, cold, new air. And the bottom was not muddy. It was dry. Deep sand, it felt like. Charity sat down and ran some through her fingers. In the blackness it gave out a comforting, small sound.

Her hands were tied together, but not tightly. She poured a stream of sand onto her foot. The antinomial was quiet, finally. "Sweet God, deliver us," prayed the stranger, next to her ear.

Thirty feet above them shone a ring of orange light, where the manhole cover made an imperfect seal. The light was not enough to penetrate the darkness or allow Charity to guess the dimensions of the well. She could not see her two companions.

Hearing about this new form of punishment from Mr. Taprobane, she had pictured it a different way. She had thought she would be gagged and trussed and lowered down into a space barely larger than herself. She had thought that she'd by lying on her back, watching the workmen pick up shovels above her head, and then there would be dirt in her face—it would be over in a moment. She had not pictured it like this, lying in the comfortable sand, and everything so quiet. She poured some sand onto her foot.

"It's not so bad," she said.

"Just wait," murmured the stranger, close to her ear. He was calmer too. He too had been expecting something worse.

The air was cool and had a faintly sour smell, as if it came to them over a stagnant lake.

"It's as if we'd come into another country," said Charity after a while. "There must be an opening somewhere."

She put her cheek down on the sand. She watched the orange ring, suspended in the dark.

Once, not long before, the last time Paradise was close to Earth, she and her cousin Thanakar had gone out on the balcony, when Paradise was rising above Monmouth Hill. For a moment they had been alone. Then Paradise had been as big as the whole world, when they were leaning on the balustrade, their elbows almost touching. The light from the planet had been on his face when he turned towards her, smiling. That was all.

In another moment her husband and her brother had arrived, laughing and making fun. With mock seriousness, the old man had pointed out a scar on Paradise's surface—the Ocean of Iniquity, where his family once had a beach-house. His grandmother had seen it in a dream.

It was with thoughts of her cousin Thanakar that Charity fell asleep, and her head was full of thoughts of him when she awoke. She had no recollection of where she was, until she turned onto her back and saw the glowing ring above her. It had lost its orange color; it was a milky gray.

She strained her ears to hear something of the festival, but there was nothing, only the sound of a deep muttering close beside her. Turning her head, she could see the outline of the stranger's shape, deep black against a gentle black. Beyond him was another shape standing erect. It was the antinomial.

The stranger was saying prayers. Charity sank back down onto her elbow and listened for a while to the quick, careful rhythm of the chant, and from time to time the incantation of her brother's name. It was a blurred, restful sound, mixing with her thoughts—she was not quite awake.

"As You suffered injustice, now deliver us," chanted the stranger. "None of us can suffer as You suffered. Nonetheless we have no wish to try."

His voice went on for a long while. And then it stopped suddenly, because the antinomial had spoken too, and her voice was different.

"Some," she said.

There was breathless silence for a moment, and then the stranger's prayer started again, quick and soft, almost inaudible.

"Now," said the antinomial. "Black now bright now fire. See."

Again the prayer stopped, and there was silence. "I don't see anything," said Charity.

"Not eyes."

The antinomial's speech had none of the sweetness of her music. It was deep and very rough, with an uncouth rumbling at the back of it. Yet even so, there was some music in it, Charity was sure. She could feel it rubbing at the back of her neck, tingling on her skin, as if it existed in a frequency beyond the range of Charity's ears, so that she perceived it only indirectly.

"See," said the woman.

Charity looked, and for a long time she could see nothing. She stared at the woman's outline in the dark. After a moment she thought she could distinguish the antinomial's outstretched arm, and so she looked in that direction, trying to penetrate into the darkness layer by layer. At length she saw the faintest glimmer of a light.

"There is something. Over there," she said.

For a while it burned unsteadily, a beacon marking the farthest limit of her sight. Then it sagged and glimmered out, and reappeared again, lower down. Then it seemed larger, shaky and more blurred, until it split apart into two separate lights, closer now. For the first time she could hear a noise, the sound of lapping water.

She was lying in a stone chamber. She could see that now. Its diameter was not more than forty feet. But a large, jagged hole had been broken through the wall. She saw its outline as the lights came closer, the blocks of fallen stone, the low boundary where the hole approached the sandy floor. Beyond the hole she could distinguish nothing, for soon all that space was filled with light.

The light came from two guttering lanterns held on poles. It was not bright, but even so, Charity turned her head away because her eyes had been made sensitive by so much darkness. She looked instead at her companions, their faces illuminated by the long red beams, their bodies half in shadow. More than ever the stranger looked like Prince Abu, for the light was bleaching out their differences and covering the marks of surgery. His terrified expression was very like the prince's, the way his mouth flapped open.

Charity's hands were still bound together at the wrist. The stranger's hands were also bound; he put them up together to block out the light. But the antinomial had loosened hers. She was standing with her arms crossed on her chest. One of her eyes was swollen shut, and her face was covered with bruises.

Yet she stood in an attitude of fierce indifference, almost of inattention as she stared into the light. It reassured the princess. Awkwardly, because of her tied hands, she rose to her feet.

Two men were climbing through the hole and down into the chamber, while two others held the lanterns on the other side. They were dark-skinned and almost naked. Their hair was yellow, hanging straight to their shoulders, and their faces were sharp and cleanly formed. Their cheeks were covered with a kind of powder or dark paint that made them shine like masks. Their eyes were large and very pale, blue or gray, one of the illegal shades, Charity couldn't tell which. Their movements were quiet and sure, and they said nothing as they dragged the stranger to his feet.

"Come quietly," said another man, a fifth man standing framed outside the hole between the two lanterns. He was a different kind of man, older, with white hair, and he was dressed in a white robe. It was a type of clothing that Charity recognized from Starbridge funerals when she was young—the ritual garments of the corpse of some great gentleman, pilfered from some underground sarcophagus a long time ago, she guessed. The material was ripped under the sleeves. Nevertheless, the man's face was kind.

"Nobody will hurt you," he said. He gestured to his men. One of them was leading the stranger, cowed and unresisting, over the barrier of broken stones, while another put his hand out for the antinomial.

"Do not touch me," she said softly, her voice resonant with music, and the man drew back uncertainly. He pulled a flashlight from a pouch at his waist and shined it in the woman's face, while the man in white stepped over the barrier into the tomb. He spoke a few words in some foreign language, and then he smiled. He put his hands together in an old-fashioned gesture of greeting. "Welcome, sister," he said, and then he added a few notes of music in a high voice. But he stopped when he saw the woman's face fill up with fury and contempt and loathing.

"Barbarian!" she cried. "Barbarian!" She reached out suddenly and grabbed away the flashlight that was shining in her face and then leaped over the barrier between the two men with the lanterns. One put his hand out to restrain her, but she slapped it aside. Then she stepped out beyond the circle of the lamplight and disappeared into the darkness.

The man in white stared after her. Then he turned back to Charity, and again he made the same gesture of greeting, joining his palms together and bowing slightly. "My name is Freedom Love," he said.

The name meant nothing. But the gesture reminded Charity of something, a description from some book, or perhaps an illustration: an old man joining his hands together in front of him, hiding his tattoos.

She tried to speak, but the man shook his head. "Come quick," he said. "Let's see if we can find her. Otherwise, she'll starve to death here in the labyrinth." He turned and led them out over the barrier through a gap of broken stones. On the other side the lanterns illuminated a low, straight corridor, hacked out of the rock.

They walked single-file, the lanterns first and last. Charity was behind the man in white, looking at him, searching for a clue somewhere, his clothes, his hair, his way of walking. And then she found it: a chain of amber beads around his neck. In her religious history text, when she was a girl at Starbridge Dayschools, there had been a picture of a man joining his hands and bowing, and underneath a diagram of a necklace of small beads. Underneath that a caption was printed in small black letters—"The Cult of Loving Kindness."

As she walked along the corridor, Charity cast her mind

back to the book. Six generations before, in winter, the twenty-third bishop of Charn had had a dream, a chain without end, wrapped around the girdle of the Earth. After six days of meditation he had made a proclamation. He declared the existence of a great chain of precedence, a hierarchy in which every living creature was arranged according to its rank. He postulated a social language of infinite gradations, with forms of address peculiar to each individual, and gestures of respect or contempt that differed only by fractions of millimeters.

The twenty-third bishop had devoted his life to sorting out these differences. Subsequent bishops had abandoned the attempt. Such a structure was impractical on Earth, beyond the subtlety of mortal minds and fingers. But even so the dream had become part of the mythology of Charn. It was a vision, some said, of Paradise, where the soul of every creature would be arranged according to its worth, in a structure so harmonious and perfect, it would bring tears to the eyes of everyone who witnessed it.

Nevertheless, some sections of the Song of Angkhdt were open to quite different interpretations. In Charity's great-grandmother's time, St. Gossamer Marquette had preached another gospel, claiming that all human souls were equal in God's love.

St. Gossamer Marquette was burned to death on the first day of autumn, 00015. Her disciples had scattered, and two seasons later her followers were so few as to be almost mythological. But the saint had worn an amber necklace, Charity remembered that from books. The necklace was the only thing that had survived the flames, and it had become the symbol of her heresy. That and a way of bowing she had preached.

"Where are you taking us?" asked Charity. The walls of the corridor had broadened out of sight, and the gravel underfoot had given way to coarse blocks of quarried stone. The way still led straight on, without a twist or a turn. From the burial chamber she had seen a light shining, far away. She had seen a distant light, and she had heard the sound of water lapping. Later, that sound had been obscured by the shuffling of their feet, but now she heard it again close by. In front of her, Freedom Love stopped walking and took a flashlight from his robe, while the lanterns drew off some way ahead. Outside the compass of their light, Charity could see more clearly where she stood, a triangular stone chamber perhaps fifty feet along each side, the ceiling perhaps twenty feet above her head. Near her, a stone stair was let into the wall. She guessed it led up to the surface, because some light was dribbling down it. It dribbled over rows of simple graves along the floor.

"We've lost her," said Freedom Love. "She must have gone another way."

They were in the tomb of some important bourgeois family. The cover of the grave where Charity had sat to rest was decorated with a list of modest privileges, together with some modest optimism that the dead man's punishment would not be hard or long. Charity ran her hand over the stone. A chart of the solar system was etched into the dusty surface. The dead man's soul had been consigned to Mega Prime.

The chamber was the terminus of an underground canal. Freedom Love climbed down into a ditch between the graves and gestured with his hands. Charity got to her feet and followed the lanterns towards the entrance of a low tunnel. There the water had receded back into the dark, leaving a scum of mud along the bottom of the ditch. But the men with the lanterns jumped down into it, and so did Charity and the stranger. They followed the lanterns into the tunnel's mouth, where the light seemed to burn much brighter. Fifty feet along the ditch the water was around their ankles. Then the tunnel widened to the right, and they clambered up onto a stone landing, where a boat was drawn up into a stone trough.

"It took us thirteen days to find this place," said Freedom

Love. "It's not on any of the maps. The Dogon don't come up this far. But Sarkis remembered from his childhood, and after that we had to find the execution chamber by dead reckoning, under the pilings of the Morquar Gate. It took us three days with picks and shovels to break through. You have Gudrun Sarkis to thank—that man there."

He pointed to the edge of the landing, to where one of the men was fussing with the boat. He was a squat, unlovely person of indeterminate age. His chest was decorated with a chain of bones and fur, and when he grinned up at Charity, she saw that his teeth were pointed, sharpened with a file.

"Why?" asked Charity.

"Human life is sacred, is it not?" replied Freedom Love vaguely. "Great Angkhdt tells us to succor those in pain. They were killing men and women for no reason—burying them alive. There were forty people in that room when we broke through. All but six of them were dead."

"Not for no reason," said the princess. "My family had a lot to answer for."

"And his?" Freedom Love motioned towards the stranger, who was squatting by the water's edge.

"He has no family."

"An antinomial? Surely not."

"Of a kind," said Charity. "Not by choice. His memory was surgically removed."

The stranger was less frightened now, though still his voice was trembling as he spoke for the first time. "I hate these stupid ropes," he said. Again Charity was amazed by his resemblance to the prince, his childlike way of talking, the futile motion of his hands. He was pulling his hands apart, straining at the ropes, fluttering his fingers.

"I hate these ropes," he repeated sulkily. But he shied away when Gudrun Sarkis, responding from a word from Freedom Love, drew a knife from his belt and came towards him. The stranger's face took on an expression of slack terror, and the men around the boat started to laugh.

"Don't torture him," said Charity, for Sarkis was rolling up his eyes and twisting his lips in an expression of ferocity while the others laughed. "He has no memory of how a person should behave," she said. She held out her own wrists, and at another word from the old man, Sarkis drew his knife under the knot and cut her hands apart. Then she went down to the edge of the landing to where the stranger was crouching against some fallen stones. And as she fumbled with the knotted ropes around his wrists, she tried to soothe him. She whispered to him and caressed his naked forearm in a gesture that was somewhat intimate, though he didn't seem to be aware of that. She could not have touched him if he had not reminded her so strongly of her brother, who had been teased so cruelly when they were children.

"What are we waiting for?" she asked aloud. "Why are you all just standing around?"

Freedom Love was consulting his wristwatch. "We are waiting for the wind," he said. In fact, the men had let the boat into the water, and they had pulled erect a flimsy mast.

"There is no wind down here," said Charity, but at that moment there was a booming noise above their heads and a grinding of harsh gears. Immediately, the dead air around them seemed to move a little, and the lanterns flickered in their chimneys.

"Five-seventeen," commented Freedom Love. "Every afternoon they open up the garbage doors below Saint Morquar's Square, where the river runs underground. When the doors are open, there is a draft over this pool."

Charity looked down into the water. It stretched away into the dark, as perfect as a sheet of steel. The light upon its smooth black surface seemed less an effect of shadow and reflection than of paint, as if the semicircle of lamplight were just painted on. When finally, after a moment, a pattern of ripples spread across the surface of the pool, it was like the swirl left by some unseen brush. Charity could see no hint of three dimensions, until Gudrun Sarkis pulled the boat against the stones and leaped aboard. Then thick black waves smacked up against its wooden sides as the vessel found its equilibrium, jostling the lamplight into a million shapeless dots.

As Gudrun Sarkis raised the sail, the rest of the men jumped down. They gathered up the lanterns and suspended them from poles in the bow and stern. Freedom Love reached out his hand to help Charity aboard, but she hung back. The stranger was still frightened. His eyes were shining, and he was tugging on her sleeve.

"Where are you taking us?" asked Charity again.

For the first time, Freedom Love evinced some irritation. "Come quick," he said. "The doors only stay open thirty minutes. Do you want us to leave you in the dark?"

"Where are you taking us?" demanded Princess Charity.

"To safety. Come. Great Angkhdt tells us that we must trust each other."

The sail flapped lethargically over to one side. It was a narrow triangle of red cloth, ragged and much patched. But the wind was gathering strength, and soon the boat started to draw away from the stone bank. Gudrun Sarkis leaned on his paddle to keep it in close, but still Charity hesitated. It was not until the last possible moment that the stranger jumped aboard, and Charity stepped after him.

"That is good," said Freedom Love as the boat heeled away. It was a wide, shallow craft, sluggish and unresponsive, but it rocked as the stranger stumbled forward and sat down in the bilge. The four tribesmen sat on benches with paddles on their knees, while Freedom Love moved aft to take the steering oar. Charity sat at his feet as the boat moved out over the water, and she was listening to him sing under his breath. After a few false starts the melody came clear, and then the words:

*What can I do to make you trust me?*
*Is it not enough to give you pleasure*
*Six times out of seven?*

He had to be singing from the Song of Angkhdt, Charity decided. In Charn, before the revolution, it had been a criminal offense to duplicate the rhythm of a verse of holy scripture, even in casual conversation. Nor had it been the fashion for at least a generation to set the words to music.

"You talk about religion in a new way," she said aloud, finally, after the song had drifted down to nothing. "What did you say before? 'Great Angkhdt tells us to help those in pain.' I never heard of that before."

"It is from an old translation," replied Freedom Love, staring straight ahead over the bow. "Soon these verses will be common knowledge, now that it is spring."

"What do you mean?"

The old man rubbed his head, and waited a while before speaking. "The word of God is like a living thing," he said at last. "It has its seasons underground."

All around them the water stretched away into the dark. From time to time the wind seemed to shift direction, so that the sail flapped and rattled overhead. But still the boat moved slowly on as Freedom Love tugged upon the oar. "Winter is a barren time," he said. "If people turn for comfort to these phallic images, is it any wonder? When the Earth is sterile for a man's entire life, is it any wonder that he makes a cult out of fertility? That is his need, and in winter, the Song of Angkhdt adapts to it. The subtler verses are all stripped away. Our God becomes a phallic monster, deformed, inhuman, cruel, but with a supernatural vitality, a potency that covers all the Earth. It fills the sky. His sperm is in the rain."

"And now?" asked Charity.

"And now the world is changing. Our faith is changing, too. But as always, the change is very difficult, because men and women are always ready to die for what they think is true. It makes it hard for them to let go of the old ways. There has been violence and bloodshed, and there will be more. But you are young enough. You'll live to see the

Earth become a garden. Your children will know verses of the Song that you have never heard. And even the crudest of the verses now, you will find that they have changed. The crudest and the most obscene—you will find they are about love."

"That's not what I meant," said Charity. "I mean, what happens now? There has been a change of government in Charn."

The old man shrugged his shoulders. "It was to be expected," he replied. "There were some grave abuses. Spring is the time for atheistic governments. But the people are still with us in their hearts."

"I'm not sure. When they brought the great brass statue of Immortal Angkhdt down from the temple into Durbar Square, ten thousand people stood in line for seven hours in the rain, just to file past and spit on it."

Again the old man shrugged. "But that too is a kind of worship. It goes deeper than that. You will see. Every week dozens come down from the streets to hear me preach. They risk their lives to bring us food. How do you think we live?"

The boat was moving faster now. It had reached some kind of current; the water was turbid up ahead, and the boat was carried by its own momentum as the sail lolled and flapped. "I hadn't asked myself," said Charity. "Who are these men?"

"They are a tribal people called the Dogon. They have lived down here for generations. I am a newcomer by contrast. A refugee. I was censured by the bishop's council, four, almost five months ago. I was condemned for heresy, but I escaped. These men are my converts."

They were entering a channel where the current flowed more rapidly. The lanterns on the stern and forward poles swung wildly back and forth. All was in darkness beyond their flickering reach, and out of that darkness came a constant roaring sound. The wind was stronger now, and damp and hard to breathe. Charity's hair was slick with moisture, and there were beads of water on her clothes.

"They call themselves the Dogon," continued Freedom Love. "They speak another language, far more ancient than our own. And until I came, they had no inkling of the truth —they fished in these lakes and ate the roasted carcasses. They worshiped pagan gods."

"How many of them are there?"

"Seventeen. At least there are many tribes down here. The labyrinth stretches for fifty miles. But not all tribes are so receptive to the truth. These are the first. They are my children. I have taught them to grow mushrooms in the lower crypts."

Charity was asking questions to keep herself from thinking how Freedom Love could steer his boat through total darkness underneath the earth. But there must have been something in her face, for he laughed as he pushed upon his oar, and the boat scudded out into the roughest current. "I put my faith in God," he said. "Besides, look there."

He pointed up ahead to where some greenish lights were shining in a row. At first they were very small, and seemed to jiggle in the darkness like a row of dots along the inside of her eyelid as Charity turned her head. She raised her hand to block out the glare from the forward lantern, and then she saw them clearly, thirteen pinpricks in a line, growing all the time as she rushed towards them. After a few minutes she could see that they, too, were lanterns, strung out along the width of the vast cavern.

"It is the Morquar Dam," said Freedom Love.

The current was gentler now, and in the gathering light, Charity could see the water breaking apart into a series of small whirlpools, losing its momentum, turning back upon itself. In front of her the lights were strung along the top of a white barricade. She could see the pumping station and the weir.

Freedom Love turned the boat in a wide, slow semicircle,

and the current brought them around close to the dam. Charity could hear the rushing of the water through the sluice. Up ahead the current was slowly wheeling back upon itself, turning back out into the darkness behind them. But Freedom Love was keeping the boat along the barricade, which rose a dozen feet above their heads. There was no wind in the sail, but the Dogon had taken up their paddles. They pulled the boat into a stagnant stretch of water below the east end of the dam, where Charity could see for the first time the rock walls of the cavern, and even its ceiling far above. The water around them was full of dust and bits of wood.

From the house above the sluicegate, the keeper of the lock was peering down at them. She was a tiny, ancient woman, with white hair braided down her back. Freedom Love called up to her in a language he seemed to speak only indifferently, for he could only manage a few words. But the woman said nothing. There was no expression on her face either; she just leaned on the railing of the dam and stared down at them. The Dogon were pulling down the sail.

In the bottom of the boat the stranger looked up anxiously. "What's happening?" he asked, but Charity shook her head. She was looking at the woman, studying her colorless, enormous eyes, wondering how many generations of living underground it took to develop eyes like that. The Dogon didn't have them. They were a dark-skinned race.

The woman held up five colorless fingers, and Freedom Love threw her a coin. It was a wide, copper penny, and he flicked it with his thumb so that it turned over in the air. The woman caught it overhand and rubbed it between her fingers before thrusting it away into the bosom of her dress. Then she bent over the wheel, straining with her skinny arms until the sluicegate opened up.

The dam was made of concrete, but the doors were wooden and elaborately carved, and painted with scenes from the life of the Beloved Angkhdt. Once on his journey through the universe, the Prophet had come to a planet where there was no light. The only light in all that world came from the Prophet's mouth when he spoke the word of God.

The door into the Morquar lock was painted to represent this episode in the immortal life. The outer panels were all decorated with barren landscapes and frozen cityscapes, painted black so as to be invisible. But the Prophet's open mouth was on the central panel, golden red behind a fence of canine teeth. And when the gate split open, Charity could see that the inside of the lock was painted red.

"Ah, God," she murmured, as the Dogon pulled them inside. The air was dank and close, and an oily foam covered the top of the water. Behind them, the doors churned closed, leaving them in a small red room.

"The lock is four hundred feet high," said Freedom Love, as the water started to suck away beneath them. The sides of the shaft were painted from top to bottom, circles of orange and red. They seemed to glow brighter as the boat descended. Something in the paint reacted with the lantern light, a phosphorescent sheen mixing with the orange of the Prophet's throat. But as the air got worse, the lanterns flickered low, so that the color was lost. Soon all that remained was the gleam of the phosphorescence on the dripping walls. "It's from the rain," said Freedom Love. "It drains into the river lower down."

After many minutes the lock let them out into a small pool at the bottom of the dam. Behind them the great white wall stretched out of sight, out of reach of their lanterns, while in front all was in darkness. Around the boat, bubbles rose and broke constantly on the surface of the pool, filling the air with a noise like crackling fire.

The boat swung sharply around. The Dogon dug their paddles deep into the water. The stranger was sitting in the bilge, staring back at the dam with a look of empty wonder. His mouth hung open, and there were beads of sweat along his upper lip. "D-do people live down here?" he asked. Freedom Love pushed on the steering oar. He was looking for the channel down out of the pool, and he slid the boat into a gap between low banks of fitted stone. It was only a few feet wider than the boat. The Dogon scraped their paddles along the channel's sides, yet still they made swift time, moving as if haste were important.

"In ancient times," said Freedom Love, "there was a period of seven years when the weather was far harsher than it is even today. Winter and summer, the extremes of temperature were much harsher. It is a periodic fluctuation; the last time was many years ago, and at that time, it is recorded, half the population of the city lived underground. Even more, at certain times of year. Half a million people lived down here. Rich people, mostly. They had tunnels dug as far as Caladon."

He pulled his flashlight from the breast of his robe and shined it up above their heads. "Look," he said. "Look there." The lanterns in the boat had guttered low, and the beam of the flashlight pierced the darkness where they could not follow. It illuminated the ceiling of the tunnel they had entered and played among the carvings and the painted figures with their eyes of mirrored glass. "The dam fed an electric generator," said Freedom Love. "This tunnel was once called the Prince's Walk."

He was steering with one hand, while with the other he shined his flashlight at the pictures on the wall and into the doors of abandoned galleries. He told them the history of the place, and took detours into other, smaller corridors to show them special things: a crystal chandelier still hanging from the dome of one small chamber; the portals of the summer house of Lord Berylliam Starbridge; the winged, porcelain statue of the Snake of Relativity; and one enormous cavern where the vault was set with moving lanterns, long extinct, to duplicate the constellations of the winter sky.

As he explained these wonders, Freedom Love seemed calm and at his ease. But Charity noticed that the Dogon were paddling as fast and as hard as they could. They had turned down the lantern on the prow until it was scarcely bright enough to guide them, and they looked back anxiously at their leader's powerful flashlight. Yet they had no way of expressing their disapproval except by the energy of their work, their bent backs and the sweat along their arms, the flash of their paddles and the power of their stroke.

"They are afraid of something," remarked Charity.

Freedom Love made a careless gesture with his hand. "The woman," he replied. "The white-faced woman. It is true, she has been seen near here."

How to measure time in that black hole? Charity was hungry and exhausted by the time they reached their destination, an island in the middle of a lake. The stranger was asleep in the boat, but Charity was awake. She had seen the island from far away, lighting up the vault, shining over the surface of the lake. On its beaches, acetylene torches hung from poles stuck in the sand.

The Dogon had paddled without ceasing until they came into the reach of a long spit of sand. Then they put their paddles on their knees and let the boat drift up onto the beach. Gudrun Sarkis stepped out into the shallow water and dragged the boat the last few yards, until its bottom groaned ashore.

Men and women came to greet them down the beach. They all greeted Charity in the same way, a little bow with their palms joined together. But when Freedom Love descended from the boat, they got down on their knees in the dark sand. They made a line on either side of him, and as he walked up the beach between them, they put out their hands for him to touch.

When he had passed, one got up and came forward and

took Charity by the hands. She was a dark, handsome woman, younger than Charity and still dressed in the remnants of a rich, embroidered gown. She too had pressed her palms together, but not so carefully that Charity had failed to glimpse the flash of gold and silver in the lamplight.

She was a Starbridge of the soldier's blood, a member of Charity's own clan. But still she did not introduce herself that way. "My name is Varana," she said, and then she laughed when Charity looked puzzled. "It is the name my master gave me," she explained. "It means 'the bell that God rings,' in I don't know what language. Don't you think it suits me?"

She was a constant talker, but kind, too. She took Charity to her own house, a wooden hut down by the water's edge. She made Charity lie down in her own bed, and brought her soup and basins of hot water. And all the time she chattered constantly, a blithe, comforting sound, until Charity fell asleep.

"I've been here a long time," said Varana, hours later. Charity was sitting up in bed. Again the girl was feeding her with mushroom soup and talking all the time. "I came here the same way you did, just the same. It's hard to tell how long ago—thirty days, a month, oh, I don't know. My trial was October eighty-third. I was buried in that pit, just the same as you. Only worse, of course, because my mother and I, we were among the first the master saved." Suddenly there were tears in her eyes. She swallowed and went on more slowly: "There were people in the pit, many people who are gone. I was there six days, my master told me. I was with my mother, holding her hand, touching her as I am touching you, but we were dying. My mother died that morning, and I didn't know. I couldn't tell. There were people crying out. And I heard someone banging on the stones. It was my master, breaking down the wall with hammers. He broke down the wall."

"You don't have to tell me if the memory is painful," said Charity after a pause.

"No. Let me finish. I want to tell you why I love him, so that you will love him too. It is because he gave me life. He took me from my grave; if there is pain, it belongs to my past life. Before me there is nothing but joy," she said, the tears still on her cheeks.

Charity put down her bowl and spoon and held her hand out tentatively. The girl seized it in both of hers. She turned it palm up on the coverlet and started squeezing it, kneading the muscles in between the bones. "My master says that this is good for stress," she continued. "He is full of knowledge. Relax your hand—let me show you. The reason I'm telling you this is because I want you to stay. The people that he rescues, he gives them their choice. I want you to know this is the best house in the village if you want to stay. I've been so lonely. Some of the people are kind but they are not my kin. My father was Baroda Starbridge. I cannot talk to them as I can talk to you."

The hut was ten feet square, lit with oil lamps. Charity sat on a low bed, a metal frame strung with strips of cloth and covered with a woven mat. There were some quilts and blankets. On a block of stone next to the door, Charity could see, neatly arranged, a broken piece of mirror and a comb.

"Who lives here?" asked Charity. "Who lives here on this island?"

"Refugees," Varana replied. "Every Monday the tribunal condemns another batch of prisoners. Every Tuesday they are buried. On Wednesday my master brings them back. Then on Fridays, he goes up to Bishop's Keys. People come to hear him preach, and always one or two come back with him. They bring food from above."

"And the Dogon?"

Varana wrinkled her nose. "They live here too. But they are primitives. Not worth the time he spends—did you know, until he came, they ate the flesh of animals? They hunted fish with spears. Their kin still do, across the lake."

Charity shrugged. "And now they live on gifts from other people. What do they do all day, the ones that used to hunt?"

Varana frowned. "You don't understand. They had strange rites and strange beliefs. They had no knowledge of the truth. How could you know? You've only just arrived."

She let go of Charity's left hand, picked up her right hand, and started rubbing it. But soon there was the faint sound of a bell, and she got to her feet. "My master sends for me," she said.

When she was gone, Charity got up and dressed herself. She washed her face in a basin of cool water. She combed the dirt out of her hair. She washed her hands and feet, and then she left the house.

The stranger was walking on the beach below the town. Charity called out to him, and he turned his head. He was carrying a lantern, and looked as if he were searching for something in the sand.

Near him a line of wooden pilings stretched out into the lake, and the sand gave out onto a stone pier. The stranger stepped onto the pier and squatted down next to the water's edge. As Charity came close, he was throwing sand into the water, scattering it a few grains at a time. Wherever the sand hit, the lake glimmered briefly, a silver gleam deep beneath the surface. "I've been trying to understand why it is not colder here," he said without turning around. "You'd think it would be freezing so far from the sun."

"The lakewater is warm," said Charity.

"Yes. I noticed it when we arrived. Perhaps it flows over some deep thermal activity. Look at this." He dipped his lantern down over the edge of the stone pier, illuminating a green scum of algae on the surface of the lake. "It's what they eat," he said. "I had a bowl of it."

"How was it?"

"Not good. Look at this." With a flick of his fingers he scattered some sand into the water, and immediately a fish rose to the surface, a small, slow beast with a back of luminescent scales. The stranger frowned. "Hah," he said. "What could that creature be expecting?"

Bats played over the lake, dipping low onto the shore, calling to each other in susurrant voices. Occasionally they came to rest, their long legs clumsy in the sand. One fell over onto its back, and Charity watched its struggles to get up.

"We can leave here if we want to," she said. "Freedom Love gives us the choice."

"Hah. Some choice. We'd never find our way."

"But we could try. I don't want to eat algae till I die."

The stranger looked up at her. "It's not so bad for you. But I'm in a stone barracks, with fifteen other men. Our host has an eye for a pretty face, I've noticed."

"Perhaps he'll give us a guide."

"Who'd go? They're terrified. They're afraid of the white-faced woman. I don't blame them."

"Who?" asked Charity. She was watching the bat as it struggled on the sand. By pushing with one wing, it had managed to right itself. Now it stood on one leg, cleaning the skin of its small body with the other.

Again the stranger flicked some sand into the water, and the luminescent fish came to the surface. "It's a superstition," he replied. "A superstition come to life. My guards were telling me about it when I was in prison. They're not stupid. Every week they'd put a new consignment of prisoners into that pit, and every week it would be empty. They thought the white-faced woman was stealing them away."

Charity was watching the bat. "You are afraid," she said.

Furious, the stranger turned on her. "Of course I am," he cried. "What's wrong with you? Don't you have any feelings?"

For an answer, Charity touched her lion's-head tattoo, and wondered what it would be like to be without it. "Freedom Love," she said. "You heard what he told us. He said there are tunnels here that take you all the way to Caladon. They take you all the way across the border."

"If you can find them," grumbled the stranger. But Charity wasn't listening. She was watching the bat, how it gathered itself into a jump and leaped away into the dark.

"He wants to see you," said Varana. "You and the other one."

The princess had wandered down to the end of the island, and Varana came up behind her as she stood watching the Dogon women working in their garden. The rows of pallid plants were marked by tiny oil lamps set in the ground, six to a row, and the women moved up and down between them, shoveling out fertilizer from baskets on their backs. Unlike the men they wore a lot of clothing, shawls and shapeless robes, and their heads were veiled. They made somber, shrouded figures, for they chose always the darkest colors. Sometimes Charity would lose sight of them entirely in the gaps between the lamps, and sometimes she could only guess at where they were, as the lamplight snatched quickly at the opalescent thread and the bits of mirror that they used to decorate their clothes.

The circle of Dogon houses stood out on a peninsula into the lake, poor huts of clay and broken stone, away from the rest of the village. Charity stood on a small embankment with Varana at her side, looking out over an open space of trampled dirt. There, while the Dogon women worked, the men sat idle in small groups, laughing and conversing. Some played a game with spears and a small wicker ring. The ring was soaked in oil and set on fire; it flickered with a bluish flame. One man would set it rolling in an area of darkness, while another tried to throw his fishing spear so that its double barbs would catch the rim.

That whole section of the town was darker than the rest. The women grew their plants almost in darkness. As for the men, Charity could barely see them, though she could hear their laughter and their shouts as someone missed his cast.

"He wants to see you," Varana repeated, for Charity had not turned around.

At the sound of her voice, one of the women stopped working below them and looked up. Varana muttered part of a prayer and made the sign of the unclean. "Let's get away from here," she said, putting her hand on Charity's arm. "I hate them," she confided. "They made me feel dirty when they look at me, especially the men. One man exposed his penis to me—there, that one. Come, let's go. I want today to be a happy day. My master put his hand on me today."

Charity turned to face her, mildly surprised.

"Oh, not like that," continued Varana, leading her away. "I mean he touched my head." She gestured towards her forehead. "Here. The place is still on fire. He can touch the energy resources of the brain. Ask him when you see him. Perhaps he'll do the same for you."

Charity smiled and shook her head.

"Why not?" asked Varana. "It's perfectly safe. His hands are clean."

"How do you know? What caste is he?"

"I'm not sure. Some kind of scholar. He has a candle marked under his thumb."

"A teacher!" exclaimed Charity, still smiling. "And you let him touch your head?"

Varana frowned. "There are some distinctions that we should transcend," she replied with dignity.

They had reached the main street of the village. Here the dark was chased away by lanterns hung from poles. Walking with her arm through Charity's, Varana nodded to everyone they passed.

At length they stopped in front of a long building, the

grandest in the town. This was the meetinghouse, and inside a meeting was in progress. They passed under the portals of the central chamber and found themselves among a small crowd of respectful listeners. Freedom Love was standing on a wooden dais, talking to his people.

"When I was young," he said, "I lived with my family on the northwest frontier, south of the River Rang. We were a community of shepherds, very poor, for it was wintertime. I would take the sheep up into the meadows to feed on insects incubating in the snow.

"My family's land overlooked the river. It was at the bottom of a steep crevasse, and there were cliffs upon the other side. Occasionally you could see people there, wild tribesmen, antinomials, riding their horses close to the cliff's edge.

"Our priest told us that they were devils out of hell, atheists and heretics. When the river froze, we were always afraid that they would ride across and murder our livestock. We would build huge bonfires in the fields, and our priest would ring the bells all night, but they never came. They never came.

"Stupidity that tries to justify itself, we call it fear. Ignorance that justifies itself, we call it hate. This sounds like foolish insight, but you must understand, in those days it was part of our catechism that every morning upon rising we would recite aloud, at six-fifteen precisely, the forty-second verse of the Song of the Beloved Angkhdt. You know it: 'Listen to me, my love, and to no other. I am the only one. These others tell you lies. They want to use you for your beauty, that is all.'

"Nowadays these lines admit a myriad interpretations, as you know. Then we believed what the priests told us. Later when I came to Charn, I saw the remnants of these tribes. Defeated and starving, they had migrated down into the city, and they were selling their own bodies and begging in the streets. It was a sad sight, for once they had been proud.

"Perhaps you don't remember the antinomials, how they spoke with music, and danced and played music all night long. They are few and scattered now. Then, they were creatures of denial, savage in so many ways. They had no families, no names. They had no interest in such things. As I say, they were primitive in many ways. But it was a willful kind of savagery, as if they had passed through civilization and stepped back. Or stepped forward, who can tell?

"A man can learn something from people who are not like him. In Charn I took them into my house. I fed them, and in return they taught me to love freedom and freethinking. They taught me a man is what he does. They taught me to judge men by their uses, for we must live forever in the present tense, and there is no point in pretending otherwise.

"When people ask me to define God, I say to them, 'God is a creature who lives in the past and in the future, as we live in the present.' That is why we never see Him face to face. That is why He always seems to be receding from in front of us or traveling close behind. That is why sometimes it is as if we are entering a room where He just left, and the scent of Him still lingers."

"Isn't he incredible?" asked Varana, giggling and poking Charity in the ribs. But she quieted down when Freedom Love looked down at her and frowned.

"Now, here in our community," he said, "I have heard something that reminds me of the way we used to be when I was young and we had corralled our sheep into their pens and were waiting for the antinomials to attack across the river. There is a superstition in our town. People are talking about the white-faced woman, as if she were a devil or a witch. Once more, it is foolishness and ignorance. It is hate and fear. . . ."

As he talked, Charity found her attention wandering. She looked around the room. Some of the Dogon were sitting on the floor, scuffling their feet in the dirt, smiling at each other, looking bored. The others listened more attentively.

Like Charity, they were refugees from Charn; they had been rescued from the burial pit, or else had followed Freedom Love of their own will, down into the dark. They were a dirty, ragged lot, thirty-seven men and women, most past their first youth. Charity looked them over with faint stirrings of distaste.

The stranger was standing by the door. As Charity looked at him, he raised his eyebrows, as if to signal his desire to speak with her. But Varana had pushed her in the ribs again, and Freedom Love was asking her a question.

"Well," he said, "now that you have seen us, what do you think? Charity Starbridge, tell me, have you decided? Will you join our poor community? Believe me, we are nothing now, but we will be important in the days to come."

Before replying, Charity detached herself from her companion's arm and moved a few steps forward, so that she stood in a more open space. "You saved my life," she said.

"Then you'll stay."

"No."

A spasm of annoyance passed over the face of Freedom Love; then he was calm again. He motioned to the stranger. "And you? What about you?"

"I think I'll stay," the man responded, staring down at his feet.

"Speak to me," said Freedom Love. "Look at me when you speak to me."

"I think I'll stay," the man repeated, raising his face.

Freedom Love gave him a long, contemptuous look, and then he nodded. "I wish that it were otherwise," he said. "We have many like you; few like her." He glanced at his wristwatch and then shook his wrist. His voice was sulky as he turned away: "You all have duties to attend to, I believe."

Charity avoided Varana in the crowd as the hall emptied out. Once in the street, she walked through to the lake and turned onto the beach, moving swiftly and purposefully, as if there were someplace to go down there. But when she heard the stranger's footsteps behind her in the sand, she turned to face him, furious.

"I'm sorry," he began, but she interrupted him. She said, "You have decided. You have decided what you are."

"What do you mean?"

She made an impatient gesture with her hand. "Tell me you weren't listening," she said. "A man is what he does. Not what he thinks or what he feels. Not a family or a name. Judge men by their uses—weren't you listening? Freedom Love! He may be a liar, but he's not a fool."

"I'm sorry. I don't understand."

Again she made a gesture with her hand. "You're like my brother, the way you apologize. Listen—you're a coward, like my brother. But even he was a hero at the end."

"I want to be like him in all things," said the stranger humbly, looking at his shoes.

Again Charity interrupted, too angry to listen. "When I first met you, I felt sorry for you. Because you had no mind. Because so many things that go towards making up a person had been stolen from you—your face, your memory, your past. Your name. But now I envy you. Don't you understand? You have been given a new chance. So many people, they wake up in the morning cursing God because they haven't changed. They're locked up inside their characters; by the time they're grown, the traits of their personality are like heavy stones, impossible to budge. They're like the bars of a cage. But you are different. That cage is unlocked for you. The memories that made you cowardly and foolish have disappeared. A man is what he does. If you want to be brave now, you can be. You can be loyal to your friends. You are free."

The stranger had been looking at his shoes, but now he turned to her. "Why are you so angry?" he asked.

"Don't you understand?" she said. "It's a long way. It's a long way in the dark."

He gave them warmer clothes. With relief, she moved out into the darkness beyond his lantern, onto the dark beach. She stepped out of the dress she'd been arrested in and put on her new Dogon dress. Over it she put a black cotton jacket, and on her feet new rope-soled shoes. She wadded her old clothes into a ball and handed it to Freedom Love when she went back.

He gave them blankets and flashlights and a bag of food. "It's all that I can spare," he said. "You'll lose weight, but you'll live. It's only eleven days. Look here." He showed them on the map that he had drawn for them. "This way. The second tunnel and then back. It will bring you up just twenty miles from the Caladonian frontier. The way is marked. And there'll be water, too. You cross water here and here."

She folded up the map and put it in the inside pocket of her coat. "Thank you," she said.

"Angkhdt tells us to share everything we have," responded Freedom Love, scratching his lip.

He was standing on the pier holding a lantern. Varana had not come to see them off. But seven people from the town were there, and some of the Dogon too, for Freedom Love had lent them Gudrun Sarkis to ferry them across the lake.

The boat was pulled up on the sand, and the Dogon stood around it, talking. Gudrun Sarkis was already there, looking nervous and unhappy. He was stowing six long fishing spears aboard the boat while his companions spoke to him. Once Charity heard the only word of their language that she had learned: *onandaga. Onan* meant "face," *dag* meant "milk" or "whey," and *a* was the ending for all feminine nouns.

Freedom Love frowned. "They are a superstitious lot," he said. "They think she is some kind of devil. But she is a mortal woman, just like you." He took his wallet from his robe and removed from it a tiny glassine envelope filled with yellow powder. "If you meet her, give her this and she will let you pass," he said. "It is heroin. I have heard she has a . . . partiality."

The stranger was standing with his hands in his pockets. He looked ill and frightened, and in the lantern light the scars stood out all over his pale forehead and his cheeks. The hair grew in patches on his jaw, a result of the uneven skin grafts there. The Dogon brewed a stuff called raxshi, and he smelled as if he had been drinking it. "I try to emulate your brother in all things," he had said when she asked him.

He bent down to wash his face in the lakewater. Gudrun Sarkis stepped into the boat. He was setting lanterns fore and aft, in metal brackets atop poles. The townsfolk had all moved away except for Freedom Love and the Dogon, who were waiting for his signal to push the boat adrift.

Charity stepped aboard and sat down in the bow. She held her hand out to the stranger, and he followed her and sat down next to her, avoiding her eyes.

On the pier Freedom Love turned around and walked towards the town. He didn't say goodbye, didn't look back as the Dogon pushed the boat along its groove of sand and out into the water. But Gudrun Sarkis raised his paddle in the air, and the people on the shore responded, crying out as if in mourning as he backed water and then swung the boat around.

There were other paddles in the bow. Charity took one and gave the other to the stranger, who held it in his lap. "Like this," she said encouragingly, dipping hers into the water.

"Do I have to?"

"Come on," she said. "I want to get away from here as fast as possible."

"Where are we going?"

"The entrance to the tunnel. I don't know. But Gudrun Sarkis knows. Don't you, Sarkis?"

"*Ma,*" came a coarse voice from the back of the boat.

The stranger tried a few halfhearted strokes and then gave up. "Do I have to?" he whined. "I feel so awful."

Charity smiled. "Come on, don't be lazy. I think you must have been a priest in your past life. Does that sound right? Lord Chrism must have found you in the temple."

Charity stroked steadily. Gradually the shore lights started to recede. "Thank God for that," she said. "I hated that place. Freedom Love! There's no freedom there, and no love either, that I saw."

"He saved our lives."

"For reasons of his own. He wanted converts. I never asked him to interfere."

"Nevertheless, it doesn't change the fact."

Charity burst out laughing. "You *are* a priest. I knew it. Where else would Chrism Demiurge have found you?"

"Believe me, I've considered it," the stranger said. "But aren't there some physical differences? Besides, there would be something left. Some special knowledge, something.

"I seem to know a lot of numbers," he continued after a pause. "I can see them in my mind, big numbers, and they seem to mean something. Sometimes I can see them in my dreams."

"What are they like—your dreams?" asked Charity.

"Unsettling. They are full of people I don't recognize, places I don't remember. But sometimes I know that it's important. How can I tell? I wake up with an empty feeling. I could be dreaming about my father or my mother, my wife or my children, and I'd never know."

From time to time the light from their lanterns would

catch on something overhead, a low part of the roof, a stalactite or a mass of sculpture. They were in a complicated area of currents and crosscurrents. In places the water was as sheer and shiny as black glass. In others it had a stippled texture, and the boat swung back and forth. Charity guessed that the lake had narrowed suddenly. According to the map, the way they were to take rose from above a waterfall, where the river drained out of the lake. Already she could see a hint of shoreline to her left, black against a darker black.

"Tell me," said the stranger. "What was your brother like when he was young?"

"Fat," responded Charity. With her paddle, she cut long strokes in the water, though her arms were beginning to get tired.

"That was all you remember?"

"No. But he was . . . very fat," she said. "I didn't like my brother much when we were children."

"And later?"

A lock of Charity's hair had fallen down over her eye. She pushed it back before she spoke. "He was my only friend. He and my cousin Thanakar. After my marriage, they were my only friends."

"I didn't know you were married."

Before replying, Charity tried to summon up her husband's face out of the darkness ahead of her, without success. Yet she remembered him so well; her mind was full of memory, but the image wouldn't come clear. It was the opposite of the stranger's dreams.

She frowned. It was as if she could remember every feature, but couldn't structure them into a face. "He was a kind old man," she said, and then instantly she saw him in her mind. It was as if the image had been liberated by the words; she remembered a drawing that Thanakar had made, a pencil sketch on the flap of an envelope. It was a caricature, but in her mind, Charity shaved away the excess, until she saw her husband's smiling gray face, his melancholy eyes.

"He was an army officer," she said. "Three times my age—it was the custom in my family. He died on the Serpentine Ridge, fighting the Caladonians. Murdered before the battle, that's what I heard. He was too old to be a soldier."

"You don't sound as if you cared."

"But I did," said Charity, staring ahead. "He was always kind to me. But there was nothing he could do."

"What do you mean?"

Charity shrugged. "Spring is not the season for sentimental marriages. That is something Chrism Demiurge once said. The weather is too harsh. 'Sterility breeds violence,' he said. Besides, the women in my family were like slaves. It was the custom. We were like slaves, except there was no work for us to do. No, it was different—my mother and myself, they treated us like patients. Mental patients. And if our doctors were considerate and kind, what difference could that make?"

She paddled strenuously for a few strokes, and then she stopped. "Of course I cared," she said. "My brother was arrested at just the same time, and my cousin. Two of them are dead, and the third, I don't know. I suppose he is dead, too. But whatever happens, what could be worse than all that waiting? All that waiting to do nothing. I'm glad to be out in the fresh air."

Dubiously the stranger looked around the boat. To his left he saw waves hitting a shelf of rock, making a low, scraping sound. The lamplight shone on a white froth of water, and something gleaming deep beneath the surface. "Did you see your brother when he was in prison?" he asked.

"No. In my own house I was a prisoner as much as he. More than he, for it was not my choice. Yet I escaped—do you understand? That's why I find it hard to forgive him, even now. He didn't have to die. He could have stopped them just by lifting up his hand."

"I don't understand."

"Don't you? Because he chose the luxury of dying in a prison he had made himself, he is a hero and a saint. Other people cling to life—you, me. Don't we deserve some credit? What we do is harder, after all."

"You are jealous," said the stranger.

"No. It's just that I was a victim far too long to value it in other people. A man should stand up for himself, especially him, a Starbridge and a prince of Charn. That's what I tried to tell him at the end."

"So you did see him."

"Yes. One time. Didn't you hear the story? Even I heard it: how a washerwoman broke past the soldiers at the very end, as they took him to his place of martyrdom. She jumped into his truck as they were driving him along the Street of Seven Sins."

The stranger stared at her, astonished. "That was you?"

"That was me."

"I heard the story twenty times," said the stranger. "My guards in prison told it to me. It was a woman of the starving class. She fell at his feet to worship him, and he raised her up and kissed her on both cheeks, and comforted her. And when the soldiers were dragging her away, he said, 'Don't be afraid. Among a hundred thousand, I will know you. And when I see you in the land of Paradise, I will kiss you on the lips.' It is a famous story."

"It is a lie. He was stinking drunk," said Charity. "You could smell the liquor on his breath," she said, tears in her eyes. "He had a mask on his face and silver gauntlets on his hands, and they had put him in a cage. I told him to stand up, to stand up like a man. He had fallen down and was leaning on his side, and I told him to stand up. Because a man has a duty to his family and his friends, and to whoever loves him."

"He was dying. You are very harsh."

"It's not what I said, it's what I thought," continued Charity, tears in her eyes. "It's what I should have said. He was my brother."

"And didn't he say anything at all?"

"There wasn't time before the soldiers threw me out. But yes, he said one thing. He said, 'This is my empty cup.'"

The stranger looked at her, baffled, and she wondered if she wanted to explain to him about the poem and the silver pipes. But before she could make up her mind, she heard a grunt from Gudrun Sarkis; he pulled upon his paddle, and the boat slid in a circle. Simultaneously there came a shout out of the darkness to their left, a challenge and a curse. And then a flare went up, dousing that low shore with silver light. Charity could see a dozen men standing naked and motionless among the rocks. The nearest was not fifty feet away. He was squatting by the water's edge, a flare gun in his hand.

*"Onandaga,"* cried Gudrun Sarkis. Paddling furiously, he swung the boat out into deeper water, pausing only to extinguish the lantern above his head. Charity reached up to do likewise, knocking the wick with the end of her paddle. The stranger was stroking steadily, tiredness forgotten. Though in fact the men on the shore were more eerie than threatening—they stood motionless as the flare settled above them, grazing the cavern ceiling, making massive shadows on the water.

The men were armed with spears and long arrows and short bows, and they made no motion as the boat drew out of range. But the man on the water's edge reloaded his flare gun. He shot it off again as the light glimmered away: a silver bead that seemed to rise so slowly before it shattered on the surface of the dark. The flare gun made no noise, only a soft puff that was lost in the creak of the boat, the slap of the paddles and the stranger's panicked whine.

But as the boat sped away, the man on the shore tilted his hand. He let the muzzle of his gun slip down a few inches, so that the third flare he fired burst not above himself, but above the boat, beyond her bow. It lit up the water for the space of forty yards.

Dead ahead, there was an obstruction in the water. It towered up above the boat, an enormous mass of painted stone carved in the shape of a woman's head. It was half sunk in the water; the lake had risen almost to the woman's eyes. She stared out over its surface, her eyes white and empty. She wore a great stone headdress in her thick stone hair, a crown and diadem in the fashion of the old kings of Charn.

*"Onandaga,"* whispered Gudrun Sarkis as the boat drifted to a halt. Charity took her paddle out of the water. There was no sound anywhere, except water dripping from the paddle blade, and the puff of the flare gun as the man behind them fired again.

This time he lit the water back the way they had come, and revealed five boats drawn up motionless in a line. They were long and very low in the water. Seven men were standing up in each, serene, attenuated figures, dark-skinned, but with their chests and faces painted white. They too were armed with spears.

Noiselessly Sarkis turned the boat towards shore. There, on an outcropping of rock, stood the white-faced woman, black-haired and dressed in black, with an onyx ring through one nostril.

So much blackness only accentuated the sick pallor of her skin, the changing color of her eyes. "Her eyes," croaked Gudrun Sarkis. Throwing down his paddle and snatching up a spear, he bounded to his feet. As quick as thought, he aimed the spear and flung it, but at the very end his throw was spoiled by the force of a single arrow passing through his chest. His arm wavered. The spear clattered on the rocks beside the white-faced woman's foot, and then Gud-run Sarkis fell over backwards into the water without even a cry, as the boat drifted in towards land. Charity stood up, but he had disappeared. Deep below the surface, he left a trail of phosphorescence.

The boat rocked gently in the water. As they drifted in towards shore the stranger hid his face, but Charity was curious. Varana had told her about the white-faced woman's eyes, how they shone in the darkness. It was a lie; as the light faded above her, Charity could see nothing. Then someone lit a torch behind the rocks, a softer, reddish glow, full of soot and smoke. Soon there was a row of moving torches: wadded cotton dipped in kerosene, carried on the end of spears. Holding torches, the men gathered in around the white-faced woman, and by the flickering torchlight Charity could see what Varana had meant.

As the boat drifted up the narrow beach, Charity watched the woman's face and saw her eyes change color. At first she thought it was a trick, a figment of the smoky light, but the woman was not ten feet away as the boat grunted to rest. Charity could see her clearly. Her eyes, which had seemed black at first, took on a reddish tinge, spreading from the pupil. Then they seemed to lighten to a nauseating pink, then lost color altogether. But then flecks of yellow appeared and spread into a pool; her eyes flashed yellow for an instant, until they were polluted by a mist of violet darkening to black—a full circle of unnatural shades.

Her skin was ageless and unlined, her face clear and handsome. Her hair was loose around her shoulders, and she was dressed in a long gown of Starbridge silk, cut low over her breasts. She was tall, with an expression of uncompromising pride upon her face. Standing in a circle of naked warriors, she made a proud and regal figure. But when she stepped down to the beach, Charity noticed that her teeth were badly stained.

The stranger was making a low, stricken whine. But he

stopped abruptly when the white-faced woman spoke. "Where are you going?" she asked, and her voice was soft without being gentle. It was almost a whisper, audible only in the perfect silence, coldly arrogant in its softness, as if it were not even imaginable that anyone could speak while she was speaking. "Where are you going?"

"To Caladon," said Charity.

"To Caladon. No. Your guide mistook the way," whispered the white-faced woman. "It is easy in the dark."

"We mean no harm," said Charity, looking back over the lake. A pale fin broke the surface near where Gudrun Sarkis had disappeared. Beyond, Charity could see the five boats slowly approaching, paddled gently by their crews.

"They were hunting a big fish," whispered the white-faced woman. "They say it lives near here—a very big one. Big as a ten-man boat. I came to watch them."

"We mean no harm," repeated Charity. "Show us the way and let us go. Please. I was told to give you this."

She reached into the pocket of her coat and pulled out the glassine pouch of heroin. When the woman saw it, a yellow stain was spreading in her eyes; she stepped across the beach and plucked it out of Charity's hand. With her fingernail she slit the tape that held it closed. She licked her little finger and scooped some of the powder onto the pad and rubbed it on her gums. "It is second-quality," she said. "Where did you get this?"

She closed the pouch and tucked it underneath her clothes. When Charity didn't answer, she continued: "This is good, but I have heard of better. There is a new medicine, a new kind of vaccine. Have you heard of it? It interrupts the hierarchy of nature. It desanctifies the blood."

"Please let us go," said Charity.

"No. I need this medicine. Come with me." She turned and walked away into the darkness. Her men came down from the rocks to help Charity and the stranger from the boat. They pulled the boat up onto the beach. Then they escorted the two travelers away, down a muddy track among the boulders and over a small creek.

In single file, they passed over an expanse of packed dirt and then entered a narrow tunnel. Countless footsteps had worn a groove in the rock floor, and the ceiling was seared by the fire of countless torches. Above their heads were cracks and fissures in the rock, and Charity could hear the scurrying of rodents and lithe bats, and perhaps even larger animals. When finally they came out into an open cavern, the air above them was full of circling white birds.

At the outskirts of a small town of canvas tents, the white-faced woman waited for them. "You are my guests," she whispered. "Though that may change. Until it does, I will prepare a place for you, with food and water. When you are ready, come to me." Again she turned and walked away, but Charity could see where she was going. The shantytown of tents was built around the base of a small hill, and there was a stone staircase leading to the top. Each step was flanked with urns of burning fire, and Charity could see the white-faced woman passing up between them, followed by two men carrying torches.

At the top of the hill was a stone mausoleum. Charity walked up there some time later, after she and the stranger had sat and rested in a tent, and naked men had brought them bowls of mushrooms. "I won't go," the stranger said. "I'll tell you that right now."

So Charity went alone, and climbed the stone staircase in between the urns of fire. At the top she stood for a while against the parapet, looking down at the lights among the tents, and listening to the shouts of children playing. Then she turned and walked along a wall, a six-foot frieze of carved obsidian depicting the exploits of the eighteenth bishop of Charn. This had been his mausoleum—Charity recognized it from photographs. In some places she recognized the story of the carvings: the bishop receiving the felicitations of the guild of prostitutes; the bishop wrestling with sleep; the bishop at the end of his life, mad and blind, grazing on grass as if he were a pig.

Again the wall was lit with glowing urns. But at the first corner stood a man with a torch, and he bowed solemnly as Charity approached, and motioned her inside a narrow door. She looked up and caught a glimpse of the roof of the cavern, high above her beyond the circling birds, and then she stooped down to enter, for the gate was low. It was just a slit cut into the stone.

Inside, Charity found herself walking through a narrow corridor, barely wider than her shoulders. It was lit with candles set in niches in the wall and decorated from the floor to the ceiling with painted friezes from the visions of Beloved Angkhdt: the constellations of the zodiac as seen from Paradise; the angel with a thousand mouths.

The corridor led her to the burial chamber where the white-faced woman sat waiting for her. A brazier of raked charcoal had filled the air with smoke and with a strange, hot odor that made Charity dizzy. The brazier was set below the bishop's black sarcophagus, next to a marble throne. On the throne sat the white-faced woman. Guardsmen came and went around her, perhaps six men in that small space, and they were tending the fire and bringing lights and vessels from a room farther back.

From a grate over the fire hung strips of some strange substance, and everywhere there was a smell of murdered animals. Charity sagged against the wall and put her hand over her nose. But she could not go back, for there was a man standing in the door behind her, blocking the whole space. "My God," she cried, "you did not bring me here to murder me?"

As she spoke, the white-faced woman was aware of her for the first time. She clapped her hands, and instantly one of the men ran forward and pulled the grate of meat out of the fire. But the smell remained. To steady herself, Charity leaned back against the wall and put her head against the stone. In that moment all her courage left her, and all she could think about was the sunlight far above her head. She had a pain in her heart that felt like hopeless love, and she was very tired.

"Come closer, child," whispered the white-faced woman, and in her voice there was a parody of real concern. "Poor child," she said, smiling softly, but again there was a tone of falseness deep within the words, as if she were trying to reconstruct from memory a gentleness that she no longer felt.

"Poor child," she continued. "Don't be afraid. It is meat from fishes. Dumb, cold, stupid fish—these men have always eaten it. It is what there is." She rose and came towards Charity, smiling. All her men had disappeared except for two, who stood as stiff and quiet as cadavers, on either side of her throne.

"It is against the laws of Angkhdt," said Charity.

"It is what there is. Besides, the laws of Angkhdt are not for you and me. Let me see your hand."

Before Charity could pull away, the woman had seized hold of her right hand and bent her fingers back. Charity could feel the aching coldness even through the woman's gloves. She shuddered and tried to close her fingers. But the woman was too strong. She pulled Charity forward into the torchlight.

"The silver rose," she whispered. "Yes—I knew your mother well. Yes. I held you in my arms when you were first baptized."

Charity shuddered at the thought. The woman, who had been scanning her face with an eager, rapt expression, scowled suddenly. She pulled her lips back to reveal her teeth, and then she turned away, back to her chair. "Come close," she whispered, and Charity took a few steps forward and then stopped.

"I hate the smell," she said.

"You will get used to it. I have."

"I'm surprised their stomachs tolerate it."

"Nonsense, child. Don't be naive. It's what keeps them strong." The woman put her hand out to the guardsman on her left, a tall, muscular figure, dark-skinned and naked, with white paint on his face and genitals.

"We others have become decadent," whispered the white-faced woman. "We have spoiled our strength. But the fire of life burns very hot here, underground."

As she spoke, she was stroking the man's thigh, fingering the muscles down his leg and on his knee. Then she reached up to hold his testicles in her left hand, weighing the sac, stroking the flesh until it came alive. She slid her fingers around the root of his sex and teased it until it stiffened, and then she put her hands around the shaft and squeezed until its veins stood out. "This one is particularly strong," she whispered. "You can have him if you like."

Charity was looking at the man's face. He had not moved, or shifted his position. He was staring straight ahead of him, not even blinking as the woman stroked his penis with her thumb.

"No, thanks," said Charity.

"You come from a family of prudes," whispered the white-faced woman. Then she let go of the man's sex, as if it suddenly disgusted her. When she continued, her voice was wistful and a little sad: "I was a prude myself."

"Who are you?" asked Charity.

"I am the white-faced woman," she answered, her mouth twisted with contempt, whether for Charity or for herself, the princess couldn't tell.

That was all that she would say. When Charity pressed her to speak further, she shook her head. "Those things are finished, gone," she whispered. "I have come so far along another road, I cannot recognize myself."

She had been studying Charity with some curiosity, but now she looked away. Her face was white and still, the only movement the changing color of her eyes, from black to red, from red to yellow. "Do you believe in Paradise?" she asked suddenly.

"I don't know."

"Then you are a fool. But I was more foolish than you. More foolish, and fresher and more beautiful than you will ever be, when I let the priests of Charn take hold of me and fill my body with their drugs. They stole my life from me. Chrism Demiurge! But he will pay."

"Some say Paradise is in the mind," murmured Charity. She was thinking about other things.

"Do they? No one ever said anything like that to me. No. They drew me diagrams of my soul's journey. The exact trajectory, they said, for Paradise was in orbit around Mega Prime. Two hundred million miles, they said; not very long. They told me I would wake up in my father's house. They told me he'd be young and happy, as he was before the accident. They said it would be summer there. Summer all year round, and there was nothing for me here, after my prince was broken from the army. Just my crippled child, and it was not enough. I chose to go. But it was lies."

In Charn before the revolution, some high-ranking men and women had been sent to Paradise prematurely, some in disgrace and some in honor. They had not waited for their natural deaths. Instead their bodies had been put to sleep, their souls set free to start the long cold climb through space. "I was asleep for fifty months," the woman whispered. "I tell you Paradise does not exist, not even in our dreams. They pumped the blood out of my body. They turned me into a monster, and for what? Only they never expected me to wake. How could they have known that I had such a clever doctor . . . in the family?"

"He woke you up," said Charity.

"Yes. He woke me up. Yes. By giving me a hunger that I couldn't bear. He woke me after fifty months of restless dreams, and I fled down here into the darkness, where I fitted like a key into a lock, into these people's monstrous superstitions."

Charity glanced up at the guardsmen, but they hadn't moved. They stood quiet and impassive while the white-faced woman slouched between them, gnawing on her fingers. Then she snarled a few words of an unknown language. Still staring straight ahead, the men fitted their hands over their ears.

"You see?" whispered the white-faced woman. "They are savages." She clapped her hands, and someone appeared in the doorway behind her, a bent old man carrying a silver tray. He came and knelt beside her chair and put the tray down on the step. On it were some stoppered vials, an oil lamp, a hypodermic, and a silver spoon.

Crooning to himself, he shook some powder from a vial into the spoon. The white-faced woman ran her thumb down the inside of her arm. But when the old man put the spoon over the fire, she jumped to her feet. "Come with me," she said. "I want to show you something." And without another word she left the chamber.

# CHRISM DEMIURGE

**6**

**O**n the 50th of October of the eighth phase of spring, in the year 00016, elements of the new people's militia had captured the Temple of Kindness and Repair. But by the time they had penetrated all that way—two miles of court-yards and corridors from Slaver's Gate to the council chambers of the Inner Ear—the council had had opportunity to flee. The bishop's private doctor had administered the sleeping drug to two hundred of the members then in residence, to start them on their flight to Paradise. By the time the soldiers had broken through the chamber doors, it was too late. The members of the council sprawled unconscious in their chairs and could not be revived. Their trials for treason and subsequent executions were a grim affair, for even the most fanatic supporters of the new government could take no joy in executing sleeping men.

At the trial the indictments against Chrism Demiurge, the secretary of the council, ran to forty-seven pages. Offering no defense, he was found guilty of crimes against humanity and was executed in absentia on the 92nd of October. This was a curious spectacle: At noon precisely, various effigies were set alight on scaffolds all over the city, for the government had never managed to procure Lord Chrism's body, though they had hunted for it in the temple for three weeks.

That season, rumors of Lord Chrism's whereabouts were as common as the rain. He had been seen disguised in Beggar's Medicine, in Durbar Square, in Caladon. He had been photographed crossing the southern border, dressed as an old woman. He had escaped into a hidden tower in the temple built entirely of mirrors, invisible to the naked eye.

Other citizens, more practical, swore that he was safely dead, that his body had been so mutilated during his interrogation that there was nothing left to burn. About an equal number claimed that he had risen up to Paradise in a golden car.

It wasn't until the following autumn that two speleologists, working for the University of Charn, proved from dental records the identity of a body they had discovered in the lower town beneath the city's streets. It was the body of an old man. The flesh of his hands had deteriorated, so that his tattoos could not be read, but he was carrying the crystal seal of the council on his forefinger, and a silver chain of office around the bones of his neck.

He was found in an old burial ground, a site important to the tribal history of Charn. By then nothing remained of the old cult of the White-Faced Woman, and the caves and crypts were dark under the city. But at the time we speak of, in the eighth phase of spring, the lower town was full of energy and light and a new species of religion. When Princess Charity Starbridge came out of the mausoleum above Tribal Site Number 471, she stood at the top of the stone stair amazed, for the floor of the cavern was lit to its far recesses with torchlight and with bonfires. On the parapet in front of her, the white-faced woman raised her hand, and from down below them came a roaring and a shouting, the clash of metal and the beat of drums.

Hundreds were gathering to see her, from every corner of the underworld. They surged towards her up the steps, chanting her many names.

"Better to lick cocks in Paradise than reign in hell," muttered the white-faced woman. It was a paraphrase of holy scripture. Nevertheless, she was a queenly figure as she started down the steps: her rich black hair, her eyes, the dead white pallor of her skin. She was supernaturally pale; the blood had been pumped out of her body and replaced with a cold, colorless fluid, a nutrient developed by the bishop's council.

Charity followed her down into the throng. The white-faced woman reached out her hands, and in an instant her people were around her, grasping, touching, plucking, struggling with each other to get near. They were desperate to touch her, to feel the cold miracle of her flesh. For it was not every man or woman, even in those days, who could claim to have touched a god and held her hand. And this was not just any god, but an incarnation of the White-Faced Woman, who had spread her legs for Angkhdt himself. *"Onandaga! Onandaga!"* they shouted, struggling in a mass around her.

At first she accepted them. She held out her hands as if to warm her fingers, and smiled back at Charity through the crowd. But when she reached the end of the stair and stepped out onto open ground, the mob around her grew. Charity lost sight of her among the flailing arms and heads, but could see by the movement of the crowd how she was jerked and pushed from place to place. Then there was a shout and a scream, and the crowd pulled back for an instant, long enough for Charity to see the white-faced woman, disheveled, with her bodice torn and her mouth contorted. She had bitten a young woman who had come too close.

But the tribal people of the caves did not require politeness or good manners from their deities. Proof of inhumanity was enough for them, and after a moment they closed in again. But the white-faced woman pulled a whistle from around her neck, a piece of silver jewelry in the shape of the penis of Beloved Angkhdt, and she put her lips to it and blew a note so high and pure that Charity could hear it in her bones and in her teeth. Instantly members of the woman's bodyguard, who had been standing idle on the edges of the crowd, cut through it to the center, cleaving their way with sticks of scented ebony. The mass of people broke apart, and some were battered to their knees. The White-Faced Woman stood in the middle, with her men ringed around her.

She looked back towards Charity and gestured for her to come closer. "Follow me," she said, as if nothing had happened. "I've got something to show you," she said. She turned as if to walk away. But then she hesitated, because a woman was kneeling in her path, a mother who had brought her child to receive the blessing of the god. Charity saw the White-Faced Woman stoop, and with a gesture that was almost careful, she brushed the hair back from the child's head and rearranged his blanket.

"I wanted him," whispered the white-faced woman. "So I found him. Two miles from here, on Bishop's Keys, there is a stair that rises to the temple. When I was a child, my mother used to visit my great-uncle, who was in the council: a long, long, spiral stair. It comes out in his bedroom. So I climbed up. I had just been wakened, and I was full of strength. But more than that—it was my hatred. My hatred made it easy to find him. Easy to drag him back; I waited for him in his bedroom. He is an old, blind man. You'll see.

I dragged him by his head, but carefully. He must not die. Not yet."

They were on a long, curving beach next to a pond. With them walked a single naked guardsman carrying a torch. The rest had stayed back to keep the townspeople from following. Looking back, Charity could see a knot of torches at the isthmus where the two ends of the pond curved back together. A small island was joined to the mainland at that point. It was a sandy, dirty place, covered with low dunes and coarse, white, noctiferous grass, perhaps half a mile from the mausoleum. The water had a strong mineral smell, for it was brackish and stagnant, with no outlet to the river.

"It's not his fault," said Charity.

"It is his fault. How can you say that it is not? He is the father of the lie that robbed me of my life."

"Some lies have no father," murmured Charity.

"No. But I was rich and proud, and he was jealous. He promised me that he would send my soul to Paradise. Instead he poisoned me with his foul drugs."

They came up over a low hill of sand. On the other side stood a row of ancient tombs in various stages of dilapidation. Some were half-buried in the sand—small stone structures with elaborate roofs. Stone columns supported the four corners, thin and delicate, and between them stood curtains of carved stone.

Most of the tombs were empty and abandoned. But here and there a light shone from the doorways, or through the holes in the stone curtains. "These are my prisoners," whispered the white-faced woman. "People who have come upon me in the dark."

In an open circle in the center of the tombs, there stood a shallow, artificial pool, still full of water. Charity bent to wash her hands. She watched the torchlight on the surface of the water. From where she was, the place resembled a small town. The light from the occupied tombs seemed sleepy and inviting: little oil lamps placed on the steps or behind the curtain walls, so that shadows from the delicate stone tracery were cast out upon the sand, patterns of flowers or fighting beasts.

Guards sat in the open doorways, conversing in low tones. They called out greetings to the white-faced woman, their voices friendly and relaxed. And there was music too, a low, melodic, coughing sound.

"What's that?" asked Charity.

"It is peculiar, is it not? I find it soothing. But he hates it. He puts his hands over his ears. Therefore I encourage her to play."

The white-faced woman had turned her head towards the sound, and Charity watched her eyes change from black to red. "Not that she needs encouraging," continued the woman. "She plays without stopping. But I have put them in together. It hurts him. You'll see."

Charity reached down to skim her fingers over the surface of the pool, scattering the reflection of the lamps. Then she rose and walked up the pathway towards one central tomb, following the music. Two guardsmen were sitting on the steps, boiling potatoes over a pot of coals. They stood up to salute as Charity passed, their fists over their hearts. The white-faced woman was coming up the steps behind her.

The music came from just inside the door. Shackled to the wall, the antinomial sat cross-legged. Light from a single candle illuminated her worn face and ragged clothes, and glinted on her flute. She had contrived to break a row of holes into a length of copper tube. It was a coarse and rasping instrument. Whole sequences of notes were missing, but it didn't matter. As always, she was using music as a way of talking; this music was like food in a broken pot. The song, the song itself was the important thing, and each coarse note was so specific, they were like words in a language Charity almost knew.

"Why do you keep her here?" asked Charity. "She means no harm."

"No harm?" whispered the white-faced woman, behind her in the doorway. "She killed two of my soldiers. Besides, look there."

She motioned with her arm. In the far corner of the tomb, in a tangle of red robes, Lord Chrism Demiurge lay on his side. His hands were clamped over his ears and he was talking to himself, reciting verses from the Song of Angkhdt. "Unclean," he moaned. "Unclean. 'By the freshness of my body you will know me. Nor am I corrupted in my heart of hearts.'"

The tomb stank of excrement and filth. But inside it was still beautiful, the marble floor inlaid with lapis lazuli, the ornate walls. Chrism Demiurge lay chained to a screen of carved marble, an intersecting pattern of triangles and squares. From time to time he banged his head against the floor.

"The shock has been too much for him," conceded the white-faced woman. "He thinks he is in hell." She squatted down and took his arm in her cold fingers, and pulled him upright so that Charity could see his shriveled features.

Charity had not seen him since the night of an official reception when she was a little girl. Even then he'd been an old man with an old, fleshless face, and she had been afraid of his blind eyes, his quiet voice. Now he looked so frail; she could see the blood vessels underneath his skin, and underneath them she could see the bones of his skull, brittle and sharp-edged. Of his authority and pride, no residue remained. He shrank from the woman's touch, fumbling and muttering and making the sign of the unclean.

Behind them the antinomial had stopped her music, and they could hear her harsh, even breath. "How long has he been like this?" asked Charity.

The white-faced woman shrugged. "My people have no

words to measure time. Days, hours, weeks—some words are useless in the dark."

Lord Chrism pulled himself away. His eyes seemed huge in his dead face; staring and luminous, they moved wildly around the chamber. "'I make no excuse, she was a monster,'" he quoted. "'I make no excuse; a hundred men could not have filled the cistern of her cunt.'"

"He has lost his mind," whispered the white-faced woman. "He thinks he is in hell."

"What is your plan for him?" asked Charity.

"I have no plan. No. One time it would have made me happy to cut out his heart for what he did to me and to my family. Instead I feed him nothing but the raw flesh of fishes, but he will not eat it. I took him down to see if I could force him to profane the statue of Beloved Angkhdt, but he would not. I tried to force him to defecate onto the altar, but he would not. He just lies here in this place, reciting poetry. No. You understand—I want him to die. Die and be damned. But when I was a little girl, my mother told me that every Starbridge, no matter what his sins, rose up to Paradise when he was dead. It is our birthright. It is in our blood. You understand—I don't want it to happen. Not to him."

Charity looked back towards the antinomial. She had not moved; she was sitting cross-legged, and with a piece of wire she was rasping out the embrasure of her flute, enlarging it, changing its shape. Her yellow eyes were slitted down to nothing, and she was breathing heavily.

"So he is still alive," whispered the white-faced woman. "He is still alive. But I have heard of a new drug. The desanctification drug—it takes away that Starbridge privilege. It pollutes the blood. So I have sent men up into the light to scrounge for it. When they come back, then we will see."

The antinomial opened her eyes. She stared at Charity, but there was no flicker of interest or recognition in her face. But she was caressing her copper flute and scratching out one of the holes with a bit of wire. Then she stopped, and looked up behind Charity to the wall, with a gaze so pointed and direct that Charity followed it. There, hanging from a hook, was a ring of keys.

Lord Chrism Demiurge had dozed off for a little while, but now he started awake. "'She had no heart,'" he quoted groggily. "'Her skin was cold, her breasts were cold, and her face was white as milk.'" Then slowly, sleepily, he put his hands over his ears again, for behind him the antinomial had started to play again, a whisper of low notes.

"I think if we went now, she would not hinder us. I think she is already bored of us. Bored and repelled, because I remind her of the way she used to be. She feeds herself upon a diet of revenge, and now she knows I am no use to her."

The stranger frowned. "How do you know? How do you know what she is thinking?"

"Since last night she's put no guards on us," said Charity. "What can that mean but we are free to go? Look," she said, "here's where we are. The entrance of the tunnel is northwest of here, no more than seven miles overland."

"And from there?"

"I don't know. It's not marked—perhaps a hundred miles to the border. But we can get outside the city limits, that's the most important thing. Perhaps then we can go up."

She was sitting in a tent in the shantytown below the mausoleum, with the map that Freedom Love had given her spread out on her knees. "We could go up here," she said. "And here, by this waterfall, if the way has not been blocked."

The stranger stood beside her. Light from a candle gleamed upon his face, softening his lost, puzzled expression. At such moments, his resemblance to her brother seemed uncanny. His fat lips were trembling, and his reconstructed chin. He held in his right hand, as he so often did,

Prince Abu's letter. It had become his talisman. Often before he slept he would whisper its injunctions: "How can our hearts be dirty if our hands are clean?"

He had folded the letter into a square. Now he pressed the greasy paper to his forehead. "Caladon," he said. "What's Caladon to you? To me it's just a word."

When Charity said nothing, he went on. "What did that man say? Freedom Love. 'We live forever in the present tense'—that's how it is for me. In these dark caves the world does not exist, except the one place where your lantern hits, the one place where you are."

He took the prince's letter down and started to unfold it. "You understand," he said, "I'm following you. I have no past; it's hard for me to have faith in my future. Just where the lantern hits: here. 'Get in touch with Thanakar. He is gone to Caladon. You should join him there.'"

He sighed, then raised his head to look at her. "It's not much," he said. "Who is Thanakar?"

She dropped her eyes back to the map. The way to Caladon was marked in red. "He was my friend," she said. "He was my brother's friend, and mine as well."

"Was he your lover?"

Charity shrugged. The question brought back Thanakar so vividly, standing with her on the balcony, their elbows almost touching. She remembered his high forehead and long nose. "Yes," she said, and then she shook her head. "What's love? Besides, he may be dead."

With her forefinger she touched the name of Caladon upon the map. "His memory serves a purpose, that is all," she said. "Like you, I have no vision of the future. Caladon, I've never been there. I can't picture it. So instead, I picture him, his face, his hands. Because I need a goal. Something to climb towards. Otherwise I'd stop. Otherwise I'd stop and die."

"There, you see," he said. "It's memory that makes a picture in the mind."

The tent was large, smelling of fish and littered with the detritus of the family they had displaced: baskets full of wood and rags and coal and bones. A child came to stare at them from time to time through the open doorway, small, serious, potbellied, with long hair and a greasy nose. He was clutching a small wagon carved from bone.

The stranger made a face, and the child disappeared. "I need my memory to survive," he said.

When Charity had told him about Chrism Demiurge, he had said nothing. Now with patient fingers he refolded the prince's letter and put it in his pocket near his heart.

"He won't tell you anything," she said. "He's lost his mind. I'm sure that he won't recognize you."

"I've got to try," answered the stranger.

"You're better off not knowing. Aren't you afraid to know?"

"I've got to try."

So later, when they left, instead of heading north along the road to Caladon, they wandered west beyond the mausoleum, back towards the prisoners and the pool. "There are guards," said Charity.

"I'll show them my tattoo."

They had thought to choose the time when there were fewest people in the streets. But there was always someone. Old women sat cross-legged in the dust, sewing strips of plastic into sheets, while men played betting games with pebbles and the vertebrae of fish. When finally they left, with their packs on their backs, a crippled child followed them along the water's edge. He followed them along the beach. But when they wandered up over the dunes, he let them go and squatted down in the wet sand.

From the top of the dune, they could see the lights around Lord Chrism's tomb. "It's no good," said Charity. "Look at them all." The paths and steps were lined with oil lamps, and the pool presented a flat circle of reflected light. It was ringed with torches, and there must have been three dozen tribesmen sitting around it in the dust. They were racing boats over the surface of the water, tiny canoes rigged with tiny sails. By blowing through long, metal pipes, they made an artificial wind.

Others sat in clusters on the steps, spears in their hands, and some even carried rifles. But the stranger was undaunted. "That's the one," said Charity, pointing to the largest tomb, and then she followed him as he walked straight ahead under the lights. And as the guards called out their challenges, he lifted up his hand, displaying the symbol of the golden sun crudely cut into his palm, the counterfeit tattoo of Abu Starbridge.

To Charity's surprise, the symbol seemed to mean something even there, so far from the sun. The guardsmen stood apart to let the stranger pass, and they knocked their fists against their hearts. Charity followed the stranger as he marched up the steps, and she stood on the top step looking back. Behind them, the tribesmen had returned to their game, though one or two looked after them with open mouths. The air over the pond smelled flat and stale and full of salt.

Charity turned to go inside. Near the door the antinomial lay back against the wall, her eyes slitted down, her flute held loosely in her lap. In the far corner the stranger knelt over Lord Chrism Demiurge, rousing him from sleep. The old man had a gash on his left eye. The blood had dried to a black powder, which had streaked his face and stiffened in his hair. And when he turned his head, Charity could see that he was wounded in the eye itself. Blood had leaked into his eye, extinguishing the fire that had always glowed there.

"'I dreamed that I had died in my own house,'" he quoted, his voice desperate and shrill. "'And in my dream there was a darkness rising up around my bed, around my cup and chair, my book and bottle and the faces of my friends . . .'"

"Hush now," the stranger interrupted. "Quiet now. B-be quiet. I mean no harm. Only there is something you must tell me."

"No harm?" cried the old man. "'I was alone. And in my dream the darkness was as cold as space, and I came down onto a world of darkness, breaking like a star. And like a star I squandered all my strength and all my light, until I was alone in that dark world.'"

"Hush now," said the stranger. "Quiet, please, and look at me. Touch my face and listen to my voice. It is not so long since you last heard it, in my cell in Wanhope Hospital. You were there when my bandages were taken off."

For a moment it seemed that he had caught the old man's attention. Lord Chrism put his fingers out and touched the stranger's face. He was mumbling deep in his throat; he coughed and swallowed, and the words came clear. "'Dark streets,'" he said. "'Dark houses. I came down onto an endless plain. Oh my beloved, how could you have left me, when the world without you has no rest or comfort, and the darkness burns like fire?'"

"Be quiet." The stranger grabbed Lord Chrism by the jaw and slid his hand over the old man's mouth. In the doorway Charity had pulled the ring of keys down from the wall and stooped to unlock the chains around the antinomial. The woman had not moved, but her eyes were open.

Charity broke the padlock apart, but the woman wasn't even watching her. She was staring at the old man, so Charity looked back to see the blood pulsing in his temples as the stranger squeezed his mouth. She saw his eyes stretched wide in fright. "Stop," she said.

But the stranger wasn't listening. He was shaking the old man's head from side to side, but when he spoke, his voice was soft and level. "Think," he said. "Just think. I am the double of Prince Abu Starbridge. But I was someone else before. I had a name, a life, a home. Perhaps a family."

He released his hand over the old man's mouth. Demiurge stared up at him with his blind eyes. "'Sweet God,'" he said. "'Make for me a Paradise in all the darkest places of my heart. Make it shine like sunlight, like the early morning sun . . .'" But then he stopped, his voice shaken from his mouth, for the stranger was slapping him across the face and battering his face against the wall. "Stop, you'll kill him," cried out Charity. But it was too late. The old man's eyes stared wildly for a moment, and then his pupils drifted up into his lids. Charity knelt down and pulled the stranger's hand away, but Lord Chrism could no longer be revived. A spasm shook his body, and then his head fell to one side.

The stranger let the corpse sink to the floor. Charity turned away. She looked up towards the stranger's face. He was trembling with frustration, but his eyes were full of tears. She put her hand upon his wrist. "Never mind," she said. "Never mind. It was a mercy," even though she knew that that was not the reason for his tears. But she hadn't time to think of any other consolation. She heard a hiss of anger from the open doorway, a cold, angry whisper, and she looked back and saw the white-faced woman standing there. She did not speak. Only she gave that same wordless hiss, and then she started forward.

The stranger stumbled to his feet. He shrank back flat against the wall, trembling and full of fear, his arms stretched out. In one hand he held a piece of rock that he had snatched up from the floor. But when the white-faced woman grabbed him by his collar and his shirt, he let it drop. She pulled him up, away from the wall into the center of the chamber; he was weak in the knees, but she supported him, and shook him by the front of his shirt. She bent her face to his and bit him on the cheek, and on the shoulder, and then she pulled open his shirt and bit him deep and hard over his heart.

Then she raised her head. She was supporting the stranger with her hands under his armpits, standing with her back to the door, so that she never saw the antinomial at all.

But Charity saw her. Charity watched her getting to her feet, stiffly at first, rubbing her knees. Charity watched her straighten up, until she stood erect behind the white-faced woman.

She was holding her copper flute in both hands above her head. Charity scrambled up and grabbed hold of the stranger from behind, just as the antinomial brought her flute down on the back of the woman's head, a single, massive stroke. For an instant Charity was aware of the woman's face next to her own, her cold breath, her lips, her eyes changing from pink to yellow. Then she went down, without noise or protest, and lay crumpled on the floor.

"Now," said the antinomial. She stood at the doorway looking out, and in one hand she held her copper flute. Charity had her arms around the stranger, but soon he found his feet. He stumbled over the two bodies on the floor, his hands clutched to his breast. He was whimpering and there was spit in the corner of his mouth.

Outside, the tribesmen stood around the tomb. They stood in a semicircle, three or four men deep, the torchlight shining on their painted faces. But still they showed no symptoms of alarm, even when they saw the antinomial kick over the oil lamp inside the door.

She kicked over the lamp, and a puddle of oil started to spread across the stone mosaic of the floor. Weak blue flames rustled on its surface, making a sound like the beating of a pigeon's wing. The antinomial stepped into the middle of it, and the fire burst around her foot, changing color as it rose. "Now," she said again, and she stalked out of the door and down the steps.

The stranger clutched his hand over his heart. His breath was wheezing and rattling, and there was a scum of foam over his lips. But Charity pushed him forward, and she took his other hand and raised it up, so that the tribesmen could see her brother's symbol on the stranger's palm, the tattoo of the sun. They didn't care, they weren't paying attention.

They moved apart and let the travelers push through their ranks. They were standing up straight with their weapons in their hands, watching the tomb, and some had tense, puzzled expressions, and some were weaving and chanting and clapping their hands, and swaying with a kind of rapture. But it wasn't until she had reached the dunes that Charity looked back and saw the reason. By then the flames were showing through the doorway and the geometric screens, and the crowd was wailing and moaning, because the white-faced woman was standing on the steps, her gown on fire and her hair ablaze.

All around her, her people had sunk down to their knees. They had cast away their weapons, and they were wailing and rubbing sand into their hair, while their god burned like a candle on the steps. And as Charity watched, the white-faced woman pulled a whistle from her bosom and blew a shrill, high, noiseless blast that thrilled in Charity's ears and hurt her teeth.

At the sound the stranger bent double, heaving and vomiting. The antinomial had disappeared into the darkness. Charity had not seen her go. She had one arm around the stranger's waist as he vomited and coughed. When he could walk, she pulled him to his feet and led him forward, up over the rim of sand. Behind them the tombs were lost from sight, and lost, too, was the light from the torches and the fire. In front of them, to the left, a single torch was burning at the water's edge, stuck at an angle in the sand. Beyond it, half a mile away, lanterns shone on the slopes of the eighteenth bishop's mausoleum, and in the town beneath it.

Charity fished a flashlight from her pack and set off down the back of the small slope. The stranger had his arm over her shoulders; he was walking, but she supported much of his weight. His legs were uncertain, and he was trembling. His face was dripping with sweat. "Cold," he said. "So cold." He clamped his hand over his heart.

And those were his last words until he died. Charity gripped him underneath his armpit and led him away from the lights, north out of the great caverns where the blind birds flew, and into the old catacombs again. She was following the map, and from time to time she had to stop and rest and study her map in the circle of her lamp, while the stranger collapsed into the dust and hugged his knees. She talked to him to keep her spirits up, showing him the map and asking his advice, although he could not speak.

But after many hours she found the way. Six miles from the mausoleum, in a tangle of small corridors, she lowered the stranger down next to some boulders and shined her flashlight around the entrance of a narrow tunnel, decorated on one side with the head of a wild pig crudely daubed in red. She pushed her hair back from her face. She shook the flashlight once; it was failing, and there were no batteries. The stranger had left them in his pack, near the corpse of Chrism Demiurge.

"Cold," he said. "So cold." He was lying on his side. His teeth were chattering, and there was sweat over his lip. His hands and legs were shaking, but he quieted down when Charity turned him over and wrapped him in a blanket. She took a jar of water from her pack and tried to make him drink, but his jaw was trembling and his teeth locked shut. So instead she washed his face and talked to him and reached down into his shirt to touch his breast. She brought the flashlight down to try to find his wound, and rubbed his flesh over the mark of the white-faced woman's teeth. He groaned and pulled away: The skin there was unbroken, but it had a bloodless, yellow look, and it was very cold. Her fingers left a mottled mark, which faded as she watched.

But in a while he was quieter. He stopped shivering and accepted water and a few morsels of food. Charity sat back against the boulder, saying nothing, only shining the flashlight down the corridor where they had come, shining it along the rows of graves, the great stone sepulchers and metal statues of Beloved Angkhdt, and angels with their scaly wings.

In time the flashlight failed. Then she sat in the dark. The stranger was unconscious, lying curled against her, and she was holding his hand. She was rubbing it between the two of hers, but in time she must have fallen asleep. When she woke, his hand was stiff and cold, and it was hard to pry her fingers loose. She had some matches in a box; she lit one and looked at his face. His eyes were closed, and he was smiling. "Good night," she said as the match burned out, and then she settled back against the rock. She ate some food. Then she must have slept again, for by the time she heard the music of the copper flute, it was already very close.

# JENNY
# PENTECOST

**7**

"**H**ear me," said the antinomial. She blew a few notes, paused, and then added two more.

Charity lay back and stared up at the roof of the tunnel, unseen in the darkness. "Snow," she said.

"Snow. Now." The tune was complicated this time. The snow was part of it, but there was something else, a variation.

"Mountain in the snow," said Charity.

"No. See rock. Big rock, black, red. Wet. Hear me. This is mountain." She played almost the same tune again, but louder this time, in a different key, an octave or so higher. "Rock is mountain-small," she said. "Sharp, flat. Red, black. Gray. No wind. Snow. Hear me." She blew a few soft notes.

"Yes," said Charity. "A snowfall. Very light."

"Snow," agreed the woman. "Just few. Five. Six. Seven. All. Clouds now. Clouds. Now falling." She played the snow song again, simply, almost clumsily. "Hear me. Nothing there. Snow. No and. Deep one. In. Out. In. Feet. Hear now: wind."

Charity lay back. She had cleared the sharp stones from an area big enough for her own body. She was comfortable, wrapped in the blanket that she had taken from the stranger. She was finishing her seventh meal since she left his body, a few squares of artificial food, the gift of Freedom Love, but welcome after all.

The antinomial had lit a fire. At intervals the roof of the tunnel was supported by a row of wooden posts. Out of a row of six, she had kicked one down and broken it apart and lit a tiny fire out of the splinters. She sat cross-legged next to it, and from time to time she took her flute from her mouth to warm her hands. The fire cast no light.

"Now," she said. Charity was using her thumbnail to clean her teeth, but she stopped so that she could listen. "This is never-know," said the antinomial. She smiled. She grinned, and then she played for about two minutes, a bitter, complicated melody in many different parts.

Charity lay back and cleaned her teeth. "I don't know," she said at last. "I don't understand."

"No. This and this." The antinomial blew the mountain theme again, so that Charity could see how it fit in.

"Think," continued the woman when Charity said nothing. "Think here, not here." The woman touched her eyes and then her mouth. "Knowing world, be world up there River Rang, and I child." She played a few notes more and then relented. "For you is never-know," she said. "This is my song. My song. No name. Hear me: broken mountain. Sun, snow red. Cold in finger and this foot. Hunger after nothing food, when I so child and free. I free."

"That sounds like a sad song," said Charity.

"No sad. Never, and I free." She played a few notes of the freedom song.

The voice of the antinomial was slow and coarse, her

words badly pronounced and hard to understand. But over the days of their journey she told Charity a story. Words were all she had at first, and at first it was hard for Charity to listen. But in time the music made a part of it, and then a larger part. Charity was greedy for the music. She suspected that she would never, ever get down deeper than the first few layers of meaning, even if she listened her whole life. But in time she could recognize the simple melodies and even a few variations. In time she could lie down and close her eyes and listen to the music making pictures in her head.

"Snow," grunted the antinomial. "Hard snow. Rock. Wet rock. Wet rock and me child." She was patient. After they had eaten, after they had slept, they walked for miles through the tunnels. The antinomial carried the pack. Charity walked in front. In one hand she held her map, and in the other the torch that the antinomial had seized from Freedom Love and managed somehow to retain—a small, intense light. It skewered rocks and boulders with a narrow beam.

They walked for miles in the dark. "Rat," grunted the antinomial. "Rabbit." And then she whistled the bare music for the word, the barest sketch. She was strong and tireless. Even at the end of a long march, she could whistle for a whole minute without drawing breath. "Ice," she said. "Black ice. Black ice, smooth." And sometimes she would sing a wordless song in her coarse voice, to illustrate the difference between words.

The torch punctured the darkness. Sometimes the air was bad. In time Charity's eyes would tire, and she would find a place to camp, to stretch out her blanket and sit on it, and portion out their food and water while the antinomial scrounged for wood and struck sparks out of the rocks. Then Charity would lie back and try to recapture the music in her mind, so that when the antinomial sat down and took her flute and rubbed it in her hands and put it to her mouth, the sound would mix with the music that was there already in the dark.

At first the sound was tentative, then overwhelming. Charity lay back and closed her eyes. She let the pictures come. After a while she no longer wondered whether they were accurate, because her head was full of them and she would never know. In her mind she pulled apart a skein of tangled images and let a world grow out of the space between them: snow. Wet rock and mountains. An empty town clasped in the fist of the high mountains, and horses slipping on the black ice, and the dogs barking and fighting over bones, and the red sun shining, and a little girl stamping with the snow around her shins, her hair wild and tangled, a flute stuck in her belt.

Jenny Pentecost woke up. For a while she lay without moving, staring at a stain in the wallpaper above her head. There was a beast in the jungle, and its head was darkened and deformed. Below, a bird had ripped its wings.

The stain had frightened her, her first night in that room. Now, after ten nights, she was used to it. The room seemed similar to others. The doctor always chose the same type of hotel—expensive, gone to seed.

The room had been luxurious once. It was large, with casement windows and a stone floor. The wallpaper was rich and richly colored, a pattern of animals and trees that never once repeated. But all the furniture was gone; the room was empty, except for the ornate wooden bed, a table, and a wicker chair.

In one corner of the room a drain was set into the floor, and next to it a fat clay jug. This was the Caladonian custom. In the early morning a chambermaid would bring a jar of steaming water and clean towels.

In the room the air was cold, and the floor was very cold. Nevertheless Jenny shrugged her nightdress from her narrow shoulders and got out of bed. She walked on the sides of her feet with her toes screwed up, and when she reached the jar, she stood on one of the towels, to one side.

She was carrying a mirror in her hand. She stood naked on the towel, her shoulders hunched, her belly sticking out. For a minute before washing, she examined her small body in the glass. The mirror was not large enough to show her more than one part at a time, and she held it very close. As a result, there was no coherence to the images. Fascinated and detached, she stared at her knee, her buttock, her still-hairless sex.

She had a scab on her right hip where she had fallen down and scraped herself the week before. She examined it carefully, tilting the mirror by its silver handle to reveal a small circle of red skin with the scab in the middle of it.

She brought the mirror to her face and stared solemnly at her left eye. Below it, a dingy, mottled mark spread to the mirror's edge, a birthmark on her cheek. In Charn it had been a sign of God's displeasure, God's thumbprint in her mother's womb, where God had touched her and rejected her. People who had seen her, even relatives, had mumbled prayers and made small gestures with their hands. Every morning her mother had painted over the mark with grease and cosmetic powder. Jenny had never gone outside, for fear of the police.

But the police had come. Her parents were both dead. She touched the birthmark with her thumb. Strange that people could be killed for such a thing—in Caladon she could wash her face and keep it washed and no one seemed to notice. People avoided her for other reasons.

In Charn her jailers had sold her to a shrine operated by the guild of prostitutes. On the top floor of one of their hotels they had built a shrine, sacred to Angkhdt the God of Children. There she had lived for many weeks, until Thanakar Starbridge had found her and taken her away. It had been a violent and painful time. Still her stomach rose when she smelled incense, and still her legs were weak from so much kneeling, so much squatting in the dark. The prostitutes had bound her feet, to please certain customers.

Now all that was over. Now chambermaids brought fresh hot water every morning to her room. It was no use. Some stains never could come clean. When she was a little girl, her mother had bathed her cheek every morning with patent remedies and solvents.

Jenny turned the mirror in her hand. Her hair was very fine. Under it she could see the contours of her head, bloated behind her ear with dreams and too much sleep. What was it? She had dreamed of tunnels underground, an empty labyrinth of tombs.

On her desk by the window lay the drawing she'd been working on before she went to sleep. She could see it from where she stood, a drawing of a human head, with the bone cut away to reveal a cross-section of the brain. In her drawing the brain was a full of caves and paths and corridors, and rows of little cells. Perhaps, she thought, a memory could be imprisoned in the brain, locked up like a murderer inside a cell, perhaps forever, perhaps not. Perhaps events and thoughts could be imprisoned in the past.

Jenny put down the mirror and picked up a clay dipper from the floor. She ran a dipperful of water through her hair and rubbed it dry. Then, before she was even dressed, she went over to the table. Shivering, wrapped in a towel, she turned the papers over. She was looking for a drawing she had made two days before, and when she found it, she took it over to the window, to see it in the light. It was the picture of two women in a cave. They were crossing a bridge over a small crevasse. In the foreground a precipice of stone led down to a pool of water, the terminus of a small stream that was boiling and rushing down the center of the page. The women and the bridge were in the background, almost lost among the carefully drawn rocks. Their faces were invisible, covered up in darkness.

\* \* \*

Fire was important to the antinomial, more than food or safety. She pulled a wooden post out of the wall, dislodging stones and pebbles from the vault above them. When Charity shouted at her to stop, she seemed angry. She took the princess by the shoulder and threw her down against the wall, but then she laughed. "Barbarian," she said. "Barbarian. You can not know. You can not think." And later, when she played her flute, the music was incomprehensible to Charity. It was full of a subsidiary tone, the song of some emotion. Through it Charity detected snatches of the melodies that she already knew—horse and mountain, snow and wind. But they were distorted by this other music. Finally, in a storm of desperate playing, all the other images were covered up and lost, and the antinomial cried out and threw her flute against the wall. "Hungry," she cried. "Now. What are you?"

Every time when they had stopped, Charity had portioned out some of her small store of food, plastic rice cakes, sugar pills, and aspirin. The woman had accepted water but had spurned the rest. "Food for pigs," she had said. Now she reached out her hand towards the four transparent squares that Charity had put out on a level rock. She picked one up between her finger and her thumb. She closed her eyes and placed it in her mouth and chewed on it for a while before she spat it out. She spat it out and made a face. "Aah," she cried. "Biter, biting. No." And then she jumped up to her feet. "I," she cried. "But I."

Lying against the tunnel wall, wrapped in her blanket, Charity groped in the dust and found a sharp-edged piece of rock. Antinomials ate meat, it was well known. Occasionally in the darkness they had heard the scurry of a rodent or a bat. Once while playing, the woman had put up her flute. Holding it poised, her fingers still over the holes, she had turned her head to listen to the noise of something moving outside the circle of the fire. "I smell life," she had said.

This time the woman snatched her flashlight from the

floor and ran away into the dark. Charity sat up with the fire for a while, and then she fell asleep.

In time she became familiar with the many songs of wanting, the hunger songs that were the heart of antinomial life. And in time she put together the woman's story, words and music.

"This love not mine," the woman said. "This place. Brother, no, nor sister. Oh my sister, when I am so child. So child in River Rang, river and I small. No more. Now black so hard, in this hard stone is dark."

"This is," she said once, sitting near the fire, relaxed, almost coherent. "River running, in my mind. Now is. Now. Right now. Ice on the water, and the red rock cliff."

Sometimes her words almost made sense. "Water," she said, and then she blew a melody that Charity had come to recognize: the name song of the River Rang, the only name the woman knew. There the antinomials had lived, far to the north and west of Charn. A cult of atheists and revolutionaries had fled up there into a wilderness of mountains. They had no law, no faith, no love, no learning. In the end they were sustained by pride alone.

And as the webs of culture and tradition loosened and let go, whole families of concepts had disappeared out of their language. Single words had become isolated. Ideas receded from each other, farther and farther, as all the ways of joining them were lost. But because the mind is devious, and because there are ideals that never, ever can be reached, a new language had grown up to reinforce the old. It was a language not of words but of music, of melody and tone. It was a way of making language personal, so that every antinomial could speak a different one, yet still could understand each other. Words remained, simple nouns and verbs, each one suspended in a web of music.

For generations they had lived alone, harsh and isolated lives, hunting in the snow. But in the first weeks of spring, the thirty-first bishop of Charn had sent an army. When

Charity was a little girl, the soldiers had crossed the river by the Anzas Bridge, and they had burned the towns and villages, and erected rows of gallows on the hilltops. The survivors they had dragged to Charn in chains, and some were locked away up on the Mountain of Redemption, and some escaped into the city's slums. There they had joined with others who had come south by themselves, and they had lived together, persecuted and despised, eating garbage, pigeons, rats, mixing with adventists, flagellants, Brothers of Unrest, playing their music in abandoned warehouses next to the abandoned docks. Many had been born there, halfbreeds of various kinds. But there were others who were old enough to remember; Charity's companion was gray-haired, and her face was seamed and scarred. When the soldiers crossed the bridge, she had been almost grown. Fiercely, with great bitterness, she played the music on her flute. Charity lay on her back, staring up at the shadows of the firelight on the rock surface of the roof.

After they slept, they went on. In the tunnels there was neither night nor day. The only clocks were in their bodies. Charity was hungry. She was tasting dirt in her mouth, and the water was all gone. But from far away they had heard a roaring sound and the wind whistling in their ears. They came out on a ledge above a stream.

Charity shined her torch across to the opposite wall, where a waterfall was boiling through a cleft in the rock. She let the light play on the surface of the current, and followed it along the floor of an enormous cavern. "Look," she said. "Look, there's the bridge."

Even without the light it would have been visible, a span of stone that crossed the cavern at its narrowest point. The roof of the cavern had pricked up into the open air, and dim light shone down from above. The water poured from a deep fissure in the roof and fell into a pool, and mixed there with the light of day. The bridge rose through a cloud of vapor, while the water thundered underneath it.

Charity walked down along the ledge. "Look," she said. But then she stopped. The woman hadn't followed her. She was standing with her hands to her head, holding her head as if in pain, and then she was scrambling down another slope, up to her ankles in loose sand and scree. She was heading for the water, shouting and crying, banging her flute against the stones, until finally she tripped and slid down into a small pool, out of the main current which the backwater had filled with scum and floating wood, and bottles and tin cans. There she wept and wailed, kneeling in the water while Charity looked on, unable to understand until she caught the music in the woman's cry. Then she took the map out of her jacket and turned her light on it and studied it until she found the cave, and found the river rushing through it, and followed it with her finger up into the world, and up through many permutations north and west, to the map's edge and then beyond, the names unreeling in her memory, for she had won prizes in geography at school: Poldan, Visser, Medong, Koo, a dozen tributaries and a thousand miles, up to its farthest source, the River Rang.

In Caladon the psychiatric arts were highly prized. On the Monday of his third week in the city, on the morning of November 45th, Thanakar took Jenny Pentecost from their hotel, and together they walked down the Street of the Harmonious Mind, searching for a block of offices that looked inviting.

Unlike Charn, Caladon was a city of straight lines and low buildings. By law, no structure could exceed four stories, that being the tallest height that Argon Starbridge, the present king's great-uncle, could climb to without throwing up. He had been afflicted with a rare condition of the inner ear, which made him sensitive to air pressure. When he was crowned king, he had had all high buildings in the city truncated or demolished, citing some scriptural au-

thority. As a result, the city had a sprawling, relaxed air.
During the winter many houses had collapsed from the
weight of snow on their flat roofs, and by the eighth phase
of spring they had not yet been rebuilt, so that even in the
center of the city there were open spaces, not precisely
parks, but pleasing nonetheless.

At least they pleased Thanakar Starbridge as he walked
along the street. The accumulating rain had covered everything, as if in dusty layers of new paint. People walked lei-
surely under their umbrellas, and it seemed to Thanakar
that they lacked the desperation of the citizens of Charn,
the wild fanaticism, the public drunkenness and frenzy. In
their clothes and in their houses, he noticed fewer excesses
of rich and poor.

In Caladon the worst of times had already gone past; the
countryside was richer than the stony hills of Charn, less
eroded, less exposed. North of the city, under long plastic
awnings, the first corn of the season was already grown—
tiny, bitter husks, but it was food. In Caladon, though distribution was a government monopoly, technology at least
was in the hands of private merchants, and even in the darkest winter they had managed to produce something—
strange hybrids grown in caves under electric lights.

In every way it was a richer city. The Street of the Harmonious Mind was lined with prosperous buildings faced with
marble and white brick. On Mondays and on Thursdays the
street was closed to traffic, and the doctors were available
for unscheduled consultations. As Thanakar and Jenny
studied the directories, the pavements behind them were
crowded with people seeking appointments. Some were
making a great show of their ailments, twitching and shouting, and striking themselves on the face. Others were
gagged, or led along by keepers, and a few spectacular cases
were dragged by in wheeled cages.

In Charn, reflected Thanakar, people were too poor to be

insane, too poor and too afraid. But here the citizens seemed proud of it; it was proof of their leisure and prosperity, for treatment was not cheap.

"Fifteen dollars," said the nurse, before Thanakar had even taken off his gloves. He had chosen Dr. Caramel out of a list of ten in the lobby of a building that seemed less pretentious than the others they had passed. The other nine were all psychic abortionists and electrotherapists; by contrast, the specialty of Dr. Caramel—cerebral massage—seemed benign.

In addition, Thanakar had hoped, from the name, that Dr. Caramel might prove to be a woman. But in this he was disappointed. After he had paid the nurse, he and Jenny were shown into a comfortable waiting room, and after a suspiciously short time, they were joined by a short, balding, middle-aged man in a white suit. He shook them gravely by the hand and peered with mild curiosity at their tattoos.

"Charnish," he said at last.

The nurse had given Thanakar a card to fill out while he waited. It had requested information of a general and harmless nature. Dr. Caramel took it and glanced at the top line. "You are a doctor," he remarked.

"A surgeon."

"Hmm. Charnish medicine is very backward, I've been told."

"In some ways."

Dr. Caramel turned the little card between his fingers and glanced at the back of it, which was blank. "What can I do for you?" he asked.

Thanakar looked at the floor. "May we speak privately?"

"Of course." The little man clapped his hands, and when the nurse appeared, he instructed her to take the child to an inner room where there were games and juice. Nevertheless Jenny kept her grip on Thanakar's finger, squeezing it until it hurt. Thanakar had to slide his finger from her tiny grasp.

"Go with her," he said. "I'll be right here." But he turned his face away, so that he would not have to watch her expression as she went out the door. In fact, there is nothing wrong with her, he thought. It is not so strange, to be unhappy.

He had brought a sheaf of Jenny's drawings, and he laid them out along a table in the center of the room. Dr. Caramel stood behind his shoulder. "You are very talented," he said.

"They are hers."

"Incredible." Dr. Caramel picked up one of the drawings, a pen-and-ink sketch of a skull, seen from the side. The bone was cut away behind the ear, to reveal a tangled web of brains. "Incredible," he repeated. He brought the drawing over to the window, where the light was stronger. A small desk was there; he rummaged in the drawer for a magnifying glass, then drew it out.

"Incredible," he said for the third time. The detail of the drawing seemed to progress towards some microscopic infinity, halted only by the failure of the human eye. Under the glass the tangle of brains spread apart into its component strands. As the doctor's eye adjusted to the fineness of the drawing, they were revealed first as a labyrinth of corridors and then as lines of little rooms, rooms without doors, each one with a prisoner inside. Some were squatting in the corners, shackled to the walls; some sat reading on their beds; some paced back and forth. Some spoke together secretly, through holes scratched in the walls. Some slept.

Dr. Caramel sat down in an armchair and held the paper to his eye. Thanakar approached him from the table, carrying more drawings. "She calls that 'The Prison-Mind,' " he said. "Look at this."

He showed Dr. Caramel another drawing, similar to the first. Again a human skull was cut away behind the ear. But this time the brains took the shape not of corridors and hallways but of tunnels and caves. The bone of the skull itself was drawn to resemble rock in some places, masonry in others. The socket of the eye, the nose, the jaw seemed built out of rotting brick, carved into the surface of a hill. Farther back, where the skull was cut away, the rock was permeated with a maze of holes: caves, tunnels, rivers, islands, waterfalls, a whole subterranean world.

Another drawing, this one in brown pencil, highlighted in red: again, a human skull. The eye was still in its socket, the teeth in its mouth. Through a crack behind the ear the brain showed puffy and convoluted, a mass of tissue caught in a net of blood.

The brain had receded from the back of the skull. There at the opening for the spinal column, an enormous insect had dug out a cavity for itself. With sharp mandibles and claws it was tearing down the wall of tissue that enclosed it.

"Here," said Thanakar. He handed Dr. Caramel the last of the sketches, a pencil drawing of the insect itself, huge, blind, and hairy, with long, segmented legs. Under it, in childish letters which contrasted strangely with the beauty of the sketch, was printed: THE FLEA.

"What are her symptoms?" asked Dr. Caramel.

Thanakar was staring out the window. In an antiseptic courtyard, a tree with no leaves on it was reflected in a rectangular pool. "She has no symptoms," he said. "But there is something about these drawings that breaks my heart."

"Tell me," said the doctor gently.

"She does not speak. She has a kind of sadness that seems morbid to me—you understand, I don't have much experience with children. She is my adopted daughter. I took her from a house of prostitution in my city. Her situation there was beyond words, but it was not for long. Nevertheless, perhaps there are some wounds that can't be healed. I had hoped it was enough just to be kind."

Dr. Caramel made a cage out of his fingers and knocked it thoughtfully against his lips. "Kindness is meaningless outside a program of therapy," he said. "And I've never heard of a mental problem that was not physical at bottom. This"—he tapped the drawings in his lap—"this is the key."

But Thanakar kept on speaking, as if he hadn't heard. "She came from a poor family. An only child; her father once was in the guild of carpenters and clowns. Nevertheless, I can't pretend they were incapable of love. There are worse things than poverty. Her parents died in prison. Is that enough to kill someone with sadness? The human heart is such a mystery."

Thanakar was staring out the window. It had begun to rain again—soft, slow drips which disturbed the surface of the pool. He said, "I took her from a house of prostitution. They had dressed her as a priestess in the shrine of Angkhdt. Yet it was a long time ago. Ten weeks. Life is hard for many people—why can't she forget about these things? I have been kind to her."

"Kindness means nothing," repeated Dr. Caramel. "Look at this." He tapped the drawing of the flea.

"I cannot think that she is mad," said Thanakar. "What is normal, in these circumstances? It is more healthy to forget, for a wound to heal and show no trace. But there are wounds that bleed and bleed."

Dr. Caramel was embarrassed by this talk. "There is always some physical manifestation," he said, rising from his chair. "I would like to examine the young lady, if I could."

"She has terrible dreams," continued Thanakar, but then he stopped. Dr. Caramel had clapped his hands again, and in a moment the nurse brought Jenny in. She seemed subdued. She came to stand next to Thanakar near the window, but did not look at him. And when Dr. Caramel approached her, she let him touch her. She bent her head forward so that Dr. Caramel could examine the back of her skull; he had a tiny flashlight in one hand, and with the other he pulled the hair back from her neck, stroking it against the grain. He had put on a pair of glasses, and his mouth was partly open. His lips were taut. "Aha," he said. "Aha, I thought so. Look. I told you."

He had combed her hair back from the nape of her neck, revealing sad, pink skin. Just where her spinal column met her skull, there was a little mark.

"Look," said Dr. Caramel. "That's where it entered in."

Thanakar took her away. In his pocket he carried Dr. Caramel's surgical diagram, drawn on tracing paper over one of Jenny's sketches. He had proposed making a small incision in the skull, wide enough for his fingers. He had proposed reaching in to see if he could grab hold of one of the insect's legs. Or if the disease had progressed, and the flea had burrowed out of reach into the corridors of Jenny's mind, he proposed tempting it out with sugar-coated tweezers.

The next morning Thanakar took Jenny to another doctor. "I'm glad you came to me," said Marcel Paraclete. "In this city you will find a scandalous number of incompetents and quacks. I pity the poor invalid who finds himself in any waiting room but mine."

At least that's what Thanakar thought he said. It was hard to tell. He was dressed in a suit of plastic overalls from head to foot, and his voice was muffled under a mask of plastic gauze that covered his whole face. His waiting room was a cubicle of white tile, without windows or furniture. He had observed them through the skylight, and then told them through a speaking tube to proceed into an inner office, where he greeted them. He motioned them to chairs, and then sat down at his desk.

On a table stood an array of surgical gloves and facemasks, under a sign that read, For Your Own Protection. Dr. Paraclete indicated the display with plastic fingers, but Thanakar shook his head. "It is...premature," he said, looking around the room. The office did not seem particularly clean, though it stank of disinfectant. There were stacks of books and papers everywhere, and dust on the carpet near where Thanakar and Jenny sat.

Inside the plastic suit, the doctor shrugged. "Contagion is a subtle thing," he mumbled.

There was an uncomfortable silence while Dr. Paraclete fished out a cigarette. His suit had a zipper over the mouth, and he unzipped it. He lit the cicgarette and blew a puff of smoke into the room; Thanakar could smell tobacco mixed with marijuana, as well as something else, some sweet anti-septic smell.

"Contagion is a subtle thing," repeated Dr. Paraclete, more clearly now that his mouth was bare. "Subtle and in-sidious. Viruses and microbes, I have devoted my life to them, classifying, analyzing, and destroying. I see from your hands that you, too, are a doctor, though doubtless of an insufficient kind. Even so, even in Charn you must have heard of me. Otherwise you would not have come."

Uncomfortable, Thanakar caressed his knee. "I under-stood you were a psychoanalyst," he said.

"Precisely. I am the first. I am the only man who under-stands the true pathology of mental illness. Microbes, sir, microbes! For generations we have treated influenza, bloodpox, cholera, sometimes with wonderful results. We have had success with many new antibiotics. Why not neur-ophrenia, paranoia, unhappiness, and hysteria?"

"You believe these to be contagious illnesses?" asked Thanakar.

"Highly contagious. Let me exemplify. One patient is an alcoholic. Well, what is the first thing I discover, but that most of his friends are also alcoholic. What is more, his father also drank. You see? It is because a child's immune system is so weak. Adults are resistant, but a child can be exposed and never know it. There is an incubation period, of course. I am working with a man who has a history of child abuse. Well, as it turns out, his uncle had abused him when he was only twenty-three months old. The period of incubation lasted most of his adult life."

"I've never thought of it like that," said Thanakar, caressing his leg.

"Think of it now. Think of yourself. Are you happy? No, don't tell me. Think. Think about your friends. I tell you, two unhappy people can infect and reinfect each other until they die."

"And you," asked Thanakar. "Are you a happy man?"

Dr. Paraclete shook his head. "Too soon," he moaned, sucking on his cigarette. "I was exposed too soon."

Thanakar spent the evening in Jenny's room. He had a stack of drawings on his lap, and they sat together on Jenny's bed, examining them by the light of the bedside lamp. Jenny was sucking on her thumb and stroking her upper lip with the edge of her forefinger. She was leaning her head against Thanakar's shoulder, and from time to time she would turn her head to press her face against his shirt, to sniff at the dark material.

"This one," said Thanakar. He had picked up one of a new series. Jenny had finished with her drawings of the head-shaped mountain, and instead had penetrated deep inside. There, among caves and waterways and rough-hewn tunnels, two women slowly struggled up into the light. Some of these new drawings showed islands and dark lakes, and cirques covered with houses, and caverns lit with bonfires, and rocky warrens full of life. They showed armies marching, and struggling together in the dark. They showed people washing livestock in the murky pools. They showed tunnels cut out of the rock, and some were dry and clean, and some were damp and fleshlike, with bulging stalactites and slick walls. And always somewhere, prominent in the foreground, distant and occluded in the back, separate from the rest of the detail, always the figures of the two women were included in the drawing, muffled in shadows and black clothes, their faces always hidden.

"This one," said Thanakar. In the middle of the page a village rose up the sides of a great cavern, built on tiers cut into the rock. A central bonfire illuminated the streets and cast its beams into the far recesses of the drawing, down into the far left-hand corner, where two women crouched among the stones. They were in a narrow passageway, separate from the rest of the cavern. One had collapsed against a boulder, hiding her face, while the other was holding up a lizard by its tail.

"This one," said Thanakar. He rubbed his finger over the image of the woman, the one holding the lizard.

Jenny shook her head and buried her face in Thanakar's shoulder. "Tell me," he said. "Who is she? Who is this one?" He pointed to the other figure, crouched against the stone.

Again Jenny turned her face against the doctor's shirt. And she didn't look again until he had reached the last of the drawings. At long last it was a landscape, a hillside above ground, and there was weather and fresh air and light. Two women struggled down a slope of gravel and shaped rock.

Then Jenny looked up. She reached out her hand to the doctor's neck, to where a golden locket hung from a chain, a tiny thing, unopened now for weeks, containing a single hair and a photograph of Charity Starbridge, taken when she was a young girl.

That evening, far away, Princess Charity emerged out of a hole in the ground into a light, fine, crystal rain. By that time she had spent several weeks in the dark, and her pupils were dilated, and there was mud on her face and cobwebs in her hair. In the hour after sunset she crossed through a barricade of planks put up in the shape of an X over the mouth

of an abandoned mine just twenty miles from the Caladonian frontier. The mine emerged into a gravel pit, a long,
broken slope stretching down into the rain. If Charity had
not been too fatigued to raise her head, if she had cared to
look, she would perhaps have noticed that the entire hillside
had been built into the shape of a woman's face. Ruined
and eroded by the rain, nevertheless it was still recognizable—the face of the fourteenth abbess of a local priory,
who had been part owner of the mine. Charity emerged
through a hole under her left eye and slid halfway down her
cheek before she was able to stop herself. She sat down
wearily in a pile of shattered rock and looked around.

Above her the antinomial labored down the slope. She
was bleeding from cuts on her forehead and her hands, and
the lines in her face were filled with grime. She was whistling through the gaps in her teeth, and she held her flute in
her left hand. Then she stopped suddenly, and crouched
down in the hump of a small boulder, and the music she was
humming changed a little. She was out of breath, and the
notes came in ragged gasps, but soon they formed themselves into a different melody, more solitary, less compro-
mising, the song of herself, which no one but herself would
ever understand. She watched Charity diminish among the
rocks of the lower slope; she made a small gesture with her
flute, and then she turned away. For she had seen in her
mind's eye a stream of water flowing from the north, over
the next hill, and in her mind she followed it, mile after
mile, back up into her own country. When Charity looked
back she had disappeared, and the princess was too tired
and hungry to go back up to find her. She didn't care, for
she had seen the lights of a town shining down below.

On the hillside Charity sat listening for a moment, to see
if she could catch a wisp of melody somewhere, an intima-
tion of the song called "now I am." But there was nothing,
only the crystal rain as fine as mist, drying to a crystal
powder on her shoulders and her hair. In a little while she

got up and went forward, down into the world.

That night, past midnight, Jenny Pentecost drew a picture of the princess eating dinner. In that little village on the slopes of the mine, Charity fell in among simple, pious folk, for whom the revolution was just distant words. She was too tired to dissimulate, and when they found out who she was they fed her the first new vegetables of that spring—potatoes as small and as precious as pearls. They made a bath for her in a tin tub, and then saved the dirty bathwater and decanted it in earthen vessels, and sprinkled it upon their hearths and fields, their children and their household gods. They bowed their heads and would not look her in the face.

In their village many houses still were empty, abandoned and not yet reoccupied. In one of these, a stone building that had been a shrine, they made a home for her. Each family brought gifts: blankets, pillows, mattresses of straw. And they were with her constantly, asking her blessing or advice, or just sitting near her, staring at her every movement. They were amazed by everything she did, by the way she sat and drank and combed her hair, by the way she yawned and slept. Sometimes when she was asleep, they would come near to touch her hands.

During the next week Jenny Pentecost drew many pictures of these scenes. But always Charity's face was hidden, so that as Thanakar pored over them, he was concerned only with trying to find some clue as to the child's illness. He had no way of understanding, nor could Jenny have told him, for by that time she only spoke in whispers, and in a language that was private to herself alone. It was based on a system of numerology that seemed to have sprung unaided from her own heart, for it had no basis in mathematics or mythology.

She had assigned numbers, arbitrarily, it seemed, to weather patterns, places, states of mind, types of food, and articles of clothing. These she would multiply and combine with the date and the hours of the day, to form a calculation for each thought and action, each event, identifying its position in a landscape of her own. "5719076 x 9191919," she would whisper to herself very softly.

She had made a catalog of all her thoughts and memories. And every morning she would draw a quick cross-section of her head, with the flea growing ever larger, its chamber at the back of her skull ever expanding. Every morning it would crack the wall of some tiny cubicle in that vast labyrinth and suck out the occupant into its mouth. The flea was feasting on her memories. Every day the number she had penciled in the margin of her sketch grew smaller.

One day Jenny came to Thanakar, shaking with urgency, and she showed him a drawing of a small town below a hill—dilapidated stone houses on a single street. And there were horsemen coming down out of the hills, carrying the flags of the League of Desecretion: a child's red hand upon an orange ground. In the cellar of a farmer's house, Princess Charity crouched under some bags of straw, her face hidden in shadow.

Thanakar was good with numbers. He made some calculations with the numbers in the margin. He was acute enough to understand them, partly. He was acute enough to understand that this was something that was happening at that exact moment in the landscape of Jenny's mind, perhaps a hundred miles to the south and west. But more than that he couldn't understand.

Though he could not bring himself to follow any of their advice, Thanakar was still taking her to various psychiatrists around the town. On the morning of November 66th, he stood out in the slowly settling rain, in the courtyard of a block of offices in the Avenue of Bliss. Jenny was undergoing a second battery of tests inside, in the office of a doctor that specialized in clairvoyance.

The results of the first test had been confusing. The psychologist had come out to Thanakar as he was pacing the halls. She was carrying a sheaf of papers.

"How did she do?" Thanakar had asked.

She had done badly. The psychologist explained. "Look. This is a test in which she tries to guess the card that I am holding in my hand. Out of ninety times, she couldn't do it once."

"Well, that tells you something, doesn't it?"

"You don't understand. There are only four choices—a circle, a cross, a square, and a dog's head. A normal person, answering at random, should achieve a score of twenty-five percent. To fail on every question, that is remarkable."

The psychologist had asked him to bring Jenny back to be retested. He had taken time away from work and come down through the crowded streets. In those days every hour brought more refugees to Caladon, sixty thousand in that week alone. Pushing through the streets, Thanakar felt new currents of resentment and unrest, and there were soldiers everywhere.

The refugees were all his countrymen. In Charn the National Assembly had banned the practice of religion. In the first weeks of November, soldiers of the Desecration League rode out into the countryside of Charn, smashing shrines and killing priests. Always they were preceded by waves of refugees, the faithful and fanatical, the wealthy and well born. Two hundred thousand refugees had cut the knot of the unravelers and crossed the border into Caladon.

When Thanakar had first come into the city underneath the Argon Gates, he had been one of a small number, for most were held at the frontier. But each day after that there had been more: Starbridges on horseback and in carriages, crowding the hotels and the restaurants. And they were followed by an endless stream of poorer folk, beggars on the road, crossing the soda plains with their pots and pans upon their heads, pushing wheelbarrows piled high with kettles and with clothes.

At first there had been room for them in the capacious streets of Caladon, but on the forty-second of November,

the Argon gates were closed by orders of the king to all but
the most influential. Under the walls the people camped in
plywood shelters and under sheets of corrugated iron.
Thanakar had found work in a miserable shantytown strung
out along the red-brick battlements. A gynecologist from
Caladon had staffed a clinic there; she was a priest of
Angkhdt, and required no certificate. She and sixteen nuns
had built a new dispensary in an abandoned brickyard.
Under canvas shelters the sick lay in concentric circles, arranged according to disease.

Thanakar had read about this doctor in the papers, which
otherwise were full of xenophobia and hate. In the fourth
week of November he had crossed the barbed-wire checkpoint, to work among his countrymen. And while the gynecologist delivered sugar children, and the nurses and the
nuns distributed fresh water and first aid, Thanakar was put
in charge of seven patients.

Soon he had them taken up, and taken to a separate tent,
where their ravings would not harm the others. For it was at
that time, among the Charnish refugees, that the first cases
of a new and strange disease were diagnosed. Later it would
devastate whole dioceses. But it was first observed by Dr.
Thanakar Starbridge, in the camp at Kethany, and he called
it black brain fever. In his diary from that time he described
the symptoms—melancholia, followed by hallucinations,
and then by catatonia. Death came rapidly, sometimes in a
few days, and when the skulls of the corpses were split
open, it was found that their brains were black and rotten,
almost liquid in their cases.

In his diary for the sixth week of November, Dr. Thanakar made a note of his own feelings, when he was working
with these patients. He was sick at heart. He feared that in
his daughter he was seeing a slow progress of the same mal-
ady. It was for this reason that he took off time from work,
to bring Jenny to all the specialists in Caladon, to try to find
some clue. In the office of one alienist, an old, obese

woman with sunken eyes and a slow voice, he had heard for the first time a theory that was later to become famous.

"I believe you," the alienist had said. Her voice was slow, without being particularly rich or deep. "I believe you. The conditions are related, that is clear. I have heard of this brain fever. It is contagious, is it not?"

"I don't know. How could it be?"

"How, indeed? I am summarizing what you told me. But perhaps your patients catch this illness from your hands."

"No," said Thanakar. "How can you say that? In most cases, death comes in sixty hours."

"And do none survive?"

"Yes. Some do. In some the symptoms have been less acute."

"And these survivors, do they have anything in common? Do they have anything in common with your daughter?"

"I don't know," said Thanakar miserably. "Two are out of danger, but they have suffered terrible brain damage."

The alienist wiped her nose with the back of her hand. "Let us look at this another way," she said. "You love your daughter, do you not?"

"Very much. Of course I do."

"Have you considered, perhaps, that it is love that is keeping her alive?"

"I take good care of her."

"I'm not talking about that. Perhaps you take good care of all your patients. I'm talking about love. I mean as medication, not as therapy."

"I don't understand."

Like most Caladonians, the alienist had disgusting manners. She blew her nose onto her hand and then rubbed her palms together. "Let me put it another way," she said. "This spring every patient that I see is starved for love. I don't mean that in a sentimental way. I mean it is a hunger that is killing them, a function of the weather and the insecurity of life. In summer we have other epidemics—surfeits and venereal diseases—not like this. But one full year ago, in spring, there was a devastation on our eastern coast that forced the evacuation of twenty fishing villages. It sounds similar to the fever you describe."

"It was not the same," said Thanakar.

"It was a fever that killed many. At that time philosophers first speculated about the cause."

"No, it is ridiculous," interrupted Thanakar. "I have read the history, and it is not the same. If love were medicine, my daughter would be well."

"At that time, Saint Carilon Bargee first speculated as to the cause," continued the woman, frowning. "He said there were many kinds of love. He compared it to a source of light. He said if we could manage to break love apart into its component elements, the way a prism breaks apart a beam of light, then we could have a panacea for all ills. If you could find the precise type of love that would most benefit your daughter. . . . It is not sexual love, I feel sure."

"No?" cried Thanakar, furious, his voice full of sarcasm and rage. "I don't see why not. Didn't I tell you that in Charn she had been terribly abused? Perhaps she feels the lack of it. Besides," cried Thanakar, "don't tell me about Carilon Bargee. He was a lunatic. Didn't he poison himself with his own serum, an injection that was supposed to duplicate the feel of being loved? He set his skin on fire."

"He was before his time," the alienist had said.

Now, standing in the courtyard on the 66th day of November, waiting for the results of Jenny's second test, Thanakar again felt some of his anger. All psychiatrists were fools, he thought. They inhabited a realm of darkness and ate despair like food. What was the alternative? thought Thanakar.

He was standing in the courtyard of a block of psychiatric offices, staring at the rain. The courtyard he had found by chance, searching for a toilet. A pair of doors had given way into an open space, a garden surrounded by windowless, white walls, where the sugar drifted down like snow. It was a rock garden: round, white pebbles like the tiny eggs of some small bird were raked in swirls around a central pile of rocks. Nothing grew. Nevertheless it was a restful place. The arrangement of the rocks was pleasing to the eye. Thanakar stood on a path of polished stones, next to a tiny spirit house of bronze.

Across from him, at the other end of a raked path, there was a marble bench set into the wall. On it sat a boy, young and handsome, with a thin, high-boned, delicate face. He was richly dressed in a uniform of blue and gold, the mark of the highest of the six varieties of Caladonian Starbridge. But the sleeves of his uniform had been extended past his hands, and they had been tied behind him, so that he sat hugging himself as if against the cold. He was staring down at the gravel in front of him, and with the toe of his boot he was obliterating the careful marks of the rake.

He kicked at the gravel with his foot, digging a trough down to the bare earth. He jerked his head back and noticed Thanakar for the first time. Instantly his face took on a look of bitter scorn, and his fine black eyebrows drew together. "Well," he said, "What are you staring at? You also, have you come to laugh at me?"

Thanakar found this question hard to answer. Involuntarily he glanced around the little garden, though he knew they were alone. But the stranger had a way of speaking that Thanakar, though he had used it often, had never heard addressed to himself—a phraseology pitched from high to low, as if he, Thanakar Starbridge, had been a jeweler or a slave. The stranger's voice was thick with drugs, and the contempt in it was almost palpable, like spittle on the doctor's face.

The doctor made a gesture in the air, one of the ninety-seven gestures of self-revelation. But the boy had already dropped his head. As he did so, Thanakar realized who he was.

The king of Caladon had had two sons. The younger one was still an infant, a strange, misshapen boy, the source of many rumors. The elder had been grown when he was born —a popular, erratic prince, a drinker and carouser, a singer and a poet. Many nights when he was growing up, he would slink down from his cold palace, fooling the ancient priests who were his teachers and his guardians with a series of preposterous disguises. Alone or with a few companions, he would pass the night among the brothels and the wineshops of the lower town. Enraged, his father had sequestered his allowance, and even at one time had locked him naked in his room, but he had always managed to escape. Once Craton Starbridge, his best friend, had held a ladder to his window, and he had come down in borrowed clothes to be among his people. Poor folk came from miles around to be with him and hear him sing. His poems were on everybody's lips—long songs, drinking songs, songs of harsh captivity. In the brothels of the lower town the prostitutes tied silken scarves to the posts of their beds, to show that he had been there.

But on the first day of July, in the eighth phase of spring, Prince Argon Starbridge had been born in Caladon Cathedral, and five days later the king had disinherited his elder son. A crowd of fifty thousand had marched in protest all the way from Starbridge Covenant to the cathedral, carrying signs and banners, and wicker cages full of pigeons and white doves. But on the steps of the cathedral, the queen had met them, heavily veiled, with her newborn baby in her arms. There she had shown the child to the multitude, and they had gone down on their knees.

And after that the troubles of the elder prince had been forgotten. He was convicted of insanity—a long list of mental maladies that had been dormant in his mother's family— and imprisoned in a lunatic asylum. In the city, new violence and epidemics claimed public attention. The Peacock Prince, as he was called, Samson Mantikor was soon forgotten, though his songs were everywhere. And in the brothels certain combinations of solicitude were still named after him: the pigeon's tail, for example, the flutter of wild wings.

Now, in his royal straightjacket, he leaned back against the stone wall of the courtyard and wagged his handsome head from side to side. It had been five months since his first incarceration, and his hair had grown down past his shoulders. It was dusted with rough sugar, and there was sugar on his knees and on his boots. Ignoring Thanakar, he was humming a tune to himself, a tune then popular in Caladonian dancehalls:

*To the wings of the wild dove,*
*The winds and rocks are cruel.*
*I have been battered without cease,*
*By flatterers and spies.*

"I am not here to laugh at you," said Thanakar angrily, at last. "I came this way by chance." He used the tone of discourse between equals, as was his birthright, and at the sound of it, Samson Mantikor raised up his head.

"Don't lie to me," he said. "The door was locked."

"It was not locked," retorted Thanakar. "I came this way by chance."

The prince stared at him keenly and then got to his feet. "Come, then," he said. "If you are not a liar, come loose my hands. Your voice is strange to me. Who are you?"

"I am from Charn," said Thanakar, limping forward across the narrow courtyard, holding up his palm. And when the prince saw the tattoo of the golden briar wrapped around the doctor's fingers and down his wrist and forearm, some of the hostility left his face, and his eyes took on a look of sober calculation.

"From Charn," he said. "Who was your father? A prince of the ninth rank—don't lie to me. Swear to me that you are not some new utensil of my father's. Swear to me—I have heard the virtues of our race are still alive in

Charn. Loyalty, courage, and singleness of heart; I have heard the Starbridges of Charn still keep their ancient oaths."

"You were misinformed," said Thanakar.

But the prince wasn't listening. He was speaking very fast, in a tone verging on hysteria. "Courage, honesty, and simpleness," he said. "When my first ancestor made his vow to Angkhdt himself, how many men were there with him? And now how many, in this sink of treachery? And yet, I can remember when I had so many friends—come, speak to me! Are you deaf? Untie my arms!"

His voice was thick with medication, and his eyes were bright. He kicked his foot and made a clinking sound; Thanakar looked down and saw for the first time that he was chained. A chain locked around his ankle was stapled to the marble wall. It was cruelly tight, for the cloth of the prince's boot was torn away.

"I mean no harm, I promise you," said Thanakar. He reached out to untie the prince's arms. But then Samson Mantikor pulled away.

"Do not touch me," he said. "You have not the tools to loose this chain, and anyway the place is full of soldiers. They must not know that you were here with me, or they will take me to some other place. But you will take a message for me, to the home of Craton Starbridge. He is my faithful friend—tell him you have seen me. Tell him where I am. Take him this." He inclined his cheek. There was an earring in his right earlobe, a golden stud in the shape of a wild bird in flight. "Take it," said the prince.

Again the results of Jenny's test were inconclusive. Sick at heart, Thanakar took her from the sanatorium, and together they walked down the Avenue of Bliss towards their hotel. Jenny squeezed his hand. But the questions had exhausted her, and so he took her in his arms the last few blocks and carried her. He was limping and his knee hurt badly. But he would not stop to rest, not wanting to disturb the rhythm of her breathing, the pressure of her cheek against his cheek. She was asleep, and when he came to the hotel he went upstairs without a word and laid her down upon her bed. Mrs. Cassimer undressed her, but she was fast asleep. Thanakar stood in the doorway for a while, and then he turned and went downstairs.

Craton Starbridge was the seventh minister for agriculture. His house was in the Baekland Road. Thanakar gave the prince's earring to a steward, wrapped in a written message, and within twenty minutes he was standing in the conservatory of the minister, a long gallery of glass at the top of the house. The room was lined with tables, from a few of which, in pots and trays, protruded feeble and malnourished plants.

The seventh minister was alone. He was a big man, burly and strong, with a wide face and a cropped head. He was older than the prince, about Thanakar's age. When the doctor entered he was fiddling with a bank of fluorescent lights above one table. But in his left hand he was holding the prince's earring by its golden shank, spinning it between his forefinger and thumb.

"How do I know that you're not lying?" he said at once. He turned, and strode rapidly across the floor towards Thanakar. "This earring could mean anything. It could mean the prince is dead."

Bored, Thanakar turned to go. "That's not my concern," he said. "I am a foreigner. I wasted my own time to bring this message. What you believe is up to you."

"Wait," said Craton Starbridge. He came into the center of the room. He had a strong, open face, but it was strange with doubt. "Wait," he said. "Don't go."

Thanakar made a bored, dismissive gesture with his hand and continued towards the door. Behind him, the seventh minister cleared his throat. "I cannot let you go," he said. "Please try to understand. I don't mean to insult you. You have given me a token of my friend. This is news that I have prayed for. It is because I want so much to believe you that I listen to my doubts."

Thanakar turned back to face him. "I have told the truth," he said.

Craton Starbridge spun the prince's earring in his fingers. "It is hard to believe that they would have left him unguarded. You say you found the door unlocked?"

"That's what I said."

"I wonder. My friendship with Prince Mantikor is well known. Don't be insulted. But if the king wanted to tempt me to an act of treason, what better tool for him than you, a foreigner from Charn? Impossible to trace. Anyone else, and I would know their sympathies."

When the brother of Prince Mantikor was born in Caladon, in July of the eighth phase of spring, there had been festivities around the clock. The story was that even in his mother's womb, Prince Argon Starbridge had recited verses from the Song of Angkhdt. Philosophers, the story went, had been invited into the cathedral. They had pressed their ears against the queen's vagina; it was a lie.

The prince's birth, the story went, was painless and uncomplicated, despite the largeness of his head. When he was just a few days old, his mother had been strong enough to hold him in her arms on the steps of the cathedral, confronting the protesting crowds. He had spoken to the protesters, calling them by name until their leaders had dropped down in the dust upon their knees, their hands clasped out in front of them.

It was all lies. On that occasion the queen had been heavily veiled. In fact, she had died in childbirth. Her labor had lasted for more than fifty hours, and her screams had penetrated from the sanctuary far into the labyrinth of the cathedral. In Caladon it was the custom for the queen to be delivered in the sanctuary of Beloved Angkhdt, behind a silver screen. It was the custom, at the perfect moment in the litany of kingship, for the nurse to bring the newborn child from the altar to his father on his throne a dozen yards away. The nurse would walk in rhythm to the drums, and the king would wait for a particular passage of the singing before he lifted up the child to his breast. All would be performed in silence, the child's mouth taped to stop its crying, until the supplicant before the altar had reached a certain section of his recitation. Then he would ring a little bell, a signal for the seal upon the child's lips to be undone.

That was how Samson Mantikor had come into the world, taking his place like an actor on a stage. But on the night of July 1st, after the queen's labor had gone on for forty hours, the supplicant had dismissed the congregation. The king had sat, immense, immobile on his throne, his expression hidden behind his golden mask, while the queen's screaming echoed to the utmost vault. The candles in the sanctuary were all extinguished, all but one. The midnight ritual and benediction were suspended, the musicians and the dancers were dismissed. The king had sat immobile in the dark. Perhaps he slept. But as the queen's delivery reached its climax, one of the acolytes reported seeing a drop of moisture run down under his mask and down his neck. And at the moment of crisis, when the screams burst out redoubled and then stopped, the acolytes saw him lurch heavily to his feet, his jeweled fingers curved in a gesture none of them had seen before.

Despite appearances, the king was not a fool. Towards four o'clock, when the litany had been resumed, he beckoned with his little finger. In the pause between the versicle and the response, Lord Bartek Multiflex, the king's first minister, inclined his ear to Argon Starbridge's fat lips, and in a few short, whispered words, he received the instructions that reshaped the kingdom.

For the king was a student of history. He had made himself aware of the progress of events. In July and August of that phase of spring, his armies reached the gates of Charn before they were repulsed; what on both sides was perceived as one more surge of strength against his ancient enemies was really an attempt to forestall a revolution there. For he was aware that in the course of seven of the past nine springs, uprisings in Caladon had quickly followed those in Charn. His own great-grandfather had ended his auspicious reign upon a scaffold. Tensions in both cities were the same —the people desperate and malnourished, the Starbridges exhausted and corrupt.

But when his son was born, King Argon saw one difference, and saw how to exploit it. What in Charn was heresy, in his city was the people's faith. In shrines and pulpits throughout Caladon, adventists proclaimed the coming of the risen Angkhdt, the dog-headed master, the new made flesh. For generations they had waited, fervently, impatiently, for God to come and tread the Earth again, as He had in the beginning of all things. They waited for His touch.

All winter and all spring the people of Caladon had turned their famished hearts to these teachings. Each change in the weather, every discoloration of the sky, was enough to bring them out into the streets. On the night of July 2nd, in the eighth phase of spring, Lord Bartek Multiflex announced the horoscope of the new prince from the steps of the cathedral. That night there was jubilation in the streets. And for months afterwards the government was born aloft, drifting on a swell of popular enthusiasm. Rumors from Charn could find no purchase. New decrees were greeted with a frenzied acclamation—taxes, laws, and military stratagems—as if even the most mundane aspects of public policy were suddenly made sacred.

And in the general euphoria, people gave no thought to the disappearance of Prince Mantikor. It seemed reasonable and just for him to surrender his claim to his divine younger brother. A golden cradle was installed in the sanctuary of the cathedral, a dozen paces from the throne. It was surrounded with mirrors, and every day the court was crowded with pilgrims seeking entrance, to prostrate themselves before the holy child. Priests and philosophers interpreted his screams and wails.

But still, there were rumors of unpleasantness. A palace servant, dismissed for drunkenness, published an account of how, at five months old, Prince Argon's eyes were still unfocused; how he cried incessantly unless his mouth was taped; how he was still incapable of reaching out his hand, of recognizing those around him. She had been, or so she claimed, a midwife at the birth, and it was she who first published the rumor that the queen was dead, that the person who had presented the baby to the multitude five days after his birth had been a fraud, a veiled imposter, a nun out of the sanctuary, or else Lord Multiflex himself.

After this account was published, the servant disappeared. Some said she'd been suppressed by the authorities, but it was more likely she had fled the city, chased by angry crowds. For days, wherever she was, people had spat on her, and pelted her with mud, and called her *Onayan Kundega*, "she who mocks the living God."

But on the morning of November 79th, the situation changed. In a front-page editorial of the leading opposition daily, Craton Starbridge announced the formation of a new political party, a coalition of reactionary and progressive Starbridge elements, unified by a new political agenda. Warlike, secular, antimonarchist, they advocated a return to ancient Starbridge values and denounced the government of Argon Starbridge, which was sunk in bureaucracy and superstition.

The editorial was widely ignored, for party politics had little use in Caladon, which was ruled by the king and nineteen ministers. Party officials were entitled to wear certain clothing and were permitted certain seats in the sanctuary of the cathedral. Certain salaries were paid them by the state, and that was their whole function. Nevertheless that same day fifteen members of the new party broke into the offices of Dr. Karan Blau and liberated Samson Mantikor, who had been held against his will. In the evening they staged a rally on the Goostep Road, calling for the abdication of the king. Samson Mantikor read several poems which he had written in captivity.

He was greeted rapturously by the crowd, which included a fair sprinkling of common people. But there must have been two thousand Starbridges, young and old, sick of the inertia of the government and bored by the expectations of their careers in civil service. They applauded wildly the speech of Major General Antrim Starbridge, who recited in his ancient voice the ancient duties of their caste. "We have sold our pride," he quavered. "Many thousands of our cousins have been martyred on the scaffolds of Charn, and what have we done to succor them? The king has sent his protests to the embassy. On many sheets of paper he has recorded his disapproval, while our armies lie idle at the frontier. But I tell you, out of the new National Assembly in Charn a wind is rising to engulf us all, while we do nothing. Now we must act. Now!" He raised his hands, and on the podium he embraced the doddering form of General Tarpon Starbridge, leader of the government-in-exile of Charn. It was a touching moment, for on the battlefield they had been frequent enemies.

This kind of language was unusual in Caladon, where even public protest tended towards certain ritualized forms. Offended, the editors of the other major newspapers rallied to support the government. The signatories of the new manifesto included the assistant chief of police and most of the general staff; nevertheless, public opinion was staunchly with the king. The next day more than ninety thousand people demonstrated around the cathedral, while the archbishop read a statement from the steps.

Later chroniclers, with the objectivity of hindsight, would

say that if the king had acted then, with the people behind him, no force could have withstood him. If, in answer to the people's acclamations, the archbishop had produced the infant prince, if he had demonstrated to the mob the new-made flesh, then the Starbridge party would have been dissolved that day. But instead the prelate discoursed vaguely on the duty of each citizen. He did not even mention the young prince. Later it was clear why he did not. But in the meantime the crowd was full of noxious rumors: The prince had succumbed to black brain fever, he was dead, he had disappeared, it was a trick, it was a lie, a wax effigy in a golden cradle, animated by some mechanism. Rumors seemed to grow up out of nothing.

The truth is, on the night of November 78th, Zenith Malagond, a junior acolyte at the cathedral and a former friend of Samson Mantikor, choosing a quiet section of the litany, stole behind the inlaid screen, bearing an embroidered pillow in his hands. That much is well known. But chroniclers of the period, and even some contemporary historians, have confused what followed, some for corrupt reasons, and some through honest ignorance. Caladonian legend has transformed Samson Mantikor into a murderer. Sixty months after these events, the play *God's Death* opened in Caladon. In it Prince Mantikor, a tragic figure dressed in black, murders the boy himself, after a hesitant soliloquy. Zenith Malagond does not appear; the prince smothers the child himself, holding a jeweled pillow over his tiny nose. In the play, the death of Samson Mantikor a month later on the battlefield of Charonea achieves a kind of tragic symmetry.

On November 79th, the body of a man, tortured beyond recognition, was buried privately beneath the stones of the cathedral. Whether that was Zenith Malagond, or else the captain of the watch, remains conjecture. The fact remains: In the morning the cradle in the sanctuary was empty. Three days later, in response to certain rumors in the capital, Lord Bartek Multiflex issued a proclamation. He announced that the infant prince had been taken to a place of safety, to an estate outside the city, following an attempt upon his life. Official historians of the period, who believed that Zenith Malagond was executed for an attempt that failed, account for the prince's disappearance in this way. They claim the prince was murdered later, after the fall of Caladon. They claim he was disposed of secretly by Charnish troops.

Predictably, the adventists present a third alternative. Later, a legend was to be retold as part of the scriptural cycle of the Cult of Loving Kindness: how the young prince, perfect in his innocence, ascended up to Paradise. Or in another version, through good luck and the power of God, he evaded all the snares that had been set for him and escaped into a far country, to the town of K——, where he grew to manhood.

It is this version that is closest to the truth. On the night of November 78th, between compline and morning invocation, while Argon Starbridge sat slumbering upon his throne, Zenith Malagond stepped behind the golden screen, a pillow in his hands. In the morning this pillow was discovered with the prince's mantle cunningly arranged on top of it. But the child was gone, stolen away, and by morning Zenith Malagond was far away inside the labyrinth of the cathedral, carrying the child underneath his robe.

On the morning of November 81st, Thanakar Starbridge was working at the new dispensary at Kethany, in a shed of fallen brick under the city walls. That day Samson Mantikor had issued the first of many public proclamations, charging that the infant prince was dead and challenging his father to produce him. Towards three o'clock, as Thanakar stood up to stretch his leg, the bells in the steeple of St. Pandolph Unguentine started to ring, a plaintive scattering of notes. From the field outside the shed the cries of fever victims rose up to the sky, mixing with the bells and the clatter of the rain.

Thanakar had been kneeling at the cot of a young woman, administering a sedative. Now he stood up, a scowl of disappointment on his lips, his head dizzy with nausea and despair. His clothes and gloves were streaked with black.

Around him in the operating shed, men and women lay unconscious on low canvas cots. Thanakar was skilled at trepanning, and he had taken several desperate cases to see if he could find, through trial and error, a way of relieving some of the pressure in their brains. In some manifestations of the fever, the victims' heads swelled up until they cracked apart. Thanakar had thought—but it was hopeless. From the eyes of the woman he had just abandoned, a black bile had poured out over his hands. Choking with disgust, Thanakar turned away. The woman had been young, a handsome woman, what was left of her. She was from Charn, with tattoos of the oil pressers' caste. The marks of her horoscope, cut into her palms, foretold the onset of a loathsome and untreatable disease. How did they know? Thanakar asked himself. How did they fucking know?

Incense smoke was rising from a brazier in the middle of the floor. It flickered slightly in the draft, and the light from the doorway was interrupted for a moment as a man bent underneath the flap and stepped inside. He was a heavy man in a rich cloak and a big hat, and he carried a small burden in his arms. It was a child, wrapped in a coarse, linen sheet, and Thanakar watched with a sense of sickening inevitability as the man pulled the sheet away from the small face.

The man was Craton Starbridge, seventh minister for agriculture, leader of the party of Prince Mantikor. Embarrassed, apprehensive, he took off his hat and looked around at the recumbent bodies, wrinkling his nose up at the stench. "He doesn't eat," he said, as if that were sufficient explanation for his presence. "He is suffering from dehydration. They told me I could find you here. I sent for you at your hotel."

The child was swaddled tightly, so that it could not move. Its head was swathed in bandages, and its lips were sealed with transparent tape. Its little cheeks were purple and distended; it was close to suffocation, Thanakar could see at once. Without a word he snatched up a scalpel from his table and, coming close, he slit the tape over the baby's lips. Relieved to take some clear and useful action after a morning full of failures, he stripped off his glove and put his fingers into the baby's mouth, clearing out a wad of vomit the color and consistency of clotted cream. He pushed his fingers down its throat to clear its nasal passages. "You people are beyond belief," he said.

"It is my son," said Craton Starbridge.

Thanakar passed his hand over the outline of the child's swaddled head. "You must take me for a fool," he replied angrily. In the distance the churchbells were still ringing, then they stopped.

Again Craton Starbridge glanced around the room. "All right," he said. "But remember, I have your deportation papers in my pocket. If you are tempted to make a public statement, now or later, just remember: Sentiment against you refugees runs high. There is a proposal in the Cabinet to quarantine this entire area."

Thanakar had taken the child into his arms. It was snuffling weakly, trying to cry, and he was cleaning its face with a wet cloth. Where the cloth touched its lips or the inside of its mouth, the skin began to bleed, it was so dry. "You people are beyond belief," he said again. "Why me?"

"Who else? The doctor's guild has come out for the king, like all the middle class. There is not one whom I could trust. But you are not like them. You are a Starbridge and a foreigner, here on our sufferance." He turned away, embarrassed. "You will be given a place of refuge, far from here.

Soon you will go. The child is not safe, not even from some members of our party. He is not safe in my own house. Yet it is clear he needs a doctor's care. It is the deepest wish of Samson Mantikor that he not be harmed."

The baby had begun to wail, a dry, clicking noise deep in its throat. "Go now," said Thanakar. "Fetch me a nurse with an IV. She'll know. I will think over what you've said."

Craton Starbridge nodded. "Very well. In the meantime I have given you a guard. At the moment he is engaged in transferring your household here from your hotel. He is putting up a tent here, for your use. It will be very private."

"No," said Thanakar. "I don't want my daughter here."

Craton Starbridge shrugged his shoulders. He replaced his hat over his face. "I understand," he said. "I understand —this is a place of death. But let me say this: You will be well rewarded."

# THE WHISPER BRIDGE

**8**

In those days at the end of the eighth phase of spring, the city of Charn was broken and divided by bitter factional disputes. East of the Mountain of Redemption, from the river to the Morquar Gate, the Desecration League had claimed its territory. Its partisans wore scarves, and feathers in their hats. They chalked their palms with reddish powder, to leave their mark on everything they touched. They swaggered everywhere, armed with knives and cudgels, urinating against walls, covering the buildings with their nihilist grafitti.

In that area they were paramount, but if they chanced to cross the Street of Seven Sins, they walked more circumspectly and pulled their cloaks around their shoulders. The fairgrounds of the Sugar Festival and south to the buildings of the National Assembly made up a narrow band of neutral ground, but farther west the sixth and seventh wards were in the hands of Rebel Angels, less numerous but better armed, dressed in coats of midnight blue.

These two companies of independent soldiery met frequently in bloody brawls. In the precincts of the National Assembly they preserved a wary peace. But elsewhere they fought viciously. There was no one to prevent them; in their respective territories, they had taken over the duties of the metropolitan police. Colonel Aspe, commander of the army, rarely came into the city and was not interested in keeping order. He sulked in his own quarters, spending most of every day in bed. His officers had requisitioned a small village seven miles from the southern gate, where their troops were more easily supplied.

In the city, the Rebels and the League fought freely. In this they reflected a political struggle that was just as fierce then taking place in the amphitheater of the National Assembly. There Raksha Starbridge still maintained a small majority, though by the last weeks in November the grotesque excesses of the Sugar Festival had changed the hearts of many waverers. During the roll call of November 76th over a minor point of precedence, five members changed their seats. The final vote, 418 to 411, was widely touted as a victory in the broadsheets of the Rim, but most political observers had their doubts. The majority had been achieved only after hours of lobbying by Raksha Starbridge, during which several delegates had had their teeth knocked in.

In those days the Desecration League provided the security for the assembly. They were everywhere in the chamber, lining the upper banks, moving back and forth between the deputies. First hired as pages, in theory they were an unarmed peacekeeping force, to be used at the discretion of the majority speaker. In fact they were the private thugs of Raksha Starbridge, and as his abuse of power grew ever stranger and more desperate, their truculence increased. In those days it was nothing, during a crucial vote, for them to physically restrain the members of the splinter opposition, locking their hands behind them, gagging them for minutes at a time, blocking out their speeches with derisive shouts.

But certain members were too powerful to be intimidated. By the middle of November the leadership of the minority had shifted away from Martin Sabian, though he still held his seat upon the Board of Health. After he had lost the vote over the Mountain of Redemption, after the gates of the great prison had been sealed, he made fewer public speeches. He devoted more time to his hospital and to his family. The members of his party changed their seats, moving up among the benches of the right side of the hall, where Earnest Darkheart sat beside his wife. The League never penetrated to that side of the chamber, where almost two hundred delegates sat together in a block, dressed in midnight blue.

Over the veto of the majority speaker, Earnest Darkheart was allowed to provide his own security, after the third attempt upon his life. The Board of Health had voted three to one, the president pro tempore abstaining. Colonel Aspe had voted for the first time that month. Standing alone at the top of the chamber, glowering down over the banks of seats, he had searched out Earnest Darkheart with his stare. The two men's eyes had met, and later in the antechamber the Colonel's adjutant was observed in conversation with a captain of the Rebel Angels.

That had been on November 63rd. By the seventh week in November, more than a dozen Rebel Angels sat around their master, blocking the steps, denying all but urgent access. They were evenly divided between men and women, for Earnest Darkheart was a man before his time. They were unarmed, but even so, their mere presence was significant, for Raksha Starbridge had argued strenuously against it. Politics is so often a matter of whim; that small victory was applauded loudly by the opposition. The exchange of glances between Darkheart and the colonel hinted to them a new axis of power. Starting that same week, the colonel came to the assembly every day. After the sessions he was often observed riding in the city with a small guard. And on the evening of November 85th, he spent several hours at the

Sugar Festival, stalking in between the booths.

That evening, at nine o'clock, a spectacle of grotesque cruelty was offered to the patrons of the festival. Coriel Starbridge, widow of the former postmaster of Charn, had been discovered hiding in a garret in the thirteenth ward. A neighbor had alerted the police after she had seen the face of a child in an upstairs window, in a house where two old pensioners, former postal employees, were known to live alone. The Desecration League had found a secret stair. Behind a bookcase in a tiny attic underneath the eaves, they had discovered the unfortunate lady and her son, a boy not seven months old.

The pensioners had been killed during the search, but on the night of the 85th, the public was invited to attend the execution of the lady and the child. Almost four thousand people crowded near the scaffold. In the words of a contemporary chronicler:

> There were so many, part of the gallery collapsed and four were trampled. Though it was worth the sight—they lit torches, and first the young man's eyes were put out with the heated iron, and then his body broke in pieces, all the time his mother was kept by. And though her hands were marked with silver, and though she had the blood of parasites and tyrants in her veins, yet still she impressed many with her beauty and her courage, for while others of her cursed race had put abuse upon their persecutors, or called out to their God to take them up, still she did neither, only turning from the crowd to hide her tears, and saying to the hangman, "Sir, do not make me wait," which sound was so pitiful, that many of the spectators wept sweet tears, and some risked death to call for her relief . . .

This passage is instructive because it shows for the first time a kind of satiation with the violence of revenge. And it is this sense of satiation, rather than any event or personality, that was responsible for what later became known as the December Revolution. But as so often happens, it is in the action of a single individual that the feeling of the time is first made manifest. On the gallery that evening, surrounded by his officers, Colonel Aspe glared down with brooding, bloodshot eyes.

The hangman, perhaps distracted by the reaction of the crowd, required seven strokes of the hammer to complete his work. After the fourth stroke, the colonel dropped his marijuana cigarette and crushed it with the heel of his boot. His adjutant, in his memoirs, describes him leaning with his elbows on the rail, staring down upon the place of death, his hard, hatchet face thrust forward, his steel hand and his gauntlet clasped in front of him. And when the seventh stroke was done, he hawked a great gob of spit out of his throat. Turning aside, he spat it down between the slats of the floor, splattering the people in the gallery below. "Enough," he whispered in his harshest voice. "Enough."

And the next morning he was up at dawn. At the sound of the whistle, when the first soldiers tramped out onto the parade grounds—a muddy, open plain outside the city, where for a month they had drilled and skirmished, and fought mock battles—he was there already, sitting motionless on his horse. His face was shaven and clean, his gray hair combed over his shoulders. All morning he sat without moving, without speaking in the center of the vast ground, while his troops drilled in concentric circles around him in the rain. Towards two o'clock he beckoned to his adjutant and bent low to whisper in his ear.

Those who saw the colonel in this period report that he had changed much from his earlier campaigns, when he had led the bishop's armies to a series of spectacular victories in the last phase of the fighting against Caladon. If anything he was less communicative, harsher, more morose, more susceptible to fits of anger. He was less active, more prone to delegate authority, often staying in his tent for days at a time, staring at nothing with his angry eyes. But at the same time he seemed more sensitive to politics, less irrational in his command. Always before, he had shown his undisguised contempt for strategies and plans, discussion and debate, preferring always action. Military analysts attribute his early victories less to his tactics, which were nonexistent, than to his ability to forge an army into an instrument of his own will, which he could then lay about himself with wildness and irrational abandon, battering his enemies into submission.

But in his later career as commander of the revolutionary armies, and later still as virtual dictator of Charn and Caladon, he showed a new political acumen. At three o'clock on the afternoon of November 86th, his adjutant rode in over the Harbor Bridge, into the sixth ward of the city, where Earnest Darkheart had his party headquarters. He stayed there for perhaps two hours, after which he rode east towards the Mountain of Redemption. There, at about six o'clock, a company of soldiers chased away a small detachment of the League, which was guarding the new masonry at Patience Portal. There, with sledgehammers and iron bars, the soldiers broke the seal on the door, reopening the mountain for the first time since it had been closed, by order of the National Assembly, seven weeks before.

It was, of course, far too late to help most of the inmates; the bells upon the mountain's summit had been silent for twenty-three days. The bonfires on its upper slopes had long burned out. For weeks hundreds of vultures had been observed passing in and out through the upper windows. Clouds of them had reeled and flapped around the Cathedral of the Holy Song, disturbing the city with their rude cries. And when the portal was finally broken, none of the colonel's soldiers ventured inside. Instead they leaped away from their battering ram and dropped their hammers and their picks, for out of the hole that they had made was issuing a huge tide of vermin, rats and surgeon bugs and furry lizards, escaping as if under pressure, scattering down the streets.

It was not until about five hours later that the first of the survivors crawled out, alive through God knew what horrors of cannibalism, and she was taken on a stretcher to Shoemaker's Hospital. Later on through the night, others appeared, singly and in groups, several thousand in all.

On the morning of the 87th, the majority speaker of the National Assembly stood up in his seat to protest. "This arbitrary action . . . ," he began, but then was overtaken by a fit of coughing. Called January First by his supporters, who had lobbied hard for a new calendar, the former priest of Angkhdt was still known in the city by his old, prerevolutionary name: Raksha Starbridge. That day he was at the height of his power—commander of the Desecration League, director of the Festival, president of the Tribunal, speaker of the National Assembly. His lectures on the liberation of the mind were reprinted every day and pasted up on broadsheets all over the city. His "New Precepts of Denial" were mumbled and misquoted at cocktail parties all over Charn. Passages from his book of essays, *Postmodernism and the Structure of Despair,* were embroidered onto people's clothes and tattooed on their skin. Painted onto flags, they hung sodden in the rain above the Morquar Gate.

Nevertheless his intellectual prestige had cloaked for weeks the frailty of his political position. For weeks his power had depended on a fragile coalition of extremists. Though his gift for parliamentary maneuvering was unequaled, still the base of his support had eroded with each vote, as the mood in the assembly changed. All through the month of November his recklessness had found a sympathetic echo in the people, as with viciousness and frenzied hate he had scattered every remnant of the old regime. But finally all that was done, the ancient structure of the state demolished. People stood in the wreck, looking for the first time towards the future.

On the morning of November 87th, the government of Raksha Starbridge depended from a bare majority of seven votes. His own supporters, called the Rim, still comprised the largest single group, but it was losing ground. In order to preserve his power, for weeks Raksha Starbridge had resorted to chicanery: bribery, extortion, kidnapping, and fraud. These devices, effective in the short run, had made him a hero to what remained of his own party. That morning, when he rose to address the National Assembly, his supporters rose with him, and they clogged the air with shouting. Two of them leaped up to bear him on their backs down from his seat along the upper rim, down through the rows of benches to the speaker's platform on the dais. And this was necessary, because in those days Raksha Starbridge could no longer walk without assistance. Weakened by drugs, his body had begun to break apart. He had lost most of his hair, and what remained was streaked with blood. Always he was bleeding, from his nose, his lips, his cheeks, his hands, as if the vessels of his blood were too fragile to contain his life. Not able to stomach solid food, he had lost flesh until his arms and legs were like sticks. His whole body had shriveled and decayed, though he was not yet an old man. And when he got to his feet, he had to hold himself upright, clasping the rim of the speaker's rail in his bandaged, shaking hands.

Yet his voice was still strong. Nasal and compelling, it rose up to the vault of the vast chamber, calling for silence as the crowd stamped and roared. "Citizens," he cried. "This arbitrary action on the part of our armed forces—my colleagues have put forward a response, which I hope you will support. Soon you will hear from them. But first, I would like to speak my mind."

At this point many members of the opposition jumped to their feet, hooting their derision and crying out, "Precedent! Precedent!" until at length they, too, were shouted down. Raksha Starbridge waited patiently until the hammer of the president was heard above the noise; then he resumed. "Citizens," he said. "For weeks our colleague Dr. Sabian, as well as other members of this great assembly have dinned our ears with their complaints. Those who support the recent actions of the army—the events of yesterday night—doubtless will justify themselves on the same grounds."

Here again he was interrupted by a rising swell of voices. He shrugged his shoulders and then turned to the table on the platform, to where a glass of water stood next to a ceramic pitcher. But his hands were shaking. He upset the glass onto the table. It rolled to the edge in a puddle of water and then broke upon the floor, as the noise of the crowd hushed abruptly. It was a trick to gain attention; in the silence following the crash, Raksha Starbridge spun back to the rail. Raising his pallid face, raising his shaking hand, he pointed towards his assembled enemies—towards Colonel Aspe, glowering on his bench, towards Earnest Darkheart and his wife, towards Martin Sabian. When he spoke, his voice was high and shrill.

"Cowards!" he shouted. "Cowards! Fools! I heard with my own ears, when Coriel Starbridge and her son died for their crimes upon the people's scaffold, how some of you cried out in pity. Are you insane? Or else, are your memories so short? One hundred days ago, when we first gathered in this building, then I promised you that I would hunt these devils down, exterminate them all, and not a man stood up against me. Even you, Martin Sabian, even you. Where was your compassion then? One hundred days, one month—is that how long it takes you to forget what you have suffered, what your parents and their parents suffered from this race of tyrants? When you were coughing out your blood upon the altars of Beloved Angkhdt, when you were swinging from the gibbets of the Inquisition, do you imagine Coriel Starbridge wept for you?

"Now, to be sure, certain of our colleagues have addressed this question, claiming that our ancient enemy is crushed, that it is beneath the dignity of this assembly to be vindictive, that we must show ourselves to be superior, after all. They do not understand. Citizens, I am not a monster. It is not that I am thirsty for more blood. But I am a student of history, and I tell you, in four years out of five in this season there has been a revolution of the people. And in four years out of five, in summer and in fall, these Starbridge parasites have crept back among us, until they were as strong as ever. This time, more than ten thousand have already escaped across the border into Caladon. How many have we caught and killed? Fewer than four thousand. Is it any wonder that I have tried to make them an example, so that other generations might not have to go through this again?

"Now of course, this question of the Mountain of Redemption is another matter, one vastly more difficult and sadder. It was my decision, and I reached it after hours of sad imagining. People say I have no heart—I ask you, is it mercy to release a crowd of half a million homeless people into the streets? I tell you, they would have starved, and we would have starved with them. If Martin Sabian claims differently, he is a liar. Even now in the sixth ward, the citizens are eating seaweed scraped from rocks, and even that has to be imported.

"Now, be that as it may, it was my opinion that if they were to starve, then better privately than publicly. In my speech to this assembly I made a comparison, saying that if a man has just enough to feed himself and gives half of it to a stranger, then both will starve. It was my opinion that the population of the mountain formed an ever-present danger to the population of this city, as well as to the safety of this government. It was my opinion, simply that, and it was taken and made law by the members of this great assembly.

"But now, because of the policies of the present government, the specter of starvation has receded somewhat. Now we can afford to be compassionate. Now we can afford to assign blame, once the problem is no more. It is true: Thousands, perhaps hundreds of thousands, have died. That is a tragedy. All death is a tragedy. I myself, I know, am soon to die. It is for this reason, perhaps, that I think differently than you, who are yet in the middle of your life and strength. Look at me! Look at my hands, look into my face, and believe me when I say that a man's life is nothing, less than nothing, and that we should not be afraid. Justice is everything, liberty is everything, but a man's life is worth nothing, for it is gone in the tremor of an eye. From inside ourselves we seem like magic beings, our brains as big as continents, and we fear death like the annihilation of the world. I thought so once myself. But now I see that men barely exist. I look about me and I see the dead, all those who died so that the state might live. I see in my mind's eye an image of the state, a huge, imperishable building of blank stone, and all about it a vast park, with all the souls of all the dead men underfoot like grains of dirt. Soon I will be one of them."

This was the final speech of Raksha Starbridge before the National Assembly of Charn. Along with some other writings it was collected into a book of posthumous essays, *The Illusion of the Self*. When his followers fled the city they took this manuscript; elsewhere it was banned. Together with his other writings, it formed the base of a new book. Brutally suppressed, nevertheless it flourished underground, and in time a cult of true believers, remnants of the League, bore its message north, beyond the range of persecution. Later that same year, it was reported, children and grandchildren of these people passed beyond Rangriver. There in that traditional refuge, they hunted and ate meat, reading the precepts of denial until language failed and they used the books for kindling.

* * *

But on the 87th of November in the eighth phase of spring, in the chamber of the National Assembly, when Raksha Starbridge had finished speaking there was silence for about half a minute. Then Valium Samosir got up to read the resolution, which was designed to make the army more responsive to civilian government. It was a complicated proposal, but nobody was interested in debating it. Both sides—the Rebel Angels and the Rim—were anxious for a show of strength and used the resolution as a pretext. After a few hours of halfhearted arguments, the president asked the delegates to stand apart. Soldiers of the Desecration League moved among the benches, stopping fistfights and disputes. The delegates returned to their places, and the tense, enervating business of the roll call was commenced, with the bailiff reading out the names. Each delegate would raise his right hand or his left.

That day there were many abstentions. People hesitated to commit themselves, for they all knew that something was about to happen, the voting was so close. And at every name, men raised their heads to stare up at the vote, which the bailiff recomputed on a board above the dais, and to stare at the combatants, who waged their struggle silently in this war of alternating numbers. Raksha Starbridge stood upon the platform, his head bent low, his hands shaking on the rail. Colonel Aspe sat immense and silent, picking his nose with the index finger of his steel hand. Earnest Darkheart, black-skinned and somber, leaned backwards to listen to his wife, who had her hand upon his shoulder.

Raksha Starbridge had voted first, which was the prerogative of the majority speaker. But finally, after half an hour, as the bailiff read the third-to-the-last name, Raksha Starbridge raised his hand. On the bailiff's board the vote stood deadlocked, 319 to 319, with 121 abstentions. But the last three delegates were on their feet. One, a solid member of the Rim, was waving his right hand. But the last two were Rebel Angels, and when he saw them standing in their places, clothed in midnight blue, Raksha Starbridge signaled to the president to stop. "I'd like to change my vote," he said.

Instantly Earnest Darkheart was on his feet. "Little fuckface!" he shouted. "It's your own law. You can't vote against it."

But again, Raksha Starbridge raised his hand. "It is my prerogative," he said. "The proposal was read by Mr. Samosir, not me."

At issue was a parliamentary device by which any delegate who voted with the majority could ask for a recount on a variety of pretexts. Raksha Starbridge had used that loophole once before, changing his vote when defeat seemed certain. During the recess the Desecration League had visited a dozen members in their houses, to ensure that at the recount the next day the Rim would be victorious.

But this time, Earnest Darkheart was prepared. "No!" he shouted. "Starbridge murderer! How long can we endure this tyranny?" And then he went storming down the rows of seats, pushing delegates aside as the president rapped his hammer. Instantly soldiers of the Desecration League went up to meet him, their truncheons in their hands.

But on the left side of the chamber, the seats around the colonel were dark with his officers in their black uniforms. As Earnest Darkheart rose, they had risen too, though their leader still sat sprawling in his chair, picking his nose. One shouted out, and at the word, sixteen soldiers of the new model army burst through the doors at the top of the chamber and spread out among the upper benches with automatic rifles in their hands. At the same time, the colonel's adjutant drew a pistol from his waist. Holding it in both hands out in front of him, he blew a hole through the captain of the League, who was charging up the steps. At that the whole hall erupted into violence, and in the confusion Earnest Darkheart pushed his way down onto the dais. Leaping over the rail, he jumped onto the speaker's platform, and he took Raksha Starbridge's head between his hands and crushed him down onto the floor, crushing him senseless and breaking his jaw.

That was the end of him. He was led away by Aspe's soldiers and kept under arrest in Wanhope Hospital, close by. That night an enormous crowd of people rioted for his release. From Morquar Gate to the assembly, they burned shops and pillaged houses, and towards dawn they tried to break into the hospital. But there they were dispersed by Aspe's troops: two companies of what had at one time been the bishop's purge. They had taken down the silver dog's head from their flags, and torn the bishop's ensign from their collars. But they were still the purge, black-coated and contemptuous, their officers on horseback, armed with whips and nothing else, the men striding through the crowd, looking for the orange badges of the League.

By five o'clock it was all over. Many of the members of the Rim had been imprisoned, on various charges of malicious mayhem. The League was scattered; even so, Valium Samosir and five hundred followers left the city by the northern gates, half an hour before dawn. They took with them a treasure of gold and works of art, reported variously at seven and eleven million dollars, looted from the public storerooms and from Kindness and Repair. Fifty miles north of Charn they joined with local cadres of the Desecration League, in the abandoned glassworks of Badgaon.

But in Charn, on the 91st, when he was strong enough to stand, Raksha Starbridge went on trial before the National Assembly. The charges against him—perjury, fraud, and possession of a hypodermic—seemed out of balance with the penalty, but it didn't matter. In the assembly chamber there were only ninety delegates still wearing the colors of the Rim. Of the rest, most were in prison or had fled away. Of those who remained, few dared to speak; they sat huddled in their seats.

The evidence took seven hours to read. When it was over Raksha Starbridge asked to be assisted to his feet, so that he might address the chamber. He was sitting in the dock below the speaker's platform, which was empty. But no one ventured to assist him, and no one could understand him when he spoke, for his jaw was wired shut. He tottered to his feet, and staggered to the rail and raised his hands, but no one could understand him. No one could hear him over the chanting of the Rebel Angels, who were stamping their feet and pounding on their chairs, and chanting, "Starbridge, Starbridge, Starbridge," till the chamber shook.

After a few minutes Raksha Starbridge sat back down. The assembly passed a vote of censure, and after that the verdict of the Tribunal was inevitable. Of the seven members, five had been appointed that same day.

On the 92nd, Raksha Starbridge met his end, grinning and shaking on the scaffold of the Morquar Gate. Spectators jammed onto the roofs of the adjoining houses, breaking the slates and kicking down the chimneys.

Two days later they climbed again onto the same roofs, to watch Colonel Aspe lead his soldiers up the Street of Seven Sins, out over the fairgrounds and northward over the hills towards Badgaon. In the evening there was a terrible storm, a hail of crystals as heavy as ball bearings, which bruised people's skin and made the roads impassable. In the poorer wards, people crouched under their shelters as the rain fell like blows from a hammer on the boards above their heads. Many small buildings fell down that night, collapsing from the weight of sugar on their roofs. In the morning the rain lay everywhere in crystal piles, smoldering from the pressure of its own mass. In the fairgrounds of the festival the canvas hung like rags from the tentpoles, and more than half the booths were beaten down. The ferris wheel had fallen on an angle, twenty degrees away from perpendicular.

* * *

This new weather lasted intermittently through January.
Every day there was some kind of hard precipitation. Sometimes the sky seemed full of glass. Some nights there was a
sound like breaking bottles everywhere, and in the morning
there were jagged shards of crystal in the streets. Children
sucked on it like candy, and some fell sick. It contained
unhealthy minerals which affected the nervous system,
causing insomnia and fretfulness. In the countryside beyond
the city, Aspe's soldiers followed the uneven ground. In
barren valleys and in rifts of clay they camped under
shelters of corrugated tin. At night they wore earplugs, and
by day they carried steel umbrellas. The rain battered them
and pounded down upon their heads, but even so they kept
strict discipline, marching north through country that had
recently been desert. Now, under the deluge, life was coming back: lichens and mosses creeping over the stones, the
cracks full of beetles and wet slugs.

And there were people, too. There were people in the
hills, returning to farms and villages abandoned by their
grandparents, trying to scratch some living off the rocks. In
a town of fifty houses, nestled in a rock ravine near the
Caladonian frontier, half a dozen families had made new
homes. They had raised new rooftops, repaired old walls.
Dry all winter, the creek was full of water, and on the morning of December 1st, Charity Starbridge stepped from rock
to rock above the stream, trying to find purchase on the
heavy sugar crust. Off balance, she waved her hands in the
air. Upstream, up ahead, a small boy waved back.

She had left the village at first light, well rested and carrying a pack. It was twenty miles to the Whisper Bridge
where she would cross to Caladon: two days' journey over
that terrain. The village had provided a guide, a young boy,
the youngest child of the family who had first taken her in.
Four weeks before, when she had first come up from underground, they had nursed her and fed her with a kindness

that had seemed bewildering in that stark land.

She had stayed in the village longer than she had intended. It had taken her a long time to regain her strength. And the villagers had been so kind; some days she had thought that she might stay forever. They had begged her to stay, and sometimes she had thought, What's Caladon to me? My cousin may be dead.

Sometimes, lying in bed, or walking with the shepherds as they took their flocks into the canyons, she had been tempted to stay. She had been lulled into a sense of peace. But in the last week of November, there were rumors of new soldiers in the area. A skirmish had been fought at Axel's Cross, between the League and Aspe's troops, and then the League was scattering northwards, refugees themselves. On the evening of the 98th, boys from the village had seen fires on the ridge. On the 99th, the village elders had brought the princess gifts: a shagweed blanket, a steel knife, and a new coat. They had knelt to kiss her hands.

Up ahead the trail left the creek and wandered up a slope of barren scree. Her guide waved back at her, and she stopped, resting, pushing the sugar from her eyes. She tilted her head, turning away from him and looking towards the ridge, searching for the music that she thought she had heard all morning, above the sound of water and the pounding of the rain. Throughout her whole stay at the village she had sought for it, the music of the copper flute. Sometimes she was sure the antinomial was keeping with her, unseen among the rocks, coming down in darkness, playing music just beyond the limit of her ears. Sometimes Charity was sure that she had gone. Why would she stay? Once Charity had taken food up to the ledge above the village, new potatoes wrapped in grass; in the morning they were gone, proving nothing.

She wiped the rain out of her eyes and clambered up the slope. At noon she rested with her guide, and again at four o'clock. At sundown they stood upon the highest ridge, under the shelter of a pinnacle of rock.

"Look," said the boy. He pointed out over the valley, and in the distance she could see the Whisper Bridge, a single, arching span of metal, built in the reign of the nineteenth bishop to commemorate some victory. Half-hidden in the mist, it rose up on the far horizon, joining the lips of a deep crevasse. On the other side lay Caladon, shrouded in darkness. For thirty miles in each direction, the bridge was the only place to cross, for the Moldau River was impassable that season, swollen by the rain.

The bridge itself, a metal span not five feet wide, was dangerous. It had been built for purposes of ceremonial, back when the road through the crevasse was dry, and it had supported a great lantern, a beacon of victory, hanging from the middle of the arch. The light had been extinct for generations, but there still existed, clamped to the outside of the span, the steel rungs that the lamplighters had used, up one slope and down the other. On still nights, travelers had been known to slip across.

In the shelter of the pinnacle, in a cave hollowed from the rock, Charity made camp. She sat with her back against the stones, exhausted, looking out towards the bridge. There she fell asleep, curled in her blanket while the boy sat guard. He was proud of his responsibility, but in the morning he was fast asleep. At dawn Charity left him behind, curled up among the rocks, and she left the steel knife, too, determined not to find a use for it. She felt lighthearted, safe: the trail ran straight and true down to the bridge, or so she thought. But by midmorning she was lost, for the rain had washed away the route. The boulders were the size of houses, and the scree was slippery and loose. At one point a whole slope of it started to move, and she fell down to her knees in bitter sand and shards of silicon.

Cursing with frustration, she continued on, choosing the way at random, searching for higher ground. And when she

heard a noise behind her, she turned around, hoping that
the boy had followed her. But it was not he. Down below, at
the bottom of the ravine, a man was leading a horse.

He was a soldier, dressed in high boots and stiff black
pants. He wore a vest of some quilted material, which left
his arms and shoulders bare. His hair was long under a
studded steel cap, and he was carrying a rifle on his back.
His horse was a good one, sleek and well fed, its horns
sharp and gilded. It was heavily loaded, with a high,
wooden saddle and many odd-shaped bundles.

Charity crouched down behind some rocks. She was too
far away to see the soldier's hands, but he was wearing an
ensign, a tattered orange scarf tied to his naked bicep. It
was the token of the League, and when she saw it, she staggered back, twisting her foot between two stones. Dis-
lodged by her heel, one clattered down the slope, a rock the
size of a man's head, and it came to rest between the soldier's boots.

He raised his face. Charity ducked down out of sight, but
the movement betrayed her. Other stones followed the first.
Peering through the sticky rain, the soldier took his rifle
from his back. "Come out," he said. "Come out where I can
see you."

Charity stayed low. But when the soldier started towards
her up the slope, she turned and ran. Leaving her refuge in
the boulders, she clambered on all fours over the uncertain
shale, diagonally up the wall of the ravine. She trusted that
the soldier would not leave his horse; nevertheless, her back
felt cold and big. She was hoping that his rifle might misfire
in the rain. It often happened, but in fact he never raised his
gun. He just stood there, up to his ankles in the slippery
rock, while she scampered on up the ravine. But after a few
yards the shale gave out onto a slope of powdered silicon,
and the rock was mixed with mud and shards of rain. She
slipped and fell, and then the whole slope subsided downwards, so that she lost her balance and fell down, sinking to

her elbows in the sticky marl. The soldier never moved. He
waited, and in time she came to him, sliding downwards in a
clatter of small stones.

"What have we here?" said the soldier. She did not look
up. But he reached down and put his fingers underneath her
jaw, and Charity could smell the dust on his hand, the cin-
nabar dye that the soldiers used to cover their tattoos. It left
a mark upon her cheek. He used no force; he didn't have
to. But she could feel his strength, and so she turned her
face to look at him.

It had been a young, trim soldier who had accosted her
with the same gesture, upon the stair in Mrs. Soapwood's
house, the brothel in the Python Road. This man was
younger still, but he looked tired. There was sugar crusted
in the corners of his eyes, and a bandage on his collarbone.
He had broken his front tooth. But his smile was the same,
and the courtesy with which he helped her to her feet.

"What have we here?" he repeated, and then he pushed
the hair back from her face.

As she had upon the staircase, she had knotted her hands
into fists. But with insinuating ease he coaxed open her
fingers and rubbed away some of the mud. And when he
saw the silver rose, he clicked his tongue. Once more he
touched her face, polluting the skin next to her eye while
she said nothing. But then his smile widened to a grin. He
took her hand again and rubbed the skin under her thumb.
Then, with a movement that was neither fast nor slow, he
forced her hand behind her, turning her around so that he
stood in back of her. He forced her hand up between her
shoulderblades and then let go, almost before she felt the
pain. She stumbled forward and the soldier followed her,
stopping, when they passed his horse, to pick up the end of
the halter. The horse had wandered a few feet away, searching for insects among the rocks.

"Straight on," said the soldier. "Don't talk." He touched
her on the back with the barrel of his rifle, and pointed up

the bowl of the ravine. It was a different way than Charity had chosen; she had been aiming for the ridge, up to the right. The soldier's way was easier, more suitable for horses. In time they reached the banks of a small stream. It had been flowing through the rocks beneath their feet. She had heard it gurgling and coughing for many minutes before it rose up through a pile of rock debris.

Behind her the soldier was singing in a sweet, gentle voice. It was a love song, but he had forgotten many of the words, and so he filled the gaps with nonsense syllables, laughing to himself. He stopped at the stream to let the horse refresh itself. Charity moved ahead, and he didn't try to restrain her, only followed her when he was through, up over the saddle of the land, and into a small valley.

In time they came to a small camp: five tents in a circle next to a clear pool. The sky was threatening and overcast, but the rain had stopped. Charity was grateful for the quiet. She ran her fingers through her hair. "Where is your commander?" she said suddenly. The valley seemed deserted.

"He was killed at Axel's Cross. We are equals—six of us. The rest are foraging." The soldier squinted at the sky. "I don't expect them back tonight."

Charity sat down on a rock above the pool. "I was lucky," said the soldier. "Look at this—real wood. I found it in a mine shaft, south of here." As he spoke, he was unloading the bundles from his horse.

Charity looked down into the pool. She took off her quilted cap and reached down into the pool to wash her face. "Wash yourself," suggested the soldier. "You can't be used to this." Then he laughed. "What are you doing here? Starbridge, aren't you?" The soldier smiled and returned to work.

He heaved the saddle off his horse's back, and from the mouth of a nearby tent he pulled a long, quilted blanket. After rubbing down the horse and combing out its tail and mane with a steel comb, he hauled the blanket over the beast's head. The cloth was fitted into sections. Long flaps hung down over the animal's flanks and legs, but they were tied up tight around its buttocks and its neck. Over its head the soldier fitted a kind of hood, covering its eyes but leaving its beak exposed, protruding through a hole in the material. Then he walked around the animal, fastening buckles, opening and closing zippers, until the beast was swaddled to his satisfaction. Then, last of all, he pulled a plastic bucket from his tent, and Charity could see that it was full of slugs.

All that time Charity had been washing herself as best she could, at first more out of nervousness than any desire to be clean. But it felt good to wipe the sugar from her face, to wash the mud out of her hair. As she did so, the familiar movements took on a kind of rhythm that was comforting. It soothed her and made her feel more powerful, as if she were preparing herself physically for what she had to do. When the soldier is asleep, she thought, I will break away. I will break away in darkness, before his friends come back.

At that moment came a groaning, tearing sound from far away, a metallic creaking on the wind. The soldier stopped and looked up towards the east, holding the bucket of slugs between his hands. "The Whisper Bridge," he said. "Is that where you were headed?"

"And you?"

He shrugged. "I've got a lot to carry. And a horse. Besides, I can't imagine that I'd be welcome at the border, scum like me."

As he spoke, he reached one hand in through the hole over the horse's mouth, and he was fussing with the bridle there. A hook was sewn into the blanket underneath the horse's head; he brought the bucket up and hooked it by its handle.

Through the open hole, Charity could see the thick, cruel beak dig down into the meat. Sick to her stomach, she turned her face away and watched the soldier rummage through her pack. He was clicking his tongue in pleasure over her small bag of food. The villagers had given her potatoes and a container filled with isinglass.

"This is good," he said, looking up at her and smiling. "We'll have a feast. I've got chocolates and candied ginger, and of course all kinds of wine, but no food—where did you find this? I've been eating candy for two days."

In the open space between the tents, the soldier made a fire. As evening fell, slowly the flames became visible to Charity as she sat by the pool. The rain had stopped, and at intervals there was a breath of wind, accompanied always by the music of the bridge. At other times the soldier sang, as he pulled wood from his canvas bags and broke it into shards, as he watered his horse and tethered it outside the circle of the light. He was boiling the potatoes in a bucket on the fire.

Yet all the time he was watching Charity closely, and his gun was always near to hand. Once, while he was squatting by the fire, he bent down with his back to her. She got up quickly, silently, but then she noticed he was staring back at her, even while his hands were busy with the fire. He was grinning back at her through his own legs, his face framed by his own body, upside down.

Then, when it was almost dark, he called to her. He came out from the brightness of the fire to stand near where she was sitting. He was carrying some clothing in his hands. She couldn't see the color, but it seemed light and insubstantial. He laid it carefully upon a rock. "Put this on," he said, and when she made no motion, he frowned. "Do as I say. People can be brutal. I want to be kind." He had a knife in his belt, a cruel, hooked blade.

Charity took the dress into her hands, unfolded it, and laid it out. It was made of spider gossamer and gold embroidery, miraculous and beautiful. "Besides," said the soldier. "I didn't think you'd be offended. It is part of the wardrobe of the bishop of Charn."

Charity bowed her head. "No," she murmured softly. "I can't wear her clothes. She's dead."

Again the soldier put his hand out to touch her cheek. "You'll do as I say," he told her, his voice no louder than her own. "You will. How can I know that I exist? By what I make you do." He was playing with her hair.

"Go change," he said. "There." He gestured towards the entrance of the largest tent, but she did nothing, only sat there with the bishop's dress upon her lap.

"Besides," the soldier said after a moment. "If it makes you feel better, she may not be dead."

He had a pouch of canvas hanging from his belt. He reached into it and pulled out a small silver ball. It was streaked with dirt and sugar, but when he knelt down by Charity she could see how fine it was, the silver apple of the world, with the continents engraved in silver gilt.

"We were the first in Kindness and Repair," continued the soldier. "Jonas and me. When we broke in, her funeral pyre was still smoking, and Earnest Darkheart offered us a hundred dollars to comb through the ashes. There was nothing there. No bones, nothing. Then we broke into the grave where they had laid her lover. The heretic. The cannibal. But it was empty."

Charity shrugged, but he went on: "I know that doesn't prove a thing. But we must have taken close to a thousand prisoners. Not one had seen her die—actually seen her burning in the flesh. They all said that they had seen a vision, a fruit tree on fire in the middle of the courtyard."

The soldier was excited. He was rubbing the silver apple on his pants, smudging its surface with his dirty fingers. "This is the fruit I found," he said. "I found it in her prison cell, in Kindness and Repair. The door was standing open and the room was wrecked. I found it underneath her bed."

A wind had sprung up from the south, full of sugar grit. Charity hugged her arms around her chest. "Tell me what it says," resumed the soldier. He turned the apple in his hand.

"Summer continents," he said. "The shorelines are all different. Tell me what it says." Charity could make out a line of Starbridge script in the ocean underneath his thumb.

"'Look for me among the days to come,'" she read.

"There!" the man exulted, rising to his feet. He tossed the apple in the air and then replaced it in his pouch. He was smiling and laughing, and then his face turned cruel. "There," he said, drawing his knife. "And here you are. You be the bishop now." With his other hand he pointed to the tent.

It was a rectangular structure perhaps twelve feet long. Outside, a small lamp was burning, a kerosene lantern with a wire handle.

Charity took it with her when she stepped inside. She ducked under the flap, but in fact the tent was almost tall enough for her to stand erect. And when she lifted up the lantern, she was astonished, for the light fell crookedly on an enormous pile of wealth: carpets, ingots, tapestries, and loose jewels; rolled-up canvases, and balls of musk; vials of attar, and carved gold. It was loot from the temples and the palaces of Charn, her family's wealth, and to Charity the sight of it was heartbreaking in a way she couldn't analyze. She sat down upon a roll of silk brocade and began to cry.

But in a little while she felt stronger, less afraid. Thousands had died, yet she was still alive. Surely that could not have been by chance—surely she was not meant to die here, after all? She put the lantern down upon an empty section of the floor.

The soldier shouted at her from outside the tent, something she couldn't hear. She blocked it from her mind. She picked up an embroidered linen towel from a pile, and with it she rubbed the sugar from her hair, and wiped her face and arms. She stripped off her wet clothes and rubbed her body clean, until her skin felt fresh and hot. Then she unrolled the bishop's dress. It was in two parts, a loose outergarment and a sheer white slip. Made for a smaller woman, it fit well enough, though it was snug around her breasts and hips. And the softness of the silk made her feel better just to touch it. Her skin remembered the old feeling. All through her journey she had dressed in borrowed clothes; this, finally, was a garment suitable for her. Putting it on, she felt a flush of strength.

In a bronzewood chest she found a necklace of gold beads and malachite. The holes in her earlobes and nostrils had grown closed; she passed over a tray of earrings and je-welled studs, and selected instead a golden bracelet, and clasped it to her wrist. It hung down over the back of her right hand, a web of interlocking chains, fastened to her fingers with gold rings. It jingled when she moved her hand.

Again, outside, she heard the soldier's voice but took no notice. She sat cross-legged on a carpet, rubbing her nails. In a lower section of the chest she found a case of aromatic powders: kohl, crushed amber, and antimony. With a rat-tailed brush she traced a line of gold along the hard muscles of her jaw, and rimmed her eyes with indigo. She put a drop of kohl into each eye.

The brush was long and made of silver, intricately carved and sharpened to a point. She held it suspended above her eye, staring into the mirror that was set into the back of the box. She had not seen her own face in a long time.

She was still sitting there when the soldier came into the tent. He too had washed and changed his clothes. He wore a satin shirt with a ripped sleeve. In one hand he carried an open bottle of champagne, and in the other a tin plate of food. He ducked his head under the tent flap and then stood in the doorway looking down at her. Already he smelled drunk, and he wavered a little on his feet. She couldn't see his face. The lantern threw a soft and peaceful light.

"I've brought you some food," he said. Two white, round potatoes rolled along the edge of his tin plate.

"You take them," said Charity. Her voice had no expression, and she didn't look at him. Only she sat with the brush poised over her eye.

"Not good enough, I guess," complained the soldier. But he shifted the neck of the bottle to the crook between his fifth and smallest fingers, and with his forefinger and thumb he picked up the potatoes, one after the other, and put them on his tongue. He closed his eyes and crushed them in his mouth, and washed them down with wine.

"There's chocolate in the bag," he said, wiping his lips. He nodded towards the corner. But when Charity made no movement, he grunted: "I don't blame you. Six weeks ago I had my first piece, and I thought I'd never get enough. Now..." He shook his head.

Charity sat still, and admired the lamplight on the canvas of the tent, and on the heaps of Starbridge treasure. The gold, especially, seemed to glow. On a pile of maps and manuscripts in the corner of the tent, fourteen golden statues lay in a line, arranged upon their backs. There was Angkhdt the Lord of Animals, and Angkhdt the God of Light, and Angkhdt the Dancing Master, and Angkhdt of a Thousand Eyes, and Angkhdt dismembered in the Warlock's tomb, and Angkhdt the God of Rapture, his penis stiff and hard, and winking with encrusted gems.

The shadows moved. The soldier made a movement with the bottle in his hand. "Take some," he said. And when Charity made no reply, he stepped forward, away from the entrance of the tent, holding out the bottle by its neck. "Take some," he repeated. "I want you to enjoy it. Enjoy it when I... when I fuck you."

At that, Charity drew her eyebrows together, and knotted her forehead into a frown. She looked at the soldier for the first time since he had come into the tent, and she studied his face and clothes and hair, and saw for the first time how young he was, how vulnerable, how dangerous. A woman has a kind of power, she thought, her mind slow and sad.

She had been holding her silver paintbrush in the air,

poised between them like a weapon. "I am not making myself beautiful for you," she said.

"No?"

"No. Tomorrow I will be in Caladon."

The soldier took another swig of wine. "We'll see about that," he said. "When the rest get back, then we'll see. The last woman we had here, she lasted a long time."

Charity looked at the lamplight on the soldier's young face. She remembered part of a song that the antinomial had taught her, one of the many kinds of fire songs, and this one was about shadows on an uneven surface when the lamplight touched it like a finger. "Not for you," she said. "Not for you and not for them. You think I am a whore, but I am not. I am Charity Starbridge, princess of the seventh rank. I am not the woman for your stupid games."

The soldier sat down in front of her. "What a pain in the ass," he grumbled, but Charity wasn't listening. The lamplight fell obliquely on the moving canvas near her head. Her mind was full of songs and wordless memories. And then suddenly she became aware of something in the tent, an object that protruded at an angle from a pile of gold and gems. It was a length of copper pipe, with a row of holes punched into its side.

With a cry, Charity lowered the silver paintbrush and reached forward. For many minutes, without seeing it, she had been staring at the copper flute. Now suddenly she understood why the fire music was so fresh in her, the presence of the antinomial so imperative. With a cry, she reached forward and plucked the flute out of the pile of gold. The soldier shied away, reaching for his knife, but Charity did nothing. Only she sat cross-legged, grasping the flute in her left hand, feeling unexpected strength course through her. "What is this?" she cried. "Where did you find this?"

The soldier looked at her warily, his hand upon his knife. Then he shrugged. "It belonged to a woman who was here."

Again Charity felt the music surge inside of her, tangled fire songs, snatches of memory. "Where is she?" she cried. "Where is she now?"

The soldier set the bottle down between them on the carpet. It was empty. "She ran away," he said. "She bit through her ropes and ran away."

He was the kind of person who finds it hard to ignore a question. He had an instinct for the truth, and he was young and nervous. Charity felt that with a reflex of her mind, and felt where her advantage lay.

More than that, there was something about this subject that still puzzled him. "Her teeth were sharp," he said. "She bit through the gag between her teeth. The ropes around her hands. She stole one of the horses. Jonas said that he would kill her. He rode after her, but never came back. That was a week ago."

"She escaped?"

The soldier shrugged. "Who knows? I didn't care. She was an ugly brute. Ungrateful. We rescued her from farmers who were trying to kill her. On the riverbank. They were hitting her with shovels, but we chased them off. That first night she bit a hole in Joney's cheek."

"But did you know? Did you understand what she was?"

The soldier frowned. "Of course. We could hear the sounds she made. She was a meat eater. Antinomial. Marco wanted to kill her right away. But Jonas and the rest—besides, I am not like them. I had read the speaker's book."

He had been staring at the flute in Charity's hand. But then he looked up at her face. "Enough of that," he said. "Besides, what do you know about it? No—don't answer that. I found you, and I want you. Before the rest get back. I want you first."

Impatient, Charity shook her head. "Tell me," she said. "Tell me what happened. Later, perhaps I'll give you what you want. You'd like that better, wouldn't you?"

A gust of wind shook the tent, bringing them the music

from the Whisper Bridge. The soldier turned his head, as if he were listening to something else, far in the distance. Charity took advantage of the moment to slip the silver paintbrush into the sleeve of her silk gown. When the soldier turned back she was frowning at him, and she put the flute down on the floor beside the bottle of champagne.

The soldier shrugged. "I'm not like them," he said at last. With unsteady fingers he reached into the top of his left boot, and withdrew a stained and battered pamphlet. It was entitled *The Redundancy of Suicide* in crude block letters. There was no author's name. But Charity recognized the coarse yellow paper on which Raksha Starbridge printed his tracts.

The pamphlet was much smudged with orange dye. The soldier leafed through it, and then ran his finger down the margin of one page. "Listen to what the speaker says," he said. And then he began to read, badly and very slowly, mispronouncing many words.

"'How then,'" he said, "'can we know that we exist? Surely not by our own sensations, for, as we have seen, such subjective information is worth nothing. God created man, but God does not exist, that much is clear. What does that say about the universe, to know that its architect and builder was fictitious? No, we cannot look for proof outside ourselves.'"

The soldier broke off in the midst of reading "You understand," he said. "Look—here in your eyes, I see something. I talk, you talk. I know that I'm alive. But what if that is part of it—just nothing, just two ghosts? Two ghosts, trying to fool themselves? But that woman—so I thought, here is a woman who is free. No future. No past. No name. We all say that God does not exist; here was a woman, finally, who knew it. Not just in her brain, but in her heart."

The soldier laid the book aside. After a little while he went on: "We tied her up. This was a week ago. The others were asleep; I got up and went outside. It was raining. So dark. Only in the darkness I could hear her breathing, in another tent. They had tied a rope around her mouth, but she was making a noise. Whistling in the dark. Music. Very slow. I went in and lit the candle. She was lying on her side. Tied up, you know. Tied hands and feet. But her eyes were open. I bent down to see. Her eyes were black from the darkness, but they got smaller as I brought the candle close. You understand—that was the only movement in her face. Her pupils closing down. Most people, their eyes are like a room, and you can go and live in there."

"You let her go," breathed Charity.

The soldier shook his head. "I hate to see an animal tied up," he said. "I cut the rope between her teeth. She did the rest. In the morning she was gone."

Charity felt a surge of hope. "Well then," she said softly. "Perhaps you'll do the same for me."

As soon as she had spoken, she realized the mistake. She had succumbed to the temptation of weakness; the soldier put his thoughts aside. He picked up the empty bottle of champagne, raised it to his lips, and put it down. Then he reached out his hand and seized her wrist.

With a single flex of his powerful arm, he twisted her around and pushed her down, so that she lay on her stomach on a pile of rolled-up carpets. He caught hold of both her wrists in one single massive hand, and with the other he grabbed her by the back of the neck, and forced her head down into the hard wool.

"There is something else," he said. "Some other way to tell." He removed his hand from her neck and drew his knife with it, and laid the crooked steel next to her ear, along her cheek. He was kneeling behind her, forcing one knee up between her legs, forcing her forward until her thighs weakened and let go. She bit her lips to keep from crying out.

Still, after all, he felt disposed to talk. "How do we know?" he said, from between clenched teeth. "How can we know that we exist? What is outside? Rocks and water and a few bugs. The speaker taught me everything, and now he's dead."

He was hurting her. His hands were hard and strong. But at every twist, every shove, they seemed to hesitate, as if his brutality were still unreal to him, an act of will and not of instinct. And still he kept on talking. "When I was a kid," he said, "I used to think, gold in my pocket, chocolate and champagne, naked women, princesses, freedom to go—I used to pray to God. But look at me. I have all that, and look at me. How can they pretend that life has meaning?"

He forced his knee between her legs. He released her wrists; with one hand, filthy, orange, he held his knife next to her ear, and with the other he probed under her dress, scraping the flesh there with his fingernails. Charity lifted herself onto her forearms. She turned her cheek against the rough nap of the carpet. It was wet from her spit.

The soldier put his hand around her tail. He was still talking, his slow, puzzled voice in contrast to his violent hand. "The speaker had discovered a new kind of sex. It's in the book." He ran his fingernail between the lips of her vagina. "Not here," he said. Then, hesitantly, he forced his bunched-up fingers into her rectum, bringing tears to her eyes, bile to her mouth.

"Here," he said. "The speaker tells us we must change our ways."

Suddenly, miraculously, the hand was gone from her. On the cushions beside her, he was fumbling with his book. "'We must take our sexuality out of the myth of procreation,'" she heard him say. He stumbled over the works and lost his place. Then again: "'Making life is an illusion.'"

As he spoke, he was unbuttoning his pants. But too much pedantry had robbed him of his urge; he pressed against her, and Charity could feel the limp skin along her back. And something else: Distracted by his own despair, he had let his knife slip from her ear. She turned her mouth into his hand and bit his thumb with all her strength. She felt her teeth turn on the bone.

He cursed, and dropped the knife. With his other hand he tried to find her face, but she rolled away under his arm, reaching for the paintbrush in her sleeve. She stabbed it up into his neck, and he let go of her, bringing his hands up to protect himself; he thought it was the knife. She rolled free, and as he struggled to get up, she jumped on him.

It was no contest. She was furious with rage, while he was drunk and dizzy. Besides, he didn't care. He thought it was a game. In the end she knelt over his back, pulling on his hair, pressing the sharp end of the paintbrush deep against his throat. He was lying face down on his open book, his shoulders shaking as he laughed.

"Do it," he said. "Starbridge cunt!" His pelvis squirmed under her legs. He was humping his stiff cock against the floor.

"Shut up," said Charity. She thrust the silver paintbrush into his neck until she thought she must be hurting him, and finally he was quiet. But there was nothing in her mind. It was empty of possibilities. She looked around the tent: There was the lamp, its chimney still intact. There was the knife, under some pillows. There was the bottle; it had rolled onto its side. There was the flute. As she saw it, a small tremor of music started in her mind, and it mixed with the sound of wind in canvas, and the distant groaning of the bridge. And something else: quite close, the sound of drunken singing.

The soldier heard it too. "Here they come," he said.

"Shut up," she told him. "Shut your mouth." She pushed his head down on the floor, but she could see that he was smiling.

Together they listened to the voices coming closer. The soldier was wriggling his hips, squirming for relief against the carpets. "Do it," he said again. And then he forced her, shouting out for help in his strong voice. She pressed down upon the paintbrush, running it deep into his neck, looking for the vein, spattering the open book with blood.

That night, in Caladon, in her oilcloth shelter, in the hospital beneath the city walls, Jenny Pentecost sat drawing. It was late. On the cot beside her, Mrs. Cassimer lay sleeping. Her fat old face was softened and relaxed. Her mouth was open, but she made no sound.

In the corner, in the crib, the baby lay, sleeping too. From where Jenny sat, she could see his pale fist through the bars, but his head was hidden by his pillow.

Light came from a single candle on her desk. Jenny turned back to her drawing. In it, three men led their horses over a rise of polished stone. One was carrying a torch. One was pointing down the slope, towards where five tents stood next to a small pool. One had stopped, astonished, his mouth shaped like an O. Above them, the wind had blown away the clouds, opening a path of blackness in the sky.

Charity leaped to her feet. The soldier was struggling wildly, rolling back and forth and screaming, stopping the blood flow with his hands. She stepped over his body. She bent to pick up the copper flute; with it she broke the chimney of the kerosene lamp. She remembered how the antinomial had broken the white-faced woman's head with that flute and set afire the tomb of Chrism Demiurge. Bending low, Charity struck the soldier on the face, and then raised the lamp up to the canvas roof. Small flames fled from a central point above her head, chased by the wind. She turned, and threw the lamp down in a pile of painted manuscripts. Then she ducked out through the door, running barefoot on the slippery stones, listening to the shouts of the soldiers—they were very near. But she thought that they would stop to save their wealth. The tent was well alight, burning in the wind. She turned and ran up past the little pool, towards the Whisper Bridge.

With a cry, one of the men sprang after her. He was carrying a torch in one hand and a revolver in the other. He raised it up, but she was gone, vanished into darkness. Without the torch, perhaps he could have seen her jump from rock to rock. Perhaps he could have brought her down. But with the torch he was as good as blind, not that it mattered. He knew where she was going. He took the straightest path while she ran up to hide among the rocks. She watched him pass beneath her.

Hugging her knees, she sat up among the rocks, waiting for the shouting to subside. She watched the man cavort around the fire, their shadows large and strange. One splashed water from the pool and pulled out treasure from the burning tent. The other knelt by their companion, bandaging his neck. Charity waited. And gradually the noise grew less, the light sank down. Occasionally a voice rang out, and clumps of darkness moved against the embers of the fire. But the man with the torch had not returned. For a while Charity had seen his light, up over the rise, glowing behind a mass of rock.

Perhaps an hour went by before she dared to move. For a while she crouched upon her hands and knees, testing each stone before she trusted it. Her feet were bare. On the slope above the camp the rocks seemed smoother and more solid than they had down in the valley. The rain had washed them clean. And she could see before her the outline of the hills, smooth and gentle, black against a lighter black.

She moved slowly, one hand and then one foot. She had no idea how long, but slowly behind her the embers of the campfire were submerged in darkness, and the voices grumbled and grew less, losing their edges as she made her way. One hand, and then one foot. She stared into the blackness, inches from her nose. There was no wind. In front of her the Whisper Bridge was silent.

Finally she climbed up over the breast of the hill. Around her a strange light began to burn, objectless, unilluminat-

ing, as if the darkness had become a different color. Behind
the outline of the horizon the sky took on a different color,
a soft, dull brown, and then a line of red. It was the Caladonian frontier.

From between two boulders she stared out. She had
reached the hilltop. Below her, half a mile away, the Whisper Bridge shone like a beacon, a span of yellow metal
glowing from within, still lit by some ancient art. Under it
the abyss was black, the river silent, but on the other side,
along the lip of a cliff which ran to each horizon, the sky
was lit by a red glow. An ancient barricade of glowing wires
sprawled out of the darkness and sprawled along the cliff.

A half mile away, up on the ridge, Charity could feel a
gentle wind upon her face, and then she could hear the
bridge, too, breathing softly in the night. She looked for the
third man, the soldier with the torch, and then she spotted
him, a small daub of fire below the first rungs of the bridge.

By the time she reached him, his torch had flickered low.
He had perched it in a cleft between two rocks: a crooked
stick from which the bark still hung in rags. At the top a
nest of straw was soaked in burning phosphorus; it cast an
eerie, bluish light. Under it the soldier sat, his revolver in
his lap.

Ten feet behind him, the bridge reached up into the darkness. From close at hand, the gleam of the metal seemed
less noticeable. It struggled dully with the torchlight, which
spread out around the base of the bridge in an uneven pool.
In the middle sat the soldier, his head sunk on his breast as
Charity crept close.

She crouched behind a boulder, watching him for many
minutes. He never moved, and she was hoping that he was
asleep, had dozed off in his waiting. Experimentally, she
moved her knee, shifting her weight and making a small
sound. The soldier raised his head. His face was illuminated
in the fitful glow, and Charity suppressed a cry. He was a
great, tall hulk of a man, and his face was terribly de-

formed. He seemed to resemble not a human being but another species, shocking in its strangeness. At first Charity could make no sense out of its face, its bumps and holes, its rough places and smooth. She shuddered and bent low, murmuring an inward prayer, making with the smallest motion of her forefinger the sign of the unclean.

She turned away her face, counting under her breath. When she reached one hundred, she turned back, and she was calm enough to see a pattern in the alien flesh—the great mane of hair, the fat fleshy nose, the small revolting eyes.

Once when she was young, her uncle had taken her into the Starlight Temple, to see the great brass statue of dog-headed Angkhdt. There had been torchlight and darkness and silence like a heavy weight. Before the altar, the image sat cross-legged, its hands clasped around the base of its brass penis. The penis was like a power in its hands; under the bridge the soldier held his gun upon his lap, the thick, ugly snout pointing at the sky. Calm and quiet, he stared out into the darkness. It seemed to Charity that he could not fail to see her, yet still he made no movement. Not daring to retreat, she was huddled up between some boulders. In her silken gown, she was shivering with cold. The wind had come up slightly, a cold breath on her face. From time to time the Whisper Bridge moaned ominously, a low sound rising out of nothing.

Charity prayed. "Sweet God of Childhood, fill me with Your love. Let me feel Your power in my body, for You are all my hope and all my pride, and all my strength is from Your seed."

She prayed: "By the rushing river I sat down, and by the clear brook I lay down. My God was like a shadow on the grass. He was like a whisper in the trees."

These were verses she had learned when she was young, how great Angkhdt came upon a woman by the water. Her lips trembled as she prayed, but her heart and mind were strangely still. As if soothed by the rhythm of her thoughts, the soldier closed his eyes. In a minute, his head fell down upon his breast. He was asleep.

Charity waited. Above him the bridge stretched away into the night. Every two feet along its span the way was studded with a steel rung, representing one of the five hundred and eleven visions of Immortal Angkhdt, incidents in his great journey through the stars. In the winter of the year 00011, the nineteenth bishop of Charn had taken the first line from five hundred and eleven verses of the holy song, and woven them into a poem of his own. It was a poem that seemed to guarantee, as if by divine right, the bishop's own vision of empire; victorious here, on the banks of the Moldau, his army had been broken on the plains of Caladon.

The Whisper Bridge still stood, the only remnant of his dream. A line of letters was inscribed above each rung, poetry in seven languages. Love lyrics from the Song of Angkhdt had been ransacked to provide words of bloodshed and conquest. The nineteenth bishop had seen an angel in his sleep, who had given him the key.

When she was young, Charity had won prizes in mnemonics. Crouching underneath the bridge, she found the words of the poem clean in her mind, rising up out of her lonely prayer. After another hour of waiting, after the torch had sputtered into darkness, after the soldier's head had fallen forward so that she no longer saw his face, she rose. The soldier slept. She could hear his snoring as she stumbled forward, her limbs recalcitrant and cold. She laid hold of the first rung of the bridge. It seemed warm to her touch, and the line of poetry above it glowed, as if cut from fire. "'I have walked in this sad place too long,'" she murmured. And then swung herself up: "'This simple garden in my lady's heart. But from an upstairs window I have seen another land. A dry land rising out of sight. A dry ridge in the desert. Love—you and me and seven others, we will smear our palms with lime, and with spikeweed in our hands we will continue up, up into the morning of the world, burned white and ocher by the laughing sun. Where women wash their clothes beside the stream, crimson, scarlet, and the nine kinds of red, we will lift them onto poles. These cloths will be our flags, for we are kings upon this earth, this bitter, worthless ground.'"

The wind shook the bridge and filled the air with groaning. Around her there was nothing, only blackness and the glowing steel, until she came up over the crest of the arch, weary and cold, and saw the wire fence below her, stretching out to each horizon, shining bright as she climbed down. Some of the rungs had fallen loose, and once she slipped and almost fell. Once her gown caught on a corner of torn steel, which opened up a gash above her knee. And always the bridge was shifting in the wind, trembling and groaning while the rungs burned her hands. And always she was chanting the bishop's poem in her mind, the words and images disjointed, reduced to their bare sounds. Sometimes she closed her eyes. And at the very end she slipped the last few rungs, twisting her ankle, falling to her knees on the sharp rocks.

Near her stood the fence, a mass of tangled wire perhaps twelve feet tall. With her back to the cliff's edge, she stared at it, adjusting her eyes to the strange light. It seemed impenetrable, tightly woven, cruelly barbed. Charity sat nursing her foot. She leaned back against a pile of rocks and looked into the mesh of colored filaments, searching for a flaw. The fence glowed scarlet, green, and cobalt blue.

Towards morning it began to rain, fluttering, small drops which sizzled as they hit the wire. Charity sat dozing, but then she started awake, cursing the rain. Cursing, she stumbled to her feet, ignoring the pain in her ankle. In the gathering daylight she found a path down the rock slope, leading parallel to the clifftop for a hundred yards, and then turning inward towards the barricade. There, for a distance of a couple of feet, the lower portion of the fence was shorted out. Several wires had been cut. They hung colorless and dull. Charity went down on her hands and knees; there was a tunnel cut into the heart of the wire. Wriggling on her belly in a slough of sugar mud, she entered in, picking her way as if into a briar of poisoned thorns. In front of her the wires had been severed and bent back, but still they caught in her clothes, ripping her fine gown to shreds, scratching her wet skin. In this way she came at last to Caladon, emerging out into the rain. Shivering and miserable, she lay on her stomach in the rain.

It was there that the district customs officer found her, after his morning walk. Tall, angular, swathed in strips of gauze, he stepped down from the porch of his cabin and raised a white umbrella to the sky. Moving with great slowness and precision, he walked out across the road. His mailbox was empty; that was no surprise, but beyond it, huddled in a culvert, lay a human woman. She was watching him as he approached, with a dazed, puzzled expression, in which curiosity had not yet given way to loathing.

She was dressed in silken rags. He bent down above her till their heads were very close, and she did not flinch away. "Good morning," he said softly, using the common tongue. "Have you anything to declare?"

In those days, in Caladon, certain noble families employed the services of child assassins, hereditary murderers, devotees of Angkhdt the God of Fire. On the same night that Charity crossed the border, past midnight on the morning of December 3rd, Mrs. Cassimer got up from her cot, in the camp at Kethany. She had heard children's voices laughing in the dark outside her tent, squealing with delight as if at some new game. Pulling on her bathrobe, grumbling to herself, she got up and went outside, and stood watching in amazement while a half a dozen young ragamuffins practiced gymnastics in an open space nearby. They had hung a carbide lantern from a pole, and by its light they somersaulted and turned backflips, and danced upon their hands.

Standing in the flap of the tent, still half asleep, for many minutes Mrs. Cassimer watched the antics of the children. A little girl stood on her brother's shoulders, juggling three rings and a rubber ball. A boy balanced a chair upon his chin. Many children lived in that camp of refugees below the city walls, and Mrs. Cassimer supposed that she was watching some of these: junior members of the guild of players, sharpening their skills.

But there was something wrong. She noticed a gold ring in the ear of one young boy. Though dressed in rags, some of the others, too, wore jewelry—sapphire rings and silver bracelets. Mrs. Cassimer was listening to a whisper in her mind, and it mixed with a noise inside the tent. Turning quickly, she ducked back inside, in time to see a small form bending low over the baby's crib.

She waddled forward with a cry of rage. The child had something shining in its hand, but Mrs. Cassimer was in time. In the darkness of the tent the child mistook its aim. With an open razor, it sliced apart the pillow near the baby's head, then twisted away, out of reach of Mrs. Cassimer, and slipped out through a cut in the tent wall.

"Nasty, filthy, thieving brat," cried Mrs. Cassimer, bursting into tears. She gathered up the infant prince and held him to her breast. Jenny Pentecost sat up in bed. She reached for a small electric torch, which she kept beside her in the night, and turned it to illuminate the figure of the housekeeper, standing in the center of the floor, rocking the baby in her arms.

"That's it, you just sit there," cried Mrs. Cassimer with some bitterness. "What's the matter, lizard got your tongue? I suppose it's too much to expect—look at the little darling: still asleep."

Her words were contradicted by the baby, who squirmed and fretted in her arms. After a moment, despite her best efforts, he began to cry, a weak, snuffling noise. "There,

there," said Mrs. Cassimer, fussing with a pacifier. "It's all over now."

In the past two weeks, unexpected quantities of maternal love had come out in Mrs. Cassimer, dormant since Thanakar was grown. And though retarded, the child was not insensible to her affection. Quite the contrary; in just a few days he had responded, seeming to recognize her, smiling and holding out his hand. The night before, for the first time, he had slept undisturbed till six o'clock.

In fact, his case did not appear as hopeless as Thanakar had feared. Some of the deformities of his great head had proved to be a ruse—painted ridges of putty and papier-mâché applied by the priests of the cathedral, to make him look less human. Thanakar had repaired his deviated septum, had stitched together his harelip. He had removed a cataract from one eye and cut through the flaps of skin that had sealed his ears. There was sugar in the baby's blood, that much was clear. But within certain limits he responded to the doctor's care. And Thanakar worked on him with a kind of gratitude, a full feeling in his heart, because in that hospital, in that stricken settlement of refugees, so much of his work was hopeless. That week he had six new cases of the black brain fever, two in newborn children.

On the morning of December 3rd he had been working in the clinic. Past midnight, he had left his work unfinished. Returning to the tent where his family was staying, he had stopped to watch two children juggle hoops of fire. Mrs. Cassimer was awake, he saw. He raised his hand, but she turned back under the flap of her tent. Laughing, the children scattered, leaving their hoops to smolder in the dirt.

Thanakar heard the voice of Mrs. Cassimer crying out inside the tent. Wearily, he turned his feet in that direction, entering just in time to catch the brunt of her attack.

"You!" she cried as he came in. "What have you to say? Up at all hours playing the fool while we get our throats cut.

A lot you care. It's bad enough to live in this disgusting place."

She was standing with the baby in her arms, illuminated by Jenny's torch. He blinked stupidly at her, and at his daughter sitting hidden by the light, upright in her bed. Then, again, Mrs. Cassimer started to cry. Wordlessly, shaking her head, she showed him the split pillow, the cut in the oilcloth of the tent.

"But he's all right," said Thanakar.

"Yes, he's all right, no thanks to you. A fine excuse for a doctor. Up all night, God knows where. Don't you ever sleep?"

Thanakar sat down upon the cot. His leg was hurting him, and he was very tired. "I was trying some research on my own time," he said. "No more. Tomorrow we will go."

"And high time too," cried Mrs. Cassimer, unmollified. She had been fussing with the baby, but now he was sucking on the pacifier and she was free to speak. "It's been weeks since that gentleman came to give you your safe-conduct. We could have left here any time. But every day you have been gone, with people dying all around, and all the riffraff of the country, God knows why—"

Thanakar held up his palm. "Enough," he said. "You don't understand. I had work to do. No more. We leave at the first light. Soon as we can. I'll send to Craton Starbridge for some horses."

"Oh," said Mrs. Cassimer, suspiciously. "And why the sudden change of heart? Don't tell me it's because of this." She motioned to the pillow in the crib.

"No," confessed Thanakar. He held up his hand. "Please, Jenny," he said, and she switched off the light, leaving them in a murky half-light, which filtered in through the oilcloth walls.

"The director asked me to go," Thanakar confessed. "She fired me. I have been experimenting upon animals, and four have died. That is still a crime, in Caladon."

In an instant Mrs. Cassimer had changed. Her voice was softer as she came to sit down next to Thanakar on the cot. "It's a crime all over the world," she said. "Oh sir, Great Angkhdt tells us to love all animals. Especially in springtime, when they are so few."

"I had thought, in this camp, that there were rats enough," said Thanakar. "Not that it matters—it will be good to go. You're right, it was unfair to keep you. Now that Craton Starbridge has provided such a . . . generous alternative."

In Mrs. Cassimer's arms the baby was asleep. The pacifier dropped out of his open mouth. Thanakar looked up and saw that Jenny Pentecost had gotten out of bed. She was standing in front of him in a nightgown, her hair braided on the nape of her neck, and she was staring intently at his face. She reached out her hand, and before he could move away, she touched with her forefinger the locket round his neck.

Later that same night, while Charity was lying in the rain outside the unraveler's house, Thanakar Starbridge got up from his cot. He couldn't sleep.

Working in the hospital laboratory at midnight, for the first time he had caught glimpses of a theory. When the doctors had broken in and found him with the carcasses of four fat rats, he had been excited. He had been too excited to explain himself, too excited to speak, though he had slapped one of his superiors across the face. But when he saw they were not interested, that they did not even want to hear what he had found, then his excitement died, and he had stumbled home, disgusted and angry with them and with himself. "It serves them right," he thought, stumbling back through the rows of tents.

That feeling had not lasted long. Coming home to his own tent, he had passed the orphans' hospital, and his lantern had reflected in the eyes and faces of abandoned children, curled up on pallets of raw straw. Once he had stopped to listen to some children laughing, and his anger had not survived the sound.

It had been replaced with weariness and a dull strange ache, which helped him fall asleep once his family was calm and he had helped them to their beds. But in the middle of the night, suddenly the excitement of his discovery resurfaced, and he jumped out of bed and paced upon the floor. It was not yet light.

He limped to the flap of the tent and stood looking out over the deserted hospital. He shook his head to clear it. Wisps of a theory seemed to surround him in the air, drifting close around him, then receding.

He shook his head, resolved to march on back to the laboratory and break in, and if the doctors were still there, to slap them in the face and make them listen. Listen to what? The theory drifted out of reach. Still, he limped back to his cot and pulled on his boots. He pulled on his overcoat. But then he paused, looking around at his sleeping family and at the cut in the tent wall. Mrs. Cassimer had taken the infant prince into her bed. Jenny was sleeping curled away from him, her long hair covering her pillow.

The tent was built like an umbrella of oilcloth and strips of steel, radiating from a central wooden pillar. Light came from a kerosene lantern hung from a nail in the central shaft, and it shone on Jenny's hair, and on her desk, and on the drawings stacked upon it.

Thanakar took the lantern from its nail, and he limped over to stand next to her cot. He put the lantern down upon her desk, and he stood over the pile of drawings, examining them one by one. He sat on the edge of Jenny's cot and held one of the drawings up to the light. It was her most recent flea, dated seven days before.

He reached into an inside pocket of his coat, where he kept a small case of instruments and specimens. Unzipping it, he removed a magnifying glass; turning the wick of the lantern higher, he studied the drawing underneath the glass.

On the bottom of the insect's carapace, between its lower limbs, there was a small protuberance, a small, sharp spiral, like the end of a small drill. Thanakar frowned, and then unfolded from a pocket of the case a piece of paper, an earlier rendition of the flea, one of the first Jenny had drawn. The bottom of its carapace was clean.

Finally Thanakar took out a pair of tweezers and a small vial full of samples. He unscrewed the top of the vial, and with the tweezers he caught the body of a small specimen, an insect in the vial. He pulled it out and stared at it under the magnifying glass. It was a small, translucent dot, one-sixteenth of an inch long, innocent of detail even under the glass. Nevertheless, Jenny Pentecost, sitting up in bed behind him, whispered, "You have found it," in his ear.

"Is it the same?" asked Thanakar, without turning around.

"Yes."

"I found it on a rat," he said. "Look," he said, indicating Jenny's drawing. "That's where it keeps the virus. In that drill between its legs."

He put down his magnifying glass, and held the flea up to the light. "Of my new patients," he continued, "four of six are members of the oil pressers' caste. They were temple servants, in Charn under the old regime. They mixed prescriptions for the priests."

He was speaking more to himself than to her, and he was holding the flea out towards the light. Then he brought the tweezers back up to his eye, until the flea was only inches from his face. "The curious thing," he said, "is that mental illness could be spread this way. By a virus."

"It is spread in many ways," whispered Jenny, close to his ear. She had put her arms around his neck. Her face was close to his. She, too, was staring at the flea.

"Yes," said Thanakar. "The king of the oil pressers had

looted drugs out of the Temple of Surcease. He kept rodents, too, sacred to the God of Animals. They were in jeweled cages in his tent. After his death I brought four of them into the laboratory and cut them open."

Jenny said nothing, but he could hear her soft breath on his neck. "Their guts were full of them," he said. "The sacred fleas of Angkhdt. In Charn they grind their bodies up for medicines. They make an anesthetic paste. Once in the blood, it can cause hallucinations."

"I know," whispered Jenny.

"These cases I have seen, the first symptoms are delusions and hallucinations. Nevertheless, the patient dies in sixty hours. It is because they have been bitten by the flea. You could not have been exposed that way." Thanakar indicated the difference between the drawings, the old one and the new. "You yourself see this is a new mutation."

"They grind them up for medicine," said Jenny, in his ear.

In the morning when he woke, she was still asleep. But she had left something for him, a black and battered copy of the Song of Angkhdt, on the floor next to his bed.

She had been asleep when Thanakar had left her to return to bed. But late at night she must have gotten up again, to find the book for him; it was Mrs. Cassimer's copy, which she kept under her chamber pot.

The book was open to the sixteenth verse. In the margin a small passage was marked in Jenny's hand, one of the so-called interjections of Beloved Angkhdt. It read,

*What is it that drives me on?*
*It is like the scratching of a flea.*
*It is like the biting of a flea.*

The night before, he had dragged his cot in from his own tent, to stay close to his family. But in the morning he went out, to wash and dress; when he returned, Mrs. Cassimer was awake, feeding the baby from a bowl of artificial soup.

He sat down next to her with the book in his hand. "What does this mean?" he asked, indicating the marked verse.

"Oh, sir, that's a naughty one," said Mrs. Cassimer.

Jenny was still asleep. She had turned over onto her back. "Tell me," said Thanakar.

"Oh no, sir, I couldn't do that. Not to you. That's a naughty one."

Mrs. Cassimer was knowledgeable on all aspects of holy scripture. But she was also prudish, and protective of her master. "No, sir," she said. "I couldn't tell you that." But he insisted. "Please," he said.

"Very well. That one's about women. That's what the parsons say. They've got a medicine for that. An ointment that they use."

"A medicine?"

"Yes, sir. They make it out of bugs. And a little sugar. Rainwater, I guess."

"But what's it for?"

"An ointment, sir. They rub it on their penises. Oh, sir, Angkhdt had fifty women in one day, the day He overcame the nunnery."

At 9 A.M., Thanakar sent a letter to the director of the hospital, enclosing several of Jenny's drawings. Then he sent a message to the ministry of agriculture. That one was fruitful: By the middle of the afternoon a carriage had arrived, a large, heavy vehicle drawn by four horses. Craton Starbridge's escutcheon was painted on the door, a white ship under sail.

At four o'clock Thanakar was packed and ready. He loaded his family into the dark, stuffy interior and then stepped onto the box, wearing an oilskin against the rain. He nodded to the coachman, and pulled his wide-brimmed hat over his eyes. He had a pocket full of marijuana cigarettes. He put one between his teeth.

Nobody had come to see them off.

From the walls behind him, the church bells rang the

hour. Then they were moving, the horses struggling in the mud, kicking through the radiating circles of huts and canvas shelters. A mist was rising from the ground. People stood half naked in the rain, gaunt, spectral figures, watching them.

Thanakar lit his cigarette, and pulled his hat down over his face. Mounted underneath him on the near horse, the postilion was acting as a guide. He carried a letter of safe-conduct in his boot, countersigned by the commander of the corps of engineers. Thanakar saw the flash of gold upon its seal, and through a dull narcotic haze he watched the soldiers at the checkpoint stiffen and salute. They pulled back the barricades of sharpwood and barbed wire, and let them out onto the road.

They were heading for the mountains. The postilion had already shown Thanakar their destination on a map, a small village north of Gaur, two hundred miles northwest of the city. In other seasons it was famous for its beauty, and wealthy Caladonians kept villas there. In spring most of these were empty, but there remained a small local population, who farmed the terraced hills and fished the lake for weeds. There was a hospital, where Thanakar had been guaranteed a job. There was also a small military garrison, largely convalescents on half-pay. Craton Starbridge's first cousin was the captain.

But to go west, first they headed south. In all other directions the roads were reserved for military transport. Even on the great south highway, in the first few hours Thanakar counted seventeen convoys of soldiers, and even a few ancient trucks.

Like the coach, these vehicles were moving towards the border. The coachman pulled aside out of the road to let them pass. At other times he halted for another reason: Crowds of refugees, heading in the opposite direction, made the horses kick and shy. It was not till after midnight that they reached the end of their first stage, twenty miles from the border where the road split west. Rooms were ready for them at the hotel. Jenny was asleep, so Thanakar carried her upstairs. They were to share a room.

Late at night he awoke from a strange dream. What was it? No—the details of it already were unclear to him, a medley of strange images that slipped and twisted from his grasp. He saw a bright light shining in his eyes. It seemed to hover a few inches from his face and disappear. He touched his fingers to his face and raised his head. In the corner of the room, under a small electric bulb, Jenny Pentecost sat hunched over a table.

Supported on one elbow, he watched her for a while—her narrow shoulders, the points of her thin shoulderblades under her slip. Her fine brown hair was twisted in a knot behind her head, out of the way. Single hairs stuck out at odd trajectories under the light. She had her back to him.

He remembered how he had found her, in a brothel by the Temple of Surcease, the night before they left the city. He had come back from the army and had searched for her, and had found her on the top floor of a brothel, near the altar of the God of Children. Was it there? It must have been there, that she had contracted this illness. It must have been there that the flea had crept into her blood. No doubt there had been a jar of unguent on the altar, where her clients had paused to anoint themselves. What kind of men could they have been, to try to duplicate the prowess of Beloved Angkhdt upon a child?

A feeling of longing rose up in his throat, hopeless, like unrequited love. "Jenny?" he whispered. "Jenny?" She didn't turn around. Adjusting his pajamas, he got up to see what she was doing.

Before her on the table a drawing was spread out. It was in black-and-sepia pencil, with traces of red ink—the pen was still in her hand. But she was staring at it without moving. The drawing was finished. It showed a woman dressed in rags, her face hidden in shadow. She was lying on the ground next to an empty bowl, her ankle shackled to a post. Beside her stood a chicken, searching the ground for insects with its curious snout. Behind her a wire fence intersected with the wall of a small building.

This was in the corner of the picture. Most of the drawing was about the sky—a study of dark clouds and sugar rain. But one more artifact was visible: At the top of the page, a span of metal drawn in red. The clouds were parted by its edge.

"The Whisper Bridge," said Thanakar. "How did you know?"

Jenny said nothing. Only she made a notation in red pen in the margin of the page: "21596." And under it, in careful print: "17.78 mi."

"How did you hear of it?" asked Thanakar. He leaned forward over the page. From his neck, his golden locket hung down close beside her ear. She turned and grabbed it, pulled it loose. The small chain snapped in her small hand.

Surprised, Thanakar pulled back. Then he reached out his hand. But she had found the locket's clasp, had opened it, and was staring at the photograph inside. Cut from the yearbook of the Starbridge Schools, it was a photograph of a young girl with long black hair, thick eyebrows, and black eyes. A wide mouth, a wide jaw; two months after it was taken, Charity had married the old man.

Thanakar reached out to grab it back, but then he stopped. Jenny Pentecost had dipped her pen into her well, and she was drawing the profile of a face under her numerical notation: Just a few quick lines, so fast, so expert, and so sure. Thanakar cried out, with a pain like a needle in his heart. Then Jenny threw the pen down on the page, spattering it with ink. She turned in her chair and put her arms around his neck, squeezing until it hurt. She locked her arms around his neck and squeezed with all her strength, and he could feel her small lips on his cheek. "Trust me," she whispered next to his ear, her voice so soft, almost inaudible. "Trust me," she repeated.

Before first light he limped down to the post station at the crossroads to barter for a horse. He left a message for his coachman and his guide, instructing them to wait two days before continuing; he would catch them up. He left a note for Mrs. Cassimer. He didn't wake her, not wanting to hear what she might say.

There were no horses. All had been sequestered by the army, or bought by wealthy refugees. But after some negotiation he obtained a bicycle. He tied his knee in linen strips, injecting lubricants into the joint, and at six-thirty he wheeled his bicycle out onto the road. It was an old, stiff, cast-iron model with enormous rubber wheels. For hours he rode it grimly over the deserted countryside, along a roadbed of crushed cinders.

The Whisper Bridge was in a range of washed-out hills, and there was no one on the road. At eight o'clock it started raining. Thanakar cursed aloud. Once, at the bottom of a long hill, with the rain pulsing from the sky like bullets of wet glass, he almost turned around. But finally, towards ten, he reached the border.

By the banks of the Moldau River, in a landscape of wet clay, the road came to an end. The fog was low upon the ground. He could not see the barricade; he could not see the bridge, but he could hear it in the wind. In front of him there was a mailbox, across the way a small tarpaper shack. Nearby, at the top of a high flagpole, flew an ensign he remembered well—the endless knot of the unravelers. Under it, the swine of Caladon, red upon a field of white.

Thanakar parked his bike next to the pole. He took off his hat. His leg was so weak he could barely stand. It throbbed and trembled under his weight.

He waited a minute and then walked around the shack. It

was a two-story, dilapidated wooden structure. In back there was an empty chicken run.

Returning to the road, he limped up the steps of the shack onto the porch. Through the screen door he could see the unraveler at his desk, stretched back in his chair, his gaunt frame swathed in bandages. His eyes were veiled, his face turned to one side. With a broken pencil he tapped idly upon his desk.

Thanakar tried the door. It was locked.

"Are you applying for a visa?" asked the unraveler, his voice high and soft. "Office hours start at four o'clock."

The screen was rotten near the clasp. Thanakar punched it with his fist and broke the lock. Already he was angry, but also he was weak and close to falling. He stepped inside the door and leaned against it, his back against the screen. "Is there a woman staying here?" he asked.

The unraveler leaned forward in his chair. "What do you mean?"

"I swear to God," said Thanakar. "Tell me where she is, and then I'll go."

The unraveler placed his pencil on his desk, carefully among the littered paper. He seemed to frown under the veil. "She is no longer here," he said. When Thanakar said nothing, he went on. "You do not understand. She was a foreign national, on Caladonian soil, without documentation. Not of any kind. I could not let her stay."

Thanakar limped forward into the room. He put his hands upon the desk, then stopped. From underneath a pile of paper the unraveler had produced a gun.

"No violence," he said. "You are the one. Yes, I have heard of you." With one hand he held the small revolver, and with the other he rummaged in the papers on his desk. "Hah," he said. "This is from the district headquarters at Sreshta Breaks," he said, naming the border town where Thanakar had spent so long. "Distinguishing marks? Tattoos upon both hands. A golden briarweed, among others.

Yes. You are the one. It says you failed to go through proper channels."

Thanakar was leaning forward on the desk, supporting his weight upon his wrists. He caught a wisp of a sweet smell. He breathed deeply. It was whiskey. A jar half full of whiskey stood upon the corner of the desk between some books. He could smell whiskey on the breath of the unraveler, though it was not yet noon.

"Here," the man continued, reading from a crumpled piece of paper. "Yes. Thanakar Starbridge. Yes, he has disrupted the morale of the entire district. Since he left, illegal penetration of the Sreshta Gate has increased more than thirty times. Thirty times! And you have the impudence to threaten me."

There was a pause. Thanakar sat down in a chair and put both hands over his knee. The unraveler stared up at the ceiling. "Tell me what this woman is to you," he said at last.

Thanakar put his hand up to his face. "Then she's still here. You didn't send her back?"

"No. It would not have been . . . humane. In your country they are murdering civilians. They have no respect for regulations of all kinds. This woman, she would not even give her name. What is she to you?"

He turned his head. His face under the veil was thin and bony, hairless and gray. "I too," he said. "I should have sent her back. No, for her sake I have broken elementary statutes numbers fifteen through twenty-one. Yesterday morning I detained her in the proper place. But it was raining. Now she is upstairs, sleeping in my bed. Last night I fed her rations that were meant for me."

Thanakar sat back. The unraveler gestured wearily with the revolver. It sank low to the desk, as if too heavy for his frail wrist. "The fact remains," he said, "she is an unlawful alien, on Caladonian soil. She possesses two items of jewelry, but otherwise no means of livelihood, not to mention very little in the way of clothes. That is why I ask you, what is she to you? Is she your wife?"

"Yes," said Thanakar.

"Papers, please."

Thanakar took them from the inside pocket of his oilskin and slid them across the desk. The unraveler peeled them apart with his long fingers and held the seal up to the window. "You come under the protection of a powerful personage," he said. "But what is this? Marital status: S."

Again Thanakar pressed his hand against his lips. Then he spoke. "Please," he said, "I speak of my intent. I have the means to support her. The government has granted me a house in K——" He named the village by the lake.

"I see that."

"Please," said Thanakar again. But there was no sincerity in the way he said the word: His teeth were clenched. Frustration had overcome his thoughts. That morning, cycling along the cinder road while his knee clanked and throbbed, his thoughts had all been routed by an army of conflicting hopes and doubts. They had driven him forward to the place where he now sat, his fingers twitching with frustration, an empty buzzing in his mind. Once again, he put his hands down to his knee, rubbing at the swollen joint.

The unraveler reached for the jar of whiskey on his desk. He tilted it in his left hand, staring at the level of the fluid. He laid down the pistol next to his right hand and once more turned his attention to Thanakar's papers. "It says here that you are traveling with your two children, both suffering from mental handicaps. Where are they?"

"I left them with my housekeeper," said Thanakar, naming the town and the hotel where he had spent the night.

"Let me see. You left Charn on October forty-seventh. I don't think so much travel can be salutary for children of that kind. Such children need a stable home. Is that what you hope to provide for them, in K——?"

Thanakar said nothing, only stared at the unraveler and rubbed his knee. Angkhdt save us, a philosopher! he thought.

The unraveler looked at him steadily over the top of his papers, and then he laid them down. In his left hand he held the jar of whiskey, and he tilted it so that the amber fluid hesitated just inside the brim. "Answer my questions, please," he said. "It says here that one of your children suffers from neurophrenia, and the other has adulterated blood. Is that correct?"

"No. Neurophrenia—it is the language of documents. How could it be correct?"

"Ah," said the unraveler, staring at his whiskey. His voice was melancholic: "Perhaps you can explain for me this difference."

Outside it had started raining, and the rain was beating on the window beside Thanakar's chair. He felt a disadvantage that he couldn't name. He shook his head. "My daughter," he said, "is suffering from an overdose of a hallucinogenic drug. But I feel that's not the source of her condition. I don't know. Sometimes I feel she is not sick at all. Is it sickness when her visions are the truth?"

"Interesting," said the unraveler. "But what difference does it make?"

"What do you mean? The difference is obvious. In one case the drug is everything, and all my effort must be aimed towards understanding it. In the other case the drug has simply aggravated something else, some other sorrow."

"You don't understand," said the unraveler. "I mean, what is the difference in her treatment? Perhaps that is the only thing that matters. For example, I have no idea whether your knee is congenitally crippled, or whether you have injured it. You are a doctor, no doubt you have a theory. But there is something you don't seem to know: In either case, the worst thing that you could do to it is to ride a bicycle twenty miles over these roads."

Once again Thanakar felt a rush of anger and frustration. Once again he felt he was losing a game whose rules he didn't know. "What do you mean?" he said. "This drug is compounded of an insect, which, in mutated form, seems to be connected to the outbreak of a terrible illness in this region. Surely you'd agree it is a link that we must trace."

The unraveler looked at him steadily, and then he shrugged. "Mutations," he said, shifting his attention to the window, where the rain was beating on the glass. "Sugar births, mutations. Life changes as the weather changes—is that not the center of all science? No doubt last spring also there was some illness like the one you mention. Yet here we are. And the only thing we've learned is that men and women can't try to bear these burdens by themselves. They need a context. They need a shield against the world."

Thanakar cast his eyes around the bare, disheveled room. "Yes," said the unraveler. "I live here by myself. That's how I know." He picked up Thanakar's passport again, stared at it, and laid it down. "Do you understand what I mean?" he asked. "Children need parents more than doctors. And they need a home."

With a sigh, the unraveler replaced his jar of whiskey on his desk. He picked up a pencil, and made a small notation in the margin of the doctor's passport; then he erased it. "Now, I know it has been difficult," he said. "But it looks to me as if you've spent a month and a half in hotels and refugee camps. We are in a war zone here. It is not a place to leave two handicapped children in a hotel by themselves."

"I don't understand the purpose of these questions," said Thanakar after a pause.

"Don't you? I am contemplating releasing into your custody a female refugee from Charn with no means of support. It is my job to determine what is best for her."

Thanakar held his breath and then released it slowly. "Can I see her?" he asked.

"No. The decision rests with me. Her wishes are of no importance. Neither are yours. Once again, I stress she is in Caladon unlawfully, with no documents of any kind. Though I admit, your name is one that she has mentioned once or twice."

Thanakar said nothing. He leaned backwards in his seat.

"That being the case," continued the unraveler, "for the sake of your children, and in lieu of any good alternative, I am inclined to grant you this request. Only I must reassure myself about the kind of life you plan to lead. It says here, in your own country, you were once an army officer. That is not auspicious. Nothing in these papers is auspicious. In your favor, only this: You have been granted an employment, and a house in K——. I have been there. It is beautiful. There is a lake."

The unraveler shook his head and then went on. "In your favor, only this: What does this woman mean to you? You have stated an intention to be married. It is a question of paperwork. As your wife, she would be free to go. I would not be able to prevent her."

Thanakar sat without speaking, conscious for the first time of a relaxation spreading through his body. His knee hurt less; his fingers felt less tight. "You are probably not aware," said the unraveler, "that as customs officer for the Whisper District, I have the power to perform marriages. It is a power I have never used. The region is depopulated."

Again Thanakar said nothing. With a sigh the unraveler took a single sheet of paper from an open drawer by his left hand and placed it on the desk. It was a printed form.

He pushed it across the desk towards Thanakar. "Fill it out," he said, "and I will witness it. There is a space for your signature and for hers, without which it is invalid. A problem," he continued, as Thanakar drew out his fountain pen. "Lack of proper identification. Does this worry you?"

Thanakar did not reply for a few moments. He smiled.

"Perhaps you'd better fetch her down," he said. "This might come as a surprise to her."

"No," said the unraveler. With his forefinger he stroked the lip of the jar of whiskey on his desk, producing a small sound. "This may help," he said. "She has a silver rose tattooed on her right palm. Also a mole under her right ear. She is a lovely woman. I have no wish to look at her again."

At his words Thanakar felt hope inside his heart, expanding like a shining gas, making him lightheaded, making his fingers tremble as he uncapped his pen. The words of the certificate seemed to blur before his eyes. His normally precise signature was sloppy and unkempt.

"Please understand," continued the unraveler. "I'm giving you a chance to make things right. I spent last night down here. Sleeping in this chair. At least—I did not sleep. But once I went upstairs to check on her. To look at her—you understand. All I have done is contrary to regulations. I do not want to look at her again."

The marriage form was very short. Thanakar signed it and pushed it across the desk, his trepidation changing to astonishment as the man witnessed the paper without reading it, and stamped it with the endless knot. He dated the paper and pushed it back. His head sank low upon his chest. "Second door on the left side," he murmured. "You can go up now. In five minutes I will go out to make my rounds. There is a break in the fence I must repair. It will take about an hour. When I come back, you will have gone."

Following the direction of the creature's eyes, Thanakar noticed a small key among the papers on the desk. He rose and came forward. "Thank you . . ." he began, but then he stopped. The unraveler had winced as if he had been slapped.

Thanakar picked up the key, along with his passport and safe-conduct. Through an open door behind the office, he found a small, steep flight of stairs. At the top a narrow corridor spanned the width of the house. Through an open door he caught a glimpse of an empty room, low-ceilinged, with checked linoleum on the floor. Blue-flowered wallpaper was peeling from the walls. Thanakar put his hand out and leaned against the jamb. He could not bend his knee, it was so stiff.

Farther down the hall, he unlocked a door and stepped inside. It led to a dark room with a strange, hot, pungent odor, like a place where an animal has slept. The blinds were drawn over the window. He stood inside the door, listening to the rhythmic sound of breathing from the bed. Tears started to his eyes, from what cause he couldn't tell.

After a moment he limped over to the bed and sat down by Charity's side. He put out his hand to wake her and then hesitated. She was lying on her back with her mouth open, her face streaked with sugar and with dirt. How she had changed! He frowned. Perhaps his memory was wrong. But no, when he last saw her, she had been a prisoner, a princess of proud Charn. And now? World traveler, survivor, her cheeks worn rough and raw, her hair cut short.

Her eyes were open. "Who are you?" she asked, her voice still full of sleep.

"Don't you recognize me?"

She frowned. "I recognize your voice." She pulled herself awake, and up onto one elbow. "Cousin," she said. She, too, put her hand out and then pulled it back. Then she laughed. "I felt sure that you were dead."

He could not meet her eyes. "I also," he said. "I heard that you had taken poison."

That was all. He couldn't think of anything else to say. She was staring at his face, smiling, her eyes bright. He fiddled with the papers on his lap. He looked into her eyes for a moment, smiled nervously, and looked away.

Her shoulder and her arm were naked, though she had pulled the sheet up tight around her throat. "Abu is dead," she said.

"I'd heard."

Thanakar chafed their marriage certificate between his fingers and stared down at his knee. Then he said, "The customs officer has released you. There's no question of your going back. Here," he said. "Here is the form."

In the dim light she had to squint to read it. She held it up close to the blind. First she smiled, and then she laughed aloud.

"It's a formality," said Thanakar. "Otherwise he wouldn't let you go. Just until you get a visa."

But she was smiling, still, and he was smiling too. "Not at all." She sat up in bed and wrapped the sheet around her. "I'm happy just to see someone I know."

# THANAKAR IN K——

**A**t dawn on January 1st of the ninth phase of spring, Colonel Aspe crossed the Moldau River into Caladon with an army of eleven thousand men. He waded his horse into the shallows of the ford and raised his metal fist. On the Caladonian side a company of rangers watched him from the hill.

The lieutenant lowered his binoculars. He ripped a page out of his notebook. Turning away, he scrawled a message on the page—a single line. Then he took from his belt a silver cannister and unscrewed the lid. Spindling the paper in his fingers, he thrust it into the cannister and sealed it with a strip of orange wax, which he took from a container at his wrist. Orange was the color of his regiment.

He screwed the silver cap back on the cannister and pressed the wax down over it. He marked it with the signet of his ring, leaving a clear impression on the wax: his initial and, underneath, a tiger's eye. Then he turned back without looking and held out his hand.

The courier was there, a short, squat man. He wore a black plastic helmet and a suit of plastic steel, surmounted by a black cloth vest. He raised the message to his forehead, then slipped it underneath his glove. A hole had been gouged out of the flesh of his forearm, especially to contain it.

The courier strode down the hill, his high boots awkward of the rock. His horse was waiting in a copse of broken trees, out of sight of the river, a huge, fierce creature, with a coat of rufous gray. As he approached, his grooms were busy with the horse, stripping off its mask, tightening its girths, giving it a last injection. The courier did not break his stride. When he reached them, they were finished, scattering away as he seized hold of the great curled gilded horn and swung himself into the saddle. The beast gave a cry, an airless whistle through the slits of its beak. It seemed to be resisting every step, as the rider kicked it down the hill and out into the road. Its pointed ears lay flat against its skull.

A fresh wind rose up from the valley. The rider paused for an instant and lowered his visor. He chafed his whip against his boot as the wind moved over him, stirring the rows of pennants on his back. From rings in his armor two bamboo rods protruded past his head. One was sewn with orange flags, and one with pennants of the arms of Caladon, a red pig on a field of white. They rustled softly in the wind. When he was at full speed they made an urgent, beating sound, audible for half a mile.

He cried out once and the horse was gone, pounding down the road. They did not stop that day. In way stations and villages, townspeople pulled their children from the mud, out of range of the pounding hooves and slashing claws of the great beast. Refugees stood aside upon the road, open-mouthed and fearful.

Near nightfall on the Kodasch Road, the courier finally drew rein. In the courtyard of the king's posthouse, when he came limping in the gate, another messenger waited in silence, his horse restive and kicking at the mud. He saluted as the first rider came up, and held his hand out for the silver cannister. Then he was off, not stopping till he crossed the Argon Bridge and stood before the gates of Caladon. In the early morning under a small rain, he stripped off his helmet in the mazelike streets near the cathedral. His horse slipped on the cobblestones; he leaped from the saddle and continued on foot through dirty alleyways, until the building stood before him. He hurried up the steps, up through the unguarded portals of the cathedral. Snatching a lighted taper from the wall, he ran down the first of countless corridors. Sometimes he caught glimpses of pilgrims along the way, lost among the chapels and the shrines, their faces pale and bewildered. He was a courier of the king. He knew the way, and when they saw him they cried out and tried to follow him, but he was faster than they were. He pushed through crowds of frightened people, turning always to the left, following a streak of turquoise in the gold mozaic of the floor. He followed traces of turquoise in the eyes and jewelry of the saints who lined the frescos on the walls, traces of indigo, traces of blue, which led him on through galleries of tapestries. He was searching for a single blue thread, and then a door with opal in its knob, which led him into rooms of icons, libraries of books. Exhausted, still he muscled forward, turning to the left and to the left. In the libraries he searched for clues among the titles of the books: *Black Bread and Lapis Lazuli*. Another, farther on: *The Man with the Sapphire Hand*. A third: *Hills Like a Row of Plums*. He smiled and reached up to touch its spine.

He paused between a double row of pillars, each carved into a likeness of Beloved Angkhdt, one of the thirty-four true incarnations. Beyond and to the left, the hall was crowded with false incarnations, carved in bloodstone, marble, and obsidian. Some held in their hands stone globes of alternate, false worlds. One beckoned with a jeweled finger, and pointed farther on into the labyrinth.

Finally, as the bells struck evensong, the courier made his way through the last portal, and staggered out into the sanctuary. There he was approached by black-robed ushers, who searched him for weapons and assigned him a place among the supplicants. Wearily he took a seat in the rotunda, along the outer tier. He sat back and closed his eyes, lulled by the chanting on the floor.

Craton Starbridge saw him enter. He leaned forward in the darkness and touched Prince Mantikor upon the arm. He whispered in the prince's ear, then rose and walked back up the southern aisle, signaling to certain spectators along the way. General Lakshman Starbridge stood up in his seat, watching the heavy shoulders of his cousin disappear into the dark. Then he turned back to the service.

The round floor of the sanctuary was ablaze with light, from candles and from candelabra, and from a line of votive lamps around the wheel of the altar. In the center of everything a great four-headed statue of Immortal Angkhdt scowled up into the house, along the four directions of the compass. In a circle around him, acolytes greased the sacred reliquaries on the altar while the choir sang the antiphon. It was the hour of the second evening offertory. On his golden throne, surrounded by courtiers, Argon Starbridge changed his clothes, doffing orange robes for gray ones. Lord Bartek Multiflex was proferring a candy, his painted face shining with sweat.

In the house among the outer seats, Craton Starbridge knelt beside the messenger. He took the silver cannister into his hand and broke the seal.

"Light," he said. One of the ushers behind him held a torch. The seventh minister for agriculture seized it, and by its light he read the message. Then he was up, moving through the ranks of worshipers, stopping from time to time to touch one on the shoulder.

General Lakshman Starbridge was the first to leave, muttering and pulling on his gloves. Others followed him. In five minutes half the hall was empty, and a strange wavering had come into the voices of the choristers as they watched their audience depart.

"How long is Your penis?" chanted the choir. "Surely it has pleased men and women without number. . . ."

It was too much. Samson Mantikor jumped to his feet, his face dark with frustration. "Father," he cried. "There is a messenger from Moldau Ford."

The chanting dwindled into silence. Stunned courtiers held their breaths. Then, almost imperceptibly, King Argon Starbridge nodded his masked head. The choir started up again, raggedly, unsurely, but then stopped abruptly as the prince came forward out of the first pews of worshipers, into the sanctuary light. "Father," he cried again. "There is a messenger."

King Argon made a tiny gesture with his hand. His courtiers moved away from him down off the dais, leaving him alone. Then, with effort, he stood up, supporting his weight upon the arms of his chair. He turned his head towards Samson Mantikor. But at that moment Craton Starbridge raised his hand, shouting from the back of the rotunda: "My lord, it's true. Aspe has crossed the Moldau, with fifteen thousand men."

Bewildered, the king turned to face this strange new voice. In the interval, Bartek Multiflex, standing by the altar, gestured to be heard. "This outbreak is unseemly," he protested. "We have the situation well in hand. As we speak, our own courier is riding south to propose a conference."

"Conference!" shouted Samson Mantikor. "He is across the river. You would talk until he reached the city walls."

He turned and hurried up the southern aisle. He did not see his father raise his hand or hear his father's soft, sweet voice—"Wretched boy. Because of you, we cannot win this fight. We have lost the people's love, because of you."

The king was right. When the prince's armies were assembled, they numbered fewer than ten thousand men, and

most of those were Starbridge officers. The desertion rate
was high among the other ranks. Many Starbridges from
Charn had joined the prince, but that did nothing for morale. When they saw the Starbridge flags unroll over the
plain of Caladon, many of the common soldiers turned
aside and spat, remembering dead comrades. Too recently
those same flags had been arrayed against them.

But it was more than that. Samson Mantikor's appeal for
power had hurt his family's authority. At the battlefield of
Charonea seven companies deserted, refusing at the last to
fight for him. Without the infant prince the monarchy had
lost its heart. Of the three of them—the father and two
sons—it was the child who had caught the public mind. He
was the innocent one, the long-awaited king, the seed of
Blessed Angkhdt. And while the other two were sunk in
bickering and accusations, the voices of the common people
rose in outrage and despair. In those days, every day at
noon, the cathedral steps were crowded with mute protesters, wearing shirts that had been printed with a single question mark. In restaurants and taverns the proprietors posted
a tally on the bar, a record of the days since the infant
prince had last been seen.

"It was a mistake," said Craton Starbridge. "It was a bad
mistake," he said, as the night rain beat upon the canvas by
his head. "We should have brought him back and put him in
a temple of our own."

"No," said Mantikor. He lay back upon his couch,
propped up on pillows, plucking idly at the strings of a small
guitar. "No," he repeated. "They would have murdered
him. My own men would have murdered him, to make my
claim more safe. A little boy, Craton—I could not have
stopped them. A little, crippled boy, crippled in his mind. I
would be ashamed to use him in this fight."

"You are softhearted," grunted Craton Starbridge.

"I am not. Besides, why think of it? It's too late now."

Mantikor lay back. Out of random notes his fingers formed a song, a wistful melody. "It's best to sleep," he said. "And yet, if we are to die tomorrow, it is a shame to waste the time."

With a grunt, Craton Starbridge paced the length of the tent—five steps—and then he stood in the open doorway looking out into the rain. The darkness below him was pricked with soldiers' fires, a reassuring sight, somewhat. His hands were restless. He rubbed them on his pants.

Behind him the young prince started to sing. His voice was supple without being strong, yet had an earnestness that made it pleasing. He sang,

*Science can grasp*
*The stars in the night,*
*But her love is without measure.*

"It's all right for you," interrupted Craton Starbridge from the door. "But I am just another soldier."

Mantikor put down his instrument. "Is that what's bothering you?" he asked. "Craton, I am sorry. I was thoughtless. Don't worry, I will keep you by me."

"I'm not afraid," grunted the older man. "But I'm restless. That is natural. I have staked my life upon this throw."

"So have I." Mantikor bit his lips. His handsome face was twisted to a frown, but then it cleared. He clasped his hands. "I know," he said. "We'll throw the cards. Then we'll sleep."

"It's atrocious luck," said Craton Starbridge, scowling down over the valley. In the distance on the hill of Charonea, he could see the bonfires of the enemy.

"It's atrocious luck," he murmured. In front of him the prince's standard hung down listless from its pole. There was no wind.

But Samson Mantikor had taken a pack of cards out of his kit. They were wound in a silk scarf. He untied it, and laid them out upon the bed. He made them into piles, discarding all but the face cards and the Starbridge suit; these he shuffled together and then reshuffled. "I will draw three times," he said. "Once for Caladon, once for myself, and once for you."

He laid the twenty-seven cards before him in a line, face down. Then he touched each one in turn, hesitating at the third and fifteenth cards. He put his fingers to his lips. Then, with a sudden movement, he reversed the third card from the end. It was the Tower. From the clouds, dog-faced Angkhdt frowned down upon a castle of black stones. In his hand he held the thunderbolt.

Mantikor closed his eyes for a moment and then opened them. He put his hand down on the card, hiding it beneath his palm. Then he turned over the fifteenth card.

"It is the Garden," he said when he could speak. "Craton, look—it is the Garden."

In the doorway Craton Starbridge didn't turn around. Mantikor gathered up the cards, reshuffled them, and laid them out again. "This is for me," he said, turning over the ninth card. It was the Dead Man.

Again he laid his hand over the card. "It is the Chair," he said, tears in his eyes. "Craton, look—some would say it is a throne, but I don't think so. To me it looks more like an old man's garden chair. What do you think? Will you come to see me when I am a grandfather?"

He swept the cards into a pile. Craton Starbridge turned around. "Once more," he said.

"No," protested Samson Mantikor. "No, you're right—it's awful luck. Besides, I'm tired."

But when the man came to stand beside him, he relented and laid out the cards. Carelessly Craton Starbridge took the last one from his hands and flipped it over. It was Paradise, shining red and gold and amber, rising above the bitter hills of Earth.

With a grunt, Craton Starbridge dropped it on the others. "There," he said. "You see?"

He turned and walked out of the tent and down the hill. Prince Mantikor lay awake after he left. He lay awake until the morning. "God grant it never comes," he prayed, but it did come. And when it came it brought a trick of nature. The rain had stopped during the night, and the ground was covered with a layer of mist. On the field it drifted to the height of a man's chest, and gave a spectral look to the assembled soldiers.

From the heights it seemed as if the armies fought the sea, the men up to their chests in foam. Samson Mantikor looked out from his tent and saw Aspe's army like a host of shadows. Only their flags were clearly visible, black and midnight blue, snapping crisply in the higher air.

Below him on the slopes of the small hill, the footsoldiers of Caladon stood with rifles in their hands, dressed in purple, yellow, blue, and all the colors of the morning. Scarlet banners fluttered from their pikes. Elsewhere the great standards of the Starbridge clans rose through the mist, figured in gold, silver, and green. Under them the horses swayed and blundered, and Mantikor could see the helmets of the captains: Antrim Starbridge, Lakshman Starbridge, Strontium Starbridge and his sons.

Towards seven in the morning, Aspe's standard on the Charonea Ridge started to move. Supported by its corners from four poles, it bellied like a sail, a great square of solid black moving slowly down the hill. Shortly afterwards, standing by his tent, Mantikor heard the first sounds of the battle: gunshots and explosions, men shouting, and the screaming of the horses. Yet through some trick of the mist, the noise was muffled and unclear, seeming more distant than it was, and full of nauseating echoes. Mantikor bit his lips and found a taste of copper in his mouth. He looked for reassurance in the faces of the men around him, and the boys too young to fight.

Above him fragments of mist tugged at the sun and seemed to harry it across the sky. Samson Mantikor climbed the hill. He looked out from a flat place of rock; he watched the battle for a long time. He listened to its hundred voices, until they all resolved into one voice.

It was a distant crashing like the crashing of the sea. And the mist seemed to suck men under to their deaths. Once a man was down, he disappeared, and the mist closed over him. Sometimes the prince would see a man throw up his hands and disappear, but then he looked away, following the Starbridge banners as they swept across the field. One of the boys called to him and pointed. He smiled and called back. The scarlet crab of Castle Blaylock nodded proudly in the wind, halfway to the Charonea Ridge.

But there was another banner, too, that seemed unstoppable. Already it had covered half the distance to the prince's hill. It was the largest on the field. It seemed to tower above the rest. Elsewhere, other, smaller flags of black contended in the mist, moving back and forth, and some broke and went down and were sucked under.

Above him on the hilltop his own flag caught the breeze—wild birds upon a sky of blue. Watching it, suddenly dizzy, the prince felt terribly alone. He knew what was happening. Around him people moved away. They were embarrassed, saddened, grieved. As for him, grief and fear were like a hunger in his guts, for there below him on the field, the golden lilies of Iskandar Starbridge fluttered down, the pole broken and the cloth in rags. Nearby, the great sea dragon of Lord Mara Starbridge, Prince of Charn, jerked back and forth and then was snapped off short.

Time seemed to stop upon the little hill. Smiling foolishly, Mantikor looked around him. He put his hands over his eyes, then took them away. The silver leopard of Mercator Starbridge had gone down. With him had ridden Lakshman

Starbridge and the high constable of Charn. Now only remnants of their force remained: single flags of animals or birds of prey, surrounded and hemmed in by hosts of black. But the dark flags were fewer too—the great black standard of the colonel stood alone, now three-quarters of the way across the field. From the prince's hilltop, men pointed and gesticulated. Someone shouted something that he didn't understand, and then he saw Craton Starbridge lurch out of the mist, coming up from below. He was with his brother and his sister's son, and they were dressed for fighting.

He climbed up to where the prince was standing, and saluted. "Sir," he said. "I see a way. There's no one between him and us; look at him." And he thrust into the prince's hands a pair of field glasses.

"Look," he said, and the prince looked. He saw the black flag looming towards him, out of focus, and he twisted the screw. Tendrils of mist coiled around the flagpoles; he moved the glasses down and then he saw him stagger into range, a tall black rider on a giant horse. His hair was gray, wild around his head, and his raised fist was made of metal.

"Request denied," said Samson Mantikor. But he spoke softly, biting his lips, staring through the glasses, listening to the sounds around him, the jingle of the saddles as men swung themselves onto their horses, the whirr of the sharpshooters' rifles near his ear.

And when he lowered the binoculars, the hillside was deserted, save for his own orderlies and guards. Below him, down the slope, he heard the hooves of many horses scattering on the rocks, and that was all. Then he saw a single horseman jump over a ridge of earth, carrying the flag of Craton Starbridge and his family, a white ship under sail upon a sea of mist.

Other horsemen followed him. Mantikor turned his face away. The sharpshooters were putting down their guns. They were staring open-mouthed, and he was watching in the mirror of their faces how that crazy little boat drove on, drove on, shuddered and drove on, and then subsided under that black storm.

Then the men were all around him, tugging at him, pulling him away. "Sir, you cannot stay," they whispered, pulling at his arms. And he suffered them to lead him, for he was thinking of a poem, and he was mumbling a final poem as he went along. Later it was to become famous, and was engraved along the arch of a stone gate, later, much later, when the sweet summer grass of Charonea made the work a joy. Then workmen brought their families from Caladon, and while their wives and children picnicked in the grass, the men erected a great marble gate, to commemorate the place where the Starbridges went down. And along the arch they carved these words, meaningless to all but one or two:

> *My heart went out to where that boat*
> *Broke on that silver sea.*
> *Above it on the clumsy wind,*
> *Wild birds are scattering.*

But in the days after the battle, the news of Charonea spread over the diocese and came at last to that small village in the mountains, where Thanakar had made his home. Early in the morning of the twelfth of January, when the light was fresh upon the windows, he sat up in bed. Then slowly, so as not to wake her, he rose up and dressed himself. Something felt different to him, and perhaps it was just the passing of a dream. He took his hat and cane. He stepped across the room. Carefully, so as not to make a noise, he opened the door and walked out onto the veranda.

The courtyard of his house was empty. He squinted up into the sun. Turning his head, he saw a gleam of artificial light from Jenny's room, through the slats of wooden shutters on the second floor. He frowned, then smiled, and imagined her asleep upon her desk, her forehead cradled in her arms, her pen still in her hand.

There was a bird in the courtyard, picking at the moss with its long bill.

He passed out through the gate and out onto the boardwalk by the lake. There he strolled along the fronts of the deserted villas, admiring the day. They had had no rain in half a week. The sun shone clear and calm over the shoulder of Mount Rigel. On the other side, the entire range of the Caryatids stretched away, visible for miles. There was no sugar to distort the air.

Thanakar raised his hand against the light. In front of him the boardwalk ended on a beach of sand. There a small crowd had gathered near a man on horseback.

As he watched, the man dismounted wearily. Someone held a sack of water, and he drank from it and splashed it on his face. His horse was pulling on its bridle, eager to get down to the lake.

Thanakar walked faster, and he switched his cane to his left hand. He soon met people coming back the other way. One was a technician in the tuberculosis sanatorium where he worked.

Thanakar raised his hat. The woman strayed from her companions. "We're having breakfast at the hospital," she said. "You care to come?" She extended her gloved hand Thanakar touched it with his own.

"What news?" he asked, turning back the way he'd come

The woman shrugged. "Events," she said. "Samson Mantikor is dead at Charonea. Strangled by his own guard— that's what they say. Argon Starbridge is deposed. Aspe sits in his tent outside the walls of Caladon. The governor has asked him in, but he won't go."

"You don't seem concerned."

The woman smiled worriedly and shook her head. "What help is it to be concerned? What can I do? These things are far away. Now I don't know—my husband's here. We'll keep our heads down. With any luck we can escape their notice."

They were passing Thanakar's house. Nodding and smiling, he slowed to rest his leg, letting them go on ahead. Then he turned aside, entering the wicker gate, walking through the hall and through the courtyard. The light in Jenny's window had burned out. Across the way, by the fountain, Mrs. Cassimer held the baby in her arms. She was rocking him and playing, but pretended not to see the doctor. They had had an argument the day before.

He limped up onto the veranda, and opened the door of his own room. It was still in shadow. The slats of the shutters drew thick lines on the floor.

He hooked his cane over a chair, removed his hat, his gloves, his jacket, and his shoes. He was fumbling with the buttons of his trousers as he stood above the bed. Charity pushed the sheets away and rolled onto her side. Her eyes were closed, her face softened by sleep. He sat down on the bed and touched her hair, and she came awake under his fingers, turning up to kiss his thumb. "What?" she said. "What is it?" and he smiled. Nothing of importance. No. Nothing that can't wait forever. He took off his trousers and lay down. Charity opened up her arms, still half asleep, still lingering in a countryside of dreams. But part of her was there with him, her body soft and strong, her skin tasting of sweat, her breath slightly foul as he found her mouth.